Last Dance

Last Dance

DAVID RUSSELL

DUNDURN
TORONTO

Editor: Allister Thompson
Design: Carmen Giraudy
Printer: Webcom

Library and Archives Canada Cataloguing in Publication

Russell, David, 1968-
Last dance / David Russell.

(A Winston Patrick mystery)
ISBN 978-1-926607-28-3

I. Title. II. Series: Russell, David, 1968- . Winston Patrick mystery.

PS8635.U877L38 2011 C813'.6 C2011-900584-0

1 2 3 4 5 16 15 14 13 12

Conseil des Arts du Canada Canada Council for the Arts Canadä ONTARIO ARTS COUNCIL CONSEIL DES ARTS DE L'ONTARIO

We acknowledge the support of the **Canada Council for the Arts** and the **Ontario Arts Council** for our publishing program. We also acknowledge the financial support of the **Government of Canada** through the **Canada Book Fund** and **Livres Canada Books**, and the **Government of Ontario** through the **Ontario Book Publishing Tax Credit** and the **Ontario Media Development Corporation.**

Care has been taken to trace the ownership of copyright material used in this book. The author and the publisher welcome any information enabling them to rectify any references or credits in subsequent editions.

J. Kirk Howard, President

www.dundurn.com

Dundurn
3 Church Street, Suite 500
Toronto, Ontario, Canada
M5E 1M2

Gazelle Book Services Limited
White Cross Mills
High Town, Lancaster, England
LA1 4XS

Dundurn
2250 Military Road
Tonawanda, NY
U.S.A. 14150

To Barbara, whose support of
and belief in me keeps me going.

And Ainsley, who brings us both such happiness.

Acknowledgements

It takes a village to produce a book — at least a good one. Lots of eyes went into making *Last Dance* a better book. My dad, Les Mushens, got the first crack and made pages upon pages of suggestions for improvement. Likewise, fellow Canadian author Lou Allin (*www.louallin.com*) graciously reviewed the manuscript and offered many helpful suggestions. Kim Culbert (*www.kimculbert.com*) not only has a keen eye behind the camera — she shot the author photo — but also for the written word. A.j. Devlin (*www.storminforms.com*) gave invaluable advice. Allister Thompson, my editor at Dundurn Press, worked incredibly hard to improve the flow of the story while maintaining its integrity. Numerous others gave suggestions and input as well. Thank you to all.

Thank you to Sylvia McConnell who took the first leap of faith with my novels.

Chianti Cafe — you're still missed.

While most of the locations in this novel are real, Sir John A. Macdonald Secondary is fictional, as are all the characters contained therein.

David Russell can be visited at *davidrussell.ca.*

Chapter One

"This sucks."

This is the reason why I got into the teaching profession: the stimulating intellectual debates one engages in with one's students. Not having the energy to concoct a better comeback, I responded with "Yeah."

"It's not fair," he continued, and his voice took on a tone that registered him in the category of big fat whiner.

"Life's not fair," I responded. "If it were, would I be a teacher?" I'd used that line many times, but it usually stopped the kids from carrying the "life-ain't-fair" debate any further.

"It isn't always about you, Mr. Patrick." Ouch. That one hit close to home. "This assignment is way too long. Six pages? That's insane."

I sighed with as little disdain as I could muster. I'm sure it was not very convincing. "Perhaps so," I countered lamely. "But look at the bright side."

"Which is?" Mercifully, the bell rang.

"Class is over." I smiled, turned, and walked away. I was heading into last period at the end of a long day at the end of a long week, and I was frankly in no mood to argue with a sixteen-year-old. Not only that, but I was about to introduce a major research project to the law class. Theirs was ten pages. I'm a glutton for punishment.

Law was the class for which I was theoretically

most qualified, given my relatively recent swapping of courtroom for classroom. Some people, principally my mother and my ex-wife, thought I was crazy for trading a promising career defending society's lower masses for teaching, well, many in society's lower masses. Nearing the end of my first year of teaching, I was beginning to believe they may have been right — not that I would ever admit that. I might not have been one hell of a lawyer, but I'm not certain I became one hell of a teacher either.

The class interrupted my melancholy, seeming insistent that I teach them something. That all changed when I gave them their final term paper assignment for the year. With only six weeks left until summer, the pressure was really beginning to mount for these senior students, particularly those who planned to go on to university in the fall. Those students are generally in the minority. In this school, those students were in the minority of the minority. Still, I might not be able to make lawyers out of them, but I ought to at least be able to help them beat a minor possession rap. But even for those students not planning a post-secondary life of advanced academia, the end of the school year, I was quickly learning, was a panicked time for just about everyone.

There was only about ten minutes left in the class when an impromptu conversation broke out among the students closest to the window. Strangely, this was the smartest section of the room, perhaps due in part to its proximity to Vancouver's limited sunlight. The conversation was beginning to get animated — which meant the word "fuck" had been used — so I thought I should get involved. Approaching the small but agitated group as calmly as possible and utilizing my best Martin Lawrence coolness, I said, "Whassup?"

The assembly of annoyed teenagers paused in their vitriol and looked at me with obvious surprise. They clearly had not even noticed my approach. Some days I'm so redundant.

"*Whassup?*" Sara Kolinsky said. Sara was one of the few students in my two different law classes I believed actually might have a law career in her future. At some point during the school year, she had dropped the "h" from the end of her first name in what I thought was a transparent attempt at hipness. Her tone told me she thought my obvious attempt at hipness was obviously not hip at all.

"What are we all riled up about?" I tried again.

Tim Morgan lowered his head in such clear avoidance, it was hard to not smile. "Nothing," he said.

"'Kay," I replied with nonchalance that even they must have seen as cool. I turned to walk away, convinced I had defused whatever conflict was brewing, with the added bonus that I didn't have to get involved at all. I might yet turn out to be good at this teaching thing.

"It's *not* nothing," Sara objected. Damn.

Tim tried unsuccessfully to thwart further conversation. "Sara, never mind." Sara, I had learned in the nearly ten months I had known her, was not the type to let sleeping dogs lie. A hybrid of Marcia Clark and Barbara Walters, she thrived on "further conversation."

"Okay." I tried once again to extricate myself from their conversation. With a glance at the clock at the front of the room, I silently counted off the few remaining minutes of the class.

"No, really, Mr. Patrick. I'd like to hear your opinion on this." Lissa was one of Sara's close friends. I could not understand why her name was spelled with two "s's", despite being pronounced the same as "Lisa." I hadn't thought of a polite way to ask. I sighed, leaned on an empty desk, and assumed my "I'm listening" pose.

Tim was fidgety. "No, really. It's okay." An uncomfortable moment passed between the four students.

"Grad's coming up," Sara began. "If we want to bring someone as a date who doesn't go to the school, we have to fill out a form that Mr. Owen has to sign." Bill Owen was one of Sir John A. Macdonald Secondary's vice-principals.

Nathan Donaldson stepped in. An outrageously rambunctious kid, he was uncharacteristically quiet. "Tim's application to bring a date was turned down."

"You guys," Tim began to protest.

"It's okay," Sara stopped him. "Patrick's cool." *Told ya.* I smiled slightly. It was probably dangerous territory to enter: the students were essentially going to ask me to defend or criticize my supervisor's decision. My cool status might well depend on my answer. Also my teaching position, since my contract was up for renewal in just a few weeks.

"Did he say why?" I asked.

Tim looked uneasily at me. "He said it wouldn't be appropriate. Some people might get upset."

"Why would your date upset people?"

"Isn't it obvious?" Nathan demanded, his voice rising enough to cover the din of the rest of the class, who had by now given up on their assignment and were beginning to pack up. Nathan made a noise that sounded like "tsk," throwing his arms in the air and leaning back in his chair.

"Not to me," I replied. "What has the vice-principal got against your date? Did he have some trouble with her in the past?" They all stopped and looked at me with poorly masked incredulity.

Tim smiled for the first time that whole period. "Not 'her,' Mr. Patrick. Him. My date's a guy."

Chapter Two

I wasn't ready for that.

It wasn't that I was homophobic. I consider myself to be a pretty hip and modern kind of guy, as I've made clear. I wasn't naïve enough to believe that at least some of my students wouldn't at some time discover their homosexuality. But my guilt-laden Catholic upbringing somehow had me not really permitting myself to believe that any of the kids could possibly be gay. It was bound to happen that a young student would "out" himself to me during the course of my teaching career. Of course, it was only my first year. I had been prepared to wait for a while. "Oh," was what I managed to muster. I had wanted to say something profound. The Prime Minister's Award for outstanding Canadian teacher did not seem imminent. Tim, to his credit, appeared to find my discomfort comforting.

"You didn't know?" he asked, barely suppressing a giggle. I tried hard not to think of his smothered giggle as girlish.

"No. I didn't, I guess."

"Oh, come on!" Nathan protested. "You didn't realize Tim wasn't straight? Are you blind?"

"Stop teasing me," Tim mockingly complained, affecting an over-the-top lisp. In a sitcom, it would be during this *La Cage aux Folles* routine that a vice-principal would walk in and wonder why I was doing little to stop this politically incorrect behaviour. "Seriously," he continued, dropping the stereotype, "I thought everyone knew."

"Would it seem horribly insensitive of me if I told you that I really never gave it any thought?" That seemed to stymie them for a moment. Since they were grade twelves, I allowed a moment of unguarded levity to pass between us. "Generally speaking, teachers contemplating their students' sexuality — whether hetero or homo — is sort of frowned upon by management." They laughed. At least something in this conversation was going right.

Nathan could not resist. "Man, if you can't pick out that Tim's gay, I hope you don't find yourself stuck in a gay bar downtown. You've got a seriously broken gay-dar."

Tim mercifully intervened on my behalf. "Leave him alone, Nate. I wouldn't expect Mr. Patrick to be checking me out." He smirked playfully. "Besides, he's not my type."

I got up abruptly. "Okay. Now I'm dangerously uncomfortable. Nice talking with you." Three minutes left on the clock.

"Mr. Patrick." Sara actually reached out and grabbed my arm. "This is serious."

"Sara, forget it," Tim protested.

"Shhh," she said. Tim was quickly becoming redundant in his own argument. "Really. It isn't right. He has no right to tell Tim he can't bring whoever he wants to grad."

I stopped and looked at them. "What exactly did Mr. Owen say about your date?"

Tim looked reluctant to carry on but finally did.

"He said that my date would not be appropriate for a school function."

"He mentioned it was specifically because of your date's gender?"

"Well, yeah, but he also tried to get around it by saying that my date was too old."

A fresh wrench in the works. "How old is he?"

"He's twenty, okay? And before you say anything, there's nothing wrong with him going out with me. It's less than three years difference."

I tossed my arms in the air helplessly. "I didn't make the rule. I'm not the bad guy here." I paused to find a way to gently put the next phrase to my disgruntled charges. "It is possible that Mr. Owen feels that having a twenty-year-old come to a high school graduation is not appropriate." My cool status was on the line.

"I call 'bullshit,'" Sara said. She had a habit of periodically forgetting I was her teacher and speaking with me in the vernacular of her friends. The perils of teaching in East Vancouver, I guess. I didn't bother to reproach her. She had already called me cool. I couldn't risk it.

"I'm just saying that having adults at the grad dance as dates may have certain ramifications."

"That's crap," Sara continued, "and Mr. Owen knows it. He doesn't want Tim's date to come because Van is gay."

"Van?" I asked.

Tim looked up at me defiantly. "That's my boyfriend."

"Okay." Quick glance at the clock — down to about ninety seconds. How much trouble would I get in if I just dismissed them early? "You're sure this isn't just about his age? This might have nothing to do with discrimination."

"My boyfriend is twenty, and he's on the approved guest list," Sara told me. That this seventeen-year-old's boyfriend was two years into adulthood was probably a conversation for another time, and by god, with another person. "What do you make of that?" Her tone was very demanding.

"It sounds like Mr. Owen is trying to avoid some potentially uncomfortable phone calls and complaints," I began. Sara arched forward in her seat but stopped when I raised a hand. "And it sounds like he's making that decision based on what could clearly be classed as a discriminatory perspective." There was a pause while they digested the fact that I was agreeing with them. Finally, Nathan spoke to Sara and Tim.

"Did he just say what I think?"

"Yep," Sara replied. "He agrees with us. Van should be allowed to come as Tim's date."

Tim looked up at me with a shy nod. "Thanks, Mr. Patrick. That does mean something to me knowing you're okay with my being gay."

"Oh, he's more than okay with it. He's gonna go talk to Owen for you." She wore a smile large enough that it risked breaking out into full laughter. She'd had me as a teacher for nearly nine months, and she figured she could read me like a book. It appeared she was right.

"You are?" Tim asked a little sheepishly.

I looked up at the clock, one of the few pieces of equipment I had come across within the building that worked with stupendous accuracy. It showed that there were some twenty-five seconds before class ended. It would be too long to stand there saying nothing. I sighed. "Yes, I am."

"Told you he was cool," Sara declared. At least there was that. It was a sad statement about my life that I was placing so dear a value on Sara, Tim, and Nathan's view of my coolness. The bell rang as she finished her proclamation. Standing, she patted me on the arm as she walked by. "I knew we could count on you." She winked as she walked away. "Let me know how it goes."

The rest of the class was filing out. Most of them never bothered to say goodbye. Clearly they did not share Sara's view of my coolness, or they would not have dreamed of leaving without a closing salutation. Tim and Nathan stood beside me as I watched Sara recede from sight out into the river of teenagers flowing past my open door toward eighteen hours of academic reprieve.

"You don't have to do this if it makes you uncomfortable," Tim finally assured me.

I turned to face him. "What the hell kind of name is Van?" I asked.

He smiled for only the second time that afternoon. "I think it's kind of sexy," he replied with a coy grin.

"Go home," I demanded. Nathan laughed uproariously at my discomfort and followed Tim out the door.

Chapter Three

Bill Owen was a big man.

He was about six foot three, and I shrank in comparison at my average barely six feet. He was also big-shouldered, enormously big-gutted, and big-voiced. He often tried to use his size as an intimidation factor in his relationships with the rest of the teaching faculty. Sometimes it worked. At least half the staff was so reluctant to meet with him, they went along with his edicts to avoid any kind of confrontation.

This was going to be fun.

Bill's office was the smallest of the three vice-principals, though he had served in his administrative position longer than anyone else, including the principal. There was a theory that anyone who remained a vice-principal for more than six or seven years was pretty much a lifer. In a large city like Vancouver, where there are over twenty high schools, it was likely true. My impression of Bill in my year at the school had confirmed the theory. In a rare moment of serendipity, his office was devoid of students or other staff taking up his time. There was no real reason to put off the conversation. I knocked gently on his open door.

Bill turned away from his computer and looked at me. It was also well known that he knew as much about computers as I knew about physics. "Oh, hey, Win," he began jovially enough.

A pet peeve of mine is being called "Win" by those I don't consider to be friends. There's something about the presumption of informality I find rankling.

"Hey, Bill. Got a minute?" I resisted the urge to call him "Billy" or "Billy-Bob." This conversation was going to be edgy enough. He looked only mildly distraught at seeing me. Despite my present vocation, few people are happy about sitting down to chat with lawyers, even former ones. But Bill smiled pleasantly and offered me a chair at his little round table. In education, round tables are considered friendlier than sitting across a desk from one another.

"How are things going?" he asked with feigned interest.

"Good. Things are good." I paused to permit a silence to hang between us long enough to be just this side of uncomfortable. I've found in both my careers that a sustained silence often indicates to the other party the gravity of the conversation about to take place. "I need to talk to you about one of my students."

Bill sighed and tilted back in his chair. His posture took on a fatherly form, no doubt preparing to pass on some kernel of classroom management wisdom. The man loved to dispense kernels. "Having some trouble in class?"

"No," I responded, making sure to not allow any defensiveness in my tone. "No, the student is fine with me. I'm actually here on his behalf." The contrived warm smile that had welcomed me only seconds before began to fade, though it did not completely disappear from beneath the eighties-style police mustache he refused to shave.

"Who's the student?"

I paused until it seemed he was on the edge of repeating the question. "Tim Morgan."

"Oh, Christ," he sputtered, grunting as he heaved himself forward from his chair's tilted position. A few more pronouncements like this one, and I could practically give him a workout. He put his beefy arm on the friendly round table and stared at me without speaking. I decided I would out-pause him and see what happened. His eyeballs finally rolled skyward in disbelief and he let out a tremendous sigh. I suspected that was the most exercise he'd had all day. "So I'm guessing this is about his choice of date for the graduation dance?"

"Yes."

"And you want him to be able to bring his, what, his *boyfriend?*" The scorn dripped off his final word.

"To be honest, I really don't care who he brings to the dance."

That slowed him down only long enough to clear the anger spittle already forming at the side of his mouth. I wondered if it would get caught in his moustache. "Then what the hell are you doing here?"

It was time to lay out the cards. I sat forward gently, saying, "I care about why he's not allowed to bring his date." Only a short pause was necessary before carrying on. "You can't tell someone that he can't bring a date because he's gay."

"I can't?" I could sense Bill's back going up. On the plus side, it was improving his posture.

"No. You can't. It's discriminatory."

"I'm the vice-principal here."

"I'm aware of your title." Oops. I had not planned to be snarky or sarcastic. I'd lasted less than two minutes. If Bill's posture straightened any more, he'd be completely standing.

"Look," he began, his voice rising slightly.

"I'm sorry. That was sarcastic and uncalled for." My mother had been reminding me lately of the need for occasional humility. My apology took the wind out of his sails. I'm known for my sarcasm, not my apologies. "I just meant to say that even as vice-principal, there may be limits to the reasons you can deny someone their choice of date to the dance."

Bill began to slouch slightly in his chair, a good sign. "Look, Win, I have nothing against Tim or his date. I've never even met him. But I have three hundred and fifty other grads and their parents to think about."

"What about them?" I asked innocently.

"If Tim brings his boyfriend to the dance, there could be a lot of upset, uncomfortable people."

I let that sit for a moment. "So Tim is being denied his choice of grad date because a few people might be uncomfortable?"

"Win, it isn't always as straightforward as it seems." I smiled slightly at his choice of words. He seemed to catch the humour, too, and smiled back. "Sometimes I have to make a decision that's best for the whole school community, not just best for an individual student." *What a load of crap,* I thought, but elected not to voice it.

"Bill, this is Tim's graduation as much as it is anyone else's. He ought to be able to enjoy it just like everyone else."

"And he can. He can still come, and there are plenty of kids who come to grad without a date. They still have a great time."

"Bill, come on. That's hardly the same thing."

"I think it is. I've been doing this a little longer than you." This was the point of any conversation with Bill Owen where he turned completely patronizing. I tried to prevent my own eyeballs from rolling skyward. "I've been through many of these types of situations, and after awhile you get a feel for them. It may not seem like the right thing to you, but you'll just have to trust me on this one. I've made my decision." His tone hovered between dismissal and challenge.

"So that's it?" I asked.

"Win, don't take it personally. The last thing we need is a bunch of angry parents calling the school, making a big fuss about gay students bringing their gay dates to the dance. I've made a decision that's best for the school."

"And possibly tortious," I countered.

"Excuse me?" he said. I sensed my tossing of elementary legal terminology was having the intended effect. You really don't need to go to law school to make use of a few well-chosen legal words. Pick a Latin phrase most people don't hear often, and you're bound to give them a little anxiety.

"If you deprive Tim of the right to attend his graduation, you could be placing yourself and the school in a legally untenable position."

He sat back up straight again. Two sit-ups in one meeting. He must have been working up a sweat. "I'm not depriving him of the right to attend the dance. He can still attend." He smiled. Touché.

"You are arbitrarily depriving him of bringing his choice of guest based on discriminatory criteria." Thrust.

Bill paused again, choosing his words. I was a little flattered. He wasn't one for pausing and carefully selecting words. He must have felt the challenge. "There is nothing in the B.C. School Act that requires the school to permit students to bring whoever they wish to a dance. I can guarantee you it simply isn't in there." Parry.

"The Charter of Rights and Freedoms guarantees protection from discrimination. It supersedes the School Act."

He looked a little defeated, which with Bill never lasts long. It generally turns to anger. "You know what? That's a load of crap. Trust a lawyer to turn something like this into a legal issue." He sounded disgusted.

"Yes. You generally would trust a lawyer to make an argument against discrimination."

He was beginning to seethe now. He leaned forward, the table no longer a friendly barrier, and practically hissed. "And let me remind you, Mr. Patrick, that lawyering is no longer how you make your living."

I couldn't decide what to say next: should I chastise him for his thinly veiled threat or inform him that my other pet peeve is people who use the word lawyer as a verb? I chose neither. It probably wasn't worth the effort.

I let out a long, slow breath before responding. "Okay." I stood up to leave.

Bill looked surprised. "Okay?" he asked suspiciously.

"I guess that's it," I replied, trying to restore the

friendly tone in which the conversation had begun. "I wanted to confirm that the kids had understood you correctly. You've made your position clear."

"What does that mean?"

"You're right. You have the authority to make whatever decision you think is best. I leave it up to you."

"Oh," he replied, still skeptical. "Well, I'm glad we can agree to disagree amicably."

"Sure," I told him. "You've got your job to do. I just told the kids I'd talk to you, and I did. No hard feelings."

"That's good. Thanks, Win. I appreciate your support." I wasn't sure how he interpreted my disagreement with him as support, but on the other hand, he was probably happy I didn't really feel like fighting.

"Yeah," I said. "I'll see ya." I walked out of the main office and headed down the hall to my classroom. I'd spent more time on this than I had really planned, and Bill did have a point: it was his show to run, not mine.

I reached my classroom and was relieved to see that none of the kids had stayed behind to hear how the conversation had gone. I was trying to convince myself I had done all that I could and hadn't sold out in the interest of employment preservation or the need for some pasta and a good Cabernet Sauvignon. I told myself the kids would understand that Mr. Owen was my supervisor and there was little I could do for them. Then I realized the truth: my cool status was about to go out the window.

By the time I got home, I had nearly put Tim's graduation date dilemma out of my mind. It was Tuesday, which meant Pasta Frenzy night at my favourite little Italian eatery in Kitsilano. I might have given up the seemingly more glamorous legal profession for the arduous task of teaching the youth of today, but I had steadfastly refused to give up some of the luxuries that had come with my former job.

I also knew I wasn't kidding anyone. I had mostly done work for Legal Aid, often working extremely long hours at provincial government Legal Aid rates. Consequently, I had forgone some of the richer areas of legal practice, but I had managed to squirrel away most of my earnings over my brief career. This was mostly because I had happily lived off the avails of my then-wife's income, or rather, income she had inherited without having yet had to bury her parents. I had grown accustomed to a certain lifestyle: near the beach, plenty of restaurants, and just about every kind of takeout and delivery food possible. Kitsilano is Vancouver's born-again bachelor's paradise.

Tuesday nights were particularly bad for getting a table at Chianti. In fact, it wasn't uncommon to find lineups of hungry patrons snaking up the sidewalk, interrupting the traffic flow of neighbouring businesses. Fortunately, I had been going there long enough that a table was pretty much reserved with my name on it, particularly on a Tuesday. I'd thrown the staff off one Friday by actually bringing a date. Both the dinner and the ensuing relationship were shortlived — neither made it past about ten o'clock that same night. Having left my one real long-term relationship with my ex-wife,

I had not yet re-mastered the art of dating. Who am I kidding? I'd never mastered it in the first place. Tonight I had lucked out. Only a few patrons occupied the multitude of tables the little restaurant held. It was still early. As my first year of full time teaching had progressed, I found myself eating earlier and earlier; today it was only 5:30. I seemed to be tempting the aging gods, pushing my eating habits perilously close to those of my parents. And they didn't even live in Florida.

Though I wasn't sitting in her section, my usual and favourite waitress approached me within moments of sitting down. As was the custom between us, she already had a glass of red wine in her hand — for me she never bothered with a tray — which she set down before me as she sat down across from me. "Professor," she said in her usual greeting.

"Teri," I replied. "Nice of you to join me."

"It's high time someone did." Teri, like a growing number of other friends, colleagues, and acquaintances, believed she was responsible for reminding me of my continuously single state. Never mind that she herself had never mentioned a boyfriend, significant other, or apartment full of cats.

"Hmmphh," was my masterful retort. "For all you know, I may very well be joined by a delightful dining companion tonight."

"Is your mother in from the suburbs?"

"I said a 'delightful,' not 'guilt-throwing, health obsessing, church bingo-running' companion."

"In that case, I shall assume this one glass is all that will be needed."

"That depends on how good your wine selection is this evening." As was also part of Teri's custom, selection of the dinner wine was not left up to the patron, at least not in my case. Our rule was simple: as long as it was red, she could choose for me. She also generally limited me to one glass. She aimed to make sure my life did not descend into an alcoholic haze in which the potential for a new life partner would become that much more limited. I sipped the wine that she had brought, a South African Pinotage, bold, given the gloomy late spring weather.

"And the charges? Are they giddy with anticipation at their pending departure lo, these few weeks from now?"

"But then they won't have me around any more."

"I guess I answered my own question." She stood up to leave. "I'll bring you the special."

"Of course."

"Is everything okay, Winston? You look a little bummed."

"Just tired. Thinking about the perils of pedagogy."

"More so than usual? Any particular pedagogical predicament?" Teri is very found of alliteration. I thought momentarily of burdening her with Tim's travails on his pending prom, mostly so I could out-alliterate her, but I knew I would also have to share my failure to persuade the vice-principal of the errors of his ways.

"Nah. I think I just need a vacation." Teri left to place my order. Dinner, of course, was excellent: a simple linguini in cream sauce with peas joined by a half order of tortellini in a pesto sauce I had never been able to replicate. Of course, I hadn't really tried that hard, given my proximity to the sauce's origin.

My body replenished, I undertook the ten-minute walk back to my condominium and found it in its usual depressing condition. Living this close to the ocean is supposed to be a blessing along with a curse; one is blessed with the view of Vancouver's remarkable English Bay but also cursed with the problem of never getting anything done wiling away the time staring out the window at the view. For several months, neither blessing nor curse had been an issue, given the large green tarpaulin hanging from roof to basement of the three-storey building. Like many of its contemporaries, my apartment building had succeeded in bringing in young urban professionals looking for a semi-upscale lifestyle but had failed miserably at what would seem the simple task of keeping out Vancouver's notorious rain.

My view was now limited to the small sliver of a seam where two tarps joined right in front of my balcony. When the wind was blowing, sometimes the view through my vertical viewfinder would blow back and forth, like a filtered panoramic camera lens teasing with little bits of view. I used to pity the poor suckers who had fallen victim to the myriad unscrupulous contractors who sold them faulty buildings. Now I was one of them. I had sought to avoid being a victim by employing an independent building inspector to give me an unbiased, thorough inspection before I signed on the dotted line. Turns out there are all kinds of unscrupulous independent building inspectors too. I had almost made it through the campsite that had once been the building's front foyer when a familiar though unpleasant voice rang out from the darkness. "Winston!" it barked.

"Andrew," I replied with as much coldness as I could muster. I'm a pretty fair musterer of cold. Andrew Senchek was the self-appointed manager of my condo building. He also had no job. Allegedly injured in an industrial accident some five years before, he now lived off the avails of the Workers Compensation Board — supported by all those folks, like myself, who contributed through deductions from their paycheques. Given his perennial disability claim, Andrew spent his days parading around our apartment building, supervising construction workers, annoying garbage collectors, and basically harassing fellow residents with complaints, queries, and general nosiness. He even limped around the premises with the support of a cane, though I was certain I had seen his limp occasionally change to the opposite leg. It wasn't uncommon to see his cane hanging on the edge of a box of groceries as he hauled them in from his car. I had already vowed that when I had some spare time I would use my lawyerly prowess to look into his WCB claim and see if there wasn't some way I could force his ass back to work.

"Why weren't you home this evening?" he demanded. Andrew asked a lot of ridiculous questions that I pretended were rhetorical. When I failed to respond, he pressed forward. "We wanted to get into your apartment."

"Why did you want into my apartment, and why would you think your desire to enter my premises would prompt me to grant you same?" Andrew paused to interpret the questions. Though he spoke with a thick Polish accent that belied his twenty years in Canada, I could not imagine he had to translate English into Polish in order to understand.

"What?" he finally managed.

"Exactly," I replied, turning to unlock the lobby's front door, though with the floor to ceiling window space next to the door covered only with a plastic orange tarp — a lovely complement to the green surrounding the rest of the building — a Swiss army knife would have been just as effective as a key.

"We needed to do some drywall work around the living room area."

"Bummer," I replied nonchalantly. "I guess we'll have to do it next time."

"You know, you are not being very co-operative at allowing access for construction." I could feel a lecture coming on.

"If you give me a little bit of notice, I will happily provide access for the construction workers to enter the premises."

"It would be easier if you would just give me a key." We had been down this road plenty of times.

"Are you bonded?"

"What?" International confusion again.

"Exactly." I planned my escape again, but Andrew followed me into the lobby. Maybe the third time I would be lucky.

"Andrew, you cannot have a key to my apartment. It is private property, and you are among the last people I would give a key to."

"Why is that?"

I resisted the urge to tell him that principally it was because I didn't like him. In the years since we had both lived in this building, I had come to refer to him as "The

Polish Sausage." It sounds childish, but I worked around teenagers all day. Some of their immaturity was bound to rub off on me. Or vice versa. I settled for a much gentler "Good night, Andrew." In movies and television, emphatically saying "good night" always seems to be a clear signal to people they are supposed to go away. I don't think Andrew has cable.

"But I need to talk to you."

"I said good night." I had opted to forgo stopping at the row of mailboxes to pick up the mail, believing it would only give Andrew those few extra seconds to harp in my ear. The elevator door opened, and I stepped inside, reaching immediately for the third floor button, hoping his alleged limp would prevent him from reaching the elevator before the door closed.

I knew that injury was a fake.

"You know, there is no need for you to be hostile," he told me as the door slid shut. I could think of many reasons to be hostile, not the least of which was that the green pepper from the sauce over the tortellini was starting to repeat on me. Though the condominium was relatively young, the elevator moved as though being powered by hamsters on spinning wheels.

"Hmm, hmmm," I muttered in response. I wished I had some mail to leaf through in order to look distracted.

"We are only trying to get the repairs undertaken as quickly as possible. No one else in the building is being as difficult as you."

"No one else is as pretty as me either." Would humour throw him off?

"You are a prick," he hissed, his poor attempts at friendliness completely dissipating. Did they not have comedy in Poland?

"Now who's getting hostile?"

"You should stop being such an asshole and let me do my job."

"If you only had one." I've never been one for taking the high road.

By that time, I had arrived at my apartment door, unlocked it, and was closing it in Andrew's face, assuring him I would contact the construction foreman to allow my apartment to be entered.

Home sweet home. Maybe I could move in the summer when I didn't have all this marking to do. And maybe by then the building wouldn't look like a set piece from *M*A*S*H.*

Chapter Four

The advantage of working on what's known as a linear timetable is that you see each of your classes every other day. Of course, if you have a bad class, you're stuck with them all year, but at least there are little gaps between your times together. I was counting on that one day gap to avoid having to see my law class, when I would have to admit I had failed them miserably in my attempt to argue their case with the vice-principal. It would be quite reasonable for them to no longer consider me the coolest teacher at the school. To be perfectly accurate, they hadn't actually labelled me as *the* coolest, but I refused to believe any of the teaching faculty could be any cooler. If I called in sick tomorrow, I would buy myself another couple of days. After three days, surely their teenaged attention spans would have forgotten all about our previous conversation. These thoughts had almost put a spring in my step as I rounded the corner of the second floor hallway leading to my classroom and saw Sara sitting on the floor outside.

"So?" she asked as I walked up to the door, keys in hand, pretending not to have noticed her. "Mr. Patrick!" she demanded when she could stand my pitiful pretending no longer.

"Good morning to you too," I grumbled, trying to muster indignation from the depths of my embarrassment. "Where I come from, we open our requests for information with a polite salutation."

"You come from East Van like the rest of us, so cut the crap and get to the point. What did Owen say?" By this time I had entered the classroom and was involved in the daily ritual of emptying my pockets of wallet, keys — anything with a hint of value — and depositing them in my locking filing cabinet. The rule of thumb in most high schools is: if it isn't locked or bolted down, they'll steal it. As with Polish Sausage the night before, my attempts to engage myself in other activities in order to disengage my pursuer were not terribly successful.

"I spoke with Mr. Owen."

"And?"

"Mr. Owen feels that Tim's date might not be appropriate for the school's graduation dance."

Sara's eyes rolled so emphatically I thought she might do herself an injury. Or she might be related to the vice-principal. "I already know that. I sent you there. How did you change his mind?" This was the moment in which my carefully cultivated nine-month journey to "cooldom" would be put to the test.

"I didn't."

She didn't respond immediately. Her adolescent eyes searched my face, and I realized she was looking for signs of an imminent punch line. She smiled slightly. "Shut up," she finally commanded, somehow making it sound as friendly as "good morning" might among adults. "What did you tell him?"

There was no holding back any more. "I told him I recognized it was his decision to make, and I quietly left his office." Sara's playful incredulity shifted to a flash of anger, and she seemed ready to let loose a pile of expletives — a skill she paradoxically practiced with as much acumen as her "A" essay writing abilities — when the sinister smile crept back into her eyes and the corners of her mouth.

"Oh, I get it. Nice one."

I returned the smile. "Thank you."

"You're pretty crafty."

"I have my moments." I didn't know what she was talking about, but I was willing to bask in her adulation a moment or two.

"Everything's about a teaching opportunity for you. Once a teacher, always a teacher."

"Occupational hazard."

She shook her head in a gently scolding fashion without losing the good humour I was certain would have faded long before now. "Fine then. I'm up to it."

"I figured you would be." I wasn't sure I liked the direction this conversation was taking. By now it was becoming clear that I might well have unleashed student anarchy on the poor befuddled vice-principal, and while I didn't particularly feel sorry for him — I still considered him an ass despite his defeating me — I knew this would only serve to make my life more difficult. As Sara turned to leave, she glanced slyly over her shoulder in my direction.

"I guess I'll see you tomorrow then."

"Yeah. You bet."

"We'll be ready. You just need to let us know how we do this." I couldn't hold out any longer.

"How we do what?" I asked to her back.

She turned, smiling. "How we use law class to tackle the school's discriminatory policies about Tim and grad." With that she was gone.

"Shit," I said to the empty desks.

The rest of the day passed in a haze, which must be what it feels like for many of my students on any given day. It's hard to imagine that adolescents and teenagers wouldn't be fascinated with the wonderful world of Canadian history, law, and literature, but somehow there it was. My head was not in the game as I pondered the following day's law class, in which I was expected to lead my students in a coup. The more I thought of ways to disengage them, the angrier I got at Bill Owen, not just for having put me in this position but because I knew the kids were right. The school had no business trying to legislate the gender preferences of any of its students. Shortly after the end of the day bell, I had packed up my bag and was skulking toward the exit when the student at the centre of Sara's furor appeared in front of me.

"Mr. Patrick," Tim Morgan began as he stepped in front of the emergency exit that was the conduit to my freedom — or at least avoidance.

"Hi, Tim," I said. He was standing right in front of the door.

"Mr. Patrick," he replied glumly, "can I talk to you for a minute?" I couldn't see any easy way to avoid the inevitable, so I sighed and motioned for him to carry on. "I know that Sara came and talked to you this morning. She said our law class was going to take on the vice-principal." Talking with teenagers is much like playing that old kid's game "telephone," in which a message is passed around people sitting in a circle to see if the content of the message is anywhere near the same when it reaches its originator. Searching my memory of my conversation with Sara, I could not think of any way I had even hinted — let alone stated — that we would be using this elective course as a means to pick a fight with my boss, but somehow that was the message that had been received. Of course, I couldn't confirm Tim's question without sinking even deeper into the mire of employment uncertainty.

"That's right," I told him.

"Look, I appreciate you taking an interest and everything, but really, I don't want you to get into any more trouble."

"Any more trouble?"

"I think you know what I mean." I did. My employers had scarcely forgiven me for my role in defending a colleague who had been accused of inappropriate conduct with a student. Both he and the student had ended up dead, and my academic career had nearly died with them. Of course, so had I. "Mr. Patrick. You're new here. The students like you, but I'm not so sure you've made the best impression on the principal and vice-principals. They'd be looking for any excuse to get rid of you. I'll survive without bringing Van to the dance."

"Look. Don't worry about me. I don't think you should just roll over with your boyfriend here." I honestly hadn't meant to introduce such obvious double entendre, but my juvenile tendencies must have been playing havoc with my subconscious. Tim, unfortunately, was one of my brighter students, and there was no way the comment would have gotten by him. He smiled instead of taking offence.

"Oh my god," he laughed.

"I just meant that …"

"I know what you meant," he interrupted, still trying to stifle laughter. He held open the door to the exit stairway for me, and we passed into the relative privacy of the echo chamber that was the stairwell. As the door clanked shut behind us, he stopped at the top of the stairs and turned to face me. "Seriously, though. I want you to know how much this means to me."

"Tim, all I've said we'd do is look into it."

"No, I mean your attitude … your … uhm … acceptance. Not everyone is as accepting. My dad hasn't talked to me in months. It's good to know that someone cares." It didn't feel like I could say nothing any longer, so I reached into the depths of my experience of watching sappy moments in television sitcoms and responded.

"I do care, Tim." As soon as I said it, a sudden panic flash overtook me, and I worried that Tim might actually hug me, always a risky act when it involves a student.

"Man, I think we just had a moment."

"I'm going home," I told him, walking past him and beginning my descent of the stairs.

"Okay, seriously though," he continued, following along behind me, "what options do we have?"

"Not a whole hell of a lot," I admitted. "I think that the best thing we can do is open up a conversation with the powers that be and see first of all if we can't negotiate our way to an understanding both parties can be satisfied with."

"Wow."

"What?"

"Attorney-speak. Why don't you just talk in Latin?"

"Once a lawyer, always a lawyer." We opened the door at the bottom of the stairs, turned right, and continued down the hallway towards the exit. "Tim, before we go much further, I think it's important that you do consider something very carefully."

"What's that?"

"The larger a brouhaha we make out of this, the less discretion about your, uhm, relationship we're going to be able to keep. Do you know what I mean?"

"Not entirely."

"I just mean that, not everyone is as tolerant as your immediate friends. Not all teenagers are known for their empathy and kind words."

"Oh. Now I see."

"I don't want to get too personal here or anything, but do you think people in the school — I mean, beyond your close friends — know that you're gay?" I turned to look at Tim, but he had stopped walking a few paces behind me. He was staring silently, ahead and to the left, his teeth clenched and the colour draining from his face. I turned back to see what had caught his attention. Just ahead of me, one of the lockers was adorned with "FAG" in bold black spray paint. I stopped too and looked back at my student. "I guess that answers my question."

"Well, holy shit!" Bill Owen's bellowing baritone could be heard all the way up the hall. It wasn't the most professional response to the situation, but to be fair, it did convey the general mood in the school hallway. By now a small crowd of educators and a handful of kids had gathered and were staring at the offending language on Tim's locker. Someone had thought to fetch one of the janitors, who had already gone in search of some paint to at least visually eradicate the slur. Tim was standing next to me, saying nothing. I would have joined the teachers to discuss the educational meaning of the act — which meant gossiping about which student we thought was the graffiti artist — but I felt leaving Tim alone to engage in speculative student character assassination might be a little insensitive.

The vice-principal proceeded towards us. "Are you happy now?" he barked as his presence filled my field of vision.

"Not especially, no," I replied casually. "Is there any reason that childish pranks perpetrated by imbeciles against targets selected on the basis of sexual preference should bring delight to my life?" As a general rule, the longer I'm in the building past three, the bitchier I get.

"You've just got to stop getting yourself in so much hot water." Tim finally spoke up for the first time since discovering the attack on his locker.

"Any guesses?" I asked him.

"How many people are there in the school?"

"About sixteen hundred."

"That narrows it down to about fifteen hundred and ninety-nine."

"Yeah. I guess so." We paused to stare some more at Tim's defaced locker. Although there are many areas within the teaching profession in which I consider myself to be lacking, making small talk with students during awkward moments is chief among them. If they covered it during teacher training at Simon Fraser University, from which I had graduated less than a year before, I must have been sleeping. This event would certainly qualify as awkward. "But you can't think of anyone in particular who has a beef with you?"

"Only every homophobe who's convinced they've 'outed' me."

"I guess they have," I said, nodding towards his locker, now being covered with a fresh coat of paint. The locker now stood out from every other in the hallway in that it had received a coat of paint sometime during this decade. By this time, Principal McFadden was approaching us, and I silently vowed not to be sarcastic and snippy with him. I needed some reserves for the inevitable follow-up conversation with his direct underling.

"Tim, I'm really sorry about what's happened," he began earnestly enough.

"It's not your fault, Mr. McFadden," Tim replied with a sigh.

"Still, no one should have to experience something like this, especially at school. We want you to feel safe here." It sounded like a prepared statement, but there wasn't a great deal more he could say. He turned his attention to me. "Maybe we can meet tomorrow morning."

"Sure," I said. Word was clearly already out that somehow I had been enlisted in this current battle. McFadden placed his hand briefly on Tim's shoulder and walked away towards his office. When it was clear the principal was out of earshot, his underling again approached us.

"Don't make this any worse," Owen scolded me without stopping to wait for a sarcastic comeback. "Just let it go." Then he was gone.

"Mr. Patrick?" Tim asked after the silence had hung between us awhile. "Mr. Owen might be right. We should probably just let it go." He said it, but his heart wasn't in it.

"I might have agreed, but the first part of your statement I just can't go along with." Confusion crossed Tim's face then quickly abated when I added, "I will never concede that Mr. Owen is right."

Chapter Five

Andrea Pearson is my best friend. And I don't just say that because she could kick my ass without breaking a sweat. Truthfully, that feat wouldn't be all that much. I've seen eighth graders who could probably do the same. But we've been friends since we were both little, and she would kick my scrawny butt each and every time I made a comment she perceived to be smart-assed, which was often.

When we were very little, my comments were of the "girls can't do" variety, and she would promptly demonstrate that I was wrong by ably completing the task and would also spend a little ass-kicking time punishing me for making the suggestion. As we grew into adolescence, the ass-kickings came following comments about how her body was failing to develop at the same rate as the other girls in our school. In our teenaged years, they were delivered in response to suggestions of how she and I might enjoy the developed parts of her body that had finally caught up to her peers in a way most teenaged boys in our school did not fail to notice. It was a history destined either to make you best friends or worst enemies. Andrea was sitting across from me in Las Margaritas Restaurant on Fourth Avenue, tossing back Coronas at a pace I didn't bother attempting to match, interrogating me, as usual, about decisions I made in my life.

"You're really gonna piss Owen off," she told me unnecessarily.

"I know. It can't be helped."

"Yes, it can," she scolded. "Why do you insist on alienating yourself from everyone in authority?"

"You're still here. You have authority."

"Don't you forget it." In addition to being best friend and self-appointed guardian of my best interests, Andrea was also a prominent detective in the Vancouver Police Department, with a clearance rate unmatched by any of her peers. "But I can only fire *at* you. This Owen clown can fire you." She smiled at her clever play on words.

"No, he can't. And that was awful." Her smile didn't fade: once she had decided her joke was funny, it really didn't matter what I thought. "I've got the union. And, of course, my secret weapon." Andrea raised her eyebrow as she tossed back the last of her Corona.

"My charm," I told her.

She put the bottle down on the table and indelicately tossed the lime wedge — rind and all — into her mouth. With anyone else I would be appalled by her table manners, but with Andrea it had a certain perky wholesomeness. "I'll be sure to save the want ads from tomorrow's paper for you," she said. "What about this 'faggot' thing on the kid — what's-his-name's — locker? You want me to look into it?"

I chuckled. "You gonna shake down the student body, Detective Pearson?"

"I'm just saying I could pick out the biggest, dumbest looking hoser of a guy and put the fear of god into him."

"That would be the Owen vice-principal clown."

"He wouldn't have vandalized a kid's locker."

"Not now, but I suspect it would have been about his speed when he was in school."

"You really got a hate on for this guy, don't you?"

"Yeah."

"Why? What's the story with you two?"

"He offends my sensibilities."

"That's it?"

"You need more?"

She shook her head. My sensibilities were not easily explained, even to me. "You got any kids' names I could work with?"

"Don't worry about it. That's the clown's job."

"What about the kid? What are you going to do about him?" I thought about that for a moment. Following my initial conversation with Bill, I had almost convinced myself that I would wash my hands of the issue. But I felt I owed Tim more. "Yo, Winnie," she barked to bring me back into focus. "Stay with me at least until dessert."

"Yeah. Sorry. I was just thinking."

"Planning how you're going to save the world?"

"Something like that."

"What can you possibly do if the VP refuses to let the kid bring his male date to the dance? He outranks you."

"A court might see it differently."

"Shit, Win. That's just not the best way to win job security. You'll be looking for career number three before long. You can't sue the vice-principal because you disagree with him."

I smiled just enough to look sly and sneaky. "Probably not. But the students could."

"I'll bring coffee and bagels Saturday morning. We can look through the want ads together."

"I think I love you."

"I think I'm uncomfortable with you loving me."

"You're just going to have to live with it." Sara was, once again, speaking her mind with little regard for her audience. The class, with the exception of Sara, was speechless after listening to the task I had just assigned them: they would be taking the very administration of their own school to court to undo an injustice. As the weight of the assignment and the gravity of what was happening sank in, the stunned looks began transforming into grins, then all-out smiles and laughter. Even Tim showed no sign of discomfort at the infamy the case was sure to bring him. The vandalism of Tim's locker seemed to have galvanized him into action. "This is exactly what we need to do to get Owen to listen to reason."

The rest of the class was spent assigning specific duties to class members, including research for relevant statutes, articles of the Canadian Charter of Rights and Freedoms, and any case law the textbook might have included that could be relevant to our challenge. I wanted to make sure the class focused on the legal issues at stake rather than personal attacks against my supervisor, but I couldn't help but feign deafness when I overhead conversations in which they slagged him. Before the period ended, we had the basis of our submission to the court that I dutifully promised to file on my way home from school in the afternoon. As the bell rang to end the period and the day, only one student remained behind and, unusually, it was not Sara. She was riding the high that came with being unanimously selected by her classmates as the representative who would argue Tim's case — with my assistance — in court, if it came that far. Instead, Jordan Kansky, a student I could usually count on for irrelevant, unfunny interruptions during lessons, sat sullenly at his desk as his classmates filed out.

"Jordan?" I asked him. "Is there something you need?" He looked uncomfortable, and I suddenly sensed my cool status was not, in fact, unanimously shared by every member of my Law 12 class.

"I want to talk to you about the lawsuit." His voice was sullen, challenging.

"Sure. What's up?" His discomfort visibly increased, and he sat silently for long enough that for a moment I thought he might have fallen asleep with his eyes open. It wouldn't be the first time; I had nearly mastered the skill while listening to any number of my students' oral presentations. "Jordan, I'm planning to go home in about sixteen seconds unless you have something important that's going to keep me here."

"Can I be blunt?"

"I wouldn't have it any other way."

"Fine. This assignment is bullshit." Silence fell while Jordan stared me down.

"I see. Are you referring to the lawsuit we are undertaking as a class?"

"Yep." I thought that would have been an appropriate moment for him to go into further details, but he went no further.

"Would you care to elaborate?" The challenging look he had been wearing gave way to one of classic teenaged deer-in-the-headlights confusion. Not that I had really held out much hope for a sophisticated debate following his opening statement. I had hoped it might at least be multi-syllabic. "Are you planning to expound on that theory?" Jordan continued to look at me in confusion. "Okay, how about would you like to explain what characteristics of the task have led you to such a negative opinion?" I sighed. "What's bullshit about it?" His mental light went on, just as surely as if I'd flipped a switch.

"It's just that … I don't agree with it."

"With what, Jordan? Spit it out."

"I don't want to work on helping some homo bring his homo boyfriend to our grad dance." He had promised to be blunt. I guess I should have been prepared for the reality that not all teenaged boys would be progressive, liberal-minded civil rights advocates. Jordan's steely resolve looked a tad shaky after making his declaration; he seemed not to trust that I might not chastise him for his redneck ways. I wondered how many others felt the same way but didn't have the balls to confront me.

"Jordan," I began, but he interrupted me before I could go further.

"I know. I know. Not very tolerant of me, but I'm not going to apologize for the fact that I don't believe in homosexuality. And I sure as hell don't think I should have to base one of my grade twelve marks on trying to get Tim to bring his lover to the dance."

"Fair enough."

"What?"

"You're right. I don't think you should have to do something that you feel strongly against. I may not like what you have to say, but I'll defend to the death your right to say it." Once again Jordan looked at me like I was a babbling idiot, and I wasn't convinced he was wrong. "Voltaire," I told him. That didn't appear to clear it up.

"What the hell are you talking about?" Sometimes kids cut to the chase way easier than their teachers.

"Look. My feelings or your feelings about Tim's sexual preferences are irrelevant. However, I believe his Charter rights are being violated, and I can't stand idly by and let that happen. It seems to me that most of the class feels the same way. But if you feel differently, I won't make you participate."

He looked at me with some satisfaction. "Okay then."

"Okay then. Are we all right?"

"Yeah, thanks for being cool about this." *Cool. Ahh.* Jordan headed for the door then stopped, turning to face me. "Voltaire? So when you quote eighteenth century French philosophers, does it make you feel powerful?"

"Yeah," I said, smiling sheepishly.

"Just remember: power takes as ingratitude the writhing of its victims." I stared as blankly at him as he had at me. "Tagore. Nobel laureate for poetry in India in the early twentieth century." He walked out the door before I could see if he was smiling smugly.

Kids today.

Chapter Six

The courthouse in downtown Vancouver is a stunning display of 1970s architecture. Glass on its western side, concrete on all the others, the building is touted as a tourist draw, with its multi-levelled walkways and roaring waterfalls cascading past office windows, a distraction more than attraction to much of the staff inside, I'm told. The courtyards are designed to be an oasis of calm amid the rush and roar of upscale capitalism on adjacent Robson Street. On a warm Monday afternoon, after school had let out for the day, Tim, Sara, Nate, and I stood at the court clerk's office, filing the papers that would form the basis of our suit against the school. My hastily organized extra-curricular field trip had failed to arouse suspicion amongst the school's administration, and if word had gotten out about what my law class was planning, it had remained blessedly quiet.

My last-minute sojourn to the courts had also required a good deal of last-minute deal wrangling and favour cashing with what few friends I still had in the legal system. My saving grace was that I had spent the bulk of my legal career working for Legal Aid, unlike the high-priced, Mercedes-driving, four-hundred-dollar-an-hour-billing defence counsel few defendants could afford. I tried to keep my convertible Saab hidden from view whenever I arrived at court so I wouldn't look too successful. Truth was, I had purchased it largely through the unearned earnings of my ex-wife. My smile, charm, and most importantly, my close relationship with Detective Andrea Pearson still carried some clout in the comparatively close-knit legal community, and I had managed to get a commitment to an expedited hearing should it be warranted due to the time-sensitive nature of our case: graduation was only a few weeks away.

"That's it?" Sara asked as we turned away from the counter.

"That's it."

"What happens now?" Nathan asked with his usual unrestrained enthusiasm. It made me want to "shhhh" him.

"We wait. Once the papers have been served on the school's administration, they'll have a shortened period to make a defense claim. Following that, we try to find resolution, or we end up in front of a judge."

"Shit, this is unreal!" Nathan exclaimed. "When will that happen?"

"Just as soon as we hire a process server to deliver the papers."

"Can't you just deliver it to the school?" Nathan demanded.

"I can, but I think I'm going to be in enough shit, if you pardon the expression, when Mr. Owen realizes what's going on. Having me serve notice on my employers probably won't help matters much." Tim had nearly flinched when I noted the predicament I was putting myself into, and I wanted to assure him that it would be okay. Of course, I didn't really know that it would be, but adults lie about Santa Claus too. "But it'll be fine. We're only doing what's right here, and there's nothing they can do to any of us."

"Are you sure?" Tim asked.

"Absolutely." *There's no Easter Bunny either.*

"In that case, let's save our money," Sara blurted out as she reached forward and snatched the statement of claim from my hands. "I'll do it."

"Sara," I told her, "this really isn't necessary."

"Are you kidding me? I'm looking forward to this." With that she headed through the automatic doors into the bright spring sunshine, conversation ended.

"Man, she can be pushy. It makes her kinda hot, don't you think?" Nathan asked, elbowing me conspiratorially. Tim answered before I could protest the direction of the conversation.

"Yeah. If I wasn't gay, I'd be camped out on her doorstep." He feigned his best lisp. "Hey, Mr. Patrick. You could stand to be a bit more pushy, you know." Both Tim and Nathan headed out the door after their friend. I could see but thankfully not hear Nathan as his head tilted back and he roared with laughter.

I run several kilometres most days through my Kitsilano neighbourhood, enjoying the quiet of the pre-rush hour west side of the sleeping city. That's my spin on it. For years I had suffered a chronic inability to sleep like a normal person, that is, more than about two or three hours at a stretch. Running was one of the many activities that had been prescribed by various specialists, quacks, and well-meaning friends to help me get some sleep and subtract several of the years my insomnia had added to my appearance. Running killed the hours between waking and working and kept me in terrific shape. That was my spin on it. My mother, my ex-wife, and my best friend all agreed I was too skinny. There's no pleasing some people.

Still, even the muggy morning air couldn't erase the simple pleasure I received every morning as I pounded the pathway from the westernmost limits of Spanish Banks down to Jericho and saw the city across English Bay, resting, though never really sleeping. The few fellow runners were up and about at this ungodly hour didn't seem surprised by the smile that involuntarily crossed my lips at the end of each early morning run as I rounded the corner at MacDonald and began the final stretch towards home, down Cornwall Avenue. My pace had been strong, and I was tempted to add another three-mile loop circuit to my run for the extra endorphin kick, but I recognized I was just avoiding facing the administrative music that would surely be blaring when I arrived at school.

I dwelt as long as possible in the shower, hoping the hot water would compensate for my usual lack of sleep, knowing it never had before. I flipped on the television to one of the city's morning news programs to keep me company while I got dressed. I had gotten as far as boxer briefs and shirt and was debating which tie I should wear when I noticed a familiar voice coming from the television. It took a few seconds to place it, but once I did, my heart skipped a beat.

Racing into the living room, knocking my uncovered right knee into the doorjamb and letting loose with an expletive, I stared with disbelief at the television screen. On the lower right hand side of the screen was the back of a reporter's head, while in the centre of the frame, complete with CityTV microphone prominently placed in front of her, was none other than Sara.

She was busy explaining to the reporter, who I noted was broadcasting live in front of my place of employment, that as soon as the school's administration arrived she would be serving the vice-principal with a lawsuit brought by her law class and — wait for it — her law teacher, Mr. Winston Patrick, in support of the civil rights denied one of the school's students. The fact that she was incredibly articulate for an eighteen-year-old in discussing the Charter issues at stake should have pleased me, but it only added to the dull, thumping pain growing in my chest. The phone rang, convincing me I wasn't dreaming, and I picked it up to hear Andrea. She was doing her best, I could tell, to keep the laughter out of her voice, but it was there right alongside the "I told you so" she was also masking.

"Are you seeing this?" she asked.

"Holy shit. I can't believe she's on the news."

"How the hell do kids know how to arrange press conferences? Did you teach them that?"

"I don't even know how to do that."

"Oh, that's right," she said dryly. "They usually find you. What are you gonna do?"

"Call in sick?"

"Chicken."

"There's no shame in cowardice."

"Yes there is. Do you need any help?"

"Are you planning to arrange an armed escort for me as I sign in at the office?"

"I could loan you a Kevlar vest."

"Wouldn't go with what I'm wearing today."

I could hear Andrea's sigh travel the nine blocks between her apartment and mine. "I guess you're going to need drinks after work."

"Oh yeah."

"My tour ends at five. I'll pick you up at your place. You're not going to want to be driving."

"You got that right."

"Jesus. Suffering H. Christ!" Bill Owen was apparently aware of the press conference that had transpired in front of the school.

"Good morning," I replied dryly. I had arrived as the television news truck was pulling away from the no-parking zone its driver had been choosing to ignore. I also knew that by the end of the day, the rest of the TV and radio stations and print media would have left messages at the school, ensuring not only the wrath of my immediate supervisors but also of the school's secretarial staff, which, from a practical standpoint, was worse.

"What in the hell have you done?" I sensed Bill did not want to discuss the educational merits of having my law students attempt to correct a wrong. First thing in the morning, I'm on my game. Nothing gets by me.

"Technically, I didn't really do much except give my students a ride to the courthouse to file papers."

"And invited the media to use guerrilla journalism to attack me as I arrived at school."

"I must have missed that part of the broadcast while I was in my car."

"It wasn't pretty."

"I can imagine." Right away I knew I had said the wrong thing; that's how perceptive I can be.

"Patrick! I am in no mood for any of your smart-assed comments. You had no right inviting the press to the school. The district has protocols for things like that."

"Hold on, Bill. I may have helped the kids get the lawsuit rolling, but I had nothing to do with inviting the cameras. The kids obviously undertook that one all on their own."

"Why the hell would they do that?" I knew his question was rhetorical, but I have a habit of stating the obvious when the only outcome is likely to inflame a given situation.

"To make you look bad." The vice-principal was beginning to shake, and for a brief moment I did actually worry that he might have a heart attack and drop at my feet on the school's doorstep. "Just calm down, Bill. They're angry. They're kids, and you've put their backs against the prom wall. They needed to make a statement, and they've done it. They might have done it a little more publicly than I would have liked, but they've done it. Now we sit down and try to hammer out our differences."

"You think it will be that easy?" he demanded. "We've just been broadcast all over the breakfast show. This won't simply roll up and go away."

"It's CityTV," I tried to tell him. "It's unlikely anyone was watching."

"Except all the kids in this neighbourhood and their parents."

"Yeah, well, except them." From the corner of my eye I saw Sara approaching from the interior of the building. She was wearing a huge smile and had both Tim and Nathan in tow. If she sensed the fury steaming from the vice-principal, she either didn't show it or didn't care. I kind of hoped it was the latter. I shook my head at her, hoping to avoid a confrontation out in the open. If Sara noticed my not too subtle signal, she again either didn't show it or didn't care.

"Good morning, Mr. Patrick," she said, smiling coyly. That she did not address the vice-principal was obvious and deliberate. The girl had chutzpah. Before I could reply, Bill let loose with the tirade that had been building since he had arrived on scene.

"Just what in the hell did you think you were doing, young lady?" I have yet to meet any teenager who doesn't think the term "young lady" sounds anything but condescending.

"Oh, good morning, Mr. Owen. Is there something you wanted to speak to me about?" Sara's pleasantness was not only phony, it was also kind of funny. I smothered the smirk bubbling up, especially given the smirks already on Tim and Nathan's faces. Bill was near explosion, and I felt I should intervene to protect my student from his rage, but she seemed to be holding her own just fine.

"Don't be a smartass with me, Sara. You had no right to invite the media to the goddamned school today."

Sara did not seem at all intimidated by the hulk of the admonishing administrator in front of her, which I had to admire; despite my bravado, people his size kind of intimidated me. Maybe I *am* too skinny.

"I'm not sure that I like your tone, Mr. Owen," Sara replied calmly.

"I don't give a rat's ass whether or not you like my tone. You're in deep sh —"

"Mr. Owen," I interjected. By now a small crowd of students had gathered to witness the altercation, and its members seemed particularly pleased that Owen appeared to be losing the bout. Now I was feeling a need to protect the best interests not only of my student but also of the school. "If Sara is not comfortable with the tone of the conversation, profanity is not likely to make the situation any better." Bill, suddenly aware again of my presence, appeared lost as to whom he was angrier with. I tried to defuse the growing melee. "Perhaps we would be better served by going inside and discussing this calmly and in private."

"Good idea," Bill replied. "You and I will go inside. Sara, you'll stay out here for the time being. You're suspended."

A slight but ever so brief chink appeared in Sara's emotional armour before she caught herself and held firm. "On what grounds?" she demanded.

"On the grounds that you held an unauthorized press conference at school," he replied tersely, self-satisfaction creeping into his voice.

"In front of the school," she corrected.

"Doesn't matter. You're still suspended." A quiet fell over our little group. Sara made her move first.

"And what section of the School Act gives you jurisdiction over the city-owned sidewalk?" For the second time that morning I suppressed a giggle at her audacity. She was at least as prepared as Bill for verbal sparring, not that that was saying much.

"Sara, have you ever heard the expression 'a little learning is a dangerous thing'? Taking one high school law class does not make you a lawyer." He said the last word with such contempt that I thought he might choke on his own vitriol. Good counterattack, though: he'd managed to hit both of us with one shot.

"So is a little authority." Her previously pleasant demeanour was gone and she was starting to adopt a similar tone. Nathan and Tim were no longer laughing. Instead they, along with the slowly surging crowd of adolescents, were smiling silently in outright awe at their classmate.

"You are seriously pushing your luck, young lady." Bill's voice had lowered to a growl, and I was beginning to wonder if he was capable of becoming violent against a student, a female one at that.

"And does the School Act also give you the authority to unilaterally quash the constitutionally protected guarantee of free speech?" A small cheer went up from the throng of students. Bill's head snapped to face them as though just now becoming aware of their presence.

"We're done here," he finally muttered then addressed the crowd. "Let's go everyone. The bell's going to ring any minute. I don't want to see anyone late for class." The crowd dispersed immediately. Bill, at least, looked satisfied that some people were still afraid of him. He turned to face me and invited me to join him. "Come on, Mr. Patrick. I'd like to speak with you before class begins." We turned to head into the school, but he stopped and quietly addressed Sara. "No. Not you. You're suspended until further notice. You're to leave the school grounds immediately. We'll be in touch to arrange the conditions under which you can return."

"You can't do that," Sara protested quietly. "I haven't done anything wrong."

"Section eighty-five, subsection three."

"What?"

"You asked what section of the School Act gave me the authority to send you home. It's eighty-five, three. Come any further onto school property, and I will consider you a trespasser and have you forcibly removed, possibly expelled." A slight smile turned up the corner of his lips.

"You are making a mistake. This is not over." Even I thought Sara sounded like she was starting to lose faith.

"So sue me," Bill Owen replied before walking through the school door.

"Mr. Patrick!" Nathan suddenly blurted, stepping forward to join us. "Can he do that?"

"I don't know," I had to admit. "I'll see what I can do."

"Do something!" Nathan demanded.

"No, don't," Sara instructed me firmly. "This isn't about you. I'll take care of it." Tim had joined our dispirited group.

"Sara," he asked her worriedly. "What are you going to do?"

Sara smiled. "You'll see." Without another word she walked towards students straggling in from the parking lot.

"This is unbelievable. Have you ever seen anything like this?" Cassandra Beaumont taught next door to me, and the two of us, like nearly every other adult in the building, were staring outside at the swelling mob of students congregating anywhere on the school property except inside in their classes. In less time than I would have thought possible, Sara had convinced a sizable part of the population to stand outside with her in protest of what she deemed an unreasonable suspension. Not only had arriving students elected to support this fiery grade twelve student on an impromptu picket line, many students who had already entered the building and their classes had, as word spread, gotten up and abandoned their studies in favour of student solidarity.

"No, I haven't. Of course, given that this is my first year teaching, my frame of reference isn't very big."

Cassandra nodded. "Yeah, well, it's my tenth, and I haven't either. Every year there's some little grassroots movement to start a student walkout, but most often it turns out to be a few burnouts who would have been smoking pot in the cemetery across the street anyway." Sir John A. Macdonald High School is located, a bit morbidly, directly across the street from Vancouver's largest public final resting place. It is known as a great place to drink, smoke pot, and party. "What do you think they'll do?"

"Admin? I'm surprised they're not up here yelling at me."

"Yeah. You do seem to have a way of getting under their skin." From below I could hear a steady bass thump as one of the students moved his car close to the crowd to showcase his auto's audio abilities. Thankfully, most of the school's neighbours wouldn't be complaining, not in this lifetime, anyway. Their protest anthem was no "Dust in the Wind," but Eminem had more 'F' words.

"Whatever they do, they'd better do it quickly." Two floors below, on the sidewalk directly in front of the school's main entrance, two television news vans had pulled up, greeted by Sara, who was still on her cell phone, no doubt gathering more press to cover her rally.

"God, she's good," I said, shaking my head in amazement. Sara seemed to have the know-how of a PR agent. Across the street, a *Vancouver Sun* newspaper car arrived, taking in the growing crowd of students beginning to spill out onto Fraser Street to disrupt the tail end of the morning's rush hour traffic. Just ahead of the front entrance of the school stood the three administrators, and they didn't have to turn around and look up for me to feel their anger.

It took a little less than half an hour of press coverage and chanting students before the school's beleaguered principal, Don McFadden, slowly approached the ten or twelve students forming the command centre around Sara, who by that time, by my count, had given at least half a dozen interviews. If she hadn't already had a date for the graduation dinner and dance, she would be in high demand after today's performance. McFadden appeared not to make any pretense of bravado, standing with his head bowed slightly and talking quietly to her. After a couple of minutes, I saw her offer her hand to the principal, who reluctantly shook it in front of the entire student body and the Lower Mainland's assembled media. Sara broke ranks from her friends and approached the sidewalk, where a gaggle of reporters quickly surrounded her. Like a seasoned pro, Sara spoke to the media scrum without taking questions, then turned to the crowd of classmates and announced loudly enough for me to hear even from the third floor, "Let's go to school!"

It was probably the only time the school would ever experience a cheer from a group of teenagers as they made their way towards the building.

Because both our social lives had little activity, particularly on a weeknight, Andrea had decided she was coming to my house for dinner. I was not to do any cooking — she wanted it to be a good meal — but I would be responsible for having food on the premises. But in honour of no occasion I could readily think of, I opted to order in pasta rather than pizza. Even non-romantic female friends need to be wined and dined on occasion.

"I ran a check on your student," she told me as she sucked down a lasagna noodle with less daintiness than I would have thought possible, "to see if he had any priors. He doesn't."

"He just turned eighteen. Any criminal activity as a young offender wouldn't show up on background check."

She looked at me as though I were an idiot for assuming things like sealed records were actually sealed for her.

"Right. What was I thinking?" She shrugged. She was used to me forgetting how powerful she deemed herself to be.

"Anyway. It was his locker that was victimized. Why look for criminal activity from him?"

"Cuz if he was arrested for something, I would be able to see who was arrested with him, what types of people he hung with, and look for any patterns of vandal-like behaviour from his peers."

"Who you're assuming have turned on him."

"Because he's turned different from the rest of us." There was a certain logic to this I had not thought of, which is why she's the VPD's star detective and I'm the principal's pain-in-the-ass teacher. As I opened my mouth to reassert my dignity, Andy suddenly raised a hand, palm forward, to shush me. Her head was cocked with her left ear towards the entrance hallway. "Did you hear that?" she whispered.

"I heard you whisper 'Did you hear that.'"

She glanced at me for a fraction of a second, just long enough to remind me I was not to make jokes when she was in police mode. She was probably just showing off. Or paranoid.

"That hissing sound," she whispered again, though I recognized she wasn't really talking to me any more. She slipped off the stool she was occupying on the kitchen side of my pass-through and walked silently to the edge of the hallway, slowly poking her head around the corner. I crept around towards her from the dining room side of the wall and strained to hear whatever was sending her into combat mode. As I approached, she raised her fist, pointed to her eyes, then to the front door, just like I'd seen Kiefer Sutherland do on *24*. It was television re-run season already, but as I recalled it, she was indicating that she alone was going to check what was going on behind my apartment's front door. A sudden burst of manhood grabbed me, and I opted to seize the moment. I quickly marched past Andrea towards the door. At that same moment, I became aware of footsteps running down the exterior hallway away from my apartment. Quickly throwing open the door, I was in time to see the backs of two teenagers as they rounded the corner at the far end of the hallway and went into the emergency exit stairwell.

Without thinking, I bolted down the hallway after them, pulling open the stairwell door just in time to hear the emergency exit door two floors down crash open, allowing the two runners to flee into the night. I halted my pursuit, knowing not only that they'd be long gone by the time I reached the ground floor, but also that I'd look like an idiot standing there looking up and down the back laneway, trying to determine in which direction my prey had escaped. I'd learned that from *24* too. By the time I returned to my own end of the hallway, Andrea had pulled my door further open and was examining the outside. It had been spray-painted with the word "fagit," a reference to what I assumed the vandals were indicating as my own sexual preference.

"Now do you believe this is a police issue?" she scolded me. "This is a personal attack on you."

"I'm not terribly worried," I replied with more calm than I actually felt. "We're not exactly dealing with master criminals here."

"How do you know?"

"Look at their spelling. How clever a plot could these two concoct against me?"

"They managed to find your home," she insisted.

"I'm in the phone book. Even my dumbest students could pull that off."

Andrea gave me a scathing look. "What? You're still listed? Why the hell are you listed when you're a high school teacher?"

"I'm a friendly guy."

"That seems to be what they're implying."

The thing about teenagers, I told Andrea repeatedly throughout the rest of the evening, was that despite how much they claim to value secrecy, they are notoriously poor secret keepers. I had been trying to convince her that using taxpayer resources to involve the VPD in the investigation of the misspelled graffiti on my door was, in fact, unnecessary. I figured sooner or later word would get out about the "attack," as Andrea was calling it, students would start posting similar messages all over the school, and all we'd have to do is wait for the correctly incorrectly spelled one to appear, and voilà: there would be the culprits.

She wasn't amused.

I continued to appear flip while the official police work was done and until Andrea finally decided I was in no imminent danger and went home. Then I lay in bed for several hours contemplating just how seriously

I should take this implied threat and how far I should continue to push for Tim Morgan's boyfriend to be included in our school's graduation dinner and dance. When it became clear that sleep was going to elude me altogether, I finally abandoned the bedroom and decided to do my weekend's long run in the middle of a weeknight instead.

Generally, I tried to run about twenty kilometres on a Sunday afternoon or evening, but I needed something to do that would not only kill the dark hours but also prevent me from purchasing anything late-night television had to offer. For someone who cooks infrequently, I owned a disproportionately large number of devices designed to save me time dicing, slicing, and chopping. I also had a chainsaw, a bit extreme for the kitchen and of no value to an apartment dweller. As with all power tools, I was also terrified of the thing, so it languished in the storage locker in the apartment's basement.

It was a few hours before sunrise, but the lights of the downtown core across False Creek seemed determined to turn night into day. I generally avoided running in the West End of downtown Vancouver, because even on Sunday afternoons the amount of traffic made street-based exercises perilous. Still, it was a weeknight, so I threw caution to the wind and headed over the Burrard Street Bridge and into Vancouver's unique mixed business and urban core. Rather than turning west after crossing the bridge, as I would normally do on those kamikaze occasions when I chose to run along the famed sea wall, I followed Burrard Street north all the way to the opposite shoreline of Coal Harbour and

Canada Place. Making a quick loop around the posh Waterfront Centre Hotel and back up to Hastings Street, I headed west until I could turn onto Georgia and into Stanley Park.

There are those who believed running in Stanley Park in the middle of the night was inviting death, or at least, a severe mugging, but the reality was much gentler. Though it had long been held that the massive urban forest was home to any number of the city's increasing population of homeless people — especially as the weather got warmer and sleeping out of doors was less unbearable than in the wet winter months — my experience told me that if it were true, the park at night was used primarily as a spot for sleeping. The begging and squeegying normally associated with the city's downcast was generally reserved for the daylight hours and in the more populated areas. How much success could you have as a panhandler if you hung out in the middle of the forest? Squirrels aren't known for carrying wads of cash.

Not unexpectedly, I was not only unaccosted by my fellow man, I ran the entire length of the park through to English Bay without seeing so much as another soul, kindred or otherwise. By the time my feet pounded the Burrard Bridge pavement back to Kitsilano, the late spring rain was pounding in November storm-like fashion. You have to be from Vancouver to understand the subtle differences in the type of rain that falls on you for what seems like fifty of the calendar's fifty-two weeks.

By the time I got home, there was still plenty of middle of the night morning remaining before my presence was required at my workplace. After drawing out my shower as long as possible and reading both of the daily papers, I finally made the trip to school, arriving in the staff parking lot moments before six, early even by my standards. It hadn't really occurred to me that I might not be able to get into the building. I found the doors to the school locked. I couldn't help but take a little offence that I was willing to give of my own time to come in and prepare a stellar set of lessons for the day and couldn't even access the school. My sleepless night was already making me cranky.

The rain had slowed to a drizzle, and the spring temperature took the crispness out of the air, leaving it feeling muggy. After one last futile attempt at pulling on the locked door — as though persistence might magically cause it to unlock itself — I turned my back on the building, leaning against the door to stand underneath the roof's overhang and avoid the misty precipitation. There was little view to take in besides the sopping wet playing field where first period students would soon cover their expensive running shoes in mud. It was odd seeing the school so peaceful, devoid of the pulse had when students were around.

Scanning across the field, something at the far end caught my eye. The sun, such as it was, was shedding enough light that I could see a large dark mark obscuring the white paint down one side of the soccer goal posts. Curiosity and locked-out boredom got the better of me, and I walked a few steps towards the field. I only needed to narrow the distance a few feet before I could tell that the dark mark was in fact an object rather than a simple smear of a vandal's paintbrush. I continued to walk onto the gravel running track that circles the field, figuring I could at least report the debris on the field to the school's administration. After my role in inciting the demonstrations led by Sara, I figured scoring a few brownie points with the principal might not be such a bad idea. Another few feet passed, and the image was becoming clearer. I picked up the pace and stepped off of the track and onto the wet field as the alarm began to sound in my head. I could feel my heart rate accelerate as I broke into a jog then a full run. "Shit," I said aloud. There was a person slumped forward, tied to the goal post.

Tim.

Chapter Seven

Though the sun was up, the sweeping lights of the police, fire, and ambulance vehicles still danced across the hedges separating the school field from the private properties beyond. A crowd had gathered on the outskirts of the field, where school staff were doing their level best to keep the onlookers as far away from the scene as possible. Already media vehicles were beginning to line the street; having heard of an attack at the very same place they had been only twenty-four hours before, they wasted no time ensuring they were present for the even bigger story.

My first call had been to Andrea, since she was in effect my own personal 911 service. Tim, as I suspected, did not respond to my pleas for him to hear me. Even had he been awake, both of his eyes were so badly swollen, there was no way he could have opened them to see who was trying to rouse him. Blood oozed from the side of his mouth, dripping onto his left knee. His legs appeared to have given up the job of holding up his body. The only thing stopping him from hitting the ground was the ropes tied in three places: his upper chest, his lower torso, and the lower part of his thighs, just above his bloody knees. The rope around his stomach was tied so tightly, it had already begun to make a groove in his clothing and, I suspected, his stomach underneath. Blessedly, the downward effect gravity was having on Tim's body had actually caused the rope around his chest to slacken somewhat, alleviating pressure so he could breathe. Had his attackers been better Boy Scouts, their knots would have held, and Tim may well have suffocated. I didn't carry a pocketknife with me as part of my daily accoutrement, but I clumsily managed to undo the restraints and reasonably gently lower him to the ground.

Andrea managed to beat even the ambulance and fire department to the scene. She handled the unmarked Crown Victoria in that expert kind of way we'd expect from Mario Andretti. The car skidded sideways to a halt next to the field, and she burst out the door. She tossed me a very quick hostile look.

The fire department and paramedics were less than a minute behind Andy's gravel- spurting arrival, which gave me no time to flee my angry detective friend. She held off her scolding long enough for us to determine from the paramedics that Tim, while badly beaten, would likely survive his attack. By the time on-site first aid had been given, a small crowd of students was being reluctantly herded off to the building. The students were no doubt disappointed this violent encounter would not somehow yield an unscheduled day off. As Tim's stretcher began its bumpy journey across the sopping wet field towards the waiting ambulance, Andrea finally turned to walk towards me to begin what would no doubt be ferocious questioning. Glancing towards the school again, I noticed that one of our school's administrators was at the front of the building, half shepherding the kids inside, half trying, unsuccessfully, to block the media's view of the event. That left the remaining two administrators, Vice-principal Bill Owen and Principal Don McFadden, marching on a direct path towards me. I couldn't decide which conversation was going to be worse, so I headed away at an angle about ninety degrees from both advancing war parties, hoping to evade at least one of them. It was equal parts obvious and childish, but it wasn't as though my day had been going particularly well. The police and crime scene personnel stayed behind as Andrea broke into a trot to catch me before my supervisors could. "Where are you going?" she finally managed when she came up alongside me.

"I'm going to go prepare today's youth for the future," I replied without breaking stride.

"Just like that?" she demanded.

"Just like what?" Another question came my way, this time from Principal McFadden, who had joined our group. Bill Owen's breathing, after taking more quick steps in one morning than he likely took most weeks, had rendered him essentially speechless. Just for good measure, I picked up my pace even more to make sure he would remain breathless.

"He's just heading off to teach his classes like nothing's happened," Andrea replied, though to the best of my knowledge, neither knew who the other was.

"I think maybe we need to talk first," McFadden said.

"I think I need to talk to him before he goes any further," she replied forcefully.

"Who are you anyway?" McFadden had stopped. Andrea stopped briefly to introduce herself. By this time

I had made it to a side door and was halfway up the stairs before they were able to come inside. I burst into a slight run to my classroom, hoping to surround myself with students and make it awkward for my interrogators to conduct their business. I didn't really think it would work, but I was quite surprised when neither Andrea nor the administrators came to my door. I managed to buy myself at least a brief reprieve.

By the time the bell went at the end of the day, I was almost suspicious that they hadn't tracked me down. True, during the lunch hour I did hide in the custodians' office behind the boiler room making small talk with a janitor I'd never met before, but really, if they'd wanted to find me they could have. I managed to get out of the building in record time, and after a couple of quick phone calls from the car, I determined that Tim had been taken to Children's Hospital on Oak Street, the facility kids of all sizes generally went to when their injuries were severe. At Tim's age, for him to be at Children's meant the damage was at least serious.

By the time I had found a place to park and walked to the hospital, a springtime rain was falling again. Springtime rain in Vancouver is different to most other seasons' rain only by the calendar; it can be pretty grim no matter the time of year. In May, it was a bit warmer than November, so while I was still damp and looked like hell as I strode into the lobby, at least I wasn't shivering. A uniformed police officer was standing guard in the hallway. I had already reached into my wallet and grabbed one of my old lawyer business cards, which I dutifully gave to the kind officer, and while never actually claiming to be Tim's counsel of record, I didn't dissuade him from thinking it. He was just about to slide the card into his shirt pocket when the door to Tim's room opened and Andrea stepped out. "Oh, you've got to be kidding me," she said.

"What?" I asked her.

My friend threw a disappointed look at the obviously freshly minted officer. "I don't want anyone but identified family in that room unless they've been expressly cleared by me. Understood?"

If he was bothered at being dressed down by Andrea in front of me, he appeared too scared to show it. "Yes, ma'am," he replied. "It's just that I thought —"

"— you thought he was the victim's lawyer, I know," she interrupted. "Any idea why the victim of the attack would have felt a need to call for defence counsel?"

He seemed stunned by the question. Of course, I had been counting on that. "Do you want me to arrest him?" he finally managed.

"I would prefer that you shoot him. He can't talk his way out of that."

I sighed. "Are you done with the Dirty Harry routine? I've only got so much time on the meter."

"Like you paid for parking."

"It's more the principle of delay to which I was referring."

"Come here," Andy demanded, and before I could protest, she took me none too gently by the arm and guided me a few feet down the corridor.

"How's he doing?" I asked.

"He's awake. He's going to survive. But he took one hell of a beating."

"So I could tell."

"Which reminds me, why the hell did you take off on me this morning?"

"Because you were going to scold me."

"I was," she confirmed.

"You were going to tell me that I had gotten involved in something that was becoming dangerous."

"I was," she confirmed again.

"You were going to further direct me not to encourage this lawsuit between the student and the school and to focus on teaching in the classroom and allowing the business of making decisions about the school dance to be made by the people in charge."

"All of this is true. And you didn't want to hear it?"

"Kinda seemed redundant."

"You forgot the part where I was thinking about trying to spring some departmental time to put a watch on you."

"My own bodyguard? Can I pick her?"

"Her?"

"Remember that constable we ran into at Starbucks? The one you said had been on the job just a few months but showed real promise?"

"You thought she was cute?"

"I thought she was yummy."

"Yummy? My god, you'll never marry again. I'm serious, Win. For the time being, I really think you should try to lay low on this."

"You still don't think this is some kind of kid stuff?"

"Win, have a look at the kid. He's lucky he doesn't seem to have permanent brain damage or something.

Whoever did this to Tim was pretty determined to send him a very clear message."

"Come on, Andy. A gay student gets beaten up? That's hardly organized crime material. We're talking about thugs."

"Who didn't stop all that short of killing your student. Your name keeps popping up in this, those same thugs may well do the same to you."

"Schoolyard fights are one thing. Attacking a teacher is something else."

"Winston. Listen to me." When she called me Winston, it meant she was especially serious. Her tone took on a slightly motherly quality. "Whether we're dealing with Einsteins here is irrelevant. They're muscle, and they're not afraid to throw weight around. I need you to watch your back and try to stay out of trouble, at least until I can track them down."

"All right," I said resignedly. "I will be extra special careful and look both ways when I cross every street."

"I'm serious," she insisted.

"Me too, especially about that cute cop you're going to send me as a bodyguard."

"I said she had potential, I didn't say she was there yet. Besides, the captain wouldn't spring for any cash. Seems the VPD doesn't consider you particularly worth protecting from a good beating. So you're getting the real McCoy for the evening."

"Oh no," I protested.

She turned from me and headed towards the exit. "I'll be there in a couple of hours. Try to stay alive until then and order in some decent food. I'll be hungry protecting your ass." Defeated, I turned and headed back to Tim's room, the still-puzzled police officer still holding my old business card and not bothering to slow my access to his protected patient.

Inside the bleak, cream-coloured room, Tim was surrounded by a woman I assumed to be his mother and by none other than his high-school-aged, uncertified legal advocate, Sara. Both looked glum. Tim, who had wakened earlier in the day, was trying to cheer up his two visitors. "Look who's here," he declared to the room. "Can't a guy get a break from school even in the hospital?"

"Mr. Patrick," Sara exclaimed. "Can you believe this?"

"No. I really can't." Turning to Tim's mother, I attempted to introduce myself, to no avail. If she heard me, she made no notice of it and instead stood staring out the window. "How are you feeling?" I asked Tim.

"It only hurts when I laugh."

"There's little danger of that if his jokes are as good here as they are at school," Sara said. At least her sense of humour was recovering.

"Tim," I said softly, "I can't tell you how sorry I am about what's happened."

"Mr. Patrick," he protested, "don't you apologize. You didn't beat the shit out of me and tie me to a goalpost."

"I know, but still, I just feel like this whole thing with the legal action and ..."

"That's crap. This happened because people are homophobic and couldn't get into the twenty-first century like the rest of us. For Christ's sake, I could get married to my boyfriend, but I can't bring him to the dance? This is not your fault. This was our decision to do this.

Not yours." He paused for a moment and tried to reach for the cup of ice water on the bedside. Sara beat him to it and held it up to her friend's lips. Tim smiled and the remnants of his sip dribbled out the corner of his mouth, where his lower lip was so swollen, he probably had no feeling of the liquid escaping. "If anything, it's her fault," he said, nodding slightly at Sara.

His mother finally spoke up. "Tim, that's a terrible thing to say."

"She knows I'm kidding. Look, you guys. I feel physically like shit, but the truth is, I'm almost kind of glad this happened."

"How so?" I asked.

"Because now it's out there. It wasn't exactly a secret, and I know people talked about me, but hell, now everyone knows. It's like a burden's been lifted." I nodded my understanding though I couldn't possibly have understood.

"I'm just glad you're okay. I'm sure you just want to put this whole thing behind you. I know I do."

"I wish it were that easy," Mrs. Morgan said to me.

"Mom," Tim began to protest.

"Be quiet!" I couldn't tell if she was angry, frustrated, scared, or all three. "Tim insists he's going ahead with this."

"This what?"

"The lawsuit," Sara interjected. "Tim says he's going to keep fighting the school over bringing Van to the grad prom." I looked at Tim lying bandaged in bed, slim, light, and looking as vulnerable as I'd ever seen any kid. Yet the spark in his eye was bright. I may not have been looking, but up until then I had never seen it.

"Are you sure want to do this? After all you've been through?"

He smiled at me with puffy lips. "Now more than ever." From her side of the bed, Tim's mother let out a groan.

Chapter Eight

It's difficult to imagine my day could have gotten much worse than it already was. Not to be whiny, mind you; I recognized Tim's day was probably much more agonizing than mine. Still, when I got home I was greeted by Polish Sausage as I stepped off the elevator into the foyer. I was hoping that my weekend would be less stressful than my violent week, but the sight of our building's limping strata chair thumping towards me was not a good omen. I was ready to abandon my mailbox in order to avoid the inevitable complaint, but before I could back onto the elevator again, the door slid shut and I was trapped between Canada Post's euphemistically described "super boxes" and the aforementioned walking pork product.

"Oh, Winston," he began, as though he had unexpectedly come across me as opposed to staking out the lobby waiting for whichever resident he could annoy on any given afternoon.

"Hello, Andrew." Still couldn't get up the nerve to call him Polish Sausage to his face. In my battles between maturity and bravado, somehow maturity always wins. Or being a big chicken.

"I wanted to talk to you about something."

"That seems a given every time I see you."

"Yes, well, I've been trying to reach you all day." I had no response to that, so I said nothing. Sausage couldn't take the silence more than a few seconds. "I haven't been able to reach you."

"I know." He looked confused, and this time I couldn't take the silence for long. "See, if you had reached me already, I'm sure I would have remembered."

The silence was uncomfortable enough for both of us, so I decided to leave. It didn't work. Despite Sausage's alleged infirmity, he was able to poke his way around our building — his kingdom — at speeds that made subtle avoidance of him impossible. Nothing short of breaking out into an all-out run was going to keep him from keeping up with me. Of course, if he ran after me, that could settle the nagging question of the validity of his disability once and for all. Before I could reach a decision, Sausage had followed me onto the elevator. "What is it you wanted, Andrew?"

"Your measurements," he replied matter-of-factly.

"That's a bit personal. Shouldn't you at least buy me dinner first?" It was clear that Sausage got my joke, but he didn't laugh. I was convinced Poland must be a very dull place.

"For one with such an upbringing, you certainly are crude," he informed me.

"Indeed."

"We need to have the measurements of your living room area for the drywall contractor."

"It's about twenty-by-fourteen," I told him as the elevator door opened to the third floor.

"We need to be a little more exact than that."

I stopped and turned to face him in the elevator, preventing his exit. "Fine. Leave me the telephone number of the contractor, and I will set up an appointment."

"That isn't necessary. I can simply come in and measure it. I have my tape with me."

"Nope. Name. Number. Appointment. In that order." Sausage's face began to bloat as his anger emerged. It made him look even more like a sausage. Before he could say anything else, the door to the elevator closed in response to a summons by someone on another floor. Thank god for small mercies. Silently congratulating myself for limiting our conversation to less than two minutes, I rounded the corner to find an even less inviting sight outside my apartment door.

Sandi.

At seven months pregnant, Sandi Cuffling still looked stunning. Her blonde hair was meticulously managed, her makeup expertly applied to give the casual observer the impression she was wearing none. Only when viewing her side profile could one clearly see her pending maternity; no fat cells had dared invade other parts of her body, or if they did, they hid in terror from whatever workout regimen even this severely pregnant host imposed on them.

She was the kind of woman who had the ability to get most men to do most of whatever she wanted. I ought to know: she got me to marry her. To this day, Andrea continues to characterize the relationship between my ex-wife and I as a hostage taking; I was simply Sandi's first long-term victim, the divorce settlement my ransom. I continue to plead temporary insanity.

For most people, divorce generally means having little or no contact with the former spouse. At the very least, the amount of contact ought to be less than prior to the marriage's dissolution. Several months earlier, however, Sandi had revealed to me her pending maternity in all its gloried detail save one: the identity of the father. That she continued to shield the father from me made clear it was a moment she was not proud of. It did give me some small satisfaction that at least I was better than the man who had unceremoniously knocked up my stuck-up ex. It wasn't enough satisfaction, however, for me to be pleased to see her at my apartment. "The cheque's in the mail," I told her as I approached.

"Funny. Like you'd have any money to send me even if I did need it," she replied. I had created that opening myself: Sandi could never resist reminding me of the cut in pay I had taken in my change of vocation. At least in my previous employment the potential was there to earn the kind of income needed to live in the wealthy enclave of Point Grey. On my teacher's salary, I would be lucky if I could pay to have my car towed away from said enclave. Good thing I'd been living largely off Sandi's wealth the whole time we were married.

Despite Sandi's insistence on remaining a part of my life — we would always be really good friends, she kept assuring me — I never looked forward to her always unannounced visits. Of course, if her visits were announced in advance, she had long since figured out I wouldn't be home when she arrived. Sandi stepped aside as I reached the doorway and followed me in as I unlocked the door. I didn't bother trying to stop her; it would only make whatever argument we were about to have that much more public.

"I see you've been redecorating," she said, pointing to the white splotches of paint that covered the previously graffiti-covered door. "Chic. It goes with the general green tarpaulin look your condo's been sporting."

"So what can I do for you?" I asked after closing the door and heading up the entrance hallway. "Are you just here to comment on my surroundings, or did you need to mess with my psyche as well?"

"Winston, that's not fair. I haven't talked to you in ages. I wanted to see how you were doing." Sandi wanting to know how I was doing was always a euphemism for her wanting to know how I could help her in some way.

"Wine?" I asked.

"Have you finally bought some non-alcoholic for me?"

"And let that swill enter my home? Perish the thought."

"I don't know what happened to you, Win. You've become such a snob." She was right, and I had a pretty good theory about how I'd gotten there, but I was just too tired to trade insults with the former love of my life. Andrea always told me it's because I couldn't win in a war of words with Sandi. "I was hoping we could talk." *Uh-oh.*

"Talk about what?" I could do little to hide the suspicion in my voice. My heart rate only heightened as Sandi took up residence on the couch with both feet planted firmly on the floor in front of her. If this had been a casual visit, she would kick off her shoes and tuck her legs up onto the couch beside her, even though the move would be awkward in her pregnant state. Feet on the floor in front of her never led to anything good.

"Relax. You look like you've seen a ghost."

"You're pale, but ghostly is a stretch." She sighed her pouty sigh, the one that indicated she was disappointed with the attitude I was taking. I had heard that sigh a lot at the tail end of our marriage; it had pretty much been the cornerstone of our communication. "I'm sorry," I told her. "I've had a hard week. You were saying?"

"I know that things haven't always been really good between us. But you know that I still love you and consider you to be one of my closest friends?" See?

I believed the question to be rhetorical, so I didn't respond. I always found it disappointing when someone didn't recognize one of my own rhetorical queries and made a generally lame attempt to answer it. Besides, the only thing I could think of was a snide comment about her needing to get some new friends if she considered me to be one of her closest confidantes. But judging from the tone of her voice, whatever was coming next was sensitive enough that I ought to at least try to appear empathetic. "So I need to ask you something very important."

"Okay."

"Win, I want you to be there when the time comes." She spoke so softly and with more humility than I'd ever heard from her that I momentarily forgot about her impending maternity and didn't follow what she was talking about.

"Be where?" Her eyes widened in astonishment. That happens a lot to me with women, it seems. In her surprise she leaned backwards on the sofa, and her distended belly protruded into my line of vision. "Oh," I said, nodding and sounding a lot, I supposed, like Edith Bunker.

The silence returned for a moment. Truthfully, it wasn't that I didn't want to support my ex-wife in her moment of need; to my own constant consternation, deep down on some twisted level, I still cared about her, much as I frequently couldn't stand her. The sad fact of the matter was that I found the whole idea of being in the delivery room kind of gross. I knew that wasn't likely to go over well as an excuse to get out of the role of Lamaze coach.

"Well?" she finally asked.

"Sandi, I don't know what to say." It was one of the few times in recent memory that I wasn't lying to her. How the hell do you tell your ex-wife you'd rather be any other place than watching her give birth to some unknown man's bastard love-child?

"It's easy, Win," she said, leaning as far forward as her pending addition would permit. "You just have to say yes."

She was probably right; I could think of no way I could get out of this without some extremely clever excuse I could not concoct on the spot. Wine. I needed wine. Sandi continued to eye me, waiting for me to capitulate. With shocking clarity, I was beginning to realize I was about to agree to watch the whole birthing blood sport that would be Sandi's spawn's arrival. Too stunned to speak, I had only just begun to nod my assent when both our attentions were diverted to the sound of a key in the front door.

"You're really going to love me," I heard Andrea already beginning before even coming into view. For all she knew I could be sitting on the toilet, but she would simply stand outside the bathroom door and let loose whatever was on her mind. "Not only am I the greatest crime fighter in the history of the city, I brought dinner. And I don't want to hear any complaints about my choice of … oh. *You're* here." Andy had made her way into the living room mere seconds before I was about to commit to my new role of midwife to the ex-wife.

"Andrea," Sandi said, making no attempt to hide her disappointment not only at being interrupted but being interrupted by Andy, a woman of whom she had never grown fond. There are people whose outward contempt for one another often masks a deep-rooted respect and admiration for the other party. That was not the case here. They truly couldn't stand one another. In deference to me, they were civil when the planets aligned to put the three of us in the same room, though I would have liked to see the two of them settle their differences with a good old fashioned mud wrestle — or at least a pillow fight. About the only thing these two headstrong women could agree on was their mutual need to chastise me for the way I ate, looked, dressed, worked, etc. The only way it could get worse would be if my mother joined them in the room.

"I didn't realize you were having company," Andy said.

"I didn't either."

"Winston and I had something very important to talk about." If Sandi thought her not-so-subtle hint would cause Andrea to leave, she had temporarily forgotten who she was dealing with. Andrea does not like me to be alone with my ex-wife. She thinks I'll do something stupid. Like get her pregnant. "Winston is going to be there for the delivery."

Andrea nearly dropped the extremely large pizza box onto my birch floor. "Him?" she asked.

"Yes. We may not be married any more, but we're still very close."

"We are?" I asked. Both Sandi and Andy looked to me for clarification. "I mean, you know, you asked me, but I didn't realize I had responded in the affirmative."

"You did."

"I did?"

"Yes Winston. Don't deny it. You can't back out now just because you've got backup. I'm counting on you to be there for me." She stood up. "Just like I've been there for you all these years." That statement was even more ludicrous than the notion of me in a delivery room, but I was too stunned to argue.

"But this is Winston," Andrea interjected. "He cries if he has to squish a spider, for god's sake."

"That's not true."

"Right. That would presume you could get close enough to a spider to do the squishing."

"Exactly."

"None of that matters," Sandi insisted as she put on her coat. "I know that when I need him, Winston will be there, strong and ready to support me in this most important moment. I can count on him. You should have more faith in your friend."

"Right," Andy replied. Sandi left in a huff, which was the way she made most of her exits. Andy continued to smile her Cheshire Cat grin, always pleased at having caused Sandi to leave a room, as she carried her takeout victuals to the small tiled area that passed for my kitchen.

"Come and eat," she commanded. She reached absent-mindedly for two wine glasses and helped herself to a bottle from the rack.

"Cabernet?" I scoffed. "With pizza?" She slid it back into the rack.

"You would suggest?"

"Something gentler, like a Pinot Noir. One mustn't overwhelm the palate with so bold a beverage without a meal of deeper substance."

"You're such a dork."

"It's true." Andy ignored my sommelier instincts and pulled out the Cabernet.

"So who's the world's best detective?" she asked.

"Sherlock Holmes."

"I meant living and non-fictional, though if I were fiction, I'm sure I'd be in the same category as Holmes."

"I would have put you closer to Clouseau."

"Certainly you should remember I'm about to crack your case wide open before you go insulting me."

"'Crack the case?' Wow. Talk about shock and awe."

"I'm about to tell you of my major crime-solving finesse, and you're busy snobbing me out about my wine selection."

"You simply cannot expect me to take you seriously if you plan to use 'snob' as a verb."

"Gerunds offend you now?"

"A gerund is the other way around. You were saying about cases being shucked?"

"Cracked. We found something at the crime scene."

"What?"

"Prints. Better yet, prints in our system."

"They left their prints on the goalpost?"

"Not that crime scene. This one."

"You CSI'd my place?" Andrea frowned at my pop culture reference; she watched just as much TV as me, but it bothered her when I felt I knew something about her job based on what I'd seen on the box. "Why would they have touched the door?"

"They didn't. They did, however, dump their spray paint cans into the bushes in your back alley."

"You *are* thorough."

"Clouseau be damned."

"But how do you know those are *the* paint cans used to badly misspell homophobic graffiti?" Instead of answering, Andy, whose mouth was full of the gigantic pizza slice she had extracted from the box without benefit of utensil, plate, or napkin, pointed at her midsection, a gesture she normally used to remind me she had abs of steel, but which this time was intended to demonstrate she had solved the great graffiti caper through her infallible gut instinct. "Oh well, at least there are sound scientific principles involved."

"Prints were left on the cans."

"So you said. But that makes no sense. Those were definitely kids in the hallway. If they're young offenders, why were their prints in the system?"

"They weren't. We found the prints of a twenty-eight year old ex-con who did time in the late nineties for drug trafficking."

"And?"

"And we got lucky. He works in a hardware store not six blocks from here."

"How is that going to help us?"

"How many cans of spray paint do you think he sells to teenagers in this neighbourhood?"

"Sounds like a bit of a long shot to me. How do you know these paint cans were the ones sold to our graphic artists?"

"Oh, they were," she replied, pointing again to her midsection. "Now all we have to do is take in your school's yearbook and have our paint-meister pick out your perps from the photo array, as it were."

"It's my first year teaching, and the year isn't over. I don't have a yearbook."

"I picked up last year's from your school library on my way here."

"Thorough," I admitted again. She tsk'd me as she crammed the rest of the pizza slice into her mouth.

Home Depot is the kind of big box store that brings out the protestors when it moves into town, perhaps not as virulently as those picketing a Walmart opening, but vocal just the same. Vancouverites as a rule love a good — or even a piddly — protest, and no matter how few picketers arrive, it's sure to make lead coverage on at least one of the nightly newscasts. Lazy journalism to be sure, but it's mildly more compelling than the oft featured weather piece.

Despite protests, sit-ins, and bullhorns, the "tight-knit" Kitsilano community, home to some thirty thousand best friends, has now a Home Depot to call its own, albeit a "greenerized," slightly smaller version of its suburban counterparts, and on this Friday evening, it was jam-packed, not with demonstrators but with consumers. Having satiated their need to rail against it, tight-knit community members were evidently inducting the corporation into the community by spending thousands of dollars on its wares. There's already talk of a second one.

Andrea walked purposefully through the doors, though I knew full well her ability to tell a lathe from a drill press was about as strong as my knowledge of what either a lathe or drill press were. Her mission senses were heightened, though, and thus she practically scented her way to the paint department and made a beeline for the clerk operating a machine that was treating a can of paint like it was mixing a gallon of martinis. I recognized him from the dated mug shot Andrea had shown me on the way over. He had gained a few years and a few dozen pounds — the paint shaking business had obviously been good to him — but there was no mistaking this was our guy. "Courtney MacMillan?" Andrea asked in her polite but unmistakably police-like tone.

"I'll be right with you," he replied politely.

Andrea flashed her badge at him. "No, you'll be with us now."

"Okay," he replied calmly. If Andy's badge routine had upset him at all, he gave no indication. I would have been offended at her brusque intrusion, but MacMillan calmly reached up, turned off the paint can shaker-upper and handed the mixed latex cocktail to his waiting customer, who herself looked taken aback by the sudden appearance of the long arm of the law. Andy looked as though she was ready to begin when MacMillan politely spoke first.

"If you wouldn't mind, could we converse in the back, away from the customers?" He turned, stepping out from behind his paint partition, and walked toward the back of the store.

"Converse?" I said to Andy as we fell into step a few paces behind the departing paint-smith. She managed a sort of perturbed "harrumph."

"Boy, he didn't seem to be the slightest bit intimidated by your bad cop bit. Maybe you want to switch to good cop?"

This time she managed a brief retort. "We'll see."

MacMillan stopped at the entrance to a hallway marked "Private, Staff Only." Turning to face us as we approached, he gracefully waved us down the hallway ahead of him. "This way," he directed serenely, "if you would not mind."

"We would *not* mind at all," Andy assured him.

"Thank you, Detective," MacMillan replied. He stepped in front of us to hold open the swinging door to the inner sanctum of the home improvement mecca. He allowed the door to gently close behind him, then, without further word, strode down the nearest aisle way between two large shelving units. As he turned to face us his eyes blazed with rage. "Just who the fuck do you think you are, lady?" he hissed.

A slight smile pulled at the left corner of Andrea's mouth. "I'm sorry," she said, her voice adopting the same placid tone MacMillan's had just seconds before. "I could have sworn I identified myself when I came in."

"Can the bullshit. You've got a lot of fucking nerve barging in to my place of work and harassing me like a fucking criminal." It was clear MacMillan's Mr. Manners routine had been an act to save face in front of the customers. Or he was a sociopath; it's hard to tell the difference sometimes between a good actor and a psycho. His diction, I noted, remained impeccable, clearly articulating the "ing" of his expletives rather than the more colloquial "in'" most often used in today's vernacular.

"Aren't you?" Andrea asked.

"I was."

"I stand corrected."

"So what the fuck do you want?" His face was reddening, and he was growing increasingly agitated by Andrea's sarcastic grace.

"I want some information. I'd like your help."

"Why would I help you?" He had a point.

"Because you want to be a good, decent citizen, and you don't want your parole revoked."

"Okay. What do you want?" he sighed.

Andrea pulled out the school yearbook from the oversized, low budget purse-cum-briefcase she kept in the car but rarely carried. "I want you to find someone for me. A few days ago you sold some spray paint."

"We're a big store. How do you know it was me that sold the paint?"

"Your prints were on the cans."

"Did it occur to you that if I stocked the shelves, my prints would be on every can?" It hadn't occurred to me, but I had to imagine it had to Andrea the super-cop. If it hadn't, she wasn't about to admit it.

"Humour me," she said. Reluctantly he took the yearbook from her and made a half-hearted effort to flip through some pages and skim the photos. "Does this mean you remember selling to some teenagers recently?"

He didn't answer but continued to turn pages and scan images. After several minutes of silence, during which I counted eight different brands of bathroom sinks, MacMillan turned the book around to face Andrea. His finger pointed to a Grade Eleven student — this year in Grade Twelve — named Paul Charters. He was in my Law 12 class. Andrea didn't speak but took out her police notebook and recorded the name. The department had issued its detectives handheld personal digital assistants, but Andy had told me that powering up the BlackBerry lacked the dramatic flair of the flipped-open notebook.

A moment later he turned the book again and pointed at another student, Krista Ellory. It hadn't struck me that any of my hallway redecorators might be female. My sexist upbringing, I suppose, had taught me that homophobia was essentially a male affliction. "Yes, I'm sure," MacMillan answered before being asked.

"So you remembered selling the paint all along," Andrea noted.

"You don't sell a lot of spray paint to teenaged girls. It's easy to remember."

"See how we could have avoided all this unpleasantness if you'd just cooperated in the first place?"

"Probably would have gotten your information faster if you'd been a whole lot more polite and less aggressive." That, of course, was my whole point all along. Andrea uncharacteristically made no response, smart-assed or otherwise. She made a few more notations on her little pad, which I recognized as the detective equivalent of counting to ten. Finally she asked, "Do you recall if they said anything about their plans for the paint?"

"Do you mean did they confess any nefarious intent to this complete stranger of a paint clerk? As I recollect, they proffered no such information."

Nefarious? Three more syllables than "bad."

"And can you tell me on what day they bought the paint?"

"No."

"No?"

"No. I recall recently selling paint to those two kids. On what day the transaction transpired I could not say."

His politeness was clearly — at least to me — starting to rankle Andrea. It was amusing to see her starting to frazzle the more polite and articulate MacMillan became. Rather than risk further confrontation, she opted to terminate the interview. "Thank you. We'll be in touch." With that she turned and headed for the door. I smiled as warmly as I could at MacMillan then hurried after my friend.

"So what now?" I asked when I met her pace. "Do you go roust the perps?"

"Tomorrow. I'm tired of crime busting for the night."

"All right. It's been a long week. You can drop me off at home and I'll begin my reward-less ritual of trying to sleep." Andy shot me a sideways glance. "What?" I asked, stepping out into the environmentally friendly, SUV-filled parking lot.

"I'm not going home."

"Ooh," I groaned. "Do we have a hot date I'm just now being made aware of?" As a rule we were both so hopelessly inept at affairs of the heart, we tended to pre-brief one another about prospective and upcoming romantic engagements, followed by an in-depth de-brief, usually the same night. If the de-brief couldn't take place until the next morning, it was considered unnecessary.

"Hardly," Andy replied coolly. "I'll be staying with a sick friend, remember?"

"Who's that?" She shot me another sideways glance. "I'm not sick."

"That's debatable."

"Is this because you feel a need to protect my front door from further anti-homosexual vitriol?"

"And/or you from the same type of anti-gay beating delivered to your little law protégé."

"I'm pretty sure I'll be all right."

"Because you're so tough? Masculine? Straight?"

"Because I'll be in my apartment, locked from the hallway and the outside."

"That doesn't fill me with a great deal of confidence, given how effective security has been at your place in the past."

"We're not dealing with the same caliber of skels."

She shot me another look across the roof of her unmarked police cruiser as she unlocked the door. "You must stop watching *NYPD Blue* re-runs. You need a life." No argument there, though I'll give up Sipowicz around the same time I give up red wine.

"Still. I don't need a bodyguard. I'm sure the people who beat up Tim have no desire to beat me."

"Your door was their first target. And few people need much of a reason to want to beat you. I think of it almost daily. Besides, I'm not doing this for your sake. If someone gets their hands on you again, your mother will never leave me alone." She had a point. A few days of living with me until she made an arrest would be much less torturous than a guilt-riddled conversation with my mother. We rode a few blocks in silence, thinking about Tim and the two students who had been identified by MacMillan. Finally I couldn't resist commenting on Andy's interviewing technique.

"Have you ever heard the expression you catch more bees with honey?"

"Shut the hell up."

"Indeed."

Chapter Nine

Saturday dawned with no attempt having been made on my life and no attempt by me to get Andy to sleep in my bed while I slept on the couch. I just wasn't that much of a gentleman, especially when it came to Andrea. Furthermore, I remained convinced her presence was completely unnecessary.

I opted to do a second long run on Saturday morning rather than on my traditional Sunday afternoon, though I had already undertaken such an extended venture earlier in the week. I thought it might shake her willingness to babysit me around the clock, but unlike me, she's never one to shake off a challenge. In theory, my chronic insomnia gave Andrea a competitive advantage, but I'd grown so accustomed to running on so little sleep, it was all she could do to keep pace. The presence of a slight sheen of sweat on her forehead, not a common sight no matter how vigorously she exercised, was an indication I'd made her work hard.

After nearly a two-hour run, showers, and a luxurious breakfast at Denny's — I order the Moons over My Hammy sandwich every time because it always makes me chuckle — we parked outside the East Vancouver home of Paul Charters slightly before nine. In case his hobbies extended beyond vandalism to weekend organized sports, Andy thought it best we hit his home earlier rather than later. If we woke him up, even better: a groggy teenager was less likely to have his guard up. "You gonna take it easy on him?" I asked.

"Why would I do that?"

"You saw how well your Dirty Harriet routine worked yesterday."

"It got us here, didn't it?"

"I'm just saying he's just a kid."

Andy shot me a serious look. "Are you going into public defender mode with this kid? Are you gonna make him hire you first? Give you a retainer?"

"Look, I just … I'm a teacher now, not a lawyer. But that doesn't mean I'm indifferent to the treatment of my students."

"Your little cabal of criminals."

"He spray-painted a door."

"He almost put Tim in a coma."

"You don't know that."

"But I intend to find out. If you're going to get in my way, just wait in the car." Andrea rang the doorbell, and by the time the door locks were turning on the typical East Vancouver forties-era stucco house — the kind of stucco that doesn't leak — I had joined her by the front door. As it opened, I flashed my friendliest smile at the woman I assumed to be Paul's mother.

"Good morning," I began, "I'm Winston Patrick, Paul's law teacher from school." I was about to continue when Paul himself rounded the corner, fully bedecked in his soccer gear.

"See ya, Mom. That'll be Steve coming …" Paul stopped himself in mid-sentence when he saw me.

Dropping his bag, he turned and ran back into the house.

"Paul, wait!" I called after him.

"What's going on?" his mother asked, half to me and half to her son. Before I could answer, there was a clattering din from the back of the house and the distinctive voice of someone yelling "Police!" I turned in surprise, ready to declare my disbelief that Andy had brought backup, only to discover she wasn't there. Recognition sank into my consciousness that the cop voice I'd heard yelling at the back of the house had been hers. The woman moves like a cat.

"Excuse me," I muttered, because good manners are always important, even when about to embark on a foot chase. Darting around the side of the house, I was able to get to the backyard in time to see Andrea disappear through an open back gate. I struck out after her and heard a decided scraping and clacking sound. Looking up the alleyway I could see the departing figure of Paul, the scraping sound I'd heard coming from his cleated soccer boots striking the cracked and broken pavement. By the time they hit the street at the top of the alley, the gap between them was closing. He may have been a fit young teenager, but no one can run down a perp like Andy, adrenaline being one of her essential food groups.

I set out after them at a reasonable pace, knowing it was unlikely I could immediately catch up but figuring what I lacked in short bursts of speed I could make up for in endurance. When I turned the same corner around which I had seen Paul and Andy disappear, the two had begun to run up the grassy hill at the front of a corner house. For a brief moment Paul appeared to gain the upper hand as his soccer cleats found purchase in the wet grass. But as he reached the top of the rise, Andy reached up and forward, grabbing his leg just above her. With a near grace bordering on ballet-like, she pulled the teen's leg up and over her head, sending Paul like a wet bag of cement onto his torso. I almost thought I could see the air expel from his body as the wind was knocked out of him.

Hitting the damp grass, he began to slide downward. Though she tried clumsily to jump over him as he slid down the hill towards her, Paul's shoulder caught Andy's left leg, tripping her and bringing her crashing down on top of my already collapsed student, violently pushing out what little air remained in his already strained lungs. The two of them slid and rolled a few feet before coming to a stop in a muddy mass, Andy's semi-automatic in hand and pointed ridiculously close to Paul's face. At the site of the gun barrel at the side of his nose, Paul's eyes widened in terror, and he appeared to hyperventilate, though I'm sure his breathing had yet to recover from his fall. To his credit, he didn't lose control of his bladder, for which, having stared down the business end of a firearm myself, I would not have blamed him if he had.

"Andrea!" I yelled.

"I'm fine!" she grumbled back at me as she scrambled atop Paul.

"I don't care about that. Put your gun away. He's just a kid, for god's sake!" In one deft move, she spun Paul over onto his stomach, face down in the slippery, muddy grass. I thought I could just make out muttered, whimpering apologies as he struggled to regain his breath. "Paul, don't say anything else right now," I told my prostrate protégé as I trotted up beside them.

"Are you kidding me?" Andy protested. "Are you defending him now?"

"No. I just … I don't know what I'm doing. Old habits die hard, I guess. Just make sure you inform him of his rights."

She threw me a scornful look. "Yeah, Counsellor. I'll *Mirandize* him." I knew she was mad because she called me "Counsellor," a title she generally put out with no small amount of contempt. She also threw in *Mirandize*, an American term that has no legal bearing in Canada, but, much to the police's consternation, is often cited by arrestees who have grown up watching television and movies from south of the forty-ninth. It was never difficult to discern when my best friend was displeased with me, especially since it happened with such frequency.

The Vancouver Police Department headquarters is just beneath the Cambie Street Bridge in a facility that opened a few years back as the department grew bigger than its less glamorous Downtown Eastside facility could accommodate. Though it maintained both the new and former VPD locations, along with a small array of "community police stations" perpetually threatened by budget shortfalls, the detective and major crimes divisions were housed in the swankier new digs that many citizens had protested were the Taj Mahal of law enforcement. Coincidentally, my own teachers' union owned the building immediately adjacent to VPD's H.Q., just on the opposite side of the intersecting roadway. It too had its vocal opponents, who referred to the office building as the Crystal Palace of educational advocacy. Neither nickname was particularly apt; having had occasion to involuntarily find myself inside both, I could attest that the two facilities were pretty ordinary.

Andrea had dispatched two uniformed patrol officers to pick up Krista Ellory while she changed into some fresh clothes. By the time Krista was ushered into an interview room with her mother, Andrea was looking her professional best: business suit and running shoes, as formal as it gets with her. The two teens were placed in interview rooms separated by the anteroom in which we stood watching through panels of one-way glass. Was there anyone on the planet who didn't know that big "mirror" in an interview room wasn't for fixing up your hair? Looking through the window at Krista and her mother, I could not place the face: I had already known by the name she was not one of my students, but her face wasn't even remotely familiar. I had to assume that she'd had no particular personal vendetta against me and was along for the spray-painting ride with Paul. "So, which one first?" I asked.

"Both the moms are here, and neither wants a lawyer," Andrea replied, smiling smugly. Kids and parents could waive their immediate right to legal advice, but police couldn't use any information obtained from a minor without some form of guardian present, the theory being that kids lacked the sound judgment to assess the merits of speaking to the police without legal counsel. As a lawyer I thought anyone — kid or adult — who allowed themselves to be interviewed by the police without counsel lacked sound judgment. "Think I'll take the girl first."

"The 'girl'?"

"Chicks like to talk. She'll roll faster than he will."

"That's quite the sexist presumption. You sure you're not distantly a Steinem?"

"I work in an old boy's club."

"And you're fighting to change all that with your progressive attitude."

She raised her arm in a salute as she headed for the door. "Chicks rule," she proclaimed. "Watch and learn, girlfriend."

Krista Ellory sat sullenly at the small table in the characterless interview room, the only furnishing beyond the table being five metal folding chairs. If there was remorse in her head for having contributed to the badly misspelled mischief on my doorway, it was well masked. Indeed, she looked as though she was ready to kill.

"Hi, Krista," Andrea's voice came sweetly through the intercom on the wall, and if you didn't know her, it sounded like a teenager's.

"Who the fuck are you?" Krista asked.

My detective super-hero friend remained calm. "I'm Andrea," she said, her name ending with a youthful upward inflection that made it sound as if she wasn't sure of her own identity. "I was hoping we could talk."

"Like that'll fucking happen, old woman," was Krista's response. I glanced towards the mother. If her daughter's language was anything out of the ordinary, Mom gave no sign. She also made no attempt to correct her daughter's behaviour.

"Krista," Andrea continued in mock disbelief, like Krista had just asked her to do her math homework. "I really want to help you here."

"Really?" Krista's face momentarily lit up then instantly turned dark again. "Fuck you!"

Andrea sighed and shook her head, giving every indication Krista's unwillingness to accept her overtures truly hurt. "I'm having a hard time understanding why you want to make me the enemy here," she said quietly.

"Because you're the fucking pigs. Is that clear enough for you, or do I need to draw you a fucking picture?" If there had been any doubt Krista had been present during the spray paint purchase, it quickly evaporated: she had taken to clearly articulating the "ing" at the end of her expletives, a trait she had in common with Courtney MacMillan.

"Mrs. Ellory, perhaps you'd like to speak with your daughter a moment to see if you can convince her to talk with me?" I wasn't hopeful, but Krista's mother sat forward in her chair as though she was reluctantly willing to try, before Krista abruptly cut her off.

"Just sit back and keep your fucking mouth shut," she told her mother. "I don't need my fucking mother to speak for me. Anything you've got to say, you'd better have the balls to say it to me." I was trying to picture speaking to my mother with that language and in that tone. Right about the time the last word of the sentence escaped my lips, I'm quite certain my father would have intervened. He would have killed or at least seriously maimed me for even thinking of speaking to my mother like that.

"Krista, please," Andrea said calmly. "I really am trying to help you here. Couldn't we just talk, woman to woman?"

"Sure. Right after you do some ditch-licking, you

fucking dyke." It took some seconds before I even understood the metaphor.

Andrea sat quietly for what I'm sure was more than a full minute, the two young women staring each other down while Krista's mom and I braced ourselves for the explosion that was certain to be unleashed at any moment. Finally she leaned forward and in a voice just as friendly as she'd used since entering the room, said to Krista, "Do you need to continue this teenaged bitch thing a while longer?"

"Fuck you," Krista replied, though with much less force than she had begun the meeting with.

"Well, that wasn't the right answer," Andrea said with a sigh, then unexpectedly got up and left the room.

"Wow," I said when she returned. "You've got a way with the chicas. She sang like a canary."

"You would have preferred I beat her?"

"I almost would have, yes. My god, she's a lovely girl. So what now?"

She sighed. "Back to plan A. I'll let her stew while I get the boyfriend to talk."

"Didn't you beat him up once today already?"

"I arrested him. That's different." She started towards the other door.

"While I watch, should I learn some more?"

She didn't answer as she disappeared through the door and immediately reappeared through the window into the adjoining interview room. Paul still sat forlornly in his chair looking as though his best friend had left him. It was kind of pathetic. Both of his parents had joined him; their emotions ran from stunned confusion

— Mom — to pacing like a caged, angry parent whose son has just been arrested — Dad. Andy was still clutching in her hands the parents' waiver of right to counsel. Inwardly, I chastised them. Outwardly, I was getting hungry and just wanted my day of crime busting to be over. I found the volume switch on the intercom into Paul's room and prepared for the show.

"Paul," Andy began. "This is how it is. That charming young woman over there has given you up as the perpetrator and mastermind. She says she was only present because she's your girlfriend and felt she couldn't tell you no."

Paul looked up at Andrea, and his eyes began to well up with tears, something you don't often see from twelfth graders. "But that's not true!" he protested. Of course it wasn't.

"Well, Paul. I don't know what to do. Krista tells me you have this big hatred for gays, and she couldn't do anything to stop you. Are you telling me she's lying?"

He hesitated briefly, weighing what this unknown cop was telling him against the feelings he had for the foul-mouthed monster we had just left. If he was having difficulty imagining his girlfriend would sell him out, it was clear he didn't really know her that well: Krista was the type of kid who'd sell her grandmother if she could see some value in the transaction. She'd probably make a great realtor.

Paul didn't have too much time to reflect before his father's hand smacked him harder than I would have thought possible in this day and age. "Paul!" he commanded. "Answer the detective." My favourite television cops would have intervened at this point to thwart further child abuse from transpiring in their police station. My favourite real-life cop just stood and watched it happen. If the hit was a surprise to Paul, it didn't show. His father looked as though he would be as likely to slap his son upside the head as he would to say good morning. It all of a sudden made his teenaged rebellion and potentially violent acting out against Tim seem understandable.

Paul retained enough dignity to not reach up and rub what was surely by now a calloused spot on the back of his cranium. "It's not true. I can't believe she would say something like that." Andrea just stood quietly waiting for the rest of Paul's story to come out. "Krista thought it would be funny to paint 'faggot' on Mr. Patrick's door."

"Why?" Andrea asked.

"Because he was defending Tim, trying to get his boyfriend to come to the grad dance."

"And you're vehemently opposed to same-sex dates at grad?'"

He shook his head slowly. "I guess. I don't know. Krista thought he'd be scared off."

"By people who can't even spell faggot?"

"Krista says he looks like a pansy who'd scare easily."

Andrea tossed an ever-so-quick glance through the two-way mirror that conveyed her delight at his general assessment of me. "And Krista is so outraged at the idea of a gay couple at the grad dance, she thought she would take matters into her own hands?"

"I guess. She says she hates gays."

"And you?" Andrea asked. "Do you hate gays too?"

Paul paused again. "I guess."

"So whose idea was it to beat Tim to within inches of his life, yours or Krista's?"

Paul looked up, the tears that had been welling now overflowing and running down his cheeks. It was growing increasingly more difficult to picture him as a rabid, gay-bashing assailant. "That's what I've been trying to tell everyone. I ... we ... had nothing to do with that. I wouldn't do something like that to Tim. Or anyone."

"So your painting Mr. Patrick's door and Tim getting assaulted are just coincidences?" Andy asked with obvious skepticism.

"I guess." I was starting to wonder if he guessed as often on his in-class law tests as he did in police interrogations. If it worked as well in the latter as in the former, he was in good shape: he was currently an A student in my class of general underachievers.

"So if not you, who?"

Paul paused again, searching for any answer that would appease the adults in the room. Before he found it, he was struck by another of his dad's swipes. "Answer her!" he demanded. "No more bullshit, and stop protecting that bitch of a girlfriend. You think she's doing the same for you?" One more hit from Dad, and I was going out in the hall to get uniformed help if Andrea wouldn't step in to protect and serve.

"I don't know," Paul finally managed. "I don't know who beat Tim. I just don't know. I just know it wasn't me."

"And Krista?" Andrea asked.

Paul delayed his response again, and I worried he

was about to feel his father's wrath once more when he finally admitted, "I don't know."

Andrea nodded and headed for the door. "Okay," she told him as she turned her back. "That'll be all for now." She opened the interview room door, and Paul's mother finally spoke.

"Does that mean we can go?"

"*You* can," she replied calmly. "Your son's under arrest, and we're going to book him."

"But I told you I didn't hurt Tim," he protested weakly.

"But you did trespass and commit vandalism on private property. That's still a crime." Andrea nodded to a uniformed police officer. "Get these two in the system for me, will ya?"

"Sure thing, Detective," the officer replied.

We walked down the hallway towards Andrea's workspace. "What do you think?" she asked. "You buying his story?" I was kind of flattered that she wanted my law-enforcement opinion. Things were looking up.

"Honestly? Yeah. I kind of do."

"Yeah. Me too. I can't tell if he's honestly in love with that monster bitch girlfriend or if he's terrified of her."

"Maybe both."

"Sound familiar?"

"Ouch."

Chapter Ten

Whether Andrea's presence acted as a sufficient deterrent or due to the arrest of Paul and Krista, no further attempt was made to vandalize my apartment door that night, and by Sunday evening, the only one likely to make an attempt on my life was Andrea. Nonetheless, she insisted she was staying with me for the time being, convinced that Tim's assailants were still on the loose.

Having a houseguest — or armed bodyguard — is uncomfortable for most people, but it's particularly difficult for insomniacs. Not having given up my bedroom for Andrea, by Sunday night I was beginning to feel especially confined during my nightly battle for slumber. Living alone, I'd felt no need to install a television in the bedroom. When sleep eluded me, I simply wandered out into the living room — regardless of my bed wear — to partake of the pitiful offerings of late night television. Even for insomniacs with hours of night to kill, speed boat racing just doesn't cut it for entertainment. Having paced the room as many times as I thought my downstairs neighbours could tolerate, I made one futile attempt to sneak through the living room to the front door in order to do my usual middle of the night time-killing run, only to be blocked by the should-have-been slumbering Andrea the moment my bedroom door opened. Since I didn't want her to join me — the purpose at least in part being my desire to be alone — coupled with her steadfast and resolute refusal to pound the pavements of the city's west side at three in the morning, I was relegated once again to my bedroom cell, where I worked my way through about fifty-five pages of the G-H volume of the Encyclopedia Britannica set I had a acquired during my apartment building's annual spring garage sale. Yes, I was reading them in alphabetical order.

I was actually looking forward to going to work, which I finally did around six thirty. Andrea hung around the back of my classroom reading the paper until about seven forty-five, when she was convinced enough people were in the building that should I emit any cries for help they would at least likely be heard, if not necessarily responded to. Finally freed from my round-the-clock security detail, I had a few minutes of peace and quiet before the first of my students began to arrive. No one could have been more surprised than me to see one particular student.

Tim, walking with the aid of crutches and under the careful supervision of Sara Kolinsky, made his way awkwardly into the room. "Good morning, Mr. Patrick," Sara said.

"Tim, I really didn't expect to see you here. Are you sure you're all right?"

Sara answered for him. "He's fine. He wanted to be here."

"*He* did?" I was hoping he might answer for himself sooner or later, but Sara had taken to answering for me too. I wasn't holding out too much hope.

"He did," Sara replied assuredly. "He wasn't about to let what those bastards did to him keep him from getting a quality education."

"No. I can take care of that on my own."

There was a pause before she replied. "I'm a little bit busy with Tim right now, Mr. Patrick. I don't really have time to look after your self-esteem at the moment." She smiled for the first time since she had come in. We appeared to still be on the same team.

"Tim," I asked again in what would surely be a futile attempt to engage him in a conversation that would run through his advocate. "If you're worried about missing work, you needn't be. We can make arrangements for homework to be sent to you. You're not in any danger of failing or anything."

"He's more concerned with the momentum of his case slowing down," Sara interjected again. I had kind of been hoping he would be willing to drop the court injunction, given what had happened to him. "Did you really think he was going to drop the case just because of what happened to him?"

"Never even crossed my mind."

"Good. Because he's not about to be scared into giving up by anyone."

"Has he retained the ability to speak?"

"Not funny, Mr. Patrick."

"Not intended to be. I was aiming for serious inquiry."

Tim finally spoke. "She's smarter than I am. Why bother wasting my energy contributing to the debate?"

"I've never allowed someone's superior intellect prevent me from voicing an opinion. Otherwise I'd be a mute."

"I really do want to be here. I think it's important."

"You're sure?"

"Yes," they answered in unison. It was a done deal. In my brief teaching experience, I had already learned that entering into an argument with a determined teenager was more or less pointless. We spent the remaining few minutes before the bell rang discussing the next step in the legal process. I knew I was continuing to stir the shit more than was contractually wise, but I couldn't help but believe in the righteousness of the kids' cause. I was also feeling pretty pleased with the practical legal opportunity this was providing the class. A narcissist at heart, I was easily distracted by the thought this might be written up as a case study in a high school legal educator's journal, if there even was such a thing. The bell had just rung when Sara dropped the next bombshell of her legal strategy on me.

"By the way, Mr. Patrick," she began. "I hope you can get someone to cover your first period class tomorrow morning."

"Why?"

"I've booked us all as guests on CKNW. They're expecting us at eight thirty." I put on my best lawyerly cool face so as not to show my dismay at her ability to attract media attention. CKNW radio, the Top Dog, as it's known in broadcast circles, is the province's number one radio station, talk or otherwise. Its morning talk show is heard all over B.C., and it surely would not go unnoticed that we were drawing yet more critical attention to the school. Sara stared me down, waiting for my resolve to diminish. I wasn't about to be undone.

"Sounds like an excellent strategy. I can't wait," I lied. I wondered who would kill me first: Andrea or Bill Owen.

CKNW broadcasts from the twentieth floor of an office tower in downtown Vancouver. Its lobby, gleaming white with banners promoting it and its three sister stations, gives visitors the impression of having entered some sort of radio heaven. When I arrived, Tim and Sara were already sitting in the reception area, nervously anticipating the fifteen minutes of fame that awaited them. Brian Winter, the station's morning talk show host, could be seen on closed circuit monitors delivering the start of the broadcast editorial.

"Good morning, Mr. Patrick." For a change, Tim managed to get in the first words.

"How are you feeling?"

"He's fine," Sara replied.

"You didn't bring Nathan with you?" I asked. Since he had been part of the original plot, I thought he might have liked to share in the public glory.

"We figured we wouldn't get a word in edgewise," Sara replied. Coming from her, that was quite a commentary. We passed the remaining moments in the waiting room in small talk. Finally, a producer emerged from the hallway and invited us into the studio.

Brian Winter sat behind an enormous console, a wall-wide window behind him showcasing a panoramic view of the downtown core. We were ushered into three chairs, and a microphone was lowered in front of each of our faces.

In the first ten minutes or so of the interview, Winter delved into the issue, and my students responded ably to his questions. He saved his tougher probes for me, including asking me how my employer was feeling about my involvement in this legal challenge.

"Well, I certainly cannot presume to speak for the school or the school district," I replied. "I imagine this scenario is providing some challenges to people, to be sure. On the other hand, I'm sure that the school community appreciates and admires that these students are taking a principled stand on an issue they feel strongly about and putting what they've learned in class to practical use. It's really been a tremendous educational opportunity, on top of everything else." Professional spin doctors, eat your hearts out.

With that, Winter invited phone calls on the issue and went to a commercial break. "That went well," he told us, and to the kids specifically added, "You guys did great. Just keep it up, and you'll do fine. The next segment could be a bit tougher."

He wasn't wrong. The very first caller was much less than supportive. Through the speaker on the console, an elderly-sounding female voice asked Tim, "Did you not know that homosexuality is an abomination in God's eyes? We shouldn't be encouraging that type of behaviour by welcoming gays to the dance."

"Tim," Winter asked. "How do you feel when you hear comments like that caller's?"

Tim didn't hesitate to respond to the first real hardball question he'd been thrown. "Well, the reality is, whether or not I'm able to bring my date to the grad dance, I will still be gay. Not going to the dance will not *straighten* me out." Winter couldn't help but laugh.

The calls during the remaining portion of our time on the show ranged from overtly supportive — there were even offers of financial assistance that made me think I should be charging fees for my legal counsel — to outright vitriol. But as quickly as it had begun, time flew by, and before we knew it, our interview was over. By shortly after nine thirty, we already found ourselves standing on the sidewalk in front of the station's building. It happened so fast, we all stood in stunned silence for a moment trying to determine what to do or say.

"So," Sara said. "What now?"

"For starters, you should be able to make it back partway through second period and be there for the rest of your classes."

"My god, you can be such a teacher sometimes," she complained.

"Imagine that."

"What about you? Don't you have classes to teach?"

"Nope. Why take part of the morning off when you can take the whole day? It's been a long week."

"It's Tuesday."

"Yes." I didn't tell them I couldn't find anyone willing to cover my class. Helping me out had become the proverbial hot potato among my colleagues. The only way I was going to be available for this interview was to take a discretionary — read unpaid — day off. With luck, I might be able to pay off some sleep debt, but it was more likely I would end up trying to catch up on my marking. There's always marking.

"Maybe we all should take the day to rest and reflect," Tim suggested, only half-jokingly.

"He does need to recover and preserve his strength," his advocate added.

"I think if you're well enough to be on the radio, your health will probably sustain math or chemistry class."

"What about law?"

"You might even have a decent, qualified teacher for a change."

"Oh for god's sake," Sara exclaimed. "Go home and find some self-esteem!" She was starting to sound like my ex-wife, minus the hostility.

I had chosen not to bring my car across the Burrard Street Bridge, relying on my bodyguard and temporary roommate to drop me off at the radio station. I opted to go home via a leisurely stroll from downtown to Kitsilano. It was mid-morning by the time I made it home. As I approached my building, I noticed Polish Sausage lurking near the front door to the lobby. I was ready to duck around to the rear entrance, but I had gotten close enough that there was no point; his cane-assisted limp notwithstanding, he would surely figure out my escape route and intercept me on the way. "Hello, Winston," he called out.

"Good morning, Andrew," I said, adopting a tone I hoped made it clear I was being polite but was in no way interested in further conversation, especially if it was going to involve access to my home.

"Can I speak with you a moment?"

"I'm in a bit of a hurry," I lied.

"Really? I figured you weren't going to work today, since you're here in the middle of the morning. Are you not taking the day off? Playing a little hooky?" He smiled.

"Your ability to detect employment avoidance is astute. But then, I guess you have a good deal of experience in the field." Andrew paused as though counting to ten. I held the lobby door open for him as a reluctant gesture of no hard feelings.

"I heard you on the radio." There was no question or commentary requiring my response, so I just grunted. "You sure know how to piss people off," he continued.

"I have good role models."

"As long as you're here," he pressed on, "maybe we could look at getting the drywall contractor into your suite and get measured for the repairs."

"Sure," I told him. "Whatever."

The Reno Nazi looked stunned by my acquiescence. "Well, that's good then," he replied cautiously. "We'll be right up." I knew I had that much to look forward to. I picked up my mail and took the stairs up to my third-floor unit, knowing at least that he wasn't likely to follow if he had to fake-hobble up two flights. By the time I entered my apartment, I had torn open an official-looking envelope from the strata corporation. Just what I needed: it was probably yet another bill for the continuously escalating costs to repair the climactic sieve that was my home. It was only the ringing telephone that prevented me from seeing just how extensive the damage was going to be.

I dropped the mail on the side counter and scanned the condo for the handset to the cordless phone. Having a cordless gave the impression of having more space than I really did. Not seeing it, I turned to the phone hanging on the kitchen wall. Having two phones in seven hundred square feet made me feel more important than I really was. Well, three phones, really, but I keep the ringer off in the phone in the bedroom-cum-office; three ringers would alert the entire floor of my incoming calls. Given the calls I got generally came from Andrea, my mother, or my ex-wife, I had as many phones as I did people who called me with any regularity. “Hello?”

“Hi, Winnie.”

I cursed under my breath at my negligence in not purchasing a call display service. It would reduce by a third the number of regular callers, but I could live with one fewer phone. “Sandi. To what do I owe this unexpected pleasure?”

“I heard you on the radio,” she said.

“Shouldn’t you be working?” I asked. It was a joke, I knew, given that Sandi had rarely held any gainful employment beyond shopping.

“I could ask you the same thing. Are you trying to get yourself fired?”

“I do seem to have a way, don’t I?”

“Do you think you’re going to get in shit at work?”

“Oh, yeah. This could seriously cut into my year-end performance bonus.”

“I hope you hadn’t spent in advance.” We shared a laugh that brought a brief flashback to happier times. “If you get fired, you could always go back to the law. Clearly that’s where you belong.”

I knew she would ruin the moment. “So you were calling about?” It was time to move this along. On a scrap of notepaper next to the phone, I had already written "subscribe to call display service" and underlined it twice.

"I just wanted to let you know that I've signed us up for pre-natal classes. It will be Thursday evenings, starting next week."

"Say what?"

"Did you just say, 'say what'?"

"Don't evade the question."

"What kind of question is 'say what?' Is that some kind of black thing you're trying on?"

"No! It's … I work with kids."

"You're telling me kids today use the expression 'say what'?" Nearly all my conversations with Sandi left me tongue-tied. "So, next Thursday at seven in the Kitsilano Community Centre. I even found a class close to your home."

"So I can be further humiliated near people I know?"

"Ha. Ha. You're funny. You know I love you for this." If that was supposed to be comforting, it seemed to me to be more of a threat. She hung up before I could protest further, another tool held over from *discussions* during our years of marital bliss.

I now had a significant portion of the day in front of me, which for normal people would entail kicking back with a good book, but for teachers any bank of unexpected time was usually seen as an opportunity to catch up on marking. I had yet to master an effective marking management strategy or system. To my disappointment, I'd spoken to many colleagues with up to twenty years experience who had yet to either. It didn't give me much hope. To put off the inevitable just that little bit longer, I returned to the pastime I found more enjoyable: the mail. Most was the usual stuff: bills, offers from realtors willing to take on what was surely the monumental task of selling my leaky condominium, and the already opened letter from my strata corporation. I took a deep breath before reading the contents of the letter, bracing myself for the notification that would deplete my savings account even further than my divorce. To my unutterable surprise, the letter did indeed include a demand for more money, but not for increased costs in the repair process. Instead I was being fined by the strata council, chaired by none other than Polish Sausage, for being uncooperative and obstructive with regard to the ongoing repairs to the building. Me. Uncooperative. My "attitude," the letter told me, was going to cost me fifty dollars.

During my divorce, it had cost me a great deal more.

I was so tired, I could not even muster up outrage. I suppose I should have kicked something or at least cursed, but instead I picked up the phone, calmly called the property management company and informed them that under the Strata Properties Act of British Columbia, there was no provision for fining an owner because the council did not like their attitude. The property manager, a local car salesman miraculously turned residential real estate management expert, was about to argue with me when I reminded him of my profession and asked if he really thought it would be in the strata corporation's best interests to have to fend off a lawsuit. Within twenty minutes he had called me back, assured me there would be no fine levied against me, and apologized profusely for the inconvenience the council had caused under his stewardship.

Poor guy. I knew he likely had little to do with the decision to charge me for being me. The thing reeked of Polish Sausage. No wonder Andrew had looked so uncomfortable at the end of our conversation downstairs. He had been spoiling for a fight, knowing full well he had what he thought was an ace up his sleeve. He was likely now getting the phone call from the property manager informing him his plan had been foiled. I felt stupidly powerful.

Not unexpectedly, I'd not had much success sleeping the night before, anticipating my broadcast debut and the effect it would have on my already strained employer-employee relationship. Just about everyone else's opinions notwithstanding, I really didn't relish getting myself into hot water. I just managed to do it somehow. A lot.

I spent the better part of the afternoon marking dismally poor quality ninth grade social studies papers, most of which had thesis statements of such stunning profundity as "the English were bad to the Natives when they settled," the vague pronoun reference generally acting as foreshadowing of the quality of the argument to be presented. It made one wonder why we punish ourselves by having to read this kind of work, but somewhere in the deep, dark recesses of my mind, I knew that I myself had learned how to properly craft an argument by doing it over and over. Still, I had a hard time imagining I could have written some of this crap. When the telephone rang again, I realized several hours had passed and the pile of papers had significantly diminished. It was hard to believe that even these had failed to relieve me of my insomnia. I nearly picked up the phone and changed my mind. I couldn't bear another conversation with Sandi.

As soon as the call had gone to voice mail, I listened to the message and immediately called back.

"Why the hell didn't you answer the phone?" Andrea demanded. "I knew you were home."

"How did you know that?"

"Where else would you possibly have been?" She meant it as an insult and it sounded pretty clearly like one. If I wasn't at work and wasn't with her, where would I be?

"I was worried you might have been Sandi calling. I didn't want to talk to her."

"I know how you feel. I never want to talk to her. Why don't you get call display like the rest of the population in the twenty-first century?"

"I'm going to. I assume there's a reason you're phoning?"

"Several. One: I needed to ensure you're still alive, all the more reason you need to answer the damned phone when I'm calling."

"Call display is now triple underlined on my list."

"Two: I have news. I'm on my way over, then you're taking me for dinner and a workout."

"You romantic fool."

"Uhm-hmmm," she muttered then suddenly cursed. "You asshole!"

"Ouch."

"Not you, the dumbass who just pulled out in front of me. They give anyone a license these days."

"Why don't you pull him over?"

"Can't be bothered."

"Beneath you?"

"I'm hungry. I'll be there in ten minutes."

•❧❧•

When she arrived, I was pleased to see that she'd left the car parked out front — Andrea being one of the few Vancouverites I knew who could ever immediately find parking in Kitsilano on her first try. That meant we were heading out on foot, meaning eating local, which also pleased me, because it meant there was a reasonable chance we were headed to Chianti. Tonight I could potentially stun the regulars by bringing Andrea with me, though those who were as regular as I knew full well who she was and that she in no way qualified as a date. Things were looking up as we crossed to the south side of West Fourth Avenue and headed towards Burrard Street. To my shock and dismay, we strolled right by the front entrance. There was not much remaining in our direction: Mexican on the corner, which was okay in principle, but the Mexican restaurant three blocks behind us was far superior; sushi, which wasn't really an option given that even Andrea couldn't get me to eat raw fish, or the Touch of India curry house. I had yet to sample its wares, mainly because my bland Irish upbringing considered garlic to be a seriously hot spice. Yet Andrea turned into the Indian restaurant's doorway as though we'd been there a hundred times.

"You've got to be kidding me," I complained.

"You need to expand your horizons."

"I really don't. It's Tuesday. I eat Italian."

"Why? Why do you have to do that every Tuesday night?"

As I resigned myself to the culinary ordeal about

to befall me, mentally taking inventory of my medicine cabinet at home to convince myself I had sufficient quantities of antacid, we took a table overlooking the busy thoroughfare.

"Do you want to order, or will you just leave it to me?" she asked.

"Do you think they'd be offended if I had Chianti deliver their pasta special?" She shook her head in disgust and waved over a young woman. Andy cared enough about me to at least attempt to find a dish mild enough that it would not set my insides completely on fire. She, on the other hand, would surely have sought food with enough spice to kill the aroma of an entire garbage dump. Her abs of steel were both external and internal. I finally pressed her into the business portion of our evening. "So you mentioned on the telephone, while spewing profanity at your fellow commuters, that you come bearing news."

"Why can't you speak like a normal person?" she asked.

"It's part of my charm."

"Says the perennially single guy." She added, "If you mention anything about pots and kettles calling each other colours, I'm going to kick you right here under the table and make you limp during your late night insomniac trek through the city."

"Why can't *you* speak like a normal person? You know imitation is the highest form of flattery."

"I have fingerprints," she declared. "On the goalpost where your little friend was tied and beaten."

"You science types are amazing. Tell me, oh magical one, if I may question you yet again, how do you know the prints on a school goalpost come from our skels?"

"It was raining heavily all that week. Any other prints would likely have been washed away. We got two clean prints from two perps and one set of partials."

"And they belong to?"

"Don't know."

"So what you really have is bupkis." My years in the legal defence field had trained me to detect bupkis in a case.

"No, what I have is two clearly identifiable prints I have yet to identify, as they were not in our system."

"Which is highly likely, given that we're probably dealing with minors whose records, if they had them, would be sealed."

She gave me a sly look. "They weren't in any juvenile files I could find either." I was about to protest about violating the rights of young offenders when she raised a hand. "Spare me the lecture, okay? I struck out anyway."

"Why don't you just search the Child Find database parents use to protect their kids and troll for suspects there?"

"Come on, you know even I wouldn't go that far." She slumped back in her chair. "And I couldn't even if I wanted to. Those files are not in any way connected to ours."

"Couldn't find a computer hacker with no conscience?"

"Nope. Stupid techy got all Charter of Rights on me."

"Wow, a detective with a moral conscience. There are some left."

"He's a civilian." We paused as the young server brought us our food.

"Ahh. So, that leaves us back to you having bupkis. I think for bupkis I should have gotten to choose the dinner locale."

"What I have is solid physical evidence, so that when I shake down one or more of the little delinquents you teach and get something resembling a confession closely enough, I'll be able to get a warrant, get some prints, and prove who beat the snot out of your kid."

"A warrant? My heavens! What a conversion you've had."

"And by the way, have you talked to Tim again about the attack? I mean, could he really have seen nothing of who grabbed him? Do you think he's holding back on us?"

"I can't imagine why."

"Cuz he's afraid?"

"Because he got beaten nearly half to death and might be afraid there would be retribution for identifying his attackers. She was fully engrossed in dipping something into a pile of something else and shovelling it into her mouth. I was starting to sweat just watching her. "Eat up," she ordered. "If we're going to work out you're going to need the energy."

I glanced glumly at the vegetarian-looking meal that had been placed before me. I was at a loss to identify what the vegetables were. "I may just take my chances on having a lighter workout."

"If you faint on the Stairmaster, don't expect mouth-to-mouth." A greenish-brown sauce had dripped onto her chin.

"Do you promise?"

Chapter Eleven

The Saab 9–3 convertible is a machine to be reckoned with. An argument could be made — and frequently was by my mother and Andrea — that the number of days of sunshine in the Vancouver area hardly warranted the purchase of a convertible. They were right, of course. Nonetheless, no one was going to tell me that it wasn't a cool vehicle, and driving it upped my cool quotient significantly. Or, if they were going to tell me, I wasn't about to pay them any heed. Even my ex-wife's appreciation of the car was not enough to dissuade me from my Swedish vehicular ownership.

Wednesday arrived warm and sunny, not entirely unusual for Vancouver in May but certainly enough of a bonus to imbue the city's inhabitants with a general feeling of satisfaction. Naturally, I had been awake to see the nighttime clouds dissipate over English Bay, and while the bulk of suburbia to the east prevented unobstructed views of the coming sunrise, it was clear the day was going to be one worthy of top-down driving. In overly optimistic sartorial confidence, I had donned the lightest of my lightweight summer suits, despite the morning chill I knew would persist until at least nine. But a pre-school latte would take the bite off the temperature, and a rag-topless commute would put me in a healthy frame of mind to face what would no doubt be the storm of protest from colleagues, students, and supervisors.

My apartment is outfitted with underground "secure" parking. My Saab was in its assigned location, directly under one of what seemed the few garage lights and within line of sight of the building's security cameras. I knew this because on many occasions, finding little else worthy of my attention during sleepless nights, I'd passed interminable minutes viewing the security channel and ensuring roughly every two and a half minutes that my beloved car was safe. Last night had been the exception. Having achieved the usual cumulative total of about two hours sleep, I had engrossed myself in a broadcast of *The Best Little Whorehouse in Texas,* an eighties vintage musical starring Dolly Parton and pre-toupee Burt Reynolds, thus missing the opportunity to actually see who had beaten the living crap out of my precious car.

My first call was to Andrea, who responded in her usual spry manner and pulled up beside me in her police issue Crown Victoria within minutes. "Who says people don't listen to talk radio anymore?" she said. I stood staring dumbfounded at the multitude of dents on every metal surface. "They take anything?"

"My pride. My joy. My reason for being."

"It's a car, Win," Andy sighed.

"It's a Saab 9–3 Turbo convertible. Turbo!"

"Is your life so empty that your car is your *raison d'être*?" She gave me the hairy eyeball in disgust. "Oh yeah, sorry about that. No offence."

"None taken." I had done a cursory search of the vehicle and noted that nothing had been taken. Of course, not trusting the claim of "secure" underground parking, I really had left nothing of value in the car. The car *was* the value. Andrea had already moved away from me and was beginning to examine other cars. I had not yet thought to do so. I really didn't care about any of my neighbours' cars — none of them were the Saab 9–3 Turbo convertible.

Satisfied that a rash of automotive vandalism had not transpired, Andrea returned to my side. "Nope. Looks like it was just you."

"How am I going to drive to school with my car looking like this?" I asked.

"You're not. The car's going to have to be processed for prints and anything else we can find that could point us to your increasingly hostile anti-gay students."

"You sound pretty confident this is related to Tim's lawsuit."

"Come on, Win," she insisted. "Yours is the only car that got hit. Your apartment was the only one to be vandalized. You're leading the charge to get your little gay buddy to the dance with his little gay buddy." I cocked a disapproving eyebrow her way. "Yeah, yeah, I know. Not politically correct, but I haven't had enough caffeine to think about what I'm saying before I actually say it."

"You said yourself this could be the work of some whacko radio listener who didn't like what I had to say on NW yesterday. It could be completely unrelated to Tim's actual assailants."

"Or Tim's assailants could be sending you a message to back off from ruining their grad dance."

"How is Tim's choice of date going to affect their enjoyment of the grad dance?" I demanded.

"Sorry," she pleaded, raising her hands. "Again with the speaking before thinking. You don't need to fight your case with me. I'm just trying to not let you get killed."

"They're not going to kill me."

"They did a helluva number on Tim. This could be your early warning."

I sighed. Whatever measures she decided were most prudent were ultimately the measures I would be taking. Besides, I hadn't had any caffeine yet either, and my Saab 9–3 Turbo had been beaten up. I couldn't take a losing argument on top of all that. "How am I going to get to work?" I whined.

"It's still early. I'll get you to a car rental place so you can get a replacement while we check out your precious Saab and you get it repaired."

"Saab 9–3 Turbo," I corrected. "I can't get a replacement car until I make an insurance claim. I don't have a claim number or anything yet."

"You've got something better."

"What's that?"

She moved over and put her arm around my waist. "A best friend who can wave a badge in the rental agent's face."

"You can't possibly be serious."

The smile quickly evaporated from the overly vivacious clerk's face. "Sir, did I mention it's brand new? You will be its first renter."

"You did, but you neglected to mention that while new, it is also a mini-van."

Andrea was having difficulty suppressing giggles. Soon she would stop trying.

"Oh, are you worried about the increased cost? We'll only charge you the rate for a compact. Since we didn't have one available, you get to drive the roomier vehicle at no extra cost!" The clerk tried the perky smile again. In addition to acquiring an acceptable mode of transportation, I was also seeing it as my mission to quash the young woman's persistent perkiness.

"I drive a Saab," I told her, with the expectation the statement would clarify the predicament she was placing me in.

"The 9–3 *Turbo* convertible," Andrea added. Both of our comments rendered the supra- helpful clerk speechless.

Finally the barely twenty-something girl spoke again. "So you don't want to rent the car then?"

Andy snatched the key that had been proffered. "He'll take it." Turning to me, she added, "You. You'll need to stop being such a snob, at least temporarily. You have a class in half an hour. I think you're in more than enough shit without adding truancy into the mix. Swallow your pride, get behind the wheel of that minivan ..."

"Caravan, actually," the clerk interjected helpfully.

"Caravan!" Andrea practically shouted. She raised an invisible glass. "To good old American-made quality."

"Fine. Where do I sign?" The clerk's joviality returned with a vengeance as she indicated the place I needed to sign to legalize my descent into vehicular humiliation. Turning to Andrea, I said, "But if you think I'm going to consume domestic wine just because I'm driving domestic, you're dreaming."

"I'll meet you after work for some Coors Light," she said, punching my shoulder.

School was not the media circus it had been just days earlier, and for that I was truly thankful. I had drawn enough publicity for my beleaguered principal and school and worse, I couldn't imagine friends and family catching sight of me on the evening news pulling into the staff parking lot in a beige mini-van. I could see no way to live that down. I thought the coast was clear as I pulled into my parking spot, but no sooner had I exited the motorized monstrosity than Sara appeared as if she had been stalking me, Tim and the ever-gregarious Nathan obediently at her side. I was expecting her to launch into what she perceived to be the latest developments in our crusade, but she appeared as taken back by my ride as I had been when it had pulled out in front of the rental office.

"What the hell is that?" Nathan demanded, bursting out laughing before I could even begin to concoct an explanation for my newfound mode of transportation.

"I don't know what you're talking about," I replied.

"Where's your car?" Sara asked. "The ragtop. The Saab?"

"It's a Saab 9–3 Turbo," Tim corrected her. I kept liking him more and more.

"How come you guys know what kind of car I drive? Do you keep tabs on all your teachers' vehicle choices?"

"Only the cool ones," Nathan assured me. Damn it, I knew I was right: the car *did* improve my cool quotient. "I meant the cars, by the way," he continued as though reading my mind. "The teachers with cool cars. Though, having a cool car doesn't hurt."

"So?" Sarah demanded. "Where is it? Why in god's name are you driving this ridiculous thing?"

"I decided to make a few changes in my life, that's all." I wasn't sure Tim needed to hear my car had likely fallen victim to the samc angry homophobes he had.

"Please. I don't believe you could suddenly turn that pathetic."

"Hey," I protested. "What do you drive?"

"A mini-van," she replied. "But it belongs to my mother and everyone knows that. People don't know that about you, and frankly, if this is your mom's, that makes it that much more pathetic. You're a divorced guy on the prowl, Mr. Patrick. You can't afford to make these kinds of radical changes right now."

"Yeah, can't see you scoring with the chicks in this cruising vessel," Nathan chimed in, then laughed uproariously again.

I turned to Tim. "Are you going to help me here, or am I pretty much on my own?"

Tim smiled. "Sorry. I have no expertise in chick-cruising." At this Nathan roared even harder. "But I don't think you'd be terribly successful recruiting from my team with this thing either." We had well since crossed the line of appropriate teacher-student discourse.

"I'm leaving. I have a class to teach, and in theory you have some classes to attend."

"Notice how he gets all teacher when he's uncomfortable?" Nathan asked.

"It's such an obvious defence mechanism," Sara

agreed. “Seriously though, you didn’t really buy this thing, did you?”

“No,” I finally admitted. “I’m just having some work done on my car, that’s all.”

Sara was immediately skeptical. “What kind of work?”

“Car work, okay?” Her eyebrow was raised, and I could tell she knew I was being evasive. My history at successfully lying to women, even teenaged ones, was full of episodes of the gentler sex calling bullshit.

“How much work can your car be getting that you have to rent one?” she probed further. As though sensing Sara’s shift into interrogation mode, both Nathan and Tim stopped laughing and seemed to drift into the background as she walked backwards in front of me to slow my escape. “Did something happen? Were you in an accident?”

“No, I wasn’t. It’s nothing.”

“But it’s not mechanical. It’s body work.”

“That depends on how you define body work. Sara, you’re going to make me late for class.”

She actually put her hand on my chest to block my progress towards the building. If I was in charge in this situation, it wasn’t readily apparent to any of us. “Stop, Mr. Patrick. What aren’t you telling me?” She was remarkably strong. Andy would probably say it had more to do with my lack of strength, but that’s splitting hairs. I finally relented and decided to come clean.

“My car was vandalized at my apartment last night.”

“What?” Tim practically yelled. “How badly?”

“Bad enough.”

“You love that car,” Nathan added.

"What makes you say that?"

"You have a picture of it on your computer desktop," Sara noted.

Tim looked absolutely crestfallen. "I don't believe this," he muttered barely audibly enough to be heard over the din of the passing traffic. "This has gone too far."

"Tim," I said, "I think we passed the too far benchmark when they put you in the hospital. This is just a car."

"Or a warning to you not to continue with the lawsuit, or they'd do to you what they did to me." We were all quiet a moment as we reached the door to the school, even Nathan, who as a rule was nearly always talking or at least laughing.

Finally Sara spoke. "Tim, this isn't your fault, is it Mr. Patrick?"

"Of course not. Taking on a just cause is never without a cost," I told my protégées, trying to sound inspiring. "Besides," I continued, "we don't really know my car's vandalism is even related to your case at all. This is Vancouver, and I park in an underground lot. It's quite possible this was just a random act."

"Right after you help us launch a lawsuit and appear on a talk show defending teenaged gay rights. That seems a little too coincidental," Tim said.

"Hey, don't flatter yourself," I said, trying to raise his spirits. "It's not all about you."

"Yeah," Sara joined in. "Try to imagine the number of people he's pissed off for any number of reasons. I'm sure your case is just the tip of the iceberg."

"That's right," I agreed.

"Students unhappy with their marks," Sara suggested.

"Former criminals that weren't happy with how he defended them," Nathan offered.

"Someone he cut off in traffic."

"Any number of ex-girlfriends."

"Well, I'm sure not 'any number,'" Sara interjected. "There surely can't be many angry ex-girlfriends. That would have required many girlfriends to begin with."

Nate started to laugh. "Good point," he agreed, and even Tim began to smile a little as the insults accumulated. Andy would have had a blast with this crowd. I decided this was an opportune time to leave.

"Hey, where are you going?" Nathan called as I turned away from them in the school's main floor hallway. "We're just getting warmed up. I'm sure we could think of plenty of people who'd want to get back at you for something."

"Like his ex-wife!" Tim chimed in.

Glad to be of service. By then I was jogging up the hallway stairs, and the cackle of Nathan's laughter was fading away in the cacophony of teenaged voices that hung perpetually in the hallways of Sir John A. Macdonald Secondary. If I listened intently, it was often difficult to delineate actual conversations from the adolescent hum, and when I could, I generally found the substance had not been worth the effort. "Mr. Patrick?" I heard Sara's voice call from a few steps below.

"Did you forget to let loose one more zinger that couldn't wait until after lunch?" I asked, slowing slightly to allow her to catch up.

"No, but I'll think about it during Biology, and I'm sure I can have plenty by Law class." She stopped walking at the top of the stairs before we opened the tempered glass doors leading to the third floor hallway. I interpreted that as a desire for at least a semi-private conversation and stopped too. "I wanted to say thanks for making Tim feel better there."

"It was nothing."

"He's really starting to feel stressed about all that's been happening, and having it hit home to you again is just going to make him feel worse."

"He shouldn't. It's really not a big deal," I lied, though I wondered if I would ever look at her — because clearly my car was a "she" — the same way again, if she would always remain damaged goods, even if, of course, her disfigurement was through no fault of her own.

"I know. But I'm worried about him. He's taking it really hard."

"That's understandable. Whoever did this to him damn near killed him."

Sara shook her head at the thought then said, "I wish this would all just be over. I wish that big dumbass of a vice-principal would just realize what an idiot he's being and let us get back to planning our graduation like normal people." I opted not to rebuke her for her profane description of Bill Owen. "I don't know how much more Tim can take," she said.

We paused while two students reached the top of the stairs, their voices echoing in the stairwell. "Sara," I asked when the door had closed once again. "Is there anything else Tim isn't telling us about what happened to him that night?"

"What do you mean?"

"I mean is it possible he saw more than he's told us about who beat him up?"

Sara thought for a moment before responding. "I don't know," she confessed. "Tim and I have been best friends since before kindergarten. We tell each other everything. I was the one he came out to first."

"What did he tell you about that night?" I figured I could compare Sara's version of events with Andy's notes from interviewing Tim in the hospital — maybe there'd be something that could help.

"Just that when he left his job at the movie theatre that night, there were people who must have been waiting for him, 'cause they grabbed him as he was trying to open the car door and started beating on him. The next thing he remembered, he was waking up in the hospital."

"He doesn't remember how he got to the school field?"

"No, we just assumed he was driven, because his work isn't exactly walking distance. He works at Oakridge Mall."

"And he never got a look at them at all?"

"Not that he told me. Mr. Patrick, why are you asking me about all this? Don't you believe Tim's telling the truth?"

"Of course I do. It's just that I wonder if he might be reluctant to identify his attackers because he's scared."

Sara didn't hesitate to respond this time. "He *is* scared, Mr. Patrick. He's scared shitless. But not because he knows who attacked him, but because he doesn't. He knows they're still out there and this could happen again. We're constantly looking over our shoulders. We don't trust anyone, even here at school. *Especially* here at school. It sucks thinking one of your own schoolmates may have tried to kill you." Her voice had risen with fervour, so much so that its echo in the stairwell startled us both, as though some third party was mocking from the lower floors.

"I know," I said quietly. "I guess I'm just grasping at straws."

"Tim's afraid, but he's no coward. If he knew something, he'd tell us. He has a real sense of justice." She paused a moment then punched me what she likely assumed was lightly on the arm. I did my level best not to flinch. "You may have had something to do with that," she said, smiling.

"Aw, shucks." We paused for an awkward moment.

"You're not planning on giving up, are you?" she asked. "With all that's happening, do you think we should consider throwing in the towel?"

A side of me recognized the practicality of such a decision. But that hardly seemed the kind of thing I'd spent all those years studying law to do. It didn't seem a lesson I'd want to teach either. "I'm in as long as you guys are. Maybe longer."

Sara smiled once again, and the effect was invigorating. "You're really not such a bad guy. Maybe I take it back about your car damage being unrelated to all of this. There really can't be that many people who'd want to hurt you."

"Tell that to my ex-wife."

Looking around to ensure we were alone, she reached out and lightly touched my arm. "Seriously. You've got to stop talking trash about yourself. I bet you're actually a pretty decent guy beneath all those layers of self deprecation."

"I have a feeling my ex-wife would …"

"Don't!" she interjected. "See how easily you fall into that? Just accept a compliment."

I decided to go along with her assessment, if only to bring this uncomfortable conversation to a close — and to get her hand off of my arm. "Thank you," I said.

"See?" she asked while, thankfully, pulling her hand away. "That wasn't so hard, was it?" As she spoke, she opened the hallway door, and we both headed out of the echo chamber stairway. It occurred to me that while I hadn't been aware of the tone ringing to signal the start of first period, the hallway was all but devoid of students, save for the few stragglers who always appeared late, of which today we were two. Late for class. That was all I needed: another reason for the administration to be angry with me. "So tell me," Sara asked, walking beside me. "Why did you and your wife break up?"

"She refused to squeeze the toothpaste from the end of the tube. She was a middle squeezer. A person can't be expected to live like that."

She smiled. "Okay. Too personal?"

"A little."

"Fair enough. At least you insulted her that time instead of yourself."

"That's something I'm always happy to do." Sara stepped into the classroom two doors away from my own. I hurried the remaining few steps down the hall to face students who were counting down the few remaining weeks in the school year even more expectantly than I.

"You're not going to like it," Andrea told me as she tossed a hockey gear-sized duffle bag through my bedroom door roughly in the vicinity of the bed, though the resulting sound indicated it had not made it that far. I resisted the urge to go in and move it. The size of the bag holding her clothing told me she was here for the long haul in her capacity as Patrick protector. I almost wished Tim's attackers would go ahead and come after me, if only so Andy'd be here to get them, and I could have my apartment back.

"I didn't like it this morning. Why would I like it now?"

"Because now not only has your car had the shit kicked out of it, we didn't find any useful prints on it."

"You weren't really expecting to find prints, were you, especially since we've pretty much figured we're dealing with young offenders?"

"It was worth a shot."

"It's good to know they didn't lay their grimy little hands all over my baby."

"At least not any hands we could identify."

"Excuse me?"

"There are always *latents* on cars, Win. People brush up against them in parking lots, gas station attendants handle them."

"Perish the thought. I exclusively use self-serve."

"Yours had a particularly high number of different prints on it. We picked up seventeen different individuals, none of them in our system, but plenty of people fondle your car, Win. That's seventeen people beyond you and me." I shuddered at the thought of unknown miscreants laying hands on my car. "I told you you wouldn't like it."

"What kind of world are we living in where people feel free to grope other people's Saabs?"

"Maybe you should think about getting a less appealing set of wheels."

"Like a Crown Victoria?"

"You could do worse. At least people would get out of your way thinking you're one of us." She spoke the final words as though the VPD was a secret society to which we all should want to belong.

"Did you find out anything useful at all?"

"They did determine the damage was likely done by a blunt instrument."

"Wow. The wonders of modern science."

"Which they determined largely on the basis of the lack of scratches or paint breakage. Plenty of dents, but the finish was more or less intact."

"Which tells you what, exactly?"

"That it's likely whatever he used to beat up your car was soft-edged or tipped, kinda ruling out baseball bats and golf clubs."

"Well that's a relief. I'd hate to think someone's handicap was ruined by the harsh surfaces of my car. Any guesses?"

"That's what it would be, guesses."

"Natch."

"Something like a rubber mallet, maybe. Or the rubberized handle end of a floor hockey stick. Or the small heel of a boot."

"Wouldn't that leave a footprint?"

"Not necessarily. Depending on whether or not the boot had much of a tread on it or how hard they kicked the car, or if they swung the boot like a weapon."

"So we're looking for a rubber boot owning, mallet wielding construction worker who plays floor hockey in his or her spare time. That should narrow it down some."

"I said we were at the guessing stage."

"I bet Bernard and Lupo would make an arrest based on that," I said, referencing the most recent cast of the original *Law & Order*, mostly because I knew it would annoy Andy, and she was enjoying my torment too much.

"Oh, we're closing in on him."

"Or her. Let's not rule out fifty percent of the city's floor hockey players."

"Pardon my sexism. Seems natural to assume homophobes are male."

"You met my grandmother, right?"

"Yeah, but her death two years ago gives her a solid alibi. And yes, I checked on your little door sprayers, and both Paul and his shrew-friend have decent alibis. Krista was at work and went straight home. Paul is so grounded, he's practically locked down."

I digested that a moment. It seemed a natural progression from vandalism of my door to brutality against my car, but I hadn't been seriously considering Paul and Krista; theirs had seemed a childish prank. The attack on my car had been so much angrier, fuelled by a rage not really evident in the misspelled epithet on my door. True, criminals often escalate their criminal behaviour, but this one had seemed too quick, especially after having been caught the first time around.

"Yeah," Andrea interrupted my thoughts. "I didn't really think they were our car bashers either. Too much rage. From Bitch-face maybe I could see it, but not from him. He seems a bit more afraid of his dad than he is of her, at least for now." She seemed frustrated at her lack of progress. Andy is a doer, and when she has no leads, it affects her psyche. After a moment, she finally blurted out an action plan. "Let's go for a run."

I was rarely one to avoid running, but I did have one principal concern. "What will I do during the night if we run now?"

"Maybe if you run now, you'll be tired enough to sleep at night." I had planned to respond sarcastically along the lines of "gee, why didn't I think of that?" but I realized she knew such an exercise-induced sleep wasn't the solution to my insomnia. Her frustration with the case was speaking. I opted instead to don my running gear and pound the pavement with my best bud through the early evening. And of course I was right — running in the warmth of the spring evening no more made my body want to sleep than an Avril Lavigne song made it want to dance. But at least I had something to occupy the wee hours of the night, barricaded in my bedroom awaiting dawn. I lay awake worrying about Andy worrying about me worrying about Tim. The circle of life.

Even Charter rights cases have a lifespan in the media, and it doesn't take long before a hockey player's legal problems or a pop singer driving a car with a baby on her lap displaces the public's fickle interest in your cause. Within a day, we were no longer front page news; by day three we were no longer front section news; by day five we weren't news at all. The media was no longer hovering around the school in the morning in anticipation of further violence or at least a protest. My driving a beige Caravan had never caught their attention, and I arrived at school in my new ride looking like any one of the soccer moms and dads who felt their kids could not walk to school, even though they were eighteen years old. With what had happened to Tim still reasonably fresh in their memories, I couldn't really blame them, but it's not like they all had kids trying to bring same-sex partners to the grad dance.

A week after our radio appearance, life more or less went on as before. Even Sara and Tim, with graduation exams imminent, found themselves more focused on their educational, rather than political pursuits. It was in that vein that I was discussing the intricacies of employment law — as intricate as I'm willing to get with high school students — when the school's rather archaic PA system interrupted my snide commentary on the current provincial government gutting the British Columbia Employment Standards Act.

"Mr. Patrick?" the unmistakable bark of Bill Owen growled through the ancient speaker. Some thirty years ago, the school had installed a two-way talk system which could, of course, be initiated only by the office. Who's more likely to have an emergency, after all, an office with five middle-aged secretaries or a teacher in a room filled with thirty hormonal students? They had given each of us a beat-up computer in the classroom, so if a fight broke out between students, I could always send the vice-principals an email, assuming the fight lasted the six to eight minutes it took the computer to boot up and allow me to log in to the school's network.

I tapped myself in the chest and responded, "Go ahead, Number One." There were some slight chuckles from the Star Trek fans in the room and blank stares from the majority. There was also a pause from the PA, during which, no doubt, Owen was trying hard to determine whether or not he was being mocked in some way in front of the students. But to my horror he eventually responded in kind.

"Would you please come to the bridge right away." My god, not only was I being seen as a Trekkie but so was my arch nemesis. Even thinking the term "arch nemesis" surely raised my geek factor.

"Now?" I asked, hopefully dropping Star Trek pretense of any generation. "I have a class."

"I'm aware of that, but you're needed a moment. Make it so." With that, the PA clicked off. I gave the class the homework assignment to start while I was gone, and most attempted to give the cursory impression that they were getting down to work, though I did hear a few mutters of the "what a geek" variety. Sara raised a questioning eyebrow at me as I headed to the door. I tried to toss her a nonchalant shrug in return, though being publicly beckoned to the office to see the vice-principal — even this one — was having the effect on me it likely had on any of them in the same position: annoyance coupled with a sense of trepidation.

After travelling the more or less empty hallways, I entered the office. All eyes turned to me, secretaries, a couple of fellow teachers, and a stranger who also appeared to be awaiting my arrival with growing impatience. The principal and both vice-principals stood in their respective doorways watching my entrance. I felt as though I'd accidentally stumbled upon my own surprise party, by the looks of anticipation on the assembled faces. "Mr. Patrick?" the stranger asked. The lawyer in me was immediately wary and opted not to respond.

Bill Owen stepped forward from his office doorway. "He said he had a delivery for you that he couldn't leave with anyone else," the already agitated vice-principal blurted out, pointing to the stranger. A process server. Great. I hoped this wasn't some new legal issue sideswiping me, and if it was, Owen had just removed the possibility of me not identifying myself.

"Yes, I'm Winston Patrick," I sighed, extending a hand for the envelope I knew was about to be offered. The server thrust the envelope with the unmistakable seal of the B.C. Attorney General's Ministry into my hand. The deed complete, he turned and exited without further word, and I imagined a smugness in his gait. The office remained quiet, and I felt all eyes on me, awaiting explanation. Because of my immature tendencies, I decided to silently open the envelope in front of them without providing any hint as to its contents. When I unfolded the document and confirmed my expectations, I wordlessly turned on my heel and headed for the door, but not without offering up the slightest smile from only the corner of my mouth visible to my audience, a skill I had honed and used to effect often in front of juries and ninth graders alike.

"Mr. Patrick," Bill Owen called out. "Is everything okay?" His attempt to couch his desire for information as concern for my well-being was entirely transparent, but I played along anyway.

"Everything is fine, thank you for asking," I replied more politely than he was likely expecting.

"It's just that he was so insistent on seeing you right away, we knew it must have been important," Owen continued. Fiona, our matronly head secretary, nodded. She was also our head gossip, so I knew a good deal of her concern was based on her need to manage the flow of information. "Does this have something to do with our, err, situation?" Owen pressed on.

"I'm afraid I'm not at liberty to discuss any matters pertaining to our 'situation,' as you describe it. The school board, as you are no doubt aware, has retained counsel on that matter, and it would be improper of me to discuss anything without the board's counsel present." Of course I knew I had just confirmed the delivery was related to Tim's suit. At this point Andrea would tell me I was going beyond simple immaturity and straight to childishness in my taunting of the office bully.

"Winston," he sighed, "can't you just not be a lawyer a minute and do something that's right for the whole school?" That was pretty decent manoeuvring, I had to admit, dividing my loyalties and appealing to my altruistic care for the welfare of all of Sir John A. Macdonald's population. Maybe he was smarter than I was giving him credit for.

"Fine," I acquiesced. "Since the board's counsel is no doubt receiving this as we speak, what I have here is a notification of a court date to hear our application for an injunction against the school."

"What's the date?" Fiona suddenly demanded. This information would no doubt be common knowledge before the school day was through, though it being already halfway through last period, that would require a fair amount of dedicated effort.

"Friday."

"So soon?" Bill wanted to know. "I didn't think our legal system would be able to move that fast."

"I applied for an expedited hearing in order to have the matter resolved quickly, given the pending date of the grad dinner dance." Bill muttered something that sounded like "asshole" under his breath. Mercifully, the school phones, which had been unusually silent during our initial exchange, suddenly awoke. "Anything else?" I asked and pretty much heard the expected response before Bill could utter it.

"Yeah. Do you have to be so goddamned smug about it?" The answer was self evident, so I didn't bother to reply.

"So what happens now?" a familiar voice said from behind me, and all heads turned to see that Sara Kolinsky had surreptitiously trailed me from class. "Are we prepared to go to trial?" She spoke as though she was co-chair instead of witness for the claimant, but she reaffirmed what I already knew: she was prepared to take on whatever was needed of her to see Tim win his case.

"We will be," I assured her then turned to Bill Owen and for cheesy dramatic effect said, "See you in court."

"My god, Patrick, are you really going to go through with this?" Owen demanded, as though everything that had happened thus far was one gigantic bluff.

"That much should be obvious. I respect the court too much to have wasted its time with pretend pleadings. I respect the rights provided by the Charter even more." It was a little self-righteous, but it had a nice rhythm to it. I made a mental note to keep that line for opening arguments.

"Don't you think you've done enough?" he continued, his tone hardening.

"Clearly not, given that one of my students is having his civil rights violated by this very institution."

"This isn't a civil rights issue," he insisted. "It's an authority issue. Mainly who has the authority to set policy and procedures for the school, and I do have those rights."

"Yes, well, I don't want to offer my client's opponent legal advice, but I don't recommend you try to trump the Charter with that argument. On second thought, use that: it should wrap this up even more quickly."

"Did it occur to you even once that I'm actually not trying to persecute Tim, but trying to do what's best for all the students?"

"The road to hell ..." I started but didn't finish. I find clichés much more effective when left dangling. "Your motivation for your actions does nothing to negate their illegality." Andrea would be practically rolling on the floor at my zealously pious tone. The office, however, was spellbound by my first year law school-level rhetoric. "There's a much larger principle at play here than a challenge to your authority. Tim has the right to choose his grad date like any other student, regardless of that date's gender."

"You know you're not the only lawyer on this. The

board's lawyer doesn't agree you've got such a rock solid discrimination case."

"As a taxpayer, I truly hope the board is not paying much for its legal advice. It's going to need to divert funds to a communications strategy to explain why they're wasting scarce precious funds on such a ridiculous cause." I turned once again to leave, ready to deliver one last TV drama-worthy line but was coming up dry.

"Hold on a minute, Mr. Patrick." Don McFadden, the principal, was poised to enter the fray. I showed him the respect of stopping and listening. To my surprise he said, "You're right."

Bill Owen and I spoke in unison. "Excuse me?"

McFadden sighed and walked forward. "I'm sorry, Bill, but I think Mr. Patrick is right. This has gone on long enough."

"Don," Bill began, "I understand this has been difficult, but there's a principle at issue here."

"I agree," the beleaguered principal replied. "And the more I reflect on it, the more I realize Mr. Patrick is right." Reflect is education-speak for "think about," and it's supposed to sound a little more intellectual.

I thought Bill Owen might explode. I mean actually, physically explode. The mess would be unimaginable. His head was almost shaking as he kept his temper in check in front of his boss.

"I don't want to see anything else happen to Tim or any other students as a result of this battle," McFadden said. "Mr. Patrick? Please tell Tim he may bring his date to the grad dance."

Owen didn't carry the conversation further, which was odd, given that he was not one known for backing down nor was Don McFadden one who was particularly known for holding his ground. I'm sure Bill was worried he might completely lose control in front of a room full of colleagues and a student. He went into his office, and more quietly than I would have thought possible under the circumstances, closed the door. For a moment the main office was still, save for the occasional ringing telephone, the assembled staff and student in the room uncomfortably looking at one another.

Finally, Sara spoke. "So that's it then?" I almost sensed slight disappointment, like Mussolini being handed the Italian government without really needing to march on Rome. Of course, he'd marched on the capital regardless. "Do we go to court anyway?" It seemed Sara might have had the same idea as Il Duce. You've got to make a point, after all.

I turned to Don McFadden, who was now standing immediately in front of us, separated only by the office reception counter, as though keeping a safety barrier between us and him lest we launch one last constitutional attack that could be repelled by a partition. Leaning across the counter and speaking softly in a voice designed only for him to hear, I asked, "Do you have the authority to make this decision?" I hadn't intended it as a slight, and to his credit McFadden didn't appear to take it as one.

Just the same, he sort of puffed up and declared, "You're damned right."

I smiled at him. "Then I suggest you call the board's lawyer." Then turning to Sara, I added, "It's over."

Chapter Twelve

If I had any notion that our time in the spotlight would be over with the termination of our suit, I would have been sadly mistaken. As quickly as our star had faded prior to the principal's dropping of the issue, it rose like a nova as soon as word leaked out that we had won. For Don's sake, I had kind of hoped we could just quietly fade away into obscurity and let the kids focus on enjoying their grad dance and preparing and studying for their pending final exams. And yes, in most students' minds, the priority was in that order. But once your case finds its way into the media spotlight, it's followed through to the bitter end, especially if the case had certain key ingredients: civil rights, an oppressed group, especially if the oppression is perceived to be based on sexual orientation, significant violence, or kids and teens. This case had all of the above.

The local media's court beat reporters had been closely monitoring the action. Within an hour of my conversation with Don McFadden, I had spoken with the Vancouver School Board's in-house legal counsel — even I thought it was sad a school board needed to retain full-time counsel — and had gotten confirmation that the board would not interfere with the principal's authority to allow Tim to bring his boyfriend to the grad dance. I had also informed the court clerk of my intention to withdraw the civil action and had Sara and Tim drafting the document that would formally terminate the suit. By late afternoon, I had faxed the senior clerk, who I knew from my legal practice days. He agreed to file the faxed form to save me having to take another day off from work to do so in person. I had also hand-delivered a copy of the well-drafted — by student standards — document to McFadden, so he knew for certain that the suit had been cancelled. I thought it wise not to do the same for Bill Owen, though I did place a copy in his letterbox, since he was personally named in the suit. There would be plenty of time to make nice later, and I didn't really feel like it yet anyway.

By morning the city knew. Though the filings had occurred too late in the afternoon to make the newspapers' press deadlines, news radio and the morning television news shows had picked up the scent and were running the withdrawal of the civil action as their lead stories. The principal was referring all requests for comment to the board's spokesperson, who in turn kept referring requests back to the school principal. My home phone had no doubt begun ringing by seven, but by then I was on my way into school, and this time the non-descript minivan allowed me to sneak past the small but growing assemblage of reporters near the school's entrance.

I skulked into the office around eight to check for messages and found requests for interviews from the two Vancouver dailies, the national papers, the producer who had booked us on the Brian Winter radio show, and a host of other magazines and news programs, national and international, who wanted comment from me. I planned to ignore them all.

Even Tim and Sara found it exhausting those first couple of days, politely making every effort to respond to everyone who wanted a piece of them. To their credit, they handled themselves with grace, with not a hint of smugness, playing down the media's constant reference to their "victory," instead stating they regretted having been unable to reach this important decision through negotiation and discussion rather than redress through the courts, though they were quick to point out the issue had bolstered their faith in the Charter and the court's ability to protect the rights of Canadians. In short, they did me proud.

Through it all, Andrea had made no more progress on catching Tim's attackers. By Friday night we were each spending an equally depressing evening discussing my school and her work. Since my week had ended with a victory of sorts, I got to choose the dinner venue, and unsurprisingly it turned out to be Italian, though this time I went exotic, and we travelled all the way to Gastown for the culinary pleasure. Incendios offered one of the best Italian dinners in town, reasonably priced, enhanced by the focaccia it baked in its own stone oven that was the centrepiece of the restaurant's decor. It also held an impressive wine selection that more than made up for what panache it may have lacked compared to pricier establishments in the downtown core or in trendy Kitsilano. To be sure, it rested just on the ugly side of the border between tourist-friendly Gastown and Canada's poorest, most drug-addled postal code, the Downtown

Eastside. It surely had some impact on customers' desire to park their cars outside while enjoying the good dining. We brought Andrea's unmarked cruiser, so we didn't have to worry about losing our own personal property. Of course, the VPD's forensics teams was still holding my car; I would happily have had my increasingly less temporary beige minivan stolen, though with my luck they'd simply supply me with an even uglier minivan, if such a vehicle existed.

"Who would have thought teenagers could pull off the perfect crime?" she was lamenting as she double and triple-dipped her focaccia bread into the oil and vinegar on the plate between us.

"Was the crime really perfect, or are you giving it that title simply because you cannot solve it?"

"Have not solved it *yet*," she corrected me after ferociously tearing off another strip of bread. "I can't believe kids can continue to keep a secret this long. Sooner or later one of them is bound to talk. They can't protect each other forever."

"Remind you at all of a famed blue wall?" I teased.

Andrea ran two fingers around the bottom of the dish, sopping up the scant remains of the extra virgin olive oil and balsamic vinegar, then none too delicately rammed her fingers into her mouth and slurped the treasures off her skin. "We don't have a blue wall. That's an urban myth. Our uniforms were changed to black a long time ago." She furrowed her brow into a look of disappointment as she viewed the empty breadbasket. "We need more bread."

"And a new dish for oil and vinegar," I added.

"You're becoming quite the germophobe."

"Indeed."

"You haven't heard anything new today?"

"Tim was invited to be a marshal in this year's gay pride parade."

"I meant anything germane to the case."

"In that case, no."

"Because you would have told me immediately anyway."

"At least once the wine had been delivered."

Andy took what could be charitably described as a sip of wine. Try though I might, I had yet to convince her that wine was not a thirst quencher. She had fine taste in wine, but she consumed it faster than seemed culturally appropriate. "I'm going to get pulled off the case full-time next week."

"So soon?"

"Crime goes on. They need my super sleuthing elsewhere."

"You're okay with this?"

"Do I look like I'm okay with this?" She looked like she would eat the tablecloth if we didn't order soon. A running conflict when we dined was my desire to enjoy an entire glass of wine before ordering — a prepared palate helps one make better menu selections. It wasn't so much that my dinner companion disagreed with my method so much as the difference in speed with which we each consumed that first glass, Andy downed a Shiraz like it was Gatorade. "I'll be able to work it until something else pops up that requires my attention. Next body is pretty much mine."

"Pray it isn't Tim's."

"You're worried?"

"Aren't I always?"

"They haven't done anything against Tim since the initial attack. That was two weeks ago," she said.

"And now he's getting to bring his date to the prom. He's won."

"Maybe they got it out of their system."

"Do you believe that?"

"Nope."

"Do you think it's likely to escalate?" I asked.

"Normally I'd say yes."

"But?"

"But I'm still operating on the assumption we're dealing with teenagers. They're much less predictable in some regards. Sometimes that works in our favour."

"How so?"

"As much as teenagers are less likely to follow the usual patterns of escalation in terms of degree and timing, they're also just as likely to abandon their action altogether when something more interesting comes along."

"Perps with attention deficit disorder," I remarked. "Any chance we could get him some kind of security detail?"

"Until when? Until people accept homosexuality?"

"Ideally, but I'd be happy with at least until the grad dance is over. Once they meet their objective of going through with the dance, the people who beat up Tim will have no further reason to want to hurt him."

"Except sour grapes," she offered. "Or long-lasting

violent intolerance."

"Yes, except that." We ordered dinner and spent the next hour and a half reviewing, rehashing, and dissecting every tidbit of information and evidence she had, a process she went through many times during the course of an investigation. Since she generally worked without a partner, I was frequently the wall off of which she bounced ideas and theories as she worked her way towards an arrest. I liked to think I was part of the reason Andy's case clearance statistics were still the best in the department, despite her working with half the manpower of other detective teams. By the end of dinner, a bottle of wine — all but one glass of which was consumed by me, since it would not be good for Andy to be pulled over for impaired driving at the wheel of a police car — dessert, and lattes, we were absolutely no closer to figuring out who Tim's assailants had been than we were on the morning we had found him. At least we were better fed.

Two of the three major newspapers ran feature length pieces on Tim's victory, variously describing it as a win for civil rights, gay rights, homosexual teenager rights, and those of high school students in general. The third paper, national in scope, editorialized about the Supreme Court being too activist, typical, though no suit had even been heard in a B.C. court, let alone the Supreme Court, and thus no ruling had even been made, activist or otherwise. It went on to lament the limits of local authority making it too difficult for principals to run their schools according to local needs, forgetting conveniently that it was the principal himself who had made the decision to allow Tim's same-sex partner to attend the graduation, not a ruling by a judge. I had read all three in their entirety, including the many stories that ran in more than one paper, often by the same writer, by the time Andrea the bodyguard finally graced me with her presence. I say finally because it was late by my standards, seven fifteen.

We were on the road running by eight fifteen. I had missed the Vancouver International Marathon and was determined not to miss the Portland race in August or the Victoria in October, in which I planned to run my first sub-three hour race. Thus Andrea was continuing her protection duty, even on my long runs, often occurring on Sunday afternoons, but this weekend a planned visit to my parents' house would prevent that. I had already failed to convince her that her protection services would be put to better use guarding Tim, so for the time being there was no escaping being joined at the hip. I offered to do a road run so she could park her ass in her cruiser and escort me down the road. She, of course, took the offer as a challenge and immediately geared up for the two-and-a-quarter-hour run.

Running in Vancouver on a Saturday was a more formidable challenge than on a Sunday afternoon. Once tourist season began, it really didn't matter which weekend day was chosen for running: it was traffic bedlam regardless. We decided to risk a run across the downtown core and into Stanley Park, given the relatively early hour. By the time we reached Georgia Street, the sun was warming our joints and the pavement, and the traffic crawling north towards the single available lane of the Lions Gate Bridge was leaving a visible trail of noxious fumes for us to inhale as we made the gradual incline towards the downtown core. Thus we dropped as quickly as possible to the waterfront near the shipping terminals, shaded from the increasing warmth of the sun by the overpass above us and missing much of the traffic of the business district. We wound our way away from the city core, through the warehouse district, and finally back down into Kitsilano.

The competitive spirit we refused to relinquish had us both sprinting madly the last block to my apartment as though our very lives, and not just our egos, depended on arriving first. I edged past her by hurdling the hip-high hedge that lined the sidewalk to my tarpaulin-shrouded condominium building. Unbeknownst to me, a fellow resident had chosen the moment before our arrival to stoop down to closely examine a piece of the hedge, and the precise moment of my airborne arrival to straighten up, catching me with his right shoulder and sending me spinning in mid-air. I crashed and skidded across the sidewalk, coming to a stop only when my face met and inserted itself into the matching hedge on the opposite side of the walkway. I felt the skin tearing on my left side, even before I came to a complete stop. The business end of a leafless stick on the hedge had gashed my right cheek, narrowly missing puncturing my eye, though at that moment I was having difficulty feeling grateful for that small mercy. From the very edge of my awareness, I heard an accented voice bellow, "What the hell is the matter with you?"

Polish Sausage.

I was momentarily unable to respond as I mentally took inventory of my body parts and felt reasonably confident in the functionality of each of my limbs. Andrea was suddenly at my side and had adopted professional mode, though I knew laughing outrageously at me could not be far behind. “My god, Win. Are you okay?”

I rolled my head to the side and looked up at her, though the wind that had been knocked out of me and I couldn’t respond. I noticed her eyes were scanning the vicinity, as though my clumsy fall might have actually been the result of an attempt on my life. I thought she might shoot Polish Sausage, and in my foggy mind, I kind of hoped she might.

“Hey!” Sausage snapped from behind us both. “What are you doing?” Andy continued to assess my injuries. “Hey!” he repeated. “I’m talking to you. Who are you?” Sausage, always the nosey neighbour, would have, of course, known full well that Andy was my friend and constant visitor, despite never having been formally introduced. I’d found it gave people a sense of power and authority when they demanded that others identify themselves.

Andrea rose to her feet and put her face in front of Sausage’s. “Detective Andrea Pearson of the Vancouver Police Department,” she told him. “Who the hell are you?” See? She knew full well who she was speaking to by my description and constant mocking of my condo’s self-anointed guardian. It’s all about the power trip.

I recovered my breathing sufficiently to sit up and join the fray. “Andrea, Andrew,” I said, weakly waving my arm between them. "Andrew, Andrea." They glared at each other. "I'm fine, thank you," I added dishonestly.

Andy reached out and pulled me to my feet. "Are you sure you're okay?"

"More or less. Nothing's broken but the dignity bone." I turned to Polish Sausage. "Andrew, I'm very sorry. You're not hurt, are you?" He thought a moment before replying, probably calculating what this little collision could net him.

"I don't think so, no," he said. "What were you doing?"

"Trying to beat her to the door. Just a little friendly competition between friends, which I won, by the way."

"Doesn't count," Andy interjected. "Taking short cuts automatically d.q.'s you. And no extra consideration or sympathy credit for wiping out."

"Crap."

"Doesn't all this seem a bit childish?" Sausage asked.

"Therein lies its charm," I informed him. Don't they have fun in Poland?

Sausage, his feelings of superiority once again confirmed, abruptly changed the topic. "I see you are all over the papers again today." There was no question asked, so I fell back on what I always instructed my clients to do in those situations and said nothing. My silence did not dissuade him from continuing. "Aren't you concerned you may anger a lot of people with your little crusade?"

"No."

"I think you're mistaken. Plenty of people won't like what you did."

"I have no doubt that will be the case. I'm just not

concerned about it. Unreasonable people will always have unreasonable opinions."

Sausage's superficial attempt at concern faded. I was seeing a lot of that from people this week. He twisted his lip into its customary sneer. "You know, many people think it's not the school's place to legalize homosexual behaviour."

"And many more people already are aware homosexuality is not illegal. Discrimination is."

The Sausage sneer increased. "In Poland we have a word for gay lovers. It's called *Pedal*; it's meant as an insult."

"In Canada we have a word for assholes," Andrea piped in. "It's called 'assholes.' It too is meant as an insult."

"You would think," Sausage snapped, "an officer of the law would speak more respectfully to people."

"You'd think," she replied.

"You had better be careful," he cautioned ominously.

"Really?" Andy took a step closer to him. "And what is it I should be careful of, a middle-aged, out of shape man with a fake limp? Should I be afraid you might poke me with your little cane?"

He took a deep breath to control his rising temper. "What I meant to say is there are many people who probably don't share your point of view, who may not be as reasonable and civilized as you and I, Mr. Patrick. I would hate to see unpleasant events follow you home like what happened in the past." He just couldn't let go of the past. Geez, you drop one dead body on a guy's patio, and you hear about it forever.

"I'll be sure to keep an eye open," I assured him. Then as an afterthought, and because I felt a need to re-establish some semblance of manhood after Andy had stood up for me, I decided to take one last shot at him. "By the way, Andrew, before you decide again to take some form of punitive strata action against me for your own gratification, you should remember that I'm a little better versed in the law than you give me credit for. Do it again, and not only will I have it struck down but I'll take legal action to have you removed from your imperial perch for gross misconduct and threatening the financial health of the strata corporation." That was street tough talk as far as lawyers go.

Polish Sausage actually began to go red. "Don't you threaten me! I work in the best interests of all the home-owners, even you, who tries to block me at every turn!"

"You're a pompous ass who's living off the public teat and justify your pitiful existence by driving every-one else insane. Do me, yourself, every other owner, and society at large a favour for god's sake, and get a job!" There. I'd said it. It was juvenile, it served little purpose, and I knew I would regret it later, but for the next few minutes I would ride a euphoric wave of perceived vic-tory.

"You're a bastard," he practically bellowed.

"That seems a step up from the 'prick' you told me I was before," I said calmly. Andy tugged on my arm to pull me away from the fracas. I don't know if she was worried I would do something foolish and illegal, or if she thought she would have to step in and save my ass and be faced with mounds of paperwork for her

y on our movie viewing for the evening, selecting
ntic comedy — as we did at least once per month
ur the irony — that was about as romantic as
t Burger King and as comedic as anything with
neider in the opening titles. The viewing palate
een tempted, we moved into the main event, a
e-mastered version of *Out of Africa*, which, it
was as numbingly dull twenty years later as it
luring its theatrical release when we had both
a lonely Saturday night in the ninth grade,
lly in the same theatre at which Tim was
nployed. I thought that with our increased
might be better able to appreciate the film.
ally weren't much more sophisticated, or
lly was a stinker. To its credit, the film did
e something relatively rare: falling asleep
t.

und that woke me up. It was smell.
the clock on my bedside table, I was dis-
that slightly more than two hours had
etired to bed. Once my sleep was inter-
ever returned.

tment turned to curiosity as the
t of smoke invaded my dozy nostrils.
thin enough that I wasn't sure I had
bout it. But as I sniffed the air again,
ke-like wisps seeping from the vent
lluminated eerily by the faint beams
hrough the vertical blinds. I sat up
noke from my own mind, which
pting what it was being asked to

superiors. The latter was a bit of an affront: I might not be tough, but surely she didn't think I couldn't hold my own against Polish Sausage.

"Let's go," she told me. "He's not worth it."

"Have a good day, Sausage," I told him as Andy pulled my arm. If Sausage noticed I'd started using my nickname for him to his face, he gave no specific indication.

"*Chuj ci w dupe,*" he said, and I could only assume it must have meant more or less the same as what I was thinking about him. Andrea bent down, untied my running shoe, and pulled my apartment's front door key off the lace where I secure it for running, then untied my other shoe to get the key to my apartment itself. Some might argue living in an apartment made it more awkward for running; I thought having one key on each foot made me more balanced. On a house, I'd have to have a second lock installed.

"My god," she said, standing up and giving me the once-over as she rose. "Look at you. Your mother's going to kill me. I'm supposed to be protecting you."

"From falling down and getting a boo-boo?" I made light of it, but the burning from my cuts was already beginning to make my eyes water. Some might say cry. "You're here to stop the bad guys from getting me, not the pavement."

"Do you think your mother will make that distinction?"

"No."

"In that case, is it too late to decline her invitation to dinner tomorrow?"

"Yes."

She sighed as I hobbled ahead of her into the elevator. "I'm screwed."

I hated for Sausage to be right, but he was. In the
time that Andy and I had been out running, my voicemail had filled to capacity with messages from readers of
the weekend papers, all three of which had mentioned
me by name. Seems that folks opposed to my involvement in Tim's case were early risers and readers and
had neither technical nor ethical difficulties locating
my telephone number. Most of the callers were of the
"homosexuality is an abomination" and "you're going to
go straight to hell" variety. Andy listened to each one
carefully, taking shorthand notes and vowing to record
all of the messages for evidentiary purposes and to pay a
personal visit to two of the callers who not only figured I
should burn in hell but had suggestions about how they
might be willing to expedite the process. She also used
her considerable clout to contact my telephone company, and even though it was a Saturday, garner a promise to have available a new, unlisted telephone number
within a couple of hours, this time with the added feature of call display so as to be easily able to track most
calls, if they did manage to track me down.

Outwardly I protested at her overprotectiveness,
but inside I kind of felt just a little bit safer knowing she
was taking measures. It was difficult to believe any of the
callers were the kids who had beaten Tim, but some of
the them sounded like a whole new fresh set of reasons
to have people worry about my safety. I hit the shower
while Andrea worked her detective magic, including

putting some kind of trap on m
could track all of its activity. S'
to the homes of both Tim and
received equally vicious pho
being the most virulent. Ge'
she managed to arrange s
ence around both their ho
and his family to move a
nights, on the assumptio
a legitimate threat, the
immediate future. At
left; try though she
Tim's father not to
stead. In his words
his own home by
agreed with. Ah'

Leaving my
telephone nur
ening phone
doubt was
nently atta
herself to
self sick
opinior

A
rity
rem
gle
to

process. But it was quickly becoming apparent that this was no sleep-induced optical illusion. The smoke was thickening. I brought my feet to the floor, still mesmerized by the growing cloud of smoke, when the clock radio suddenly went dark, and from somewhere within the building there was a loud clunk, as though one giant circuit breaker had been thrown, throwing the already darkened building into complete blackness.

Seconds later the door to my bedroom flew open with a violent crash as it swung into the dresser against the far wall. Andrea flew in a split second later, the gun I hadn't known but suspected she had with her drawn. Before I could even get to my feet, she was on me, one arm yanking me hard onto the floor, the other still pointing her gun at the open bedroom door. "We lost power," she hissed, and even in her whisper I could hear a tense, combat-ready tone. It seemed she had just noticed the smoke. "What the hell?" she demanded.

"There's smoke coming through the vents," I told her. "I'm sure it's probably nothing to worry about, a ventilation problem or something."

She reached onto the wing chair beside my bed and grabbed the pants I'd been wearing when Redford and Streep had wooed me into slumber. "Put these on," she ordered. "We're getting out of here." I struggled into my pants with no time to spare as she dragged me forcefully towards the bedroom doorway, gun still held in front of her in her right hand. The room was warming as we made our way back across it.

"Are you planning on shooting the fire if we come across it?" I asked.

"Something's not right," she answered as we paused in the living room and she put on the sweats she had been wearing before bed.

"Yeah. My apartment is on fire."

"Listen, this could well be a ploy to drive us into the open, or it could just be an attempt to burn you alive."

"Or it could just be a fire," I said. I was starting to believe her, and it was freaking me out.

She shook her head. "Where are the sprinkler systems? The fire alarm? Your building is equipped." The smoke was getting thicker and was starting to sting my eyes. Andy picked up my telephone. She must not have heard a dial tone, because she slammed it down and reached for the cell she had left on the coffee table, all the while training her weapon on the front door. She dialed 911 and told the operator an officer needed assistance in a burning building and gave the address and our physical location in the building. We headed for the door.

"Wait!" I told her. "I didn't put on a shirt."

"No time," she told me and yanked me down the short entrance hallway to the door. "Stay low," she commanded, and I didn't know if that was to avoid smoke, bullets, or both. In the back of my head I was remembering something about fire safety that had been drilled into my head since I was a kid, but it didn't seem the right time to "stop, drop, and roll" and I couldn't remember much else. Was it smoke low, sell high? Wait and count to sixty before exiting? Feed smoke and starve a fire? Whistle while you burn? Andy put her hand on the doorway and, satisfied it was not dangerously warm, slowly opened it.

"There's an exit to the right," I told her.

She shook her head. "We need to alert your neighbours." I nodded, which was braver than I was actually feeling, but she was right: with no fire alarms ringing, we had to warn the building's other occupants. The hallway was smokier than my apartment, and we ducked over like the flying monkeys of Oz and began feeling our way down the darkened passage, the only illumination coming from the emergency lighting at either end of the hallway. My apartment was the last at the corner of the building, with no neighbour opposite. We quickly found my immediate neighbour, and though I couldn't see it, I knew an apartment was immediately across the hallway. We both began pounding on the doors.

"Vancouver Police!" Andy yelled, more or less to both doorways. "We have a fire in the building. You need to evacuate immediately!" I adopted the same phrasing, figuring it sounded more convincing than me simply trying to identify myself as "that guy on your floor in the corner unit who never talks to you." Both neighbours opened their doors and were even more shocked by the thickening smoke in the hallway than by us awakening them. I turned to look quickly back towards my apartment and saw flames crawling out from under the exit door immediately outside my unit. At least we appeared to be heading away from the fire. The metal doorway seemed, for the time being, to be doing its job of holding back the fire from getting into the hallway, but the amount of smoke that was coming off the walls on either side of the fire door told me the walls were not going to keep it back much longer. It struck me then, limited though my understanding of the physics of fire was, that the origin of the fire did appear to be right near my apartment, more or less confirming Andrea's assertion that this was no accident and that I was an arsonist's intended target.

"Win!" Her voice cut through my pyrotechnical musings. "Come on! Let's go!" The four people we had aroused from the two suites had been pushed ahead of us into the hallway. They looked only vaguely familiar, and I found myself vowing to be more neighbourly when all this was over. After two years, it seemed a bit late for a housewarming, despite the ironic relevance of the term.

The eastern end of the hallway was thickening with smoke as the fire spread its way behind us, while we moved on to the three remaining suites on the top floor of the building. As we reached the next two suites I allowed myself another furtive glance towards my own home, and my fears were confirmed: the fire had escaped the stairwell, and the end of the building that had been cloaked in smoke-drenched darkness was now alight with leaping flames, forking their molten tongues towards our location as if daring us to continue. I tried to imagine I could hear the sound of approaching fire engines, but above the roar of the flames and the pounding of my own heart, it was difficult to determine much of anything. The apartment door on my side of the hallway flew open before I could knock. A confused woman in a T-shirt and pajama bottoms stood before me, and I recognized her as the yoga fanatic who had frequently invited me to attend classes with her. Just at that moment it struck me that those invitations might have been nothing more than a ruse to ask me out. Funny how an emergency has the capacity to bring out either the best in a person or their ego, but I assured myself that if we all lived, I would attend yoga.

"You need to get out of here," I ordered as I heard Andrea do the same across the hall. "There's no time to gather belongings. Come on!" The woman stared at me and I reached out to grab her arms. "Come on!" I ordered. She shook her head, and I could not comprehend why anyone would refuse an order to leave a burning building. "What's the matter with you?" I pleaded. "The building's on fire! Stay low and let's go." I pulled her towards me, trying to push her down towards the hallway floor.

Finally she managed to speak. "My daughter," she wailed. "My daughter." Flames were eating their way up the walls at a rate faster than I would have imagined possible. It seemed they would overtake us in seconds.

"Where?" I demanded. "Where is she?"

"In her bedroom. On the left!" Tears were running down Yoga Lady's cheeks, and in the growing light from the approaching flames, I could see the tears were staining black down her cheeks from the smoke hanging in the air. I looked across the hallway to where Andrea had evidently kicked open the adjacent apartment door to search for heavy sleepers. To my right the approaching flames seemed close enough to reach out and touch. Yoga Lady was trying to push past me as fear finally roused her from half-awakened confusion. "Go!" I ordered her. "I'll get your daughter."

"No!" she protested, and just then a piece of the hallway ceiling panel collapsed, where seconds before I had made my way up the hall.

"Go!" I ordered again, grabbing Yoga Lady by the arms and tossing her forward down the hallway. "Stay low to the ground and take the exit. I'll be right behind you with your daughter!" Yoga Lady crawled away from me, and I stepped into her apartment entryway.

Though smoke-filled, the two steps inward brought me momentary respite from the intense heat of the hallway, enough that I almost felt safe. The feeling evaporated as quickly as the breathable air around me when I turned back towards the hallway and saw the flames licking their way around the corner of the doorjamb, seeking me out like some science fiction alien's tentacles. The apartment was a different layout from mine, and I vaguely recalled that the middle units had three bedrooms, which made me suddenly unsure how many daughters Yoga Lady had told me were in the apartment.

I worked my way forward through the smoke, dropping low to the ground again and trying to orient myself. The smoke was thickening, and I could feel the slow, acidy burn at the back of my throat, making my airway feel smaller. I told myself not to panic and tried to focus my breathing, a skill my lungs were accustomed to, having spent many an hour trying to regulate the flow of air as I ran the city's streets. I slowed my breathing to allow for fewer intakes while I searched the unfamiliar territory. As the smoke thickened, I was beginning to doubt the wisdom of my decision to stay behind when I heard the whimpering of a scared child coming from my left.

I was finally able to make out the form of a young girl of about five or six. If I had seen her in the building before, it had certainly never registered with me. I went to call for her and realized I hadn't thought to get her name. "Little girl!" I called. I'm sure that was comforting. She did not immediately respond to the stranger's voice in her apartment, so I tried again. "Little girl! Over here."

She looked at me, and I thought I detected a glimmer of recognition. "Winston?" she asked. Apparently I had registered with her. Excellent. I'm a hit with the five-year-olds.

"Yes," I told her. "It's me, Winston." Glancing again over my shoulder, I saw the flames had reached and now filled the doorway leading back to the hallway and our exit.

"Where's Mommy?" she asked.

"Your Mommy is waiting for you outside. We have to go." By that time I had reached her, and she stepped into me, wrapping her little arms around my neck. She clearly had more confidence in me than was warranted. I turned towards the door, but in those few seconds it had taken to reach her, the flames had completely engulfed the doorway and small hallway and were making their way towards us in the living room. "Okay," I told her calmly. "You want to know what's funny?"

She nodded very seriously, I guess hoping some humour might dispel the fear that was causing her to shake in my arms.

"With all of this smoke, I can't remember your name. Isn't that funny?" It wasn't really, but I figured I needed her help getting us out of there in one piece, and having a name seemed more useful than repeatedly calling her Yoga Lady's daughter.

"Aspen," she half whispered.

"Of course," I told her gently. "How could I forget such a beautiful name? Do you have any brothers or sisters?" She shook her head. "Okay, Aspen, I'm going to need you to hang on tightly to me, can you do that?" She nodded, and I picked her up and turned towards what was left of the apartment's hallway. The flames had fully entered the unit, and I recognized with a growing sense of panic that going out the door and into the hallway was no longer an option. The flames had formed a wall. The sound of the fire created a din, but through it I thought I could just hear Andrea's voice from the other side.

"Winston?" she yelled. "Christ! Are you still in there?"

"I'm in here. I can't get back out into the hallway!"

"You have to get out of there! What the hell are you doing?"

I tried to put a semblance of calm into my voice. "I'm just hanging out with my friend Aspen. She's five, and she's just a little bit scared. But I've told her it's okay; we're going to be fine. You need to leave."

"I thought you were already ahead of me!" she yelled, and I heard the rarest of things in her voice: fear.

"Just go on ahead of me. We're going to wait here awhile." I far from relished the idea of biding our time in the increasing inferno waiting to be rescued, but my options were limited.

There was a pause before Andrea answered, and I knew she was calculating what for her was an impossible situation. There was no way she would leave me there to face danger alone, but there was no way she could stay there with me either. Finally she yelled back. “Stay low. Our friends from the red truck will be up here any minute!”

The din made it almost impossible to hear. “Go!” I ordered and retreated from the encroaching flames deeper into the apartment, carrying my cargo towards the sliding glass patio door beyond the dining room table.

“Who was that?” Aspen asked quietly, her voice growing hoarse as more smoke made its way into her throat.

“That was just my friend, Andrea. She’s going to wait for us outside.”

“Is she the police lady?” This kid never missed a thing.

“That’s her. She’s one of my very best friends. Who’s your very best friend?”

She paused and thought about it a moment. “My mommy.”

“Well that’s great,” I told her reassuringly. “Because your best friend is going to be waiting outside with my best friend.”

“I want to go see her,” she told me.

I gave her a bit of a hug, a gesture I’m sure felt forced, since my experience with small children was limited to seeing re-runs of *Full House* during moments of insomnia. “I know, sweetie. Me too.” The living room was becoming a blast furnace. I knew that if Andrea got out of the building, she would make absolutely certain the firefighters knew exactly where we were. Still, it was becoming harder to keep my own state of panic at a manageable level. I wanted to open the patio door and wait outside, but the flames, now tickling the ceiling, might only grow larger should I feed them more oxygen.

I began rocking Aspen to calm both of us, and I almost thought it was working until a piece of the living room ceiling, just a few feet from where we were huddling near the patio door, suddenly yawned open and dropped a burning mass onto the living room floor. Both Aspen and I let out a bit of a scream, mine only moderately quieter than hers, as the flames seemed to poke along the floor towards us, teasing us with their forked tongues, almost daring us to make a run for it.

There was a sudden flash as the flames climbed their way up Yoga Lady's sofa, as though she'd chosen gasoline as a spray-on fabric protector. Aspen burrowed her head into my chest, and I stumbled backward from my crouching position onto the floor, banging my head on the sliding glass door and rolling over to attempt to shield her as best I could. I decided we could wait no longer. Trying to cover as much of her as possible, I reached up with my right hand, fumbled open the lock on the door and slid it open. I closed my eyes, waiting for the backdraft that might come with the sudden influx of oxygen. The fire was continuing to consume the room, but we still had a small, safe space to ourselves.

"Aspen, Sweetie. Listen to me. We're going to go out on the patio now, okay." In response she clung even tighter to me. "It's okay, Sweetie. You can stay with me. But I'm going to take you outside now, okay?" I thought I sensed the feeblest of nods, and I half raised myself up and stepped over the threshold onto the patio. I reached backwards and slid the door closed, knowing that patio glass was ultimately no match for fire but hoping it would buy us a little more time. To my horror, looking down over the balcony railing, I did not see the fire department raising a ladder to us. In fact, I did not see the fire department at all. I heard sirens, but it was clear that the trucks had arrived at the front of the building. People from neighbouring buildings were gathering in the lane behind our condo, but it did not appear we were getting down any time soon.

I took some comfort in the relative safety of our new position, determined to wait it out in the relative comfort of the sundeck, when an explosion to my left grabbed my attention. Aspen screamed, and I once again dropped to the floor to shield her. Peering up from below the railing, I saw the window of the neighbouring apartment had smashed outward, and the flames that up until now had satisfied themselves with staying in the building were now reaching for the starry sky.

"I'm scared," Aspen whispered just loud enough to be heard over the roar of the flames shooting out of the neighbouring window. I was too, but I didn't tell her. Instead, I eyed the closed patio door in front of me and suffered a quick flashback to a high school science class, where we learned something about heat building up pressure to an explosive point, and suddenly realized closing the patio door was probably a bad idea. Opening the door again seemed an equally bad idea: I could no longer even distinguish the individual objects. It was just orange. Clutching Aspen tightly, I looked down over the railing trying to calculate how many places my bones would be broken should I try to jump the three stories to the ground. I also wondered how far one has to jump before the landing is fatal.

At the same time, I saw there was a second floor balcony directly below the one on which I was standing. I wasn't sure I could climb down, particularly with a five-year-old hanging onto my back, but I wasn't sure I couldn't either. Turning around, I stared back through the patio door and could only see floor to ceiling flames. As if to punctuate the urgency of what I needed to do, two more windows, including the dining room window of Yoga Lady's apartment immediately beside us, exploded in a fountain of shattered glass followed by the angry roar of the flaming beast released from its cage. I decided. "Aspen," I told her forcefully. "I think it's time for you and I to get down from here. I need you to do something for me."

"Okay," she told me through smoke-stained tears.

"I need you to climb onto my back and wrap your arms really tightly around me. We're going to climb down to your downstairs neighbour's balcony."

"You mean Kelly's place?" The kid seemed to know everyone.

"That's right. We're going to go visit Kelly's place. But you need to hold on really, really tight, okay?"

"Okay," she agreed. Crouching down, I let her climb onto my back and wrap her tiny arms around my pathetically tiny neck. I took one last look at the increasing threat of the flames, firmed my resolve, and swung my leg over the top of the railing.

"Are you holding on, Aspen?" I asked one last time.

"I'm holding on," she told me. "I'm okay." Before I could change my mind, I lowered myself off the edge of the patio, one leg at a time, holding on to the railing and quickly finding myself dangling from the third floor. I had not put a great deal of thought into how the descent would work, but once I was on the outside of the railing, crouching down, I recognized that the lower balcony was not directly beneath me but would require me to swing inward if I were to jump onto the floor rather than the railing. I wasn't entirely sure I could make it work, when the loudest explosion we'd heard yet rocked from above, and I felt thousands of minute pellets of glass hit my hands and wrists as the glass patio door gave up the fight against the air pressure. I could feel specks of glass embedding in my fingers, but I took solace in the knowledge that both our bodies would have been the recipients of the glass assault rather than just my fingers.

I realized that getting to the second floor balcony was looking less and less viable, and it struck me the architect had probably very much designed it that way. It also struck me that I was pretty much going to need to hang around off Yoga Lady's balcony until the fire department arrived. On the plus side, the back side of the building had not yet been draped in the green leaky-condo tarpaulin that had for some time been adorning the front side of the building outside my window. On the downside, as a long distance runner, my legs were likely much stronger than my arms, and I should probably be hanging from them instead of the bamboo sticks that were my arms.

"How ya doing, Aspen?" I croaked.

"I'm tired," she told me. "When are we going down to Kelly's?"

"Here's the thing," I replied. "I'm not sure I can get us there. We're just going to have to hang on for a few minutes. Can you do that?"

"I don't know."

"I think you can. You know how your mom can stay in the same position for a long time while she does yoga?" I had no idea what happened in yoga, but I needed to take a shot.

"You mean like in the lotus?"

"Yeah! Just like the lotus. I want you to think of yourself as just being in a different kind of lotus position. You need to just hold on. Concentrate on holding on, and we'll be fine." I'd always thought yoga was a load of crap, but it couldn't possibly have been as much as crap as I was trying to feed my cargo.

After a few seconds I became aware of a siren, and I managed to turn to my left and see a ladder truck of the Vancouver Fire Department entering the alley. I also made out the plaintive wail of Yoga Lady as she rounded the corner of the building, running neck and neck with the fire truck. "Aspen!" she screamed.

"Don't look down, honey," I said soothingly. "Just focus on staying on my back. Keep your focus." I could hear Andrea, who had arrived alongside Yoga Lady, shouting at me to hold on, and I promised myself I would chastise her for shouting such stupidly obvious commands. Did she think I was going to let go if she didn't tell me otherwise?

After an eternity and a half, the VFD's lifesaving ladder found its way beside me against the patio, and a firefighter reached over and lifted Aspen from my back. Seconds later my feet found purchase on the ladder rungs and I climbed to the ground, where Andrea shoved me so hard, I nearly fell backwards into the waiting arms of paramedics. "What the hell is the matter with you?" she demanded. "You scared the shit out of me!"

"It must be the smoke or something," I replied. "I thought you were Sandi for a minute, the way everything was all about you."

Andy did something then she almost never does: she hugged me close and tight then whispered in my ear. "I've told you before. Don't you ever come that close to dying on me. I couldn't take it."

"I'll do my best," I whispered back. We stepped back from the building, and I sucked on an oxygen mask for a few minutes while the fire department drenched the building with hundreds of thousands of gallons of water. When my hands had been cleaned and I convinced all and sundry I was going to survive, Andrea sat down on the bumper of the ambulance beside me.

"You know what?" she asked.

"Nope."

"I am not going to your mother's house for dinner tonight."

"Good call."

Chapter Thirteen

There wasn't much left.

As daylight was breaking on the Lord's Day, the extent of the damage to my apartment building became evident. Where the third floor of the building had been — my floor — there was the ceiling of the second floor, and that was about it. The residents of what had once been touted as a luxury condominium were gathered in groups on the front grass staring forlornly at what had once been their homes. The proximity to the nearest Starbucks had been a factor in my decision to purchase this apartment, and they were proving to be good neighbours, arriving shortly after dawn with hot coffee, muffins, and pastries for the middle class homeless standing in stupefied silence.

People had reached the phase where tears had stopped flowing, outrage had yet to set in, and most were quietly contemplating what the immediate future held for them. Remarkably, injuries were limited to minor smoke inhalation and the twisted ankle of the old man from the second floor who in his hurry to escape the flames had stumbled in the concrete stairwell. Andrea was deeply engrossed in a discussion with fire investigators, convinced that the fire was deliberate. I was sitting alone, mostly by choice, but also because my involvement in Tim's defence likely had my neighbours convinced their loss was due to me, and it would be hard to argue with them. I had just finished my second cup of Good Samaritan coffee when I felt someone sit down beside me. I didn't bother to look up, hoping my lack of response would show that I was not in the mood.

"Good morning hardly seems like the appropriate term just now." I recognized the voice of Peter Carson, pastor of the Fairview Presbyterian Church where Andrea and I, long-lapsed Catholics, had taken up more or less regular worship. Peter was younger than I thought ministers were supposed to be. In my Catholic youth, church elders were just that: elder. I didn't recall ever seeing anyone at the pulpit with anything less than white hair. Peter, at thirty-three, looked more like a promising soccer player than a spiritual flock leader. While our religious upbringing differed in Christian flavour, Peter and I had one serious common trait: he slept maybe even less than I did. It was, in fact, on one of my many middle-of–the-night expeditions that I had quite literally run into him, him trying to walk off his insomnia, me attempting to pacify mine through running. Talking through my post-run stretch, we had discovered a common bond of belonging to the night, at least as far as our sleep patterns were concerned. Peter, then an associate pastor, invited me to attend his church, and the welcome long having been revoked from my Catholic days, I took him up on his offer. Since then, Peter had assumed the role of head pastor in the church and had learned to love running through the nights more than his previous leisurely gait. Neither the increased activity level nor the closer relationship to the Big Guy upstairs seemed to cure him of his inability to use the night the way normal people did. It was a frequent topic of conversation, and it drove Andrea crazy that I had found a friend with the same frustrating habits as me.

"Shouldn't you be getting ready for church?" I asked him grumpily.

"If I were more aggressive in my evangelical zeal, I might be asking you the same question. Are you hurt at all?"

"Spiritually or physically?"

"Either or both."

"Neither. I think."

"That's a start." He was quiet for a moment, likely resisting the urge to drape his arm around me as I let out an involuntary shudder in the cool of the May morning. We didn't have that kind of demonstrative relationship. "I guess this probably has something to do with the cause you've recently taken up." I tensed slightly, sure he was about to embark on a biblical lesson on the righteousness of anti-homosexuality, though I was pretty confident neither testament offered any prohibition on same-sex partners at graduation dances.

"One would assume," I replied quietly.

"Man, that is so ridiculous." He shook his head and let out a small tsk. "People get themselves wound up over the most inane of issues."

I turned to look at Peter for the first time since he had sat down. "Coming from a man of the cloth, that seems an odd description of things."

"Live and let live, Brother."

"That kind of talk could get you in trouble with your bosses, no?"

Peter smiled. "I'll take that up with Him when I meet Him someday. I suspect He wouldn't approve of this either." He made a sweeping gesture towards the dilapidated structure that had been my home. Then we were both quiet again, watching as the wind knocked free a piece of charred timber that dropped with a thud right onto Polish Sausage's ground floor patio. "What now?" Peter asked when the dust had settled.

"Now?" I replied. "Now I guess I'm homeless. Maybe there's room under one of our fair city's many bridges."

"Could you perhaps stay with your parents?"

"I might prefer the underside of bridges. It'd be quieter, with less guilt." Andrea chose that moment to drop down beside us.

"Good morning, Reverend," she said with a formal mimed tip of the hat.

"Andrea. How are you holding up this morning? I understand you were here too."

"I'm fine, thank you." She touched my arm in a motherly manner not generally part of her emotional repertoire. "How you doing?"

"He's thinking about bridges he can squat under."

"Temporarily," I insisted. "I have insurance. Eventually I'll *purchase* my own spot beneath a bridge." I sensed their exchanged glances. "Oh relax, you two. I'm just kidding. I'll be fine." I wasn't convinced, but it seemed appropriate to say. At that moment I felt nothing but sheer exhaustion, and the stale smoke smell hanging in my clothing reminded me why I didn't go camping.

"He'll be staying with me," Andrea told Peter, as though I had no choice.

"Are you sure? Your apartment is pretty small. You two could kill each other, which would sort of defeat the purpose of the protection service you've been providing him of late." He had a valid point. My smouldering condo was nearly twice the size of Andy's tiny one-bedroom.

"There is that," Andrea conceded. "Hey, Win, your rented mini-van survived. I'll bet you could sleep comfortably in there. I could park outside in my cruiser."

"Once more to the bridge," I told them.

"I'm going to mention it to the congregation this morning. I'm sure there will be a flood of offers for assistance."

I wasn't so sure. "Given my causes of late, I have to think many of the flock won't be so anxious to see me. I've already noticed some stares lately."

"That's just because the women in the church can't figure out why you don't just settle down with Andrea and be happy."

"Go back to your first concern about me residing in her apartment. Don't worry about it. I'll sort something out."

"He'll be staying with me." A fourth voice entered the discussion, and I didn't have to look up to recognize the insistent tone I had endured through several years of wedded bliss. "Winston, are you okay?"

"I'm fine," I told Sandi, who had inexplicably arrived on the scene. Her presence was confusing not because I thought she didn't care about my well-being, but because it was not yet seven. For Sandi to rise before ten on any day, least of all a weekend, was miraculous. Pregnancy must be wreaking havoc with her sleep clock. Maybe she could finally relate to me. I glanced at Andrea, who returned my questioning look with a slightly apologetic glance of her own. Clearly she had called my ex-wife.

"You know I have room. Besides, when you're staying with me, we'll be able to work on our birthing plan and practice labour techniques." Aha! It had to be about her somehow.

"Where he goes, I go," Andrea offered. The thought of these two women bidding for my tenancy was almost laughable, given their barely contained tolerance of each other.

Sandi smiled with what passed for her as hospitality. "There's plenty of room. I think it will be fun." Good god, had she just included Andrea in her offer of accommodation?

"I guess it's settled then," Peter said. "If there's anything I can do, you know where to find me."

Sandi Cuffling lived in a glorious condominium overlooking Coal Harbour and Stanley Park. Though I was too classy or depressed to ever ask what the place had cost, news reports at the time of the building's opening pegged prices from the upper eight hundred thousands to over a million per condo. Sandi's being a three-bedroom with den on the nineteenth floor surely put hers at the upper end of the scale. I had never actually set foot in it, hoping unsuccessfully that my divorce meant I would see little to nothing of her. Still, choosing between here and the back of my rented min-van, or worse yet, my parents' place, made Sandi's offer of lodging seem welcome. After depositing me securely inside the lobby, Andrea left for home to gather supplies for the next leg of her protection detail, leaving me to settle in, alone with the love of my former life. For the first few moments I stood staring out the floor-to-ceiling windows overlooking the harbour as a seaplane silently descended past my line of sight, bouncing once on the black water and taxiing to one of the floating gas stations that bobbed playfully in the chop. "You could probably use a drink," Sandi said from behind me, breaking my moment of soundless awe at her luxurious digs.

"It's eight o'clock in the morning," I replied.

"Of course," she said, sounding a little disappointed. "I haven't been able to drink anything stronger than juice for so long, I was just excited to get to use the bar." The northwest corner of the unit was taken up by a wet bar with a granite counter-top, and the blown glass shelves on the wall were stocked with what I knew from experience would be the best-quality brands of nearly every liquor. If Sandi were ever to take a stab at earning a regular paycheque, she could certainly survive as a bartender. Never during our time together had any guest requested a drink for which she didn't know the exact ingredients. I may never have mastered the intricacies of what made a really good cosmopolitan, but I had learned more about red wine from Sandi's upper crust family and friends than an apprenticeship with a sommelier could have provided. We let an awkward silence hang between us for a few moments while we tried to come to terms with the unusual situation. Finally Sandi said, "So what now?"

I shrugged noncommittally. "I don't really know. I guess I need to find a place to live."

"I meant with your case with the gay student."

"There really isn't anywhere to go. The case is over. There's really nothing left for me to do. We won."

"And look what it got you."

"Yes. Look."

"I just mean, do you think people are still going to try to keep Tim from going to the dance?"

"I don't know. I wouldn't have thought a high school grad dance could generate this kind of animosity. But we're certainly not going to turn around now and tell Tim he can't bring Van to the dance."

"Van?"

"That's his, uhm, boyfriend." I still hadn't quite come to terms with the terminology. I wondered if I would ever become as progressive as I believed myself to be.

Sandi nodded. "You know you don't need to rush on finding a place to live. I have lots of room."

"And I appreciate that. I don't want to get in your way any longer than necessary."

"You won't be in my way." She paused a moment then carried on. "Have you considered maybe staying here for the longer term?"

"Excuse me?"

"Oh, don't get all freaked out or anything. I'm just saying I think we could handle living together for awhile."

"It didn't work out too well the last time."

"I'm not talking about us getting *back together*. I'm just saying it would be nice for me to have some help around here."

"Oh, so you're looking for a nanny." I could feel my back going up already. We'd been living together again less than five minutes.

"No, but don't you want to be part of the baby's life at all?" This was dangerous territory, and I still required a place to live in the short term.

"I don't even think I like babies. I'm probably the last person you'd want to have here looking after your child."

"You work with kids all day."

"My kids are eighteen years old. They speak, they rarely cry, and I have yet to have to change one of their diapers. It's really not the same thing."

"Okay, okay," she acquiesced. "I just thought it would be nice, that's all. It's not like I would expect you to be looking after the baby all the time. I've got Ingrid to help me."

"Who's Ingrid?" I asked.

"My nanny."

"You have a nanny already? The baby's not even born."

"I believe in being prepared. There's a huge demand for good nannies. I didn't want to be stuck on some agency waiting list."

"You don't work. What's the nanny for?" I realized it sounded a bit accusatory, but I couldn't help myself.

"I can't possibly do this on my own, Winston. I can afford help, I hired it." She gestured towards the hallway leading, I assumed, towards the bedrooms.

"She's here now?"

"Don't be ridiculous," she replied with exasperation. "It's Sunday. She has the day off." Of course Sandi would already have had the live-in nanny living in. Someone was going to have to prepare a nursery, buy diapers, formula, or whatever it was that newborns needed.

"So, with Andrea, there's going to be four of us here?" I asked.

Sandi smiled and patted her swollen belly. "And baby makes five."

Contrary to nearly everyone's advice, I went to work Monday morning, mostly *because* everyone had advised me against it.

Staying at Sandi's overnight had provided me temporary shelter from the elements and from Vancouver's media, who, unable to track my whereabouts after the obvious arson of my home, had camped themselves again at my workplace, this time early enough to precede my arrival. Not even the relative anonymity of my ride in Andrea's unmarked cruiser could deflect their attention as we pulled through the phalanx of reporters at the entrance to the staff parking lot at Sir John A. Macdonald Secondary.

"Mr. Patrick," a familiar-looking young woman called to me as I stepped out of Andy's car and it pulled away. I ignored the reporter and made my way to the school as a small chorus of media voices joined in shouting my name. Another familiar young woman was standing just inside the school door awaiting my arrival.

"Jesus," Sara Kolinsky called me as I entered.

"Wow. That's high praise for a lapsed Catholic like myself."

"You could have called. We've been worried sick about you." I looked over her shoulder to see who the second worrier might have been, but she was clearly alone.

"Is it hipster teen jargon to speak of yourself as a collective noun?"

"Funny, Grammar Boy," she replied. "I mean the fire has been all over the news, and we, Tim and I, haven't heard from you."

"If you were paying close attention, you would have heard that no one was badly hurt."

"Not physically anyway," she retorted.

"Did we get married while I wasn't looking?" It was chauvinistic and immature. And I regretted the comment as soon as it was made.

"Okay, truce," Sara sighed, holding up her hands in surrender. "It's just with all that's happened, we were worried, that's all. I didn't mean to come after you like a charging rhino first thing in the morning."

"Or a pit bull."

"Or an ex-wife?" She was smiling now, and though I was trying, it simply wasn't possible to stay mad at her.

"You're nowhere near as tough as her," I replied then filled her in on the details. She actually laughed when I told her I was staying at Sandi's.

"Oh my god, that's insane," she told me. "My parents would kill each other if they had to live together again."

"It's only been a day," I told her. "Give it time." We reached my classroom without having seen another living being in the empty hallways. "Why are you here so early anyway?"

"The media vultures were at my house this morning too. I just wanted to get away from them."

"I thought you were the little media darling? Queen of the talk-show circuit."

"Tim's the queen. I'm just a princess." We both chuckled. "Seriously, though. It gets old really quick. I just want my life back."

"Hear, hear."

"But really, Mr. Patrick. You're okay? Tim's talking about not coming to grad. All day long yesterday, he went from complete guilt about what happened to you and blowing off the dinner dance to flying into a rage and wanting to do something about it."

"I don't like either of those options. I'll talk to him."

"I hope you have more luck than I did. He's not listening to reason."

"He's a teenager. We don't expect that of him." She was about to protest, and I cut her off. "Present company excepted," I added.

She sighed. "The dance is in three weeks. Think we can stick it out without burning down half the city or seeing any more cars trashed?"

"I think we're going to have to. I don't think the media would let Tim skip the dance now. At least all your fancy duds are likely to be on TV. It'll be like the media is your own private video service."

"Small mercies. I'll see ya later." With that I was alone with my thoughts, ready to plan the day. The first order of business would be to explain to my classes that they wouldn't be getting their homework assignments back because they'd burned in the fire. It was an excuse I think I might have used once or twice already, but this time they could turn to the newspapers if they doubted the veracity of my claims. It was probably unrealistic to think that I could spend the day putting the weekend events behind me and focus on my teaching, but I was determined to make that attempt. By the time I had reached the top of the stairs to my third floor classroom, I had what in my head seemed a solid set of lesson plans ready to stimulate my charges when I noticed none other than Bill Owen standing at my door.

"I'm almost surprised to see you here," he began by way of greeting.

"And I you."

"It wasn't my apartment that burned down. Why wouldn't I be here?"

"I have to imagine I'm not exactly your favourite person after our, uhm …" I resisted using the word "victory" but couldn't think of a viable alternative. I finally settled on "Situation with the legal challenge."

"Winston," he said, adopting the patronizing tone I had not missed during our period of incommunicado. "You were never my favourite person to begin with." He laughed at his own little joke, and I smiled to show no hard feelings. "I guess I just wanted to see that you were okay." That sounded suspect, but I nodded my apprehensive appreciation.

"Thanks. I appreciate that. I'm fine." I started to walk past him through my classroom door.

"I guess I also wanted to say just one little 'I told you so' too." I turned to face him, feeling a fight coming.

"You told me so, what?"

"That not everyone agrees with your point of view," he said, sounding like a disappointed father explaining the obvious to his less-than-bright son.

"Intelligent discourse might simply have had those in opposition write a letter to the editor of the paper — which many did, by the way. Arson is an extreme."

"Still," he continued, "it kind of tells you something, doesn't it?"

"What should it be telling me?" I demanded, trying to keep my own temper in check as Owen continued to bait me.

"That sometimes it doesn't pay to piss people off."

"You know, Bill, some people could construe your desire to have this conversation as suspicious behaviour."

His smile dropped. "Are you accusing me of being an arsonist?"

"*Some people* could. But I just think you're being an asshole." With that I turned and walked towards my desk, waiting for the verbal barrage to follow. To my surprise, none came. I didn't really believe our desperately out-of-shape vice-principal had anything to do with the attack on my abode — I couldn't imagine him moving his enormous bulk quickly enough to escape the flames he would have set. On the other hand, he was such an ass, I couldn't help but antagonize him.

The rest of the day passed with my students, bless them, showing at least feigned relief at my well-being and less hostility towards the issue that likely caused it.

If any of the students I taught possessed enough animosity towards Tim bringing his male date to the prom that they would have taken violent action against me, the attitude didn't show in class. As I packed up the plastic shopping bag into which I was piling student homework awaiting my attention, I was feeling almost beloved of my students, judging by their expressions of empathy. I was almost smiling when I opened the classroom door and walked smack into Tim himself. He'd apparently been lurking in the hallway waiting for my departure.

"Tim!" I said. "How are you doing?"

He met my look of concern head-on, with eyes that looked angrier than I had seen at any time. "How am I doing? How are *you* doing?" He was nearly shouting.

"I'm fine. I really am. Everything's fine."

"No," he continued, voice rising, "it's not fine. Somebody tried to kill you! How the hell can you think that's fine?"

"Tim, relax," I said, trying to calm him, though after thirty-six hours of self-pity, I was finding his righteous indignation a little contagious. "There's a significant difference between someone *trying* to kill me and being successful. I try to look at the bright side."

"This has gone on long enough," he continued.

"With that, I can agree."

"I'm serious, Mr. Patrick. I've gone beyond the point where I'm willing to be the scared little queer waiting for someone to take a shot at me. I want whoever did this to pay, and I want to make it happen."

"Tim. The police are working on finding the responsible party, and they will be held to account."

"Yeah, and look how well that's worked so far. There was a cop in your apartment, and that didn't stop them from burning it down."

"You can bet your ass, Tim, that it's gotten a little personal. If you knew Detective Pearson the way I do, you'd be feeling a bit sorry for the neighbourhood arsonist right about now. The only thing she takes harder than someone attacking her is someone attacking me. His ass is as good as cooked."

"You sound pretty sure of yourself." He still sounded angry, but the venom was dissipating, at least a little.

"No. I'm pretty sure of my friend's need for justice. Leave it to her. Don't concern yourself about it." That sounded patronizing even to me, and I regretted it as soon as the sentence was complete. Clearly it sounded that way to Tim too, because the pinhole through which his anger had been evaporating slammed shut, and he headed again towards a full rolling boil.

"You know, I'm not some helpless little princess who can't take care of himself," he began.

"Tim, that's not what I meant. I'm just saying …"

"Forget about it," he interrupted, and it was just as well. I didn't know what I was "just saying." "I'm sorry I got you involved in this in the first place. I really am."

I decided not to push him any further. "I know you are. And I appreciate it. I really hate what this has done to your grade twelve year." We were quiet for a moment. "Go home. Do your homework."

"You too."

"On the plus side, my homework was destroyed by the fire. That's not something you can claim." My attempt at levity just seemed to anger him further.

"Yeah, whatever. Whoever ... whoever did this better hope your cop friends find them before I do." With that, he turned and stomped away into the stairwell. I heard his heavy footfalls down the two flights of stairs in the now quiet corner of the building. I turned to take my own leave before I remembered I needed to wait for Andrea. On Sunday afternoon, Sandi had insisted on shopping for me — just like the olden days — so I already had about a week's worth of clothing to see me through. But I was still immobile in the vehicular sense. My rental car had survived the domestic inferno, but my car keys had not. Even had my keys been available, my wallet had not been recovered, and there was no way my cop friend would have let me trundle around the city in garish mini-van *sans* licence.

So I spent the next forty minutes waiting for Andy, trying to restore my virtual identity, arguing in vain with bored telephone operators to convince them I was who I claimed to be. By the time I looked up to see Andy standing in the doorway, I had arranged for delivery of a new credit card, bank card, and cell phone. The young woman at the phone company had convinced me I needed to upgrade to a full blown PDA, complete with Internet and email, mobile services I had resisted to that point, but which I now recognized as useful.

"You ready to go?" Andrea asked.

"You ready to hang out at Sandi's for another evening?"

"Not so fast. First we eat. What do you feel like?" I didn't respond, because she would not likely appreciate my answer. "Winston," she sighed, "there is more to life than Italian food."

"Unless you're Italian."

"Even then. And you're not." I stacked some unmarked tests into a neat pile that sat flush with the upper right hand corner of my desk. Andy watched without commenting. "Fine," she finally said. "Where do you want to go?" I looked at her and smiled. "My god, it's not even Tuesday."

"I've been traumatized," I whined. "I need comfort food." Her nascent and all too rarely displayed sense of Patrick pity made an appearance, and she agreed to mollify my need.

"Do you think we should call Sandi and let her know we're going to be late?" she asked. It felt too much like domestic un-bliss to do so. Surely Sandi would anticipate my thoughtlessness.

"Nah."

"What if she's making dinner for us?" There was a moment of silence before we both burst out laughing.

Chianti sat about a half block west of Burrard Street on West Fourth, and until the day before, it had been walking distance from my home. As usual, while I was not sitting in Teri's section, she was still assigned to serve me. "Well, look. If it isn't Vancouver's finest," she began when we were seated. "And you too," she added with a nod in my direction.

"It's amazing I'm seen with him, isn't it?" Andy asked. When she dined with me, it was always two against one.

"You'll like the combination special tonight," Teri said. "We're trying something new with prawns." It was offered not so much as a suggestion but as a directive.

"I'm certainly not here for the service," I lied.

"That was your place that burned down yesterday? I saw the pictures but haven't read the news yet."

"It's been in the media all day."

"I haven't been up with the journalists."

"Tough night?"

"You don't know the half of it," she said.

"I can't imagine."

"Don't try, Professor. It'll only depress you by comparison."

"Amen," added Andrea. "Prawn action in the special?"

"Fresh from market today."

"I'll have the same."

"I'll have them add some fire for you. Not for him." Most Italian dishes didn't come near to meeting the level of flammability Andy required for an exciting meal. For her they'd break out the explosive seasoning.

"Should I select a wine?" I asked futilely.

"Don't be absurd," Teri replied, turning and walking away. The busboy silently glided by, depositing a basket of fresh-baked buns on the table.

"So you said there was more?" I asked Andrea. In the short drive, Andrea had begun to bring me up to speed on the progress of the investigation. It had not even taken as long as the short drive.

"The Fire Marshall sent us the results of the initial investigation," she had told me as we pulled away from the illegal parking spot of her unmarked cruiser.

"And?" I had asked.

"Arson."

"And amidst the reams of paper needed to record that profound finding, I suppose there also lay some indication about who the guilty party may be?"

"You mean like a clue?"

"A clue. Easy with the jargon. You're dealing with a layman here."

"The initial findings did not provide any such indication, no."

"You want to know something funny, in the coincidental sort of way? I actually suspected arson myself."

"Me too."

"We could work together, you and I. Think of the reduction in the crime rate we could foster."

"Fire Marshall says the perp used an accelerant of a petroleum-based nature," Andrea continued.

"Gas."

"Did he send you a copy too?"

"You'd almost think so."

She paused a moment. "To be fair, it's just an initial report. There's more work to be done in the fire investigation. There could be more to come."

"So a clue could be forthcoming?"

"There's still time." She paused again. "But as of yet, there's nothing definitive linking the arson to your case with Tim."

"Oh, come on," I complained.

"I'm just saying there's nothing forensic to prove you were definitely the target. And no witnesses either."

"But the accelerant was placed where?"

"Pretty much right outside your unit."

"So unless the perp, had, say, the wrong address, it's likely he or she was after me."

"She?"

"If I wasn't targeted because of my relationship to Tim and his legal challenge, I should leave open the possibility of a scorned lover or paramour."

"Don't you have to, I don't know, go on a date or something before that's going to be a serious focus of an investigation?"

"Probably."

"But yes, you're right. There's nothing definitive linking the arson to you, but there isn't anyone who thinks it isn't. And naturally, no one is thinking it has to do with a current, previous, or even future romantic encounter."

"Naturally." I stopped to think about this *new* information, such as it was. "Gasoline seems kind of a simplistic approach, doesn't it?"

"As opposed to?"

"I don't know, some kind of remote detonator activated by cell phone?"

"Still enjoying re-runs of *24?*"

"If Sandi lets me, I'm going to name her child Jack Bauer."

"You might be surprised that arson is generally not a terribly sophisticated kind of crime. Gasoline is most often the accelerant of choice. Arson also isn't often used as a way to kill someone. It's too unpredictable. Even the least likely of people can sometimes show miraculous feats of ingenuity in the face of flames." She didn't need to gesture towards me, but she did anyway.

"So your point is?"

"Arson is more often a threat, a way of showing someone you mean business, or that you have a serious point to make."

"Like gays shouldn't bring gays to the prom."

"Like that, yes."

"So we're right back to Tim's case then."

"Yes." She paused. "And I have news on that front today as well."

"Do tell."

"I think we need to wait for wine first," she said as Teri approached the table.

Teri deposited two glasses of red. She stayed while I made the usual big show of sampling her selection. I wouldn't have sent it back even had it been crap, and there's no way it would have been. Still, this particular one was exceptional. "Wow," I told her. "This is fantastic. What is it?"

"Are you sure you like it?"

"Teri, it's beautiful. Tell me."

"Quail's Gate. Okanagan."

"Dear god, woman! Domestic? Why do you do this to me?" It was a running theme between us that I tried to be an unbearable wine snob and reject anything born of this continent, but B.C.'s wines, in particular, were gaining world renown, and while I didn't admit it to Teri, on the way home from dinner I frequently purchased the Okanagan wines she brought me.

"An award winner, no less." She turned and left Andrea and I to the half litre — and no more — we would consume.

"She's a gem," Andrea told me over the glass.

"So about Tim?" I asked.

Andy took another swig from her glass that drained it then reached for the carafe. I wanted to flinch but resisted. "He's not the golden boy you thought he was."

"What does that mean?"

"We did some more background checking on him, found some stuff that was a little surprising."

"A record? I thought he didn't have one. And it would be sealed anyway. The kid is a victim here. You shouldn't be violating his civil rights."

She waved me off dismissively. "Relax, Win, put the cloak and wig away. We didn't go unsealing sealed records. Your kid's clean record-wise."

"So if not criminal, what did you find?"

"One of our info-tech geeks went online and started seeking out your kid, and it turns out he has quite an online presence."

"Meaning?"

She pulled out her little notebook and flipped it open to a recently dog-eared page. "Ryan, that's our geek, is on Facebook. Tim has a Facebook page. He's uploaded all kinds of photos of himself and friends at various parties, camping trips, etc., though Ryan did note that Tim had quite a number of photos in which he was shirtless, kind of posing."

"Is this in comparison to other kids' photos, or is this a supposition Ryan is making because he knows Tim is gay?"

Instead of raising an eyebrow, she rolled her eyes. "Let's just say they were of the provocative nature. But that's not the worst of it." She glanced up from her notebook, challenging me to interrupt again. I thought better of it. "Many of the kids on Facebook have links to their own web pages or to other social networking sites. Tim had a link to a personal page in ylife, same kind of idea, but a little more edgy. As you might expect if you saw Tim's Facebook page, the pictures on his ylife page were a bit on the racy side."

"What do you mean by racy?"

"Nothing pornographic, but a lot of long sultry, maybe inviting, looks at the camera, sometimes just in his boxer shorts. Almost solicitous, you could say."

"But this is all legal?"

"You're asking me?"

"I'm pseudo-retired from the profession and stroking your ego so you'll pay for dinner."

"You've got work to do then."

"The night is young."

She consulted her notebook again. "Anyway, so far, nothing's there that would get my attention. Tim's ylife page is actually pretty text-heavy, long paragraphs of Tim talking about his life. A lot of teenage angst kind of stuff. But within the text is where it gets interesting."

"How so?"

"Ryan found embedded links in the text."

"Which are?"

"They're links embedded in the text portions of the page that take you to another site. Except they're hidden from view. Normally when there's a link in text on a website, it's underlined and usually in a different colour, like blue."

"Right."

"It tells the reader there's more information to be found by clicking on the link. Except on Tim's ylife page, the only way you'd know the links were there would be if you stumbled upon them accidentally, say by running your mouse over the exact portion of text that contains the hidden link. Even then you'd have to have the status bar open on the bottom of the page before you'd know there was a link there."

"I'm still not getting it."

Teri came by with our salads. She must have sensed the heaviness of our conversation, because she put them down without a word, a monumental act of restraint.

"If you read the portions of the text where Tim's hidden the links, they're meant to be suggestive of something better to be found. More in depth. More personal. More intimate."

"And where does the link take you?"

She put down her notebook and looked at me solemnly. "To a personal pay site. He's doing porn online for money."

Chapter Fourteen

The "something new with prawns" Teri had brought was probably delicious, but I hardly tasted it. Andrea, at least, seemed to like it. She ate hers and most of mine, since I had lost my appetite.

Tim's website, titled "Tasty Tony," allowed users, for a fee, to view unlimited numbers of photographs Tim had taken of himself in various poses, from suggestive to outright sexual. We stopped by the police station on the way to Sandi's, and Andy showed me the site. After clicking through a couple of pages, I had seen more than I wanted. Though I asked her not to, she proceeded to tell me in great detail about the rest of the site, outlining the kinds of acts that Tim performed in front of his webcam. From her law enforcement perspective, the material was comparatively tame compared with much of the hardcore content available on the web.

In nearly all of the photographs, Tim was alone, and in those where he wasn't, his partner seemed to be not only around the same age but also fully aware of the camera, which meant that Tim at least was in the clear so far as unlawfully posting lewd content without that person's consent. Tasty Tony offered initial previews that were relatively tame — fully clothed, shirtless, boxers-only poses, and a few nudes with visual effects blurring out the parts one would need to pay to see. For $24.95 per month, "subscribers" were entitled to a seemingly endless array of archived photos, videos, and live scheduled webcam shows, during which Tim would perform sex acts mostly solo but occasionally with the aforementioned partner. The site also had a discussion board where members could chat with Tim and with each other, giving reviews of his latest photos, video, or live performances. It was from this discussion board that Andy and her tech geek Ryan had determined that membership to Tim's site was strong. Tim, it turns out, had what appeared to be a lucrative sideline business. It made the job he had at the movie theatre seem superfluous. It made my job teaching him seem nearly impossible.

Officially, Tim's assault was Andrea's case, and while I wasn't officially acting as counsel, she thought it appropriate to invite me to accompany her while she paid Tim a visit. Since the threatening phone calls and torching of my home on the weekend, Tim and most of his family had uprooted and found temporary lodging in a Vancouver hotel. I was initially surprised when Andy drove across the Burrard Street Bridge and into downtown Vancouver, pulling into the space outside the Four Seasons Hotel reserved for valet parking. The valet, dressed in a ridiculous outfit that indicated he would be more likely to park a horse and carriage than the chariots of twenty-first century patrons, opened his mouth to speak when Andrea pocketed the keys to her cruiser but quickly thought better as she flashed her badge, and we made our way through the sliding glass doors into the luxurious entryway. As we ascended the escalator two steps at a time — Andy never being one to actually *ride* the escalator — I couldn't help but comment on the choice of hotels. "Nice digs," I said. "Somehow I don't think Victim's Services is picking up the tab."

"Apparently web porn pays well," she replied.

"You think Tim's picking up the family tab?"

"You tell me. They live in J. Mac's catchment area. How likely is it that his family is rolling in dough?" She had a point. While certainly not downtrodden, the neighbourhood around my school could only be characterized as working class. She flashed her badge again at the front desk clerk and instantly received Tim's room number. Unlike the way shows like *Law & Order* portray it, the average citizen will almost always give up whatever information is sought at the very sight of a detective's shield. When I was defence counsel, it drove me crazy. As the elevator doors closed, Andy let out a little whistle.

"What?"

"He's got a suite. I can tell by the floor number."

"I guess web porn does pay well," I said.

"You should think about it. Who knows how well your insurance will pay out on your apartment? You might need some extra cash."

"I think it would be frowned upon by my employers."

"Not nearly as much as by those people who actually stumbled onto your site and saw you *au naturel*." Blessedly, the elevator doors opened just then, and we could focus on preparing for our conversation.

Tim opened the door himself after the first knock and registered genuine surprise at my presence. "Mr. Patrick?" he said. "What are you doing here?"

"Hi, Tim," I said quietly. "You remember Detective Pearson."

He looked uncomfortable. "Sure. Of course. Did you want to come in?" We took him up on his invitation and crossed the threshold as he stepped back from the doorway. We stepped into a living room larger than my entire apartment. A bar stood in the corner. I noticed there were drinks on the counter, but Tim appeared to be alone.

"How are you feeling?" I asked. "After this afternoon, I was a little worried about you. You sounded pretty angry."

He laughed a little. "So you brought the police to restrain me?" Andy had yet to say a word, she just looked silently at Tim and scanned the room. "You don't have to worry," he continued. "I was just really upset about your place. I've calmed down. I haven't done anything too rash yet."

"That's good." I was waiting for Andy to jump in. When she didn't, I resisted the urge to make more small talk. I couldn't muster up anything, given the image I now had of Tim in my mind. Tim met my gaze, and when I didn't continue, he turned to Andy.

Finally she broke the silence. "Do you mind if I sit?"

"No, of course not. I'm sorry. Where are my manners? Please, sit down." We both took a seat on the oversized elegant couch that backed the window to the west, with its view of the rooftop of the old Georgia 5th Hotel across the street. The room was strangely quiet, and I wondered where the rest of Tim's family was. "What is it you wanted to talk to me about?" Tim asked as the silence became increasingly less comfortable.

Andy made a show of taking her time opening her notebook and reviewing her notes before speaking. "Tim," she finally asked gently, "is there anything you want to tell us about your means of earning income?" She offered no further explanation.

"What do you mean?" Tim asked, but I could tell his heart wasn't in it. Clearly he knew what this police detective knew, but he seemed uncomfortable more at my presence than by her question. I felt the same and was starting to regret coming along. When she made no effort to elaborate, Tim sank back into the couch in resignation. "So you know, then."

"We do," was all Andy said.

Tim turned his attention to me. "It's not what you think, Mr. Patrick." Since I didn't know what I thought, I didn't know how to respond to that, so I left the statement hanging. "It's nothing illegal."

"You sound pretty sure of that," Andrea replied. "Have you sought legal counsel?"

Tim looked to me. "Do I need to?"

"Not if you're not doing anything illegal," Andrea replied. "But I'm sure your teacher here is a better judge of the legality of your online activities."

Tim looked as embarrassed as I felt. "So you've seen my website then?" My discomfort was growing, so I just nodded slightly. "God, this is embarrassing," he continued. Then, like the good-humoured student he always was, he added with a smile, "So, what'd you think?"

I got up. "I think I should go. Tim, Detective Pearson really needs to talk to you some more, but I'm feeling really uncomfortable here."

"Oh relax, Mr. Patrick. I'm just giving you a hard time."

"Tim, why didn't you tell us about this earlier?" Andy said.

Tim looked quietly between her and me for a moment before answering. "I didn't think it was relevant or germane to your investigation." He was using some of his high school law learning.

"Someone beat you to within mere inches of your life, and the fact that you're an online porn performer couldn't possibly have anything to do with it?" From anyone else, the question would have sounded judgmental, but somehow she managed to make it seem banal.

Tim shrugged slightly. "I guess not. It certainly wasn't one of my clients who hurt me."

"How do you know that?" I asked.

He looked at me as though the answer should be obvious. "They're paying to watch me, Mr. Patrick. They're fans. Why would they want to hurt me?"

I had no response. Andrea did. "Jealousy? Worried you might be involved too seriously with your on-camera partners? Someone upset he couldn't have you for himself?"

"Or herself," Tim countered.

"You have female clients on your website where you perform sex acts with other men?" Andrea asked.

"The world is a strange place. You'd be surprised." I was sure I would be. "My clients pay to see me because they enjoy seeing *me*. Beating me to a pulp certainly isn't going to enhance the picture they get. It doesn't make sense."

"It wouldn't be the first time a spurned lover took to attacking the love interest rather than the proverbial other woman, or man, as the case may be," Andrea assured him.

"But that's just it," he insisted. "I'm not involved with any of them. I've never met a single one of my online clients. Never. There is no relationship."

"At least in your eyes. In the minds of one or more of your clients, who knows? Do you think people pay to watch sex on the web because they're all necessarily well-adjusted, happy, psychologically healthy individuals?"

"Just because someone pays to access my site doesn't mean they're nuts."

"Nor does it preclude them from being so," I interjected. Andrea could well have made that point, but I was feeling redundant.

Tim digested that for a moment before Andrea dropped the bomb he surely knew was coming. "I'm going to need a list of your clients."

"Is that really necessary? What's going to happen to them?"

"Nothing," Andy assured him. "We need to just run down the list, get an idea of who's got an attachment to you and potentially whose attachment might have turned unhealthy." Tim looked crestfallen. "We'll be discreet. I promise."

He sighed. "You really think they may be connected? To Mr. Patrick's apartment fire?"

"We can't rule it out. It's an avenue we have to look down."

"And you don't have much else to go on yet," Tim added. He probably meant it more as an institutional dig than a personal one, but it didn't sound good. Andy let it slide. If I had made the comment, I would have paid for it. I was confident I still would.

"You're right. We really don't."

He considered that another moment then looked to me. "I'm not breaking any laws by revealing who my clients are, am I?"

"I'm not sure you're not breaking any laws by not revealing who your clients are. What you're doing is essentially pornography," was my shocked reply.

"I'm eighteen years old. I'm legally an adult."

"And when was your birthday?" I asked. "Tim, unless you just recently took up this business since your eighteenth birthday, those clients were paying for child pornography. That's a felony. And before you go claiming that you've only been in show business since you legally became an adult, keep in mind that Detective Pearson is fully aware of your date of birth, and the computer investigators in the police department can easily determine at what point your website was started, what you were doing on it and when. That will change everything." Of course, I was bluffing about the last part. I had no idea what the police computer technicians could accomplish.

Tim threw his hands up in mock surrender. "Okay, okay. I'll get you a list of my clients. But keep in mind I don't know who most of them are. They're just a user name and an active PayPal account. Beyond that, I can't verify who's paying to see what."

I sighed. "Good. I really do want to see this over and life get back to normal."

He nodded. "I've got a grad dance to get ready for."

"Indeed."

He turned his attention back to Andrea. "Is there anything else you need from me?"

She smiled again. "You could refund the money we had to pay to access your site. Budgets aren't limitless, you understand."

Tim laughed. "You bought your way in? That's quite a crack commando computer team you've got going down there."

"Time was of the essence. We'd have gotten in eventually."

He laughed again. "I'll bet. I'll send you the information. And I'll refund the money too." We got up to leave. "So really, Mr. Patrick. What did you think?" His sense of humour seemed to have completely replaced the outrage he'd displayed that afternoon at school. I glanced again at the bar and wondered which of the empty glasses were his.

"I assure you, beyond seeing the opening page, I didn't look any further."

"He's got no sense of adventure," Tim told Andy.

"You have no idea."

"Detective?" he said, stopping us as we reached the door. "I'm sorry if I haven't been as co-operative as I could have been. I really do want to catch who did this to me. To us," he added, touching my arm slightly. For about the hundredth time in our short visit, I felt horribly uncomfortable. "I just, well, I really didn't want this to get out. Teenagers aren't exactly a tolerant crowd, as we've found out."

"So no one at school knows about your website business?" I asked. Gossip travelled so fast in a high school, it seemed impossible to conceive of his "work" being anonymous.

"You have to know where to look for it. Anyone who'd have found it would have been searching for it. They'd be even further in the closet than I've been. Sure, people know I'm gay, but they don't know about the site. If they did, clearly they were looking for gay porn on the web."

"I promise you," Andy replied. "We'll do our very best to be discreet. Being a teenager is shitty enough without us adding any extra shit to the pile."

"I appreciate it. Six more weeks and high school is over." We said our goodbyes and headed back to the opulent elevator in silence. When the door closed and we began our descent, I finally turned to my friend.

"Shitty? Shit? Was the profanity necessary? He's a kid."

"Yeah, that much is obvious."

"Still. It's hardly appropriate language."

"For you. I'm not his teacher. I'm the shit disturber. I've gotta turn the fan on his client list and watch the shit fly. See where the shit sticks. Wrap this shit up before grad." She smiled at me.

"You're incorrigible."

"You got dat shit right."

Andrea dropped me back at Sandi's apartment. She intended to meet a computer technician who was willing to come in the evening to work on the information Tim had promised to send. There was plenty of male police and civilian personnel willing to work with Andrea after hours, most no doubt hoping the work was a pretense to spend after hours time with them. They were always wrong.

Sandi was sitting in the living room waiting for me. "You could have called."

I took a breath and resisted the bait. "I could have. I didn't. I'm sorry."

Never one to take an apology as a cue to end an argument, Sandi pressed forward. "I was hoping we could have spent some time together tonight."

"Because?"

"Because you're living here now, you were nearly killed last night, you said you were going to help me with the prenatal classes."

"Staying here, not living here," I corrected. "Escaped from a burning building, not nearly killed, and prenatal classes are on Thursday. Today is Monday."

Still, Sandi pressed forward. "Are we going to start fighting already?"

"I was really hoping not to. Andrea and I were following up on a lead. We grabbed a bite to eat and we interviewed my student about that lead. Then I came back here."

"And where's your bodyguard?"

"She'll be back. She went down to the police station to work for a couple of hours."

"Oh good. Another night under lock and key."

"I could go stay somewhere else if you'd prefer." Sara had been right: this living arrangement was destined to fail. It had taken a little more than twenty-four hours, most of it apart, before Sandi and I were finding ourselves to be incompatible cohabitants. Both Sandi and I were about to ratchet up our dialogue to the point where simultaneous, incoherent complaints were lobbed at one another when an unfamiliar voice entered the fray.

"Ms. Cuffling? Did you need anything else? I was just going to read for awhile before I turn in for the night." The accent sounded Eastern European. I turned to the sound of the voice and was momentarily silenced by the stunningly beautiful young woman standing at the entrance to the hallway leading to the apartment's three bedrooms. Her blonde hair was tied back in a simple ponytail that was at once both casual and elegant. Her high cheekbones held just the hint of colour beneath deep blue eyes that seemed to shyly avoid both Sandi's and mine. I hoped my mouth was not agape.

"No, that's all, Ingrid. Thank you." I cleared my throat to signal to my ex-wife that she had neglected to introduce me. She looked to me with a level of disdain slightly elevated from the usual, then sighed. "Of course. How inconsiderate of me. Ingrid, this is Winston Patrick, my ex-husband. Remember I told you he'd be staying with us for a while? Well, this is he."

I believe I responded to the introduction in some fashion, but it was not coherent enough to lodge in my memory. It likely was not coherent enough to make much of an impression with Ingrid either. She smiled and said, "It's a pleasure to meet you, Mr. Patrick. I'm so glad you'll be staying with us." And that, it was clear to me, was blatant flirtation on her part. I may have had a few years on her, but clearly she found me attractive. I was thinking that years between people was hardly an important issue anyway in today's modern society. And as an obviously recent resident of Canada, being around someone who had spent his whole life in the Vancouver area was surely an improvement over dating someone her own age who would have had fewer years to get to know the city as well as I. While I was thinking all those things, Ingrid's lips were moving, and I realized I had no idea what she had said as she turned and departed. I was beginning to imagine they were more words of surreptitious flirtation, but my reverie was interrupted, as usual, by Sandi.

"Oh my god, you're pathetic!"

"What?"

"She's like twenty-four! You're standing there like a big drooling moron!"

"Hey, you're the one perpetuating the nanny stereotype by bringing in an immigrant worker. Are you paying her under the table? Is she even here legally? I don't even want to talk about this. I'm going to bed."

"I'll bet. Hey, Winston," she added as I headed down the same hallway down which Ingrid had just retreated. "Try not to use up all the cold water in the shower before you go to sleep."

If the public can be said to have a short attention span, the media's feeding of that attention span was again incredibly short-lived. By Tuesday morning, the fire that destroyed my apartment building and the prom issue that had ignited it were relegated to the B section of *The Vancouver Sun*. On Monday morning, the local morning news station had a reporter on site doing live hits with nothing new to report, but twenty-four hours later we were not even mentioned. Indeed, the institutional memory even of John A. Macdonald Secondary appeared short-lived, for even with Tim, Sara, and myself on campus, life more or less returned to normal, and I fielded progressively fewer questions about my newfound homelessness, the grad dance, and Tim's assault.

By the end of the day Thursday, with the exception of those who were directly involved, it was as though the incidents had never occurred. For those few days I had called a truce with Sandi, coming home with my police escort more or less directly after work, enjoying a quiet meal, generally ordered from a pricey neighbourhood establishment, and catching up on marking that consumed more of my evening life than I cared to admit. On Thursday evening I dutifully accompanied Sandi to her pre-natal class — *our* pre-natal class, she was quick to correct me — and learned more about the wonders of birth than I would have thought possible. Despite having averted my eyes for the better part of the forty-minute video, by the end of the class I was beginning to feel I might actually be an asset in the delivery room. And as Andy continued to make little to no progress on tracking down Tim's assailants/my arsonists, she continued to make Sandi's home her own while keeping me within arm's reach. They found uncommon camaraderie in chastising me for what they deemed my obvious infatuation with Ingrid. Though I vehemently denied their accusations, even I could not recall having strung together a complete sentence in her presence — subjects were there but verbs kept escaping me. Life, in fact, in that short period, was resembling something akin to domestic tranquillity, almost enough that I was near at times to forgetting what had brought about these unusual living arrangements.

Then I arrived at work on Friday morning.

Andy stepped out of her Crown Victoria after pulling up in front of the building. Nearly every window and available wall space on the 49th Avenue front of the building was defaced with "Fag," "Die Fag," or most alarmingly, "Leave your faggot shows on the web," and other messages of that ilk. I turned to Andrea to accuse her over the roof of her unmarked cruiser. "What the hell happened to discretion?"

"Hey! Don't look at me. We never said a word about the website."

"Then where the hell did all this come from?" I stared open-mouthed at the building. Some surprisingly artistic renderings of same-sex pornographic acts were painted on the gym wall with Tim's name clearly labelled above one of the painted participants.

"I'm telling you, it didn't come from us. Look for yourself in the papers. Nobody's been reporting this. We didn't provide this to anyone. No one but me and the computer techs even knew about this."

"So this is supposed to just be a coincidence?"

"Winston, for god's sake, it's a website. Sooner or later it was bound to get out. Tim said himself he was surprised no one had caught on yet. He just figured no one would say anything for fear of outing himself. And look around. None of this is signed artwork. Someone looking to get his jollies found Tim's site and unleashed some of his own self-loathing."

"Thank you, Dr. Phil. Don't suppose in all your psychoanalysis you can come up with an identification of our graphic artist?"

"You're pissed at me because you know I'm right. Sooner or later word was going to get out that Tim's a porn star." Of course she was right. From in front of us I watched unhappily as Don McFadden's car turned into the parking lot. The principal parked in his reserved spot, fairly leaped out of his sedan, and stood staring from his car door at the defacing of his building.

"So what now?" I asked Andrea.

"Holy shit!" I heard Don McFadden yell to no one in particular.

"Now we go and we face the music," she told me, turning on the cruiser's flashing lights to signal she would not be leaving the drop-off spot in front of the building.

"Shit," I sighed, closing the door and walking towards the principal.

"Watch your language," she told me as she joined into step. "You're incorrigible."

Chapter Fifteen

I had perhaps been naive in thinking that we would be able to keep Tim's "business" under wraps while the investigation into the hate crimes continued. Don McFadden spent a good portion of the morning in front of the school, meeting with parents demanding such immediate actions as the re-institution of Tim's same-sex date ban, the expulsion of Tim, the arrest of Tim, and, just for good measure, my immediate termination. From reports of the conversation, McFadden reported to parents that he was indeed in favour of many of the above but his hands were tied by such petty annoyances as human rights legislation, the provincial School Act, and collective agreements. As usual, I was deepening the warmth and regard my supervisor held for me. Increasingly, anything and everything that went wrong at Sir John A. Macdonald Secondary School could be attributed to my presence.

I spent the better part of the day squirrelled away in my classroom attempting to avoid the topic at hand. Tim, not surprisingly, did not attend school, having been alerted, no doubt, that he had now become the subject of nocturnal artists and the topic of raging debate throughout the East Vancouver educational community. Andrea spent the morning with crime lab types, photographing the graffiti, much to the chagrin of the principal, who only wanted the school district's maintenance crew to remove the offending works as quickly as possible.

By the end of the day, Andrea met me at my classroom door, as was becoming our routine, and planned to deposit me promptly on Sandi's doorstep while she followed some leads on Tim's case, though even she admitted the likelihood of catching perpetrators faded with each passing hour and day. The graffiti had at least provided a new development that could keep the case fresh in her superiors' minds. "Let's just say some of the people on Tim's client list we've heard of," was all she had had to say on the subject.

"We?" I had asked, pressing for further details.

"The entire 'we' of the law enforcement establishment." Which was to say, I gathered, that some of Tim's loyal viewers had had enough encounters with the law to have maintained criminal records. She went quiet after that, so I gathered she was not willing to share more information. It was a Friday evening, and god knows I had no social plans. I hardly relished the thought of sitting with Sandi in her condo. I had been divorced long enough that I had forgotten there was no Friday night on the Gregorian calendar on which she would not have a social engagement, even in her extremely pregnant state. Sandi barely uttered more than pleasantries to me as she spent the better part of the late afternoon polishing her appearance for a night on the town with Vancouver's upper crust. Thus, as the late afternoon turned to evening and I stared at the glorious view of the harbour and North Shore mountains from the luxurious splendour of her private vista, I resorted to what I did best on Friday evenings: I moped. So mopey was I that I was already into my second glass of red wine, *sans* dinner, when I heard a key turn in the lock. No way Sandi would have turned over a key to Andrea, and I encountered a brief but intense moment of heart-thumping, breath-stopping, post-arson-survivor panic, as I turned to see the door slowly open. Then Ingrid entered.

"Oh, hello, Mr. Patrick," she said. "I take it Ms. Cuffling has gone out for the evening."

"It *is* Friday," I managed. My awkwardness around Sandi's nanny-to-be had begun to abate as the week went on, but there had always been an intermediary. I felt suddenly like one of my teenaged students unexpectedly left alone with the "pretty girl." I would probably comport myself with even less sophistication.

"Well, I won't bother you. I'm just going to grab something from the kitchen and watch television in my room." That seemed a perfectly reasonable way for me to not have to spend any time very badly making small talk, and yet before I could stop it my mouth, I was replying.

"No. Don't. Why don't you join me out here? I was just going to order some dinner." An awkward eternity passed while I assumed she was weighing the merits of an evening of hanging out in her no doubt well-appointed room versus dining and clumsy conversation with her employer's rumpled-looking ex-husband, nearly a dozen years her senior. To my surprise, she opted for the latter, and I found myself hoping, and immediately chastising myself for hoping, that Andrea would find enough investigating to keep her busy for a while. I was looking forward to the company of someone with whom I could converse on topics other than gay bashing, angry principals, and the inability of the Vancouver Police Department to apprehend anyone.

"I heard about what happened today," she said gently as she sat down beside me on the couch. So much for a change of topics. "I guess it must be difficult for you as one of the boy's teachers."

"It's made my teaching life more interesting than I would have wanted it to be," I confessed. "But it's not really about me. It's about Tim."

"I think it's a very good thing you've been doing. Imagine in this day and age him being told he could not bring his boyfriend to the dance. In Canada. I never would have thought it."

"Thank you." I felt better already and could feel my self-pity lifting. I suggested we order pizza, and while we waited, Ingrid told me how she had found herself in my ex-wife's employment. With excellent grades in high school, Ingrid had immediately begun training as a nurse in Prague in the Czech Republic. Qualifying at the top of her class, she had taken the advice of a trusted aunt who told her she should move to Canada, where the working conditions, the pay, and the possibility for career advancement were all much greater than in her native country. Her English was strong, and she had also studied French. Canada was a natural fit for someone with her medical and language abilities. After months of waiting, filling out forms, and working her way through the consular system, she'd found herself in Vancouver, unable to work because the licensing body that oversees nurses in British Columbia refused to recognize her credentials.

I was sympathetic and told her so. It seemed to me the human body in the Czech Republic was more or less the same as the one we'd find on this side of the Atlantic, yet it was more than simply a case of passing a nursing exam here. In order to practice as a nurse, she would pretty much be required to do her complete training all over again, something which her savings account, already depleted from the move to Canada, could not sustain. Thus she had found this job with Sandi, which she hoped would give her the flexibility to study in the evenings or weekends when Sandi was with the baby. I hoped she was right but had my doubts. I had to imagine that Sandi would be at least as demanding an employer as she had been a spouse.

When the pizza arrived, I convinced Ingrid it would be okay to join me in a glass of wine, and we relaxed overlooking the harbour as the sun set beyond Stanley Park. I tried to tell her as much fascinating history about Vancouver as I could remember. As a lifelong resident, it's amazing how much you forget. Ingrid told me the history of the nine o'clock gun, which could be seen across the water from Sandi's abode, the sound of which could not penetrate the multi-layered panes that protected the building's residents from unwanted noise pollution. Ingrid told me how she found herself looking across the water at the gun each night, waiting for the puff of smoke that told her it had been fired. Even though the windows in her room could open and she could hear the boom, she found the anticipation of that little silent puff of smoke much more enjoyable as she took a break from her studies.

Before long she led me to the living room window to share in her nightly ritual. I found myself giddy with anticipation and newfound delight in this long forgotten landmark of my hometown. Ingrid counted down from five, and the puff of smoke erupted just as she hit zero. An odd little tune accompanied it. I was momentarily confused, and Ingrid laughed as it repeated itself. She pointed to my jacket pocket on the dining room chair. The phone, having been only recently acquired, had let loose with a rendition of "The Battle Hymn of the Republic."

"Hello?" I said, hoping it was a wrong number not destined to ruin what had turned to be an unexpectedly pleasant evening.

"Mr. Patrick?"

"Yes."

"It's Tim. I'm sorry to bother you at night." Worried for their safety, I had given both Sara and Tim my phone number weeks ago, to use in the event of an emergency.

"That's okay, Tim. Is everything okay? Are you all right?"

At the sound of Tim's name, Ingrid had moved over to the dining area to join me. "I'll give you some privacy," she whispered and began to leave.

"No, no," I whispered back, my hand covering the general area I assumed to be the mouthpiece. "I'm sure we'll just be a minute. Wait here, please." I didn't know why I was so adamant about Ingrid's presence, but the evening thus far had been bearable only because of her company, and I was reluctant to let it go. She stood demurely by the hallway. Tim was saying something, and my momentary distraction with Ingrid caused me to miss it. "Sorry Tim, what was that?"

"Really. It's nothing. I just wanted to say I'm sorry you got put through the shit pipe at school again today. I heard some comments Mr. McFadden made on the news, and in his usual dipshit way, he's blaming you again for what happened. The guy's an ass."

It was probably the influence of the wine and my desire to get back to my evening with Ingrid, but I found myself inappropriately agreeing with my student. "Yeah, he has his moments. But listen. Don't worry about me. I'll be fine. I'm not likely to be invited to sit at the principal's table at grad, but I'll have more fun at the rowdy teachers' table anyway."

He laughed in a forced way, and his tone turned serious. "On the plus side," he continued, "I think I've got a pretty good idea who's been re-decorating the school, and we're going to have a little chat."

"What are you talking about?"

"Let's just say a little birdie gave me some information, and I was a little shocked to hear who's involved."

"Who is it?"

"Don't worry about it. I've got it taken care of. I just wanted you to rest assured that the guilty party's going to be made to pay."

"Tim, what does that mean? What are you going to do?"

"Nothing. Relax. I've just set up a little meeting. We're going to have a chat, that's all. Christ, you think you know a person." He was sounding as aggressive as he had when we talked outside my classroom a few days earlier.

"Listen, Tim. I don't think that's a good idea. Why don't you let Detective Pearson talk to whoever it is, and the police can handle it from there? Remember, we're talking about people who nearly killed you."

"Uh-uh," he replied. "No, these are two different things. I'm sure of it. This little painting party was someone new, and I'm gonna make sure he knows I'm not taking his shit."

"Tim, don't do anything foolish, okay? Just stop and think this through."

"It's all right, Mr. Patrick. I'm not gonna beat him up or anything. I'm gonna make him come clean. I have my ways."

I sighed. I knew from working with teenagers — and from being one — that strategies for solving conflict were almost never successful. "Tim, can you at least hold off until tomorrow? Maybe sleep on it? Why don't we get together for coffee in the morning and chat?"

"Too late. I gotta go. We're meeting in fifteen minutes at Q.E. I just wanted to let you know I'm sorry you got dragged further into my shit today. I'll see you on Monday." He hung up, denying me any further opportunity to dissuade him. I hit the button to dial the last number received, but it went straight to voice mail.

"Is everything okay?" Ingrid asked.

"No. I don't know, really." I gave her an overview of our conversation. "I'm really worried he's going to get hurt. Or worse," I told her. "I've got to get over there and make sure he's okay."

"I'll come with you," she told me.

"No, it's all right. I can't ask you to do that."

"You're not asking. I'm telling. You've had three glasses of wine; I've had half of one. You shouldn't be driving. Where is this meeting taking place?"

I thought about it for a moment. "He said Q.E. I have to think that would be Queen Elizabeth Park off Cambie Street. He didn't say where in the park."

"How long will it take us to get there?"

"At least fifteen minutes."

"Then we'd better get going."

"You drive?"

"I have a licence, but I don't have a car. Do you?" All week long, I'd been getting chauffeured around town in Andrea's unmarked police cruiser, and I'd almost forgotten that my hideously beige rental vehicle was downstairs in Sandi's visitor's parking lot. A new set of keys had been couriered.

"Yes. We'll take my car." Even in my panic I couldn't bring myself to say "mini-van."

Even though it was after nine on a Friday night, in downtown Vancouver there's always traffic. Still, Ingrid drove with what I assumed was typical European ferocity. We made good time across the Cambie Street Bridge, where her geographic knowledge of the city ceased. Fortunately, it was a straight line to the park; unfortunately, the Cambie Corridor was strewn with traffic, stoplights, and early summer construction closures. As we sat at a red light adjacent to the art deco city hall at 12th Avenue, I found myself longing for Andrea's cruiser with lights and siren. As if sensing my thoughts, Ingrid glanced at me and said, "Perhaps it would be prudent to call Detective Pearson and let her know what's happening."

It hadn't yet occurred to me to do so. I dialed Andy's cell phone, one number at least that I had committed to memory. She didn't answer, which was probably a good thing, as she no doubt would have ordered me to abort my plan, which would have been as futile as my attempt to do so with Tim had been. I left a message detailing what was happening and promising to report in with updates, if any materialized.

A few minutes later I told Ingrid to turn left into the park at the 29th Avenue entrance behind Nat Bailey Stadium, home of Vancouver's surprisingly viable Single A baseball team. Tim hadn't specified what part of the park he was meeting in, so we slowed down to look for cars or teenagers or both. As I peered out towards the darkened, forested areas, I surmised the park might well be full of teens looking for cover and privacy. We wound our way slowly up the parkway, not seeing much of anything. For a warm spring evening, Vancouver's second largest park was all but deserted. I rolled down the window and stuck my head out the window like a Labrador retriever, hoping to see or hear something. I nearly choked on a mosquito.

We followed the meandering road past Seasons in the Park restaurant to the parking lot at the top of the park, known to Vancouverites as "Little Mountain," where, during the day, unobstructed views of the downtown core and the North Shore Mountains could be had. Tourists by the busload could also be found in the massive Bloedel Conservatory that allegedly contained over one hundred different species of birds. I could not confirm the claim. I'd lived in the city my entire life, and I had yet to set foot inside. A gate leading to the Conservatory parking lot was open, either by design or neglect, so we proceeded to the very top and found no other vehicles. Ingrid pulled to a stop in front of the covered benches adjacent to the now-dormant fountains.

"What now?" she asked.

I had no good answer. "I guess I'll just get out and have a look around." Tim could have been meeting anywhere in the park. If I were going to clandestinely meet someone after dark, this would be where I would go. I had no expectation that Tim and his rendezvous would conveniently appear where we were located. Still, I was out of ideas for practical things to do in the mini-van, and it was possible that they were somewhere just out of sight. I was disappointed to not see any cars in the lot. The natural lighting from the clear, cloudless evening provided some but not enough illumination. The fountain pools, now still for the night, reflected the moon in shimmers. We walked to each of the covered benches by the fountains and mezzanine area around the conservatory, examining them for clues. I didn't know what a clue to a secret meeting would look like, but we did find several chocolate bar wrappers, cigarette butts, and a condom package. To the south of the fountains we wandered to a concrete platform that overlooked the hillside for wedding party portraits. We walked around the platform and saw nothing. If I'd had a flashlight, I would have shone it over the edge into the bushes. I didn't have a flashlight. We stood quietly at the edge of the platform while I tried to decide what to do next. In the near distance, a car's engine roared at high speed, increasing in volume as it came closer.

"Do you hear that?" Ingrid asked.

"I suspect I know what that is." The words had barely left my mouth before the car sped into the parking lot, blue and red lights flashing in the grill. Ever an entrance maker, Andy bounced the heavy sedan loudly onto the pedestrian area and heaved to a stop, simultaneously opening the driver's door and hitting the pavement even as the car came to a complete halt. How she slid the car into park while still barely contained inside its cabin would impress any Hollywood stunt driver. Her gun was in her hand.

She bellowed as she hit the ground. "Vancouver Police! Show yourself. Slowly."

"I think Detective Pearson got your message," Ingrid said quietly.

"Yes."

"I don't want her to shoot us. Should we come out with our hands up?"

"I think she'd like that way too much," I told her, then called out to Andrea. "Easy, Starsky. You can put your gun away. It's just us."

"Who's us?" she demanded. "Is Tim with you?"

"Nope," I replied, stepping out of the shadows, pulling Ingrid by the hand. "It's me and Ingrid. We struck out with Tim. Looks like we missed him. Or if he's still here, we haven't found him."

"Why are you here?" Andy demanded as we reached the front of her car. "I left you secured at home."

"Secured?"

"You know what I mean."

"I tried to call you but you didn't answer."

"So you should have waited until I was available."

"And then we would have missed him."

"You *did* miss him."

"Good evening, Detective Pearson," Ingrid interjected into our childish spat.

We paused to consider her. "Hello. Sorry, Ingrid. Sometimes we get a lot like …"

"An old married couple?" Ingrid suggested.

"Something like that." Andrea let out a sigh. "So, no luck then?"

"No, and seriously, put your gun away." I've never really been comfortable around guns. "Suggestions for what we do now?"

"Let's look around some."

"What should we be looking for?"

"On the job, we call them clues. For you lay people, look for things that tell us that Tim might have been here."

"Wow. I always wondered what a clue was. Good thing you're here to explain it to us lay people."

Andrea popped the trunk of her cruiser and pulled out a spare flashlight, which she handed to Ingrid. "Here. This might help. Why don't you two head off towards the other end of the parking lot, and I'll check around here."

"We already checked around here."

"But you're lay people. I'm a clue finder." Ingrid dutifully headed across the parking lot. Before I could follow after her, Andrea grabbed my arm and demanded, "You brought the nanny?"

"She has a name."

"She's in her twenties."

"It's not like that. She had to drive."

"Why?"

"I'd had wine. I shouldn't have been driving."

"You were having wine with the nanny?"

"It's not like that."

"Wait'll Sandi hears you're spending Friday evenings liquoring up the help."

"You're making it sound sordid."

"It sounds sordid without any help from me. The She-Beast will flip."

"Sandi doesn't need to know anything about it. There's nothing to know." I was getting flustered. "And she doesn't need to hear anything about tonight anyway, especially if you don't tell her."

She snorted a half-laugh. "Yeah. That's gonna happen. Go babysit the babysitter." I trotted after Ingrid, suddenly embarrassed. Had I been hitting on her? I didn't think so, but why else was I sitting having wine with a twenty-four-year-old on a Friday night? Ingrid and I made a rather half-hearted sweep of the far end of the parking lot, shining the flashlight down the embankment into the bushes below, looking for something I could claim as a clue to redeem myself for the evening. Nothing appeared.

I was ready to give up anyway when Andy shouted from across the parking lot. "Win! Come here." We jogged back to Andy's police car, where she was leaning on the roof in the driver's doorway.

"What?" I demanded. "What'd you find?"

"Nothing. Not here, anyway." She was holding the microphone to the car's police radio in one hand. "What kind of car does Tim drive?" I thought about it for a moment. I was pretty sure I'd seen him driving a red Honda and told her so. She cursed quietly and shook her head.

"What is it?"

"Get in," she ordered us, opening up the back door. "I heard a call on the radio and checked it out. There's an MVA over on 49th. Red Honda. Teenaged boy. It doesn't sound good." We did as we were bid, leaving my hideous rental in the parking lot and barely having time to belt up as Andy bounced the car off the sidewalk and began racing down the park drive back to the busy streets of the city. Lights flashing and siren blaring, she travelled about twelve blocks in what seemed a blur of passing street and house lights. She glanced at me once in the rearview mirror, and the gravity of the look told me what we were going to find at the accident scene was not going to be pleasant. In Vancouver, drivers still pull out of the way for police cars, so we were able to make the drive in incredibly short order. We arrived at a scene awash in red light from the fire department's first responder vehicles. Three marked police cruisers had already blocked off the roadway, and beyond one of the fire trucks I could see what could only charitably be described as a vehicle, its front end badly mangled and roof caved in beneath the weight of the street light pole that had sheared off and fallen onto the roof of what was once a red Honda Civic. Andrea slammed to a stop and turned to look at me. "You might want to wait here," she said.

"No," I said. "I'll come."

She seemed in no great rush to get out of the car. Looking out the front windshield, I could see that the emergency personnel appeared not to be moving with the sense of urgency one might expect. Finally, she got out of the car and opened the rear door from the outside, allowing Ingrid and I to step out into the organized chaos of the emergency scene. "Wait here a second," she said softly, and I leaned on the hood of the car as she approached the scene, flashing her badge to the fire and rescue personnel. She spoke with a fireman, who looked at her seriously, then glanced quickly in my direction before turning his attention back to Andy. She glanced over her shoulder at me then followed the fireman over to what was left of the front half of the car and peered in. She only looked a moment before straightening up, and with her back to me said something to the fireman, who nodded slowly.

A moment later she touched him on the arm then turned and walked back towards us. Beside me I felt Ingrid tense as she recognized what was surely coming. Finally my cop friend stood directly in front of me. "Witnesses say it looked like a street race. Another car was involved." I nodded my head silently, waiting for the sentence I knew was coming. "I'm sorry, Winston," she said gravely. "It's Tim. He's dead."

Chapter Sixteen

On Saturday morning Detectives Michael Furlo and Jasmine Smythe appeared unannounced at Sandi's doorstep. Despite the three glasses of wine I'd consumed before Ingrid and I had gone hunting for Tim, and at least two more upon our return, sleep had eluded me. Andrea had dispatched officers to pick up my rental vehicle and return it to Sandi's visitor parking space. After some perfunctory conversations with emergency personnel and traffic investigators, Andrea herself had driven Ingrid and I home, where, despite both Ingrid and Andrea's best efforts to dissuade me from doing so, I spent the night blaming myself for Tim's accident. Once Sandi returned from whatever society event had kept her out well past midnight, we shared the entire story of the evening.

By around five I had given up trying to sleep and had quietly donned my running gear and made for the door. Andy had risen from her spot on the couch and informed me that if I made an attempt to leave without her, she would shoot me in the back. Thus I had waited while she too donned her gear, and we wordlessly ran through the quiet streets of the West End. On some rare mornings, after a particularly good run, sleep will follow, and I'll gain a couple of hours of rest. This morning, despite my body's need, my mind would not co-operate, and Andy and I were drinking coffee, watching the North Shore come to life across Coal Harbour and Burrard Inlet at seven thirty, when the knock came. After carefully checking the peephole, Andrea opened the door to let her colleagues in.

"Pearson," Furlo grunted in greeting as he made his way uninvited past Andrea and into the apartment. "Figured we'd find you here. I heard you're his babysitter." Michael Furlo was a few years older than me and a lot less pleasant. A veteran of the police force who'd made detective at an earlier age even than Andrea, he was known as a tough guy, a reputation he perpetuated whenever possible through outlandish threats and bravado that sounded like rejected lines out of vintage cop shows. He also always had a case clearance rate at or near the top of the department ranks. His partner, Jasmine Smythe, was mid- to late forties, African Canadian, and about as good a cop as Vancouver had ever had, which, as a defence counsel, had made her a name I would not like to see as the arresting officer on any case that came my way. I knew any bust of hers would be legally solid, with all the evidence and supporting documentation flawless. Though we'd had little contact during my legal career, our paths had crossed during serious events earlier in this first year of my teaching career.

"Good morning, Andrea. How's he doing this morning?" she asked, tossing a motherly glance in my direction.

"He hasn't slept," Andy replied.

"Is that any different than usual?"

"Not much. But he usually gets at least a couple of hours."

"Has he taken anything?"

"No. He's still interminably afraid of sleeping pills."

"He's in the room," I interjected.

"Of course, Winston," Smythe gently demurred. "I'm sorry. How are you doing this morning?"

Having become part of the conversation, I suddenly had no desire to talk. I mumbled something and turned my back. Smythe could have responded in kind to my gruffness, but she had too much class. Her partner did not suffer from any such inhibitions.

"Good to see you, too. I see you're as pleasant as ever," Furlo chided. "We're not here because we really care about your sorry ass."

He had a way of ending my silences with his immature barbs. "I see your career is spiralling upwards. You're investigating traffic accidents now?"

"Oh no, has something happened to your ride? I hear you've got a pretty happening vehicle now. What is it, a Caravan?"

"At least it's not paid for by the taxpayers. I make my own way."

"Slowly, with the rest of the soccer moms."

"Would you two stop it?" Andrea interjected. "My god, it's pathetic. But Winston has a point. Why are you here investigating a road racing accident?"

Detective Smythe turned her gentle glance towards me again. "Because it seems we weren't dealing with a road race. It would appear Tim was being chased when he crashed into the pole."

"Chased by who?" I demanded.

"That we don't know, at least not yet. We were hoping you might be able to shed some light."

I shook my head in disbelief. “I didn’t think Tim seemed the type to get into a road race. It just didn’t make sense to me. He’s not that kind of a risk taker.”

“That’s not the impression I got, given his extra-curricular activities online,” Furlo said.

I was ready to retort when Smythe continued. “There’s more, Winston. It looks like Tim’s accident was caused by more than just driving fast.”

“What do you mean?” Andy asked, already having produced her police notebook from somewhere unseen.

“Tim was stabbed, several times, it would appear. Obviously that took place before he drove into the pole, as witnesses were on the scene immediately after the accident. No one could have done that to him after the impact.”

“He was stabbed?” I asked. “I don’t understand. It couldn’t have been more than two hours from the time I talked to him until the time we saw him in at the accident. When the hell could he have been stabbed?”

“It doesn’t take long, Winston. It seems he got into an altercation and was attacked.”

“Damn it. If I could only have gotten there faster.”

“We’d be talking to your next of kin right now,” Furlo said.

“But I might have been able to do something.” I dropped down onto Sandi’s expensive sofa. “This is unbelievable.”

“Yeah, you do seem to have a negative impact on that school’s population.” I thought I heard the sound of a smack against Furlo’s arm or torso, but I didn’t bother to look up. I was in too much shock. Instinctively I had known that Tim might be at risk, but as each day had passed, the risk had seemed to diminish. Now, of course, our victory was moot.

We stood quietly a moment to allow time for me to digest the new information. “We don’t know for certain,” Smythe continued gently, “but we suspect Tim’s injuries are what caused him to lose control of the car. He may have actually died at the wheel before impact. We should have a better idea after the autopsy.” I nodded slowly. Ingrid entered the room quietly, took in the assembled police presence and wordlessly moved to the kitchen to begin brewing more coffee.

“Patrick?” Furlo finally cranked out. “We really need to get some information from you. This is clearly a homicide investigation now. We caught it.” He sounded disappointed to have his talent wasted on so trivial a matter as the murder of a teenager.

“Shouldn’t this be Andrea’s case?” I protested for the sake of it.

“We were next up, and let’s face it: she has a bit of a close connection to some of the participants.”

“Participants? What the hell is that supposed to mean?”

“It’s like I said earlier: you have an annoying habit of being connected to kids who end up dead. Pearson here has an annoying habit of being connected to you. She’s kind of poisoned as an investigator.”

“You’re such an ass,” Andrea sighed.

“I think what my partner means —” Smythe tried to interject.

“— I know what he means. And he’s right. But it doesn’t negate the fact that he’s an ass.”

"No. You're right. It doesn't." Smythe smiled. Her partner rolled his eyes as his colleagues agreed. He was no doubt disgusted at having to share his profession with the "weaker sex," or at least that's how I was interpreting his expression.

"I'll make sure you have all my notes and information. But I'm still going to work the assault."

"Of course," Smythe agreed.

For the next half hour I rehashed what I knew, several times, since I knew very little. Partway through the rehashing, we stopped as Sandi miraculously appeared before eight on a Saturday morning, and we provided her an explanation for why there was a party in her apartment to which she had not been invited. By the time she was up to speed, the look of disapproval she gave me exceeded even Furlo's. I'm sure with the limited information I had to offer, I was able to go through "the story" four or five times before the two detectives seemed convinced I had nothing useful to add to their investigation. When we were left alone as much as our living quarters would permit, meaning with Sandi and Ingrid still beside us, I finally asked "So where does that leave us?" I knew what the answer would be, but I asked anyway. Andrea did not disappoint.

"We don't do anything. It's out of our hands. It's not my case any more."

"Yeah, yeah. They're gone. So what do we do now?"

She stood up from the couch with a suddenness and spark reserved for her most gung-ho investigatory moments. "Well, first I'm gonna shower. Then you're coming with me. We've got people to talk to."

"Back in the saddle again."

"More like back on the short leash again. Now someone's been killed, they've kicked it up a notch. I'm not letting you out of my sight till we've got him."

Until that moment it had yet to occur to me that I might be in imminent danger, but given what had already been done to my apartment and the killing of Tim, there was no reason to believe I wouldn't be a target for someone's rage, especially now that the violence had escalated to murder. But I still found a need to protest the babysitting detail. "I've got school on Monday. Are you going to guard me there too?"

"Until we have him behind bars, I'm on you like glue."

"You really think you can just spend the days sitting in class, eyeing every student as a possible suspect?"

"Just watch me. Maybe I can help your law class get a realistic perspective on the world for a change."

"As long as you remember to raise your hand before you speak, we'll have no problems."

"It's hard to imagine who this'll be worse for," Sandi interjected. "Winston having to be babysat, Andrea having to sit through high school again, or the kids having to listen to you two argue through every lesson."

"Me," Andy and I responded at once, then I added, "She's right. This is going to suck."

"Then it'd be a whole lot better for everyone if I wrap this up before Monday," my super-cop friend declared, then headed down the hallway towards the shower.

"Isn't she risking getting in trouble with those two detectives if she continues her investigation? They seemed pretty adamant that they wanted her to stay away from the case," Ingrid said.

"It'd be better for them too," I said, though I knew Andy would need to keep her nosing around on the down-low or risk Furlo and Smythe's wrath. "First thing I want to do today, though, is check in with Sara and Nathan. They're Tim's best friends."

"You are a good teacher," Ingrid said gently, placing her hand lightly on my arm as she too moved towards the hallway and her own room. "You care so much about your students. They are lucky to have you."

Actually, I had been hoping to grill them for more information, but at that moment I felt guilty that I hadn't thought more of their hurt as much as their value as potential sources of leads.

Sandi cleared her throat behind me. "Earth to Winston," she called.

"What?"

"You're still pathetic," she told me, a not uncommon observation on her part.

"What?" I protested. "I was just thinking about —"

"— she's twenty-four," she cut me off. "And my employee. Don't forget that." And with that she too stormed down the hall, leaving me alone in the oversized living room.

Sara Kolinsky lived with her mother and two brothers smack in the centre of one of the curiously well-to-do mini-neighbourhoods that fed teenagers into John A. Macdonald Secondary. If you travelled three blocks in either direction from her front door, the houses became very working class, smaller, and usually housing at least one more extra generation of family than the principal homeowners. Sara's family obviously had no such worries, situated as they were on a double lot, making their property, despite the simplicity of its dwelling, worth into the seven-figure range should they decide to sell.

Andrea and I were greeted at the front door by Sara's mother, a very attractive woman in her mid forties who, if genetics played any kind of role, was a good omen for the woman Sara would become. Sara had, understandably, taken the news very hard, and after some initial sobbing, she had turned very quiet, spending the morning sitting in her room at her computer, researching god knew what, and no doubt communicating with myriad friends through MSN and other social networking sites. I made a mental note to look at her Facebook page to see if there was anything posted that might give some indication about who Tim had been planning to meet the night before. Come to think of it, and I mentioned it to Andy, it was probably high time we met the mysterious Van. After a couple of silent moments in the living room, Sara was coaxed out of her bedroom by her mother. Her eyes were red-rimmed, and she looked more tired than I had ever seen her. "Mr. Patrick," she said quietly. "Detective Pearson."

I stood up. "Hi, Sara. How are you doing?" It was all the prompting required for her to suddenly launch herself into my arms with a fresh round of sobs.

"I can't fucking believe this," she wailed, and none of the adults present made any attempt to stifle her profanity-laden outbursts. I lamely held her, patting her back gently, trying not to sound entirely superficial as I cooed, "It's okay, it's okay," though I knew it was not. After a few minutes, Sara's hysterics began to subside, her breathing returning to something close to normal, and she suddenly pulled away from me, embarrassed either at her emotional outburst, her hugging of her teacher, or both. "What are you doing here?" she finally managed to ask.

"Well, first, I wanted to see that you were okay," I replied.

"Guess you're not quite ready to strike that one off the list, huh?" She smiled feebly.

"Don't apologize for being upset. You just lost a friend."

"My best friend," she corrected firmly. "My best friend." She stared off into the distance for a moment, and I feared another breakdown was coming, but she just as quickly returned to the present. Andrea and I exchanged glances.

"I don't know who he was meeting," Sara said. "We were going to go out last night. He texted me and said he couldn't come over because he had to meet someone. He didn't say who. When he didn't reply to my text, I called and he wasn't answering his phone."

"What exactly did he say in his message?" Andrea asked.

"Hold on. I'll get it." Sara left the room a minute and came back with the slimmest, sleekest little pink cell phone I'd ever seen. As she re-entered the room, she was gazing down at the phone, her thumbs flying across the keys at lightning speed. When she found the message she said, "Here it is. He just says: *Can't make it. Meeting the shit who sprayed the wall at J-Mac. Loves you, T.*" She looked up at us then. "That's it. Nothing else."

"So you have no idea who he was meeting?"

"No. It just seems so, I don't know, strange. Meeting in the park in the dark. Some kind of secret meeting. Who the hell does that?" I had no answer so I didn't offer one. "So it sounds like he finally had a clear picture about who was tormenting him and figured he could put an end to it himself."

"So it seems," I confirmed.

"Why the hell didn't he just tell you?" she said to Andrea.

"I don't know. I wish that he had."

"What are you going to do now?" Sara asked, her voice regaining the commanding quality I'd heard when we were planning Tim's suit against the school.

"Well, new detectives have been assigned to the investigation," Andrea began.

"That's ridiculous," Sara spat. "You've been working this now for over three weeks. It makes no sense to remove you now."

"Well," Andy said, stammering slightly in a way that took me by surprise, making me wonder if Super Cop had met her match in a teenaged girl. "Obviously I have a personal connection to the investigation...."

"That's bullshit. You have intimate knowledge of the case. There's no reason for you to be removed."

"Well ..." Andy began again, and Sara again made what I considered a fatal error: she cut off Detective Pearson.

"No. I need you to work this, even if it's off the books." I actually stepped back a little, worried about the potential crossfire. No good could come of that. "Don't they say the first twenty-four hours are critical in an investigation? Why would we want to waste time trying to get new detectives to understand what's been happening?"

Andrea nodded slowly and offered no further commitment. "Is there anyone else you can think of to talk to? Anyone who might have an idea who Tim was meeting?"

Sara was quiet again for a moment. "Jordan Kansky," she declared. "He's been against this from the start." I had almost forgotten about Jordan, for whom I had laboriously created alternative assignments unrelated to the practical work my Law 12 classes had been doing in preparation for Tim's lawsuit.

"Your conscientious objector?" Andrea asked me. I nodded. "You think he might object this much?" I shrugged.

Sara had no such inhibitions. "He's a dumb jock. I wouldn't put it past him at all." A jock he may have been, but my experience with him had shown me he was anything but dumb. "I know I sound like the hysterical grief-stricken friend, but I think you know me by now, Mr. Patrick. I'm a pretty clear-thinking individual."

Andrea and I stepped outside into the cloudy May morning. I paused before heading off towards Andrea's cruiser. "Do we have to ride around in this thing, even on the weekend?"

"Would you rather we cruise in your mini-van?"

I sighed. "Is it really any less cool?"

"Lights and siren in mine. Total babe magnet."

"So what now?"

Andy opened the driver's door. "We go talk to your little Jordan."

"He's hardly little."

"Think I won't be able to take him?"

"Looking to be the teen take-down queen?"

"Another notch on my belt."

I sat in the passenger seat, barely squeezing my legs in amid the mounted portable police computer and assorted law enforcement paraphernalia that made up Andy's motorized filing cabinet. "Seriously, though. Checking on Sara we can justify as looking into her well-being. You don't think we should just send Furlo and Smythe? They're going to be pretty pissed if we interview him."

"We're not going to 'interview' him. We're going to talk with him."

"Yes. My experience with Furlo does tell me he'll be okay with that semantic differentiation."

She started the car. "You know what your problem is?"

"Am I limited to just one?"

"You worry too much. Who is the best detective on the force?"

I sighed. "You are."

"Then?"

"Then I guess we should go talk to Jordan."

"Damn straight," she said, pulling out much too quickly into traffic. "Until I'm expressly ordered otherwise, we move forward."

"Yes, ma'am."

Jordan Kansky lived in a much more working class neighbourhood than Sara's, more in keeping with the general character of John A. Macdonald Secondary's student body. The home sat on a standard — read, small — Vancouver-sized lot and was covered in stucco. Andrea found a parking spot directly in front of Jordan's house.

"So how do we play this?" I asked.

"What's the kid like, other than being anti-homo?" she asked in reply.

"Anti-homo?"

"You know what I mean."

"Big, beefy, kind of the class-clown, except he's really not funny."

"Bright?"

"He has his moments."

We started walking up the two little flights of cement stairs separating the two little terraces that were the Kanskys' twenty feet of front yard.

"You know," I said, "just because he didn't want to fight to have Tim's boyfriend come to the dance doesn't mean he's homophobic."

"My god, Win, whose side are you on?"

"There are sides? All I'm saying is …"

"… are you a politically correct left-winger like your union keeps saying you are or are you a free thinking individual making your own decisions on social issues?"

I stopped. "Wow. That's quite a diatribe."

"Yeah, well, when I get kicked off a case, I get a little pissed."

"So you take it out on me? And my profession?"

"You're conveniently located at the moment."

"So you're a little more worried about interfering in Furlo and Smythe's case than you previously let on."

"No. I'm a little more pissed about it than I previously let on." She raised a fist and pounded none too delicately on the front door.

"Do you have an aversion to those?" I asked, gesturing at the doorbell.

"It gets their attention better when I knock."

Jordan himself opened the front door, and his face registered complete surprise that his teacher stood waiting on the front stoop. Like doctors, so few teachers make house calls these days. "Mr. Patrick?" he stammered. "What the hell are you doing here?"

"Hi, Jordan," I replied. "I'm sorry to bother you on the weekend."

"No, we're not," Andrea interjected. "We're here to ask you some questions. Let's go inside." Clearly, she was taking the part of Bad Cop. Working solo as she generally did, I wondered who got to play the other part when she interrogated suspects without me present.

Jordan gave me a questioning glance. I shrugged. I'd rather have him angry at me on Monday than Andrea. Just the same, he stepped aside and gestured for us to follow. "Okay. Come on in, I guess."

"Thank you," I said, and Andy threw me a glance. Maybe she preferred not to have Good Cop around. Jordan led us into a small but tastefully decorated living room that opened from the entrance hallway. "Are your parents home?" I asked, to which Andrea shot me another glance. "What? I'm not allowed to ask that?"

"Why do you want his parents here?" she demanded.

"Shouldn't they be here if you're going to question him?"

"Question me?" Jordan exclaimed. "Question me about what?"

"I'm not going to *question* him," Andy told me, ignoring Jordan for the time being. "Wouldn't I have read him his rights if I was going to do that?"

"I don't know, would you, or were you planning just to browbeat him for awhile first?"

"Read me my rights?" Jordan exclaimed again in surprise. "Am I under arrest or something?"

"No, Jordan. You're not under arrest. Does a teacher have the power of arrest?" He stared at me without response the way he generally did when I asked a question of him in class. "Jordan?"

"No?" he replied with little conviction.

"Are you done, Professor?" Andrea asked.

I shrugged and gave him an apologetic look. "This is Detective Pearson. She's a friend of mine."

"Yeah, I remember seeing her around the school when Tim got beat up. Is that why you're here?"

"I'll ask the questions, Kansky. Sit down," Andrea ordered. Despite his size, he offered little in the way of resistance. Andrea flipped open her spiral notebook. "I understand you weren't too thrilled with Tim Morgan." Defence counsel in me didn't like her using a statement as a question, but I held my tongue.

"Yeah, that's true," Jordan answered tentatively.

"Why?"

"Why?" He looked to me for help. I had none to offer. "I don't know. I didn't think we should have to spend class time defending some gay guy's right to bring another gay guy to the dance."

"You were bothered by Tim's homosexuality?"

"Not really. I don't know. Do whatever you want, I guess. Just keep it out of my face."

"Tim's homosexuality was in your face?"

"I don't know," he said for the third time in as many responses. "Tim was pretty quiet about it. It was Mr. Patrick who kinda dragged the rest of us into it."

"So you're mad at Mr. Patrick?" she asked.

"No, not at all," Jordan insisted. "In fact, he was really cool about the whole thing." I couldn't help but smile just a little. Still cool. Jordan suddenly seemed to realize the direction in which the conversation was going and turned to me. "Wait a minute. You don't think I had something to do with what happened to your apartment? Mr. Patrick, how could you think I would do something like that? To you? I thought you knew me better than that."

"I … uh …" I began to reply.

"You were the one who refused to take part in Tim's defence," Andrea pushed forward. "You obviously were opposed to his situation."

"And Mr. Patrick allowed me to do an alternate assignment. Why the hell would I be mad at him?"

"So we're back to you being mad at Tim," Andrea insisted.

"I don't know if I was mad at him. I didn't want to defend him."

"But you don't like him."

"Not really, no."

"Why not? Because he's gay?" I could see Jordan's increasing defensiveness. My instinct was to intervene and protect, but I could also tell Andrea was trying to push him to open up.

"No. Yeah. All right. Because he's gay. I don't like gays, all right? Arrest me."

"Do you feel threatened by gay students?" she continued.

"Threatened? No, why the hell would I be scared of him?"

"Maybe he made you question your own sexuality. Maybe you saw some of yourself in him, and you didn't like it."

"That's fucking ridiculous. I'm not gay. I have a girlfriend."

"So do most gay men before they come out."

"You're fucking nuts. Mr. Patrick, do I have to listen to this? I didn't do anything."

Andrea threw me a quick warning glance. "You're talking to me, Jordan," she barked. "Did Tim come on to you? Is that it?"

"Jesus, lady, no, he didn't come on to me."

"Are you sure? Maybe he saw something in you that made you seem available."

Jordan started to get up off the couch. "What the hell is the matter with you? Are you deaf or just stupid? I'm not gay, all right? Me not liking Tim has nothing to do with me being gay. It has to do with *him* being gay, okay?"

"And that bothers you."

"It bothers me because he fucked my brother!" Jordan was nearly shouting. The three of us stopped, tension hanging oppressively in the air. If Andrea was surprised, she didn't show it, staring impassively at Jordan, who was now hovering above us.

"Why don't you sit back down," she said finally. He looked surprised at his own outburst, dazed by the moment of hostility and the family secret he had just unleashed. He stared at Andrea a moment longer then flopped down into the couch in that dejected way only a teenager can. He sat sullenly. "Talk to me about your brother," Andrea gently directed.

"What's to talk about?" he groused.

"To begin with, you can tell me about the relationship your brother was having with Tim."

"I'd hardly call it a relationship. Tim's not just gay, he's … I don't know what you call it with gays, but he's a slut."

"You're saying Tim was promiscuous."

"Sure, if you want to make it sound nicer, he's promiscuous. He didn't date my brother, he slept with him."

"What grade is your brother in?" I asked Jordan.

"He's not. You wouldn't know him. He graduated a couple of years ago. He's twenty."

"And how long was your brother involved with Tim?" Andrea asked.

"I don't know. Not long, I guess. If Mark was gay before Tim, he kept it well hidden. He saw Tim's website and …" his voice trailed off.

"So you know about Tim's business on the web?"

"Yeah. I hit the back button on the browser on Mark's laptop and came across it. I couldn't believe my brother was looking at gay porn on the web, but I was even more shocked by the fact that it was Tim."

"And was this a recent discovery, Jordan?"

"Pretty recent, yeah."

"How recent?" Andy persisted.

He sat up a little, the challenge returning to his posture and voice. "Hey, don't go pinning that graffiti shit on me. I didn't do that."

"Where were you yesterday morning?"

"I was here. In bed. I didn't even go to first period class, cuz I was too hung over from the night before." He turned and looked at me after his confession of truancy.

"It's all right, Jordan," I said. "I'm not worried about your attendance right now. Besides, you didn't skip *my* class." He forced a slight chuckle.

"So you were out drinking with friends on Thursday night, a school night?" Andrea returned to the matter at hand.

"It happens."

"Where did this little party of yours take place?"

"Here. In this room. My parents are away."

"And you never left here?"

"Nope."

"How much did you have to drink?"

"Enough that I didn't feel like getting out of bed at seven in the morning."

"Enough that you might have done something stupid like painting the side of a building?"

"I told you that wasn't me," he growled. "Why the fuck would I want to do something like that? It's bad enough my brother was fucking around with Tim. I sure as hell didn't want to advertise it. Besides, I found out about that like two weeks ago."

She scribbled something in her notebook. "You said your brother wasn't involved with Tim for long. They broke up?"

"I don't even think you could call it that."

"What do you mean?" He looked down, avoiding both our stares. "Jordan?"

"Christ, he's so stupid."

"Mark?"

"Yeah. I mean, this isn't *Pretty Woman*. Tim wasn't interested in Mark. He was just another source of money."

"Excuse me?" I interjected. "Your brother was paying Tim?"

He looked up slowly. "Yeah. He says it was part of discovering who he really is. Tim helped him do that, for a price."

I let out a heavy sigh.

Jordan snorted out another pained laugh. "Yeah. Still think Tim's such a great guy, Mr. Patrick?"

I didn't know how to respond, so I let it pass.

"Jordan," Andrea said gently. "Was your brother angry at Tim?"

"I suppose. I think he was more angry at himself."

"Do you think he would do something to Tim?"

"Like when Tim got beaten up a couple of weeks ago? I don't think so. He was way too into him. My brother's a bit of a pansy, obviously. I mean, I always knew that but …" His voice trailed off.

"You said it was a couple of weeks ago that you found out about your brother and Tim." Jordan didn't respond. "You were pretty mad about that?"

"Yeah," he finally said. Andrea said nothing for a few moments, and Jordan held her gaze. When he spoke, his voice was full of regret. "I guess I'm in shit, aren't I?"

Andrea nodded.

"I really didn't mean to hurt him," he said quietly. "At least not that badly. I was just so shocked about Mark. And then to find out he had been paying Tim, I don't know. It just pushed me over the edge or something."

The defence counsel in me wanted him to stop talking, but I didn't say anything. As if reading my mind, Andrea interjected.

"Jordan, I need to stop you right now and let you know you have the right to remain silent, that anything you tell me can be used against you …"

He interrupted her spiel. "No. It's okay. I want to tell you. This has been hounding me. I just want to get this over with. I'm just glad it wasn't any worse than it was."

When no one spoke further, I prodded him. "What do you mean, Jordan?"

He looked at me as though just remembering I was there, and his face registered such shame, as though he had personally let me down, that I found it difficult to return his gaze. "I found out about Tim and Mark the day Sara held her little news conference in front of the school. Then when I saw Tim on the news, I guess I just kind of snapped."

"I see."

"But Mr. Patrick, I swear to you. I had nothing to do with your house being burned down. I don't even know where you live. You have to believe me. I wouldn't do that to you." It was hard to accept that someone with so much violent rage against my student and client would draw some sort of ethical line at arson, but I let him continue. Jordan put his head back against the couch. "It haunts me, you know? When I left Tim tied up against the goal post, I thought I was making some kind of statement. But I can't get that picture of him out of my head. After I drove home, I started panicking. It was like, 'Fuck, what if I killed him?' I couldn't sleep, and I was too scared to go back and check on him in case someone saw me. What a dumb fuck I am."

We neither confirmed nor refuted his self-assessment.

He was quiet a moment then took a deep breath and lifted his head again off the couch back to face Andrea. "I'm ready to face the music. Can I ask you something?"

"Sure," Andrea replied.

"I know I have to pay for what I did. That's fine. I'm glad it's over. Is there any way you can take me to see Tim before I go to jail?"

Andrea and I exchanged glances and didn't reply.

"It's just … I know it sounds stupid after all I've said about him, but I want to tell him I'm sorry. I want to tell him face to face, not in court or something, like I'm being ordered to do it. I want him to know I'm glad he's okay and that somehow I'll make it up to him. I don't know how."

Again, neither of us said anything.

"Look, I know I can't undo what I did, and I don't have a lot of money or anything, but there's gotta be something I can do. I don't expect him to forgive me or anything, but I just really want him to know that I'm sorry I hurt him, okay? You understand, Mr. Patrick, don't you?"

I looked at Andrea for guidance, and she nodded slightly.

"Jordan," I said quietly. "Tim's dead." Jordan stared at me in disbelief, and the momentary silence was broken by the always annoying sound of the *Mission Impossible* theme music emanating from Andrea's pocket. Whipping out her cell, she answered it with her last name, then stepped out into the hallway.

"What the hell are you talking about?" Jordan whispered.

"Jordan, Tim was killed last night. He was murdered."

The words seemed to be taking awhile to register. "Holy fuck," he finally managed. He looked at me and asked, "Who killed him?"

I didn't say anything.

"Holy shit, Mr. Patrick. You think *I* killed him," he said, practically leaping from the couch.

I didn't know what to think, and I told him so.

"But that's why you're here, isn't it? You didn't come because of the beating. You came because you thought I might have killed him. I don't believe this."

"Jordan."

"Mr. Patrick, I swear to you, I didn't do anything to him. I've felt so awful after what I did to him that night, I couldn't."

"Jordan. Where were you last night?"

"Last night? I was playing hockey. We had a game at Oakridge."

"What time was the game?"

He stopped a minute to think. "Eight thirty. We had to be there at eight. I left there at about eleven thirty." It seemed ridiculously late to be playing hockey, but I also knew that in this hockey-crazed city, finding ice time for even the better leagues was challenging. It was certainly plausible and ultimately confirmable.

"And your coach will vouch for you?"

"Of course. I was there. I got a goal and an assist. Mr. Patrick, you have to believe me. I didn't even see Tim yesterday. I didn't do anything to him."

"Okay, Jordan," Andrea said softly from the doorway. "We'll call your coach and check out your story." I couldn't tell if she was being nice as part of a further interrogation technique or if she genuinely believed him, but already I found myself buying his alibi. Maybe teaching was making me soft.

"So you believe me? I didn't kill Tim."

"We'll call your coach," she reiterated. He looked shaky, and he involuntarily accepted my assistance as I led him to sit back down.

"Jordan, are you okay?" His breathing seemed laboured, and I thought he might be hyperventilating. I sat down beside him, draped my arm around his vast shoulders and gently pushed his upper body forward. "It's okay," I cooed. "Just breathe gently. Little breaths. It'll be okay." We sat that way a few moments until he got his breathing under control. I glanced up at Andrea, who rolled her eyes at me.

"I'm okay," he said softly when he had regained control. "It's just ... I can't believe he's dead. I mean, I know I didn't like him after what happened with him and Mark, but this is just unreal. Un-fucking-real."

"Yeah," I agreed.

"After all that's happened this year already," he said, and I flashed back to earlier in the year, when another student had been murdered. It was a hell of a lot for anyone to take in, especially kids. The district's grief counselling team was going to be very busy this week.

"Jordan, is your brother at home?" Andrea asked.

He looked up at her. "No. I don't think he came home last night. He probably hooked up with someone." His voice trailed off, and he kind of shuddered. I wondered if he would ever come to accept his brother's sexuality.

"Where does he normally go at night?"

"I don't know. The past couple of weeks he's been going out pretty much every night to the gay nightclubs."

I looked at Andrea and shrugged. My lack of love life still had not yet found me trying *any* nightclub.

"Celebrities?" Andrea inquired.

"That sounds familiar," Jordan acknowledged.

"Two detectives assigned to Tim's homicide are on their way here, Jordan." I knew then the serious look Andrea had acquired upon answering her phone was due to being caught red-handed in the middle of Furlo and Smythe's investigation.

Jordan looked to me, and for the first time some fear registered in his eyes as the ramifications of his confession began to unfurl before him. "What's going to happen now?"

"Detectives Furlo and Smythe will want to question you about Tim. Just be honest, tell them everything you know, and don't leave out anything. The truth is your best bet right now, Jordan."

"But I didn't kill Tim," he protested. "Are they going to listen to me?"

"They'll listen to you, they'll confirm your whereabouts last night, and then you won't have to worry about that."

"And that's it?"

"No. Then they'll arrest you for the assault on Tim. It's time to realize you are going to have to pay the price for that, Jordan. I'm sorry."

Andrea raised an eyebrow. I wasn't sorry, but it still seemed the appropriate thing to say. Then she surprised me with her next statement. "Jordan, at this point you need to get yourself a lawyer." Her offers of defence counsel were generally limited to the robotic reading of rights. But she was too good a cop not to recognize that if Jordan went without counsel or even a parent present much longer, the case might face problems down the line. "At the very least, you need to call a family member or friend and let them know what's happening."

He nodded slowly. With nothing left to do but wait for Andy's VPD compadres, I wandered around the small living room, looking at the family photos on display. One in particular caught my eye. "Is this your brother?" I asked. The question was redundant because the two boys in the photograph could almost have been twins, though Jordan was clearly the more muscular of the two.

"Yeah. That's Mark. That was taken at Christmas. Just a normal, happy family, huh?"

I nodded and wandered around the room some more until finally the doorbell rang, ending the awkward silence.

Andrea went to the door. "Okay, Jordan," I said. "This is it. Just hang in there, okay? It'll be all right. Eventually."

"Okay," he said. "Thanks." I didn't know what he had to thank me for, as I had pretty much just assured him he was going to jail. Furlo's big frame filled the doorway.

"Okay, Patrick. You can go now," he said with no small amount of annoyance. "Oh, and here," he said, handing me a folded piece of notepad paper. I opened it up, and on it was a shaky sketch of one stick man apparently holding another stick man by the throat. "Since you can't seem to understand 'stay home and out of my investigation,' I thought I'd draw you a picture of what happens if you get in my way again." He seemed pretty pleased at his little joke.

I was about to reply when Andrea ordered from the doorway, "Winston, let's go."

I smiled at Furlo. "You're welcome," I said as I walked by. "Let me know if I can clear up any other cases for you." Detective Smythe avoided my glance as I walked by, a sure sign that she too was pissed at me. We were outside on the front walk before I spoke to my friend. "How much shit are you in?"

"More than usual. Less than enough to bother me." We were almost at the car when *Mission Impossible* filled the quiet morning street.

"You've really got to get a new ringtone."

"I like this one. It suits me." She answered and tensed up immediately. Cop mode. Whipping out her notebook, she scribbled down some notes and flipped her phone shut. "Shit. I gotta go."

"What's up?"

"A body." I felt my knees go weak. Andrea placed her hands on my arm and lowered me into the car. "No, Winston. Not one of yours. It looks like a gang thing." Vancouver had recently suffered a spate of gangland type shootings, frequently in very public places and occasionally with civilian casualties caught in the crossfire. It was making headlines across the country.

"Why are they calling you?"

"I'm next up. I told you that. I'd only be able to work on Tim's case till they found another case for me. Looks like some gang-banger just took care of that. Come on, you're going home. I'm going to go waste my time looking for someone who just saved the justice system a shitload of money." She got into the car, hit the lights and sirens, and sped away from the curb.

Chapter Seventeen

Andrea did not intend to have me tag along to her latest crime scene. I had no desire to experience another one. Since Vancouver's latest homicide was in the downtown area, she was able to quickly drop me at Sandi's building then speed off. I sensed her slight perverse pleasure at approaching the upscale condominium and hotel complex with lights and siren, only to dump me at the feet of the stunned concierge and speed off again. I did my level best to appear nonchalant, but I drew stares nonetheless. Sandi would surely hear about my arrival and would no doubt have something to say. Bad enough that I was driving a mini-van while her guest; my arriving this time in such an undignified manner could potentially lower her standing with her crowd.

It being mid-morning on a Saturday, Sandi was out shopping, her late-term pregnancy no match for her ability to generate income for downtown retailers. I found myself both disappointed then surprised at my disappointment that she had taken Ingrid with her. Having made a half-hearted promise that I would not leave the apartment without Andrea, I felt at least some obligation to honour that pledge, though it was more from a dearth of places to go than any real conviction. I felt fatigued but recognized sleep wouldn't likely be on my side. That left me with marking. Facing the work of my students hardly seemed a way to spend a Saturday, especially now that the weather was promising to turn into a beautiful, warm May day. On the other hand, why should this weekend be any different from the others? Still, I managed to plow through a fair number of student papers, providing me with some needed distraction from the cloud that hung over me.

That cloud only descended further when halfway through the pile of Law 12 papers, I came across Tim's. Of course, marking it was futile, but some strange sense of obligation compelled me to read it. It was a carefully crafted examination of Canada's hate crime legislation, well researched, precisely supported with both legal documentation and media accounts of incidents when the legislation had failed its followers, and was written unmistakably in Tim's voice. On the last page of his paper was a large post-it note with a handwritten message that read: *Mr. Patrick. Without getting all mushy on you, I want you to know how much I appreciate all you've done for me this year. Not just on my grad dance issue but just in the class. I have an incredible respect for the law I didn't have before I got into your class. You've really made me think about a career in the legal profession. Thank you. Tim.*

From anyone else, I might have been suspicious that the note was intended as a way to prime me for a good mark on the paper. But from Tim, the thank-you sounded so genuine, and he had become one of the most engaged students in the class even before the subject matter had hit so close to home. In reading the work he had submitted, the potential for a promising legal career — or any career — was obvious.

Having the note appear so soon after Tim's death ended my valiant attempt at distraction, and I shoved the papers aside, determined not to cry. Instead I paced the apartment, alternately staring out the window and rearranging Sandi's kitchen cupboards in a manner that made practical sense. I knew it was unlikely she would notice, as cooking was not an activity she regularly engaged in, but I might feel better knowing there was a logical order to things. Obsessive Compulsive Disorder as grief therapy. By late afternoon, Sandi's kitchen could be run with military precision, her carpets were vacuumed, and I was ready to start on categorization of the linen closet when Sandi and Ingrid returned home, the latter laden with bags from baby stores of which I'd never heard, and which no doubt carried the finest infant apparel this side of Milan. We spent a frustrating hour over tea discussing our days and viewing Sandy's myriad purchases. Finally Sandi heaved her growing self up off the couch and announced she was going to get ready for her evening.

"You're going out?" I asked.

She smiled playfully. "Oh, Winnie, are you going to miss me?"

"No. It's just … I just thought maybe you should be resting. You can't really be keeping up the same social schedule. You need to take it easy."

"Listen to you, all concerned and daddy-like. That's so sweet. I think this whole daddy concept is growing on you."

"Sure," I grumbled. "That must be it." Truth be told, I didn't relish an entire evening talking about babies, high society, and more babies, but I was feeling sorry for myself, and the thought that anyone might be out having a good time like normal people was making me sound churlish.

"Why don't you come with me?" she said, brightening. "It's a Rotary event. My dad's winning an award for some charitable thing or another. Everyone will be there. I'm sure they'd love to see you again."

"No, thank you," I said. "Go be with your family. I'll be fine." Sandi waddled down the hallway towards her room, leaving Ingrid and me awkwardly alone.

Ingrid finally rose. "Well, I'll leave you to your evening."

"Wait. Don't go."

She stopped and looked at me. "Did you need something, Mr. Patrick? I could make you some dinner if you'd like."

"No, Ingrid, you don't need to cook for me. And you don't need to call me 'Mr. Patrick.' You don't work for me. It's Winston."

"Okay," she said awkwardly.

"Do you have plans for the evening?" As soon as the words came out of my mouth, I realized how pathetic I sounded, and how much it appeared I was asking her out. I quickly tried to correct myself. "I just mean that I'm just going to watch a movie or something. You don't have to lock yourself in your room."

She smiled. "Fair enough. Why don't we go grab a bite to eat and pick up a movie to watch?" Then, as though suddenly remembering the events of the night before, she added, "That is, if you feel up to it?"

"I do," I said, heading for the closet where I had hung my jacket, unlike Sandi, who had messily tossed hers over a dining room chair.

"Wait a minute," Ingrid suddenly said. "What about Detective Pearson? Will she want you leaving the apartment without her protection?"

A combination of pride and a slight teenaged-boy like feeling of adventure combined to renew my resolve to head out with. "It's a free country. What do you feel like eating?"

She thought for a moment. "I love Italian."

I smiled thankfully. "I know just the place."

I knew that it shouldn't. But with all that had happened, walking down Fourth Avenue in Kitsilano — my old neighbourhood — toward my favourite restaurant with a beautiful young woman, if not on my arm at least right next to it, was lifting my spirits in a way they had not been elevated in quite some time. While nowhere near as crowded as Robson Street downtown, the sidewalks were pleasantly bustling with early evening foot traffic, and many of the pedestrian-friendly stores stayed open late on a Saturday to draw the evening strollers to their wares. I sensed Ingrid turning a few heads as we walked by. I was allowing the pleasantry of attractive, intelligent company to temporarily buoy my spirits.

Had I a drink in my mouth, I'm confident I would have performed the classic *Three's Company* spit take. So wrapped was I in my little aura of satisfaction, I didn't even notice the restaurant was empty until I pulled on the front door and it didn't open. Like most men, it takes my brain a few attempts at pulling on a locked door to accept the obvious fact that it isn't going to comply. It was only after the third or fourth futile tug that I noticed the piece of eight and a half by eleven paper taped to the inside of the glass bearing the message, "Chianti is permanently closed." On the window next to the door was a bailiff's notice ordering seizure of the assets for non-payment of rent. Even after reading the notice, I found myself once more involuntarily pulling on the door handle.

"I don't think they're open, Winston," Ingrid said gently.

"This is unbelievable," I said, stunned. "How can they have closed down? I was just here earlier in the week." She shrugged, bewildered by the strength of my reaction.

"Is there somewhere else nearby we can go?" she suggested. As she spoke, two other couples arrived, one from each direction on the sidewalk, and their faces showed the same shock as mine. Each stepped up to the doorway, squeezing beside me to read the notice so coldly declaring the end of an era in Vancouver. I stepped back onto the sidewalk with Ingrid and stared through the large storefront windows at the empty tables. "Are you okay?" she asked, gently placing her hand on my arm.

"It's just so bizarre. This place has been like a second home to me for years. I'm sure it's been open for at least a dozen years. I used to see lineups out the door." As I thought about it, I recalled the lineups hadn't been as large an issue in recent months. I was always able to get a table, even when the eatery was packed, so I guess I had just always assumed it was still hopping.

But the more I thought about it, the more I realized my ability of late to get a table no longer had to do with special treatment. If a restaurant like this couldn't make it in Vancouver's increasingly expensive business climate, there was little hope for anyone save for the growing number of chains. *Just what this community needs to preserve its character,* I thought, *a Swiss Chalet or Denny's on every corner.* "I knew the staff. They never mentioned anything to me."

"Maybe you can call someone and they'll tell you what happened." It occurred to me that as much as I considered Teri, server extraordinaire, a confidante, I didn't even know her last name. Making contact with her wouldn't be easy. I shook my head in dismay and watched the other two couples wander away. I could feel a cloud of self-pity envelop me as I realized I had lost two homes in the space of a week. "Come on," Ingrid insisted lightly. "Let's go find somewhere else to have dinner."

We did, there being no shortage of establishments within easy walking distance. It was probably perfectly good food, though I barely recalled what I had ordered or its taste in my shock at Chianti's demise. Ingrid was perfectly pleasant in her valiant attempts to cheer me up, though before long we ended up in a discussion of where we stood on the investigation of Tim's death. I explained our conversation with Jordan. I wondered why Tim had bothered to keep his part time job at the movie theatre, where he'd been the night Jordan had attacked him. I supposed working at a standard teenaged vocation might have alleviated at least some suspicion about how he was getting his money.

"So you believe your student when he says that he was not involved in Tim's death?" Ingrid asked.

"His alibi is easy enough to establish, but yeah. Even just from talking to him, I don't believe he killed Tim."

"I see. Is there someone else you're thinking about?"

"I don't know," I admitted. "Though I would sure like to talk to Jordan's brother about his relationship with Tim."

"How are you going to do that?" she asked. "Won't those two detectives be angry if you go back to his home to question the brother?"

"Angry would hardly begin to describe it. Furlo would probably try to charge me with obstruction of justice or something."

"We wouldn't want that."

"Actually, it would be kind of fun, because it would never stick, and I'd end up embarrassing him in court. But yeah, it would likely mean a couple of nights in jail, which I don't relish. So I guess a visit to Jordan's brother is out."

"Unless," she began, then trailed off. "No, never mind."

"Unless what?"

She looked across the table at me, the candlelight reflecting off her blue eyes. "Well, you said Jordan's brother has been going out to the clubs every night. What if we went and found him there? It's not like we're investigating anything. We're just out for a night on the town. If we happen to bump into this Mark, it could be just a friendly coincidence."

I liked the playfulness in her voice. I liked that she was willing to go around Furlo's admonition to keep away from *his* case. I liked her genuine interest in solving Tim's murder. More than anything, I liked that she wanted to spend Saturday night out with me, even if it meant going to the city's gay nightclubs in search of a killer.

Our bill paid, we returned "home" to change. To my surprise, Sandi had not yet left, and her glare showed she was, again, entirely unhappy with me.

"You're still here," I said mock-cheerfully. "I thought you were going out for a fancy dinner."

"I am. It's only seven o'clock. Where have you been?"

"We went out to grab some dinner."

"My god, what are you, seventy?" Dinner before eight was, well, just weird in Sandi's eyes. Back when we were a couple, dinner, especially on the weekend, had so often been a social event that we rarely actually consumed the meal before nine. Ingrid quietly excused herself to go change, allowing Sandi and I time to be alone. "Why is she going to get changed?"

"We're going out," I said with just a little too much élan in my voice.

"Why are you going out with my nanny, Winston?" I thought I could see the frost-encrusted words hanging in the air.

"Do I require your permission? You don't own her, Sandi, you employ her."

"Is there a father-daughter event you're taking her to?" Ouch. "I don't want you to go breaking her heart. I like her, and she's going to be a great nanny."

"Oh for god's sake, Sandi, there's nothing going on. We were both home alone. We had dinner, that's it."

"And now you're going ...?"

"To a nightclub."

"A nightclub?" She actually laughed aloud. "Winnie, you?"

"What?"

"You're thirty-five. She's twenty-four. You're going to break a hip or something. Please, think about this. You're going to look ridiculous." She could barely control her laughter. She was right again, of course. The image of me on the nightclub floor, drink in hand, "getting down" to what passed for club music these days, even made me smile.

"It's not what you think, Sandi. We're going to look for someone." I explained my plans to find Jordan's brother among the throngs of what I imagined to be stereotypes of men dressed like the Village People in the city's gay nightclubs.

I had just finished describing our plot when over Sandi's shoulder I saw Ingrid reenter the room. She was dressed in a short black skirt and tight striped T-shirt, a wide black belt adorning her slightly exposed midriff. Her heels made her almost match my six feet. Just like the first time we met, I was rendered momentarily speechless, and I suspect my jaw dropped a little as Sandi looked at me and said, "What?" Turning around, she saw Ingrid, and her elbow shot backwards, catching me in the stomach. I barely noticed.

"Ingrid," Sandi said. "You look gorgeous." That was an understatement.

She smiled bashfully. "My little sister sent me this outfit from Prague. She's always out at the clubs, every night of the week. It drives my mother crazy. Adriana heard there were lots of nightclubs in Vancouver, so she thought I would need it. I think I look ridiculous, but I thought it might suit our mission for tonight." Her eyes lit up at the word "mission."

"Just remember not to gawk at her all night, or your cover will be blown," Sandi admonished me. I would have responded, but I had yet to recover my breath, let alone my capacity to deliver articulate speech.

"My sister tells me when she feels just like dancing and having a good time, she goes with her girlfriends to one of the clubs where mostly gay men dance. She doesn't have to worry about men hitting on her."

"Good point," Sandi concurred.

I regained my vocal capacity. "Well, I guess we should go then."

"Wait, wait, wait," Sandi ordered. "You're not serious?"

"What?" I said, my eyes finally breaking from Ingrid.

"Well, for starters, it's like seven fifteen. You're not going to find anyone at the clubs until at least ten. And look at you."

"What?" I said again, giving myself a cursory once over.

"Why don't you just wear a sign that says "heterosexual"? Chinos and a polo shirt? You're going to a nightclub, not a Conservative Party convention. We need to gay you up," she declared, her voice taking on that drive I usually heard when she was determined a room needed to be redecorated. "Come on. Let's see what we can do."

She led the three of us into my guest room, Ingrid barely stifling a giggle. Sandi opened the closet and regarded the dearth of garments, given the recent destruction of my wardrobe. She shook her head in disappointment, a gesture with which I was entirely familiar. She pulled down the black pants that, along with the chinos I was wearing, made up two thirds of my current pant collection. "These will have to do. Put these on," she declared, then turned to the shirt selection where she found one grey, one white, one light blue, one dark blue, all button down. Four ties hung forlornly on a wooden hanger beside them. I stood awaiting my next sartorial direction, not willing to drop to my boxers in front of Ingrid. "Oh, wait a minute," Sandi blurted, hustling from the room to follow the sudden burst of inspiration. Ingrid and I stood awkwardly. I smiled and shrugged.

"She's enthusiastic, isn't she?" Ingrid asked.

That wouldn't have been the word I would have used, but I suppose it fit. I smiled and nodded, still feeling awkward around Ingrid decked out in her sister's vision of nightclub clothing.

"I'll leave so you can get changed now." She glided softly out of the room, and I tried unsuccessfully not to stare after her. I had barely pulled the black pants over my hips when Sandi reentered without knocking, an indiscretion I chose to ignore. "That's a little better, I suppose," she determined. "Let's lose the shirt." She held in her hand a purple long-sleeved dress shirt made of silky material that made it feel a bit like a balloon.

"Purple?" I asked.

"It works," she told me.

"Aren't you reinforcing a stereotype?"

"Are you really worried about that going into a gay bar looking for a gay kid you've never met?"

"Good point." I pulled off my shirt, less concerned about exposing to Sandi the midsection Andrea describes as "scrawny" than if Ingrid was still in the room. The shirt Sandi gave me was, I had to admit, comfortable and felt — because I had learned to sense such things during our time together — expensively made. Its owner was clearly of a larger build than I, and the shirt draped my body like a drop-cloth drapes a sofa.

"Not quite gay," she muttered, giving me a quick once-over.

"Thank you?"

"You could pass for bisexual, I guess."

"Thank you?" I repeated. "You haven't mentioned yet why you have this man's shirt in your closest."

"That's right. I haven't."

"And to whom does this shiny apparel belong?" I pushed.

"Never mind. It's not important." I glanced at her protruding belly and cocked an eyebrow. "Never mind," she insisted and turned to leave the room.

I followed her out into the living room, where Ingrid was looking out the window at the spectacular view. When she turned, her hand went to her mouth to stifle another giggle. "You look ..."

"Gay?" Sandi offered.

"Well, less than masculine," she replied, then gave up trying not to laugh. Terrific. "I'm sorry. The shirt is a little large."

"It's all right," I said, smiling. I was sure I looked ridiculous.

Sandi reached up and undid a button. "Loosen it up.

Show off a little skin."

"You understand I'm not really trying to attract anyone?"

"You don't want to stand out, Winston. If you don't fit in just a little, no one is going to talk to you. Or dance with you," she added with a laugh.

"Don't you have a dinner to get to?"

"All right. I'm sorry." She walked over to the dining room table, where she'd left her purse. "You two kids have fun, okay?"

"Good night, Sandi." She laughed one more time then went out the door.

Ingrid and I stood awkwardly in the living room once again. It was seven thirty. "I guess we could see what's on TV," I suggested.

"Sure," she said, sitting down on the couch and carefully pulling her skirt down to respectable levels. I sat down awkwardly on the opposite side of the couch and flicked on Sandi's large screen television. I found a *Seinfeld* re-run and paused, turning to smile at Ingrid, who nodded and smiled back. "Wine?" I asked.

"Yes, please," she concurred.

"I think I'm going to need some," I said.

Celebrities is an institution in Vancouver's nightlife, known as the principal gay dance club, though many of the city's more progressive-minded clubbers are regular attendees, plus those women who like to party but don't want to worry about being hit on. As Ingrid and I approached the front entrance, it was difficult to tell what I found more discouraging: the line-up or the throbbing bass beat emanating from inside. My patience for either is limited at the best of times; searching for Jordan's brother in a dark club to question him about his involvement with Tim, which surely would put me in the bad books of at least three of VPD's detectives, made this far from the best of times. The club was located in the heart of the gay community. Davie Street not only houses Celebrities but also other businesses catering to the gay crowd. For as long as I could remember, Davie Street had equaled "boys town." However, despite its reputation, it looked exactly the same as the rest of the West End peninsula.

Arriving at about ten thirty, we stood awkwardly in line, trying to look like just an ordinary couple of friends out for a night on the town. It clearly wasn't working. My mother would have had a bird seeing her son lining up with the people shouldering their way ever closer. It seemed a long time, but in reality we only had to wait a few minutes, ten thirty apparently still being a comparatively early time to arrive at a nightclub. I must have been getting old: it seemed to me it was time to be thinking about going home, not going out. I reminded myself to get a life a little more appropriate for a thirty-five-year-old than a sixty-five-year-old. Come to think of it, my parents partied later most evenings than I did.

As much as the neighbourhood might not have fit the stereotype of the gay community, the patrons of the nightclub did. It might not have been the Village People homage I had been expecting, but it wasn't all that far removed. To be sure, there was more leather than I had encountered since visiting Florence, Italy, on a high school field trip. The leather crowd seemed to be the patrons closer to my age. The younger clubbers were more inclined to skin tight T-shirts, horizontal stripes a common theme, at least for those who were bothering to keep their shirts on, a fair number having already doffed them in the humidity of the club. Indeed, two young men, having decided their torsos were no longer in need of coverage, had also surrendered their pants and were bumping and grinding away in their Joe Boxers. There were a few women in the club, some of whom were attached to guys on the dance floor or around the perimeter, some themselves guys dressed as their opposites. I realized that despite Sandi's best efforts, my purple shirt only served to make me look like a conservative guy trying to appear gay. As progressive-minded as I had decided I was in the past few weeks, I admitted to myself I was uncomfortably out of my element.

Ingrid half-shouted something in my ear, and I had to lean in and have her repeat it. "Do you see him?" In my fascination at the nightclub, I had nearly forgotten our purpose.

"No," I replied. "Not yet. Would you like a drink?" Ingrid looked back at me quizzically, and I was pleased this young woman was having as much difficulty as I trying to hear over the pulsing thump of the music. Maybe I wasn't getting old already. Maybe the music *was* too loud. I mimed a drinking action. She flashed a beautiful smile and we worked our way towards the bar, trying if not to completely avoid fellow patrons, at least to refrain from drenching ourselves in their sweat.

We got to the bar, ordered two of the drink special, something called Aquapolitans, and made our way to the top of a three-stepped rise to survey the dance floor. It was a reasonable vantage point with close proximity to the bar, so I hoped if I missed Mark Kansky on the dance floor, I'd catch him at the bar. Surely hanging out here required serious consumption of alcohol. We stood there for about a half hour, during which time I was pretty sure the same song was playing. A few men gave me slight smiles or nods as they made their way past, but nothing so overt as an attempt to pick me up or even ask me to dance. I was having about as much luck with men as I generally had with women. I returned to the bar to get more drinks. And we waited some more. The drinks went down quickly, tasting as much like fruit punch as alcohol. I knew the alcohol content was probably high, so I vowed to pace myself. It was hard enough to see through the darkened room without getting blurred vision from too much drink. It was after midnight when I returned from my fourth trip to the bar to find Ingrid in conversation with one of the few other women in the club. I stood off to her side while the two shouted indiscernibly into each other's ears, pointing and gesticulating toward the dance floor. Finally the young woman placed her hand on Ingrid's arm for a moment then waded into the crowd. I handed Ingrid her drink.

"Who was that?" I yelled.

"She works here. She asked me who we were looking for, and I told her." If we had needed confirmation that our "disguises" weren't working, we had just been provided with it.

"Did she know who you were talking about?"

"Yes. She's going to get him. She said he's been here all night. He got here even before we did."

So much for my brilliant surveillance plan. Two hours of headache-inducing dance music, sixty dollars in drinks, and I could have just asked the staff. I watched the young woman navigate the sweat-soaked crowd, expertly traversing the floor as though on a path only she could see. Nearly in the dead centre, she reached a small group of young men, two of whom were shirtless, one of the shirtless also pant-less, clad only in bright white fitted boxer briefs, a leather belt, and army boots. She leaned into the scantily clad soldier — of course it had to be him — and from our distance appeared to be whispering something in his ear, though it surely was a shout. His head stayed still but his body never missed a beat, continuing to gyrate even as he turned his head to see us. I resisted the urge to wave, just as I had resisted the urge to make any move that might be construed as dancing. As I recalled from my own nightclub experiences a decade or so earlier, I wasn't particularly good at it, and this didn't seem like a forgiving crowd. He began to wend his way toward us, his dance partners simply closing the circle. He seemed to dance as he walked, and as he passed other dancers he knew, he would give a little grind or two or writhe up and down against a dancer for a moment then continue his journey. More than a few pairs of hands caressed his upper body as he danced his way through the throng.

"He sort of stands out from the crowd," Ingrid shouted to me.

"Yes," I concurred.

"Funny you didn't notice him."

"Yes, funny." If it was meant as a well-deserved criticism of my detecting skills, it did not come out as such. If it were Andrea beside me, it would have been a pointed insult coloured with a few expletives that would have made a trucker blush.

Finally Jordan's brother made his way to us, almost gliding up the three stairs, where he stopped in front of us, though his hips never did completely cease shaking.

"I hear you're looking for me?" he asked. Jordan had described his brother as a "pansy." While Mark's physique was not as imposing as the broad shouldered muscle man his little brother had become, he was certainly no slouch in the fitness department. His upper body was slender but appeared incredibly fit and entirely muscular, less the body-building size from pushing weights, more like someone who was just all around fit and did a lot of cardiovascular exercise. Having watched him dance, I could see why he was so fit; I wasn't sure I would have been able to keep up. At the very least I couldn't agree with Jordan's assessment of his brother's physical inability to have killed Tim. "Can I see your badges?"

Ingrid gave me a confused look and I smiled. Not only had our attempt to fit in failed miserably, the staff had decided we were an undercover police duo. On the surface it seemed the kind of lame-brained thing a pair of bumbling detectives might do: let's try to dress like we belong and infiltrate the gay scene. I tried to picture Andrea dressed in Ingrid's outfit. Overall, not a bad image, but I still preferred its current occupant.

"We're not police," I corrected him. "My name is Winston Patrick. I need to talk to you about Tim Morgan."

His eyes lit up with excitement. "You're Winston Patrick? Jordan's law teacher? Oh my god, I'm so excited to meet you." He grabbed my hand and began vigorously shaking it. I fought to keep my eyes on his face, despite the uncomfortable length of time he was holding my hand.

"Yes ..." I began, but before I could go further, Mark turned and yelled down the steps to the dancers below. How they heard him was an acoustic mystery, but next thing I knew, a growing crowd of appreciative men surrounded me who also wanted to shake my hand. A round of applause loud enough to break the bass barrier from the club's speakers turned other heads on the dance floor, and within a moment Mark Kansky had disappeared from my side and the music stopped. A penetrating silence filled the club, and my ears were ringing so badly in the quiet, I actually longed for the return of the music. Suddenly Mark's voice broke through the buzz of curious conversation, directing everyone's attention to me.

"Many of us here tonight knew Tim Morgan, a regular here at Celebrities and in our community." There were murmurs of acknowledgment. "Many of us also heard how hatred that still exists took him away last night." A few angry grumbles emanated from the crowd. "I want you all to know that his battle rages on. His tragic end won't be forgotten. A hero is among us tonight. A man who embraced Tim for who he was, who didn't judge, who led the fight for justice in his name." The hyperbole was as heavy as the humidity in the club. Hearing this speech about anyone else would have caused my eyeballs to roll. Hearing it with myself as the subject was even worse.

"I know we all want to take a moment to express our

gratitude, to pledge our continued support for Winston Patrick!" A roar of approval broke out, complete with whistles and yells. The small crowd already gathered around me took up shaking my hand and hugging me. Soon I was drenched in the collective perspiration of the crowd. The momentary adulation did little to assuage my own feelings of guilt for having contributed to Tim's death, and before long I began to worry that we should probably leave before the crowd made the same leaps in logic that had me feeling so guilty. The music re-started as Mark made his way back to my side, and as quickly as the spectacle of Winston Patrick had begun, it faded into the beat of the music as patrons resumed their bumping and grinding on the dance floor. Mark was the last to throw his nearly naked body around me in a warm embrace that filled my nose with a sickly blend of body spray and body odour.

"I'm so glad to meet you," Mark shouted again directly into my face as he pulled back from our sweaty hug. I introduced Ingrid, and to my surprise he threw his arms around her as well. I guess any friend of mine was a friend of his. I gave her an apologetic look over Mark's shoulder, but she just smiled warmly, clearly more tolerant of strangers' perspiration than I.

"Is there someplace we can go to talk?" I yelled into Mark's ear. He took both our hands and led us across the dance floor, where hands reached out and patted me on the back as we passed through. I guessed if we ever wanted to return surreptitiously to interview anyone else, our cover, if we even had had one, was now blown. The name of the club suddenly seemed even more fitting. To my surprise, he led us straight out the front door onto bustling Davie Street, where late night traffic, both pedestrian and automotive, produced less din than the nightclub's. The burly bouncer who had smiled at us before lay a gigantic hand on my shoulder as I passed and smiled appreciatively.

"Come back any time," he told me. "You'll be first one in the door."

"Thanks," was all I could muster. I was fairly certain I wouldn't take him up on his offer, but I supposed it never hurt to have friends his size. We moved a few steps away from the club's entrance and stopped against the wall. If Mark was bothered by his underwear-only look out on the street, he showed no sign. Nor did passersby.

"What did you want to talk about? You find out who killed Tim?"

Word about Tim's murder had travelled quickly. It had happened too early to make this morning's newspapers, but it had likely led the Saturday evening newscasts while we were mourning the loss of my favourite restaurant. "No, not yet. Have you talked to your brother?"

He let out a laugh that was higher in pitch than I would have thought possible, given his deep voice. "That little fucking imp," he hissed. "He phoned me when the police came and picked him up." That confirmed that Furlo and Smythe had, in fact, arrested him.

"Did you know he had beaten up Tim a few weeks ago?"

"Are you kidding me? I loved Tim. If I had known Jordan had done that to him, he would have been in jail already. Tim was so great. I can't believe he's gone. It's killing me." I glanced again at his outfit and thought of him dancing the night away, grinding against all and sundry in the club. It seemed a strange way to show grief, but who was I to judge?

"Where is Jordan now?" I asked.

"I assume he's rotting away in jail. They said he'll get a hearing on Monday to determine bail. I'm sure as hell not paying it after what he's done." He leaned in, and his voice turned conspiratorial. "Do you think he killed Tim?"

"I don't know, Mark. He says he was at a hockey game last night."

He sighed and leaned his bare back against the building. I wanted to tell him that the building was filthy, and who knew what bacteria was leeching onto his skin, but I didn't think I could sell him on my own neuroses. "Hockey. That's all that boy thinks about. I played too, but with him it's an obsession."

"Mark, I have to ask. Where were you last night?"

Like his brother, Mark seemed slow to recognize that he might be a suspect, but I could see the realization hit him like a hammer, and he stood upright off the wall, his eyes widening in surprise. "You can't be serious." I would have put my hands out to stop his advance, but the only place on his body that was dressed was not somewhere I wanted my hands to be.

"Hold on, Mark. No one is saying you did it. We're just covering all the bases."

"Why would I want to kill Tim?"

"Yes, why?"

He tensed up, and for a few seconds I thought he might take a swing at me. I wasn't particularly worried about getting hurt — I'd been through that before — but I suddenly thought of how pissed Andrea would be that I had flown the nest without my armed escort. I wasn't proud to admit that the thought of being beaten up by a young gay man clad only in underwear on a busy street in front of a gay nightclub would be particularly hard to live down.

"I understand that you and Tim were involved romantically?" Ingrid gently interjected. He turned to face her.

"I don't know that I would call it romance." Her smile seemed to disarm him immediately. Good. It didn't only have that effect on me.

"Your brother seems to think you were a little heartsick when Tim broke up with you." Since his hostility had evaporated, I decided to stay out of it and let her talk to him. Maybe she and I could open a detective agency. She could be the brains and the beauty and I could be, well, there.

He half chuckled. "My brother's an idiot."

She looked at him softly, cocking her head to the side. "Oh, I don't know. He seems kind of sweet. He has a big heart, and he worries a lot about you."

"He worries his hockey buddies will find out his brother's a fag, and he'll never hear the end of it."

"I don't think that's it. He was so upset that you'd been hurt. I could tell he just wanted to protect you. He's a good brother." I was leaning more towards Mark's assessment of his younger brother, but I had to admit that Ingrid was very convincing, especially since she'd never once met Jordan. Mark softened even more.

"But that's just it. Tim and I were never dating. Tim just … um … introduced me to things. I paid him."

"You weren't in love with Tim?" Ingrid pressed.

"No. Look, I've been fighting being gay since I was about twelve. I found Tim online, and he seemed hot. He was discreet. We could meet privately without anyone knowing. He helped me experiment, understand how I was really feeling and come out. But that's it. Now I'm free to date who I want, to find love. Being with Tim just helped me to realize and accept who I was."

I re-entered the conversation. "So last night you were…?"

He turned to face me. "Right here. Where I am most nights. You may not be able to find love in a bar, but at least here you don't have to wonder which side a guy's bread is buttered on." He smiled. "With very few exceptions. Unless …" He tilted his head and batted his eyelashes mockingly.

I gestured reflexively towards Ingrid. "I have a date tonight, thank you." Ingrid smiled widely at me, and embarrassingly, my heart rate picked up just a little.

He sighed dramatically. "Too bad. Mama may not be too comfortable with my being gay, but if I bagged a lawyer, all might be forgiven."

I attempted a chuckle to cover my discomfort. "So you don't have any idea who might have wanted to harm him? Maybe an angry client he mentioned?"

"No, that's just it. Tim provided a great service. Most of his clients are straight, or at least think they are. He's like an outlet for them. Why would they want to hurt him?"

"What if he had threatened to expose one of them?"

Ingrid suggested. "Maybe tell someone's wife or girlfriend?"

He shook his head emphatically. "To what end? Blackmail? Tim was already making lots of money from people and from his website. There'd be nothing in it for him." We stood quietly for a minute, neither of us knowing what question to ask next. Our detective agency might be short-lived. "So, am I free to go?"

"You always were. But Mark, I'm sure the detectives who arrested Jordan are going to want to talk to you. I'm going to have to tell them what we talked about. You understand?"

"Sure. I know you're trying to do right by Tim. It was true what I said in there. We're really grateful for how you were standing by him, helping him with his grad dance and all. If talking to the police is going to help in any way, it's the least I can do."

"Good. Besides," I said, because I just couldn't resist, "Detective Furlo is pretty good-looking. You might like him."

Mark laughed. "Well, I'll look forward to his visit then. You take care of yourself. Keep your head up. We wouldn't want something to happen to you too."

"No, we wouldn't," came a voice from my right. I turned and saw a familiar face nearly beside us. I hadn't even noticed him approaching. Though I hadn't seen a whole lot of it, I recognized it immediately: this was the young man who shared a co-starring role in at least some of Tim's website videos.

Mark saw the visitor and quickly embraced him. "How are you doing?"

"I'm okay, all things considered. Do you mind if I have a few minutes with Mr. Patrick?" the new guy asked.

"Of course. I'll be inside if you need anything. Anything, you understand?"

"Thank you." Mark gave him the cocked-head look of sympathy generally reserved for those who have just experienced tragedy, and I knew then who the young man was. Mark gave him another quick hug and a peck on the cheek, then glancing at me with a look that asked me to be gentle, he made his way back to the nightclub entrance. We three wordlessly watched him go before I spoke.

"Van Pedersen?" I asked.

"Yes," he replied, shaking my hand. I introduced him to Ingrid and explained to him why we'd come to the nightclub. I also informed him that Jordan had been arrested. Van looked to be around the same age as Tim, though I knew he was twenty. He was blond, blue-eyed, slender but not skinny, dressed conservatively compared to the crowd we had just left. His grip was firm, and he stared deep into my eyes, a challenge in his look, as though taking my measure. After his experience with officials from my school, who could blame him? "How did you know?"

I didn't want to talk about what I'd seen of his on-camera performance. "We're becoming quite the detectives, Ingrid and I."

"You've seen some pictures," he stated as though reading my mind.

"Yes," I admitted. "I have."

"And you want to know where I was last night to determine whether or not I should be considered a suspect in Tim's death."

"Yes. I do." We hadn't gone to the club anticipating we'd see Van, but as long as we were there, we might just as well take that opportunity.

"Even though you're having a difficult time ascertaining my motive. After all, if I'm on the website with Tim, it seems unlikely I'd suddenly discovered his means of income and went into a jealous rage."

"Perhaps you'd like to join our little detective agency."

"So me as a suspect wouldn't make a whole lot of sense, would it?"

"I suppose not. And yet you didn't answer the question you posed for us."

He nodded slowly, his eyes still never leaving mine. "No. I did not." We stood that way in the late night, an interrogatory Mexican standoff. There was a challenge in his reluctance. It was Ingrid who eventually broke through our stare-down with a question of her own.

"So if you would just tell us where you were last night, we could go home. It is getting late."

He replied to her while still looking at me. "The night is young."

"Maybe for you," she replied. "But I've been wearing these silly heels for hours now, we still have to walk home, and I need to massage my feet. And I very much want to get out of these ridiculous clothes." I smiled slightly at him, raising an eyebrow to lighten the tension that had grown between us.

"I told you I already knew about Tim's websites. Why would I want to hurt him?"

I was about to reply, but Ingrid was on a roll of her own. "The websites were not the only way Tim made money."

He finally looked away from me and turned to address her. "So you know he was selling himself." Ingrid nodded gently. "Who told you?"

"As Mr. Patrick said: we're becoming quite the detectives. It could not have been easy sharing Tim with paying customers."

"No," he finally admitted, his shoulders sagging a little. "It wasn't." Ingrid waited for him to continue. She was good. I sort of wished Andrea could watch her in action. "I'm not going to lie to you." My experience with the petty criminal element of the city had taught me that when people announced they were not going to lie, it generally led to a series of untruths. But I wanted to give Van the benefit of the doubt. "It was definitely something that didn't make me happy."

"When did you find out Tim was … umm …" Ingrid faltered, searching for the least offensive terminology.

"… whoring himself out?" Van offered.

"Okay. How long have you known Tim was taking money for sexual favours?" The combination of the gentleness in her voice and the Czech accent made it sound almost sweet, as though she had asked how long Van had known his boyfriend was, in fact, the Easter Bunny.

"Oh, I've known all along. He's been doing this ever since we've been together."

"How long has that been?"

"Since December. He had started turning tricks sometime in October." I tried to think back to the beginning of the school year and whether I had noticed any change in Tim. I racked my brain for some kind of clue that something was going on in his life, but the reality that was my first year in the classroom, coupled with the tragic deaths the school had already suffered, had pretty much had me scrambling just to get through each day, let alone notice subtle hints that one of my students might be a male prostitute.

"And this bothered you?" I had to have it confirmed again. It seemed hard to believe he could know about Tim's earning money on his back but would continue to stay romantically involved with him.

"Of course it bothered me," he confirmed. "How would you feel?"

"I'm sure it would be more than I could handle," I admitted. "I'm not sure I could stay with someone who was involved in prostitution. And yet you did."

"I loved him."

"And what changed?"

He looked at me outraged. "What do you mean, what changed? Nothing changed. I loved him, end of story."

"Which brings me to last night, and you still haven't told us where you were when Tim was killed."

"Yes, Tim and I had a fight a couple of days ago, okay? I told him again, as I've told him many times, he didn't have to sell himself like that. That we could find a way for him to pay for university without having to do that. But he was determined. He wasn't listening. He would just smile at me and tell me that he loved me and that would be it. But this time was different. He was angry. He was tired of everything that had happened — to him, to you, the whole thing."

"And so, last night?"

"Oh for god's sake, Patrick, I didn't kill him. Aren't you hearing anything I said? You've got to get off this notion that some angry gay love spat did him in. Not all gay men are homicidal love nuts."

His assumption that I was homophobic offended me. "And you just admitted you'd had a big fight."

"No, not a big fight. A fight. We fought about this a lot. But stop looking at this as a gay lover's quarrel. If anything, it's a hate crime."

"How so?" Ingrid wanted to know.

"Just about everyone who paid Tim was straight, or at least in the closet. Those are the people who are emotionally unstable. You think gay men are edgy? Try looking at men who think they're straight and find themselves paying to fuck my boyfriend." His anger and grief were escalating, the last sentence so harsh it felt like a blow to the chest.

"So you think one of his clients killed him?"

"Or one of the idiot jocks he went to school with. That's who he was meeting last night. That's who you need to be talking to. Stop trying to make this a gay crime. It's an anti-gay crime."

"He was meeting with someone from school last night? Did he say who?"

"No. He didn't."

My frustration was growing; it had felt like we were getting somewhere, and we were back to chasing our tails again. How the hell did Andrea do this for a living? "I need you to think carefully, Van. Did he say anything at all that might give an indication who had called him?"

He shook his head. "No, not called. It was a text message that set him off. But if anything, the more I think of it, it's just gotta be someone from the school." That jived with Tim telling me he knew who was responsible for the homophobic graffiti on the side of the building.

"But you suggested an angry or confused client could have wanted to hurt him. Why would a client vandalize Tim's school?"

Van shook his head at my ignorance. "You're missing the obvious. Not all of Tim's clients were dirty old men."

It just kept getting worse. "Are you telling me some of Tim's clients were students at school?" I know I was new. I could accept I was naive. It was inconceivable to me, however, that not only was Tim prostituting himself, but that the johns were students as well. Where the hell was I teaching, Sodom and Gomorrah Secondary?

Van laughed at my simplicity. "Yeah, Mr. Patrick. That's exactly what I'm telling you. Not a lot of them, mind you, but I know for a fact he told me he had had been paid for a couple of hook-ups in his school, a few other schools too, especially the private ones."

How times had changed. When I was in school, we hid stacks of *Playboy* magazines under the bed and had vivid imaginations until we were lucky enough to get lucky. We didn't purchase sex from either gender's vendors. Or maybe my classmates had and I was just as naive a student in high school as it was turning out I was as a teacher.

"Are you okay?" Ingrid asked me. I guess my stunned look was obvious enough as to make me appear unstable.

Van answered for me. "I think he's okay. He's just waking up."

"Yeah," I answered to both. "I'm fine. I guess we'll have to make sure we look into that."

"I guess," Van replied. "I just wish I had been able to stop him from going. It was yet another reason why we fought." His tone was wistful, and I could see he felt guilty for failing to stop Tim from making his final rendezvous. I knew how he felt. I'd been feeling that way all day. I wondered when Van had gotten the news and who had delivered it, him not being next of kin. But then I remembered the vast array of social networking websites and text messaging I'd seen in the past week and knew the number of ways that information flowed were endless.

I had run out of questions, beyond the one he had yet to answer, so I pushed it again. "So where did you go last night?"

He looked at me with even more guilt in his eyes. "Let's just say I wasn't alone and leave it at that. If I have to, I can get that verified."

I nodded. "It may come to that at some point. But I understand." We shook hands and Van left us on the sidewalk, heading back the way he'd come. He paused by the entrance to the nightclub to accept some well wishes from patrons but didn't go in. We watched until he was out of sight, and I turned to Ingrid. "Well, I guess we should go."

"You don't want to go in for one quick dance?" I looked at her a moment, and she smiled.

"I really do not."

"Me neither."

"I'll try to get us a taxi." It was approaching one o'clock, comparatively early for the nightclub crowd. But getting a taxi still wouldn't be easy. Vancouver's cab population had not kept pace with the number of nightclubs and patrons, and getting a taxi at night was nothing like the way it appeared in movies and television in New York. Or at least so I'd heard: I was rarely out late at night to try.

"Why don't we walk? It's such a lovely night."

"What about your feet? I thought they were killing you."

She smiled again. "A small price to pay."

We wandered down Davie Street past closed businesses and residential buildings, the occasional corner store remaining open even this late. We re-hashed what we'd learned and re-lived all we'd seen in the garish club. At the corner of Denman Avenue, we paused to take in the view of English Bay with its small brigade of container ships silhouetted against the horizon, waiting their turn to be piloted through the First Narrows to load and unload their wares. A few people were walking or running the famed seawall, shift workers, partiers, or, like me, plagued by the inability to sleep and filling the restless hours breathing the city's night air. Ingrid seemed mesmerized by the vista and the gentle wash of the waves. Finally we turned north toward the opposite side of the peninsula, nearly alone along Denman, pausing occasionally to peer in the windows of the shops. We crossed Robson Street, and Ingrid silently took my arm as we began our descent toward Coal Harbour. Surprised though I was, I took the unusual step of saying nothing, particularly saying nothing stupid, and savouring the moment of companionship, however brief it might be.

I was relieved when we quietly entered the apartment, and neither Andrea nor Sandi were sitting in the doorway waiting for us. I really didn't want a lecture about my personal safety or the lecture about, well, whatever Sandi's lecture of the moment was, to put a damper on the pleasant end to the evening. We stood alone in the entranceway.

"Well," I finally said, breaking the awkward silence as we'd snuck in like two teenagers past curfew. "That was certainly interesting."

"Yes, it was."

"Thank you for coming with me. I definitely would not have wanted to do that alone."

"No, I think not." She paused and smiled at me. "You know, I know it wasn't supposed to be, but that was kind of fun. You know how to show a girl new to the city a good time."

"Oh, I'm quite the tour guide. So far I've taken you to a traffic accident and a gay bar. I'm surprised I haven't been hired by the tourism board."

She laughed a little. "Well then next time you must promise to show me only the best the city has to offer."

"I promise," I said, holding my hand across my heart.

"Good. I'll look forward to it." She paused again. "Well, good night then." She stepped forward reached up and gently kissed me on the cheek, then turned and walked down the hallway to her room. I was so stunned, I didn't bother to even mutter my good night until after her bedroom door had closed. I felt as though a jolt had run through me, and I was suddenly alert and energized, my mind racing as I tried to analyze what was likely a friendly, meaningless gesture.

So much for a good night's sleep.

Chapter Eighteen

Not surprisingly, Andrea was not pleased with me. I had managed to rest for a couple of hours when I woke to my personal detective brewing coffee in Sandi's kitchen. She was abuzz, as she usually was, with the early stages of her investigation, which she shared while guzzling two cups of very strong coffee. As she had suspected, her most recent homicide catch had all the markings of a feud between rival criminal elements, a very "clean" kill, as she called it, the victim well known to police as a suspected member of organized crime, involved in a litany of offences from drug and gun trafficking to murder. He was himself a suspect in the unsolved killing of another known criminal a few months back. It now likely never would be, as the prime suspect would never be available for questioning.

When she had finished telling me about her day, she asked what I had been up to in the nearly twenty-four hours since she deposited me at the front entrance. I suspect she suspected I had sat quietly in the apartment, mulling over the events of the day and dutifully obeying her order to stay safely tucked away. She was slightly miffed to hear I had ventured out for dinner, quite mad when she heard Ingrid had accompanied me on what Andrea was already terming a date, and outright livid when I described our venture to the nightclub. I had, she informed me, put myself and Ingrid at great personal risk trying to meet up with the man who might well be Tim's killer, not to mention interfering in a police investigation. Nonetheless, once her indignation had dissipated somewhat, she was intrigued by what we had learned. She gave me Jasmine Smythe's cell phone number. In Andrea's assessment, speaking to Smythe first might mitigate the angry inferno that would surely spew from Furlo. She guzzled a third cup of coffee, half-heartedly asked me to stay put, and headed back out to the streets in pursuit of the gangland killer's killer.

Not surprisingly, when I reached her shortly before nine, Detective Smythe was also not pleased to hear of my exploits. As Andrea had guessed, the two detectives were still hard at their investigation, and as I described my night, I could hear Furlo in the background cursing and making threats of physical retribution. Smythe shushed him several times but eventually gave up and said they would be coming to see me. I gave her my cell phone number, because I had no intention of honouring her request that I stay put.

The apartment was unnervingly quiet, Ingrid sleeping late and Sandi clearly using Sunday as an excuse to sleep in. I showered and headed off to church.

Not surprisingly, much attention at Fraserview Presbyterian was centred on me. The mostly elderly congregation spent much time cooing over my well-being, offering support, and lamenting my marital status. A few even had daughters, nieces, or granddaughters they thought would fit the bill and promised they would work on arranging a meeting. My friend Peter sought me out at the end of the service, also to check on my state of mind.

Surprisingly, I found myself spending the majority of the afternoon with Sandi, having a more or less pleasant time. Ingrid was spending her day off at the library studying, Andrea spending hers fighting crime. We put my replacement credit card to the test, purchasing yet more clothes to replenish my charred collection. I felt my spirits lift a little. I took advantage of my buoyed psyche and spent the evening at my parents' suburban home.

The extended Patrick family gathering had the usual effect of deflating my buoyancy. I also endured plenty of maternal guilt. Sandi's Protestantism notwithstanding, my mother viewed my ex-wife as an ally in the crusade to have me exchange my current chalkboard brushes for my former barrister's robes. I suppose it was nice they could have something to agree on.

Emotionally exhausted, I returned to Sandi's apartment late in the evening, and finding it empty, I opted for an early night. The fatigue from my recent activities allowed me to fall asleep shortly after ten o'clock. I woke at one thirty, leaving me with hours of empty contemplation before any normal person could be expected to show up at work. The early morning doorman gave me the same mildly judgmental look one often encounters from non-runners. I eased into the apartment, careful not to disturb the occupants. A shower, coffee, and cover-to-cover read of two daily newspapers later, I headed off to work in sartorial splendor after the previous day's shopping extravaganza.

And there they were.

Like pine beetles attacking hapless forests, once again the media had descended upon John A. Macdonald

Secondary, though it was only six thirty when I arrived at the school. Both major television stations had live broadcast vans parked on the side street nearest the staff parking lot, their extendable antennae towers reaching skyward like giant phallic symbols. Several reporters milled around the sidewalk, and I knew I was a familiar enough face that my arrival would be documented for the day's newscasts. I would face a barrage of questions before I could reach the main doors. I drove past the school and parked on a residential street about four blocks beyond the school. Snaking through the neighbourhood on foot, I managed to arrive undetected at the opposite side of the building.

I walked through the halls as I often did upon my early arrival, completely alone, the only other occupant being the daytime caretaker. Sitting quietly in my classroom, I prepared for the day, anticipating the grief that would descend upon the school after the events of Friday night, along with deluge of questions. The school would be awash with extra grief counsellors and support staff who would do their best to make sense of a senseless killing, to reassure students that the world was not such a terrible place, that they were safe at school, and that the perpetrators of this awful crime would be caught and brought to justice. And they would say it all with a straight face. Around eight o'clock I heard keys rattling and fumbling with the lock on my classroom door, a sure sign I was about to be visited by the school's administration; anyone else would have knocked. The principal's nearly bald head already shone with sweat.

"Good morning, Winston," he said softly.

"Good morning, Don," I replied, anticipating a barrage of anger. Really, who could blame him?

Instead he continued in a gentle, caring tone. "How are you holding up?"

"Me? I'm fine."

He nodded without comment. "I understand you were at the scene of Tim's ..." His voice trailed off before he could complete the sentence.

"I was."

"And you're okay?"

It struck me for the first time that my principal might actually be checking up on my well-being. I wondered how long it would last. "I'm fine."

"Are you sure?"

"Yes. I really think it's best for my students if I'm here today."

He nodded with some enthusiasm, surprisingly. "I agree. They're going to need you here. I think it's important they have as much normalcy as possible in their time of grief. You know you're going to get a lot of questions. You've seen how the media is reporting it?"

I nodded. I'd seen the deep coverage Tim's death was getting, even in the national media. His victory over the school's grad prom policy had made him a cause célèbre, and his murder consumed not only the morning's news pages but the editorial inches as well. Most were labelling his murder a hate crime and calling for everything from increased police resources to tougher hate crime legislation. Until Furlo and Smythe were able to lock up Tim's killer, the public outcry would continue to mount. It was likely why they had yet to interview me after my phone call to Smythe: they were surely working around the clock. My name also appeared prominently in the coverage.

"You're not quoted in any of the papers."

"They haven't found me yet. I've been staying at my ex-wife's this past week since my apartment burned down. I haven't yet had to use the phrase 'no comment.'"

He glanced toward the windows. "They're looking for you here."

"I know. They were here when I arrived. They didn't find me. I'm crafty."

He smiled a little. "Do you know what you're going to tell the students?"

"More or less. I really don't know very much, despite my best efforts to find out."

He looked at me quizzically. "Your best efforts?"

"Yes, Don. You didn't think I wouldn't at least try to figure out who's responsible?"

"Winston, listen to me. Seriously. You need to be careful here." Great. Another Andrea on my hands. "Obviously whoever … killed … Tim has some serious hate issues around this whole …" He paused, searching for the least offensive terminology. "This whole 'gay' thing. You're involved. You could very well be at risk."

"You're not the first one to suggest that. I spent the evening at my mother's house last night." I was trying to lighten the mood. It wasn't working.

"Winston, we're talking about hate crime here. They've killed someone. You're the one who helped him with his cause. You're an obvious target. We've had our differences this year, but believe it or not, I do like you.

I would hate to see something happen to you. Don't do anything that's going to put yourself at risk. If not for you, think about your students."

"Is this about PR, Don? Are you pissed about the media being outside?"

He shook his head in frustration, as though I just wasn't hearing him. I have that effect on people. "No, Winston, it's not. Hell, since you've gotten here I've gotten kind of used to them being around. I might even miss them when they're gone," he added, smiling slightly. "I'm thinking about your students, their safety as well as their emotional well-being. I've asked the police to maintain an increased presence around the school until Tim's killer is caught, because I want you to be here for them, and I want to make sure both you and your students are safe."

He sounded so genuine, I felt a little guilty for doubting his motives. "Okay," I said. "I promise I will be careful. I really don't want anything to happen to me either."

"Thank you," he said. He stood up. "I guess I'd better go downstairs and get ready for the emergency staff meeting. There will be a lot of questions, and we need to move forward for the kids. You remember what this is like."

I did. Not much learning would happen today. "Don," I said, stopping him before he reached the door. He had been candid and open with me. I felt a need to be the same with him. "Listen. There's something I want to tell you."

He looked at me without speaking. "There's a chance that this isn't a hate crime. Some of what the police have found out about Tim suggests what happened may have been personal rather than political."

"I see," was all he said.

"And it's possible, according to some of Tim's associates with whom I've spoken, that it may be someone here at the school."

His eyes widened in alarm. "You don't think it's a teacher?" Until that moment it hadn't really occurred to me, but now that Don mentioned it, I guess it would have to be at least a possibility. Still, I waved the thought away for the time being.

"No, I don't. But Tim may have been involved, uhm, physically with another student or students at school. It's a possibility the police will have to check out when I tell them about the conversations I've had."

He rubbed the front of his head. His hand must surely have been soaked as he reached for the door handle. I made a mental note to immediately conduct my ritual weekly spraying of my classroom door handles with Lysol as soon as he left. "Okay. Thank you for telling me. I appreciate the heads up." He opened the door then paused. "And Winston? As long as we're sharing cautions, here I've got one for you. Try to steer clear of Bill Owen today. He's kind of on the warpath."

"He's gunning for me, is he?"

"Let's just say he appreciates your efforts less and less. Stay out of the cafeteria, and I'm sure you can avoid him," he added with a smile, then left. That wouldn't be a problem. Eating in the school cafeteria was a health hazard I was willing to risk only in the direst of circumstances.

As expected, the emergency staff meeting brought many questions from teachers, some angry they were being made to stay in a school with a potential killer on the loose, most simply worried about how to support grieving, scared kids. This was the second such tragedy of the school year, and I was once again touched by the outpouring of compassion from the staff. A few wary stares were sent my way, cautious about approaching the teacher who was still "the new guy." Several teachers did approach me as the meeting broke up, offering words of support or a gentle arm around the shoulder. To their credit, if anyone blamed me for putting Tim's life at risk, they kept it to themselves.

As was also to be expected, students had little interest in the curriculum, and I had to grant them the opportunity to vent, to ask questions, and to grieve if necessary. My first two classes that morning were junior grades. Most of them knew Tim only from the infamy surrounding his court challenge. Still, they had to be wondering what high school was really going to be like given the violence that had accompanied their early days at John A. Macdonald Secondary.

I kept to myself during lunchtime, avoiding the stares and glares of students and any contact with the vice-principal. It was certain to be only a matter of time before he found me and said something inane or profane, to which I would surely respond with equal if not greater inappropriateness. No one would win such an argument, and I wasn't in the mood for chest thumping with my supervisor. I had caught up with my marking and was finishing writing some information on the archaic overhead projector when a knock interrupted me. "Come in," I called out. When I turned, Sara and Nathan occupied the doorway. I stopped what I was doing. They walked quietly into the room. Before I could prevent it, Sara marched up and threw her arms around me in a firm embrace. I stood there stupidly for a moment, arms at my side, then relaxed and awkwardly returned her hug, maintaining as much distance between us as her firm hold would permit. Even the normally gregarious Nathan gently and quietly rested his hand on my shoulder for a quiet, uncomfortable moment.

"How are you doing?" Sara asked.

"I'm holding up," I replied. "How are you guys?"

They both nodded sombrely. "We're holding up too. It's been a tough day. Just when I think I'm holding it together, someone will run up to me and start crying, and I come close to letting go again."

"Come close?"

"I'm really not one for big public displays of waterworks. I prefer to grieve privately."

"It's okay to be upset, Sara. You have every right to be grieving, even here at school. People know how close you were with Tim." Nathan, who had yet to speak, was staring silently out the window.

Sara dismissively waved off my concern. "Ugh. It's annoying. People who hardly knew him, who hardly know me, are suddenly weeping in my arms. It's all so dramatic."

"People, especially young people, often need to have others around and need to display their emotions openly. It's part of how they absorb what's happening."

"Whatever." She waved again. "I don't have time to look after everyone else. Where are we on the investigation?" She was all business again, and I respected her reserve, even if it was, I suspected, masking her grief.

"We're not anywhere. The case has been officially taken over by Detectives Furlo and Smythe of the Vancouver Police Department. It's in their hands now."

"Oh good lord, Mr. Patrick. It's me you're talking to. Your cop buddy isn't here right now. What's really going on?"

I sighed. I saw Sara Kolinsky every second day for roughly seventy-five minutes in a group of twenty-nine students, yet in nine and a half months she'd figured she had come to know me so well. "Okay." I told them about my investigative attempts. I told Sara that while her pointing us to Jordan Kansky had led to his confessing to assaulting Tim, it did look like he had a pretty confirmable alibi for Friday night. She nodded, satisfied, before addressing Nathan.

"Any questions?"

He finally spoke. "Nope. This is what she's been like all morning. All business. It's like living with an army general." It was the most subdued I'd ever seen him, and his pained expression and tone made me long for the loud, overbearing class clown I was always having to tell to be quiet.

"Get over it," she commanded. "We've got work to do."

"Sara, I'm going to tell you the same thing that Mr. McFadden told me this morning. We don't know who did this. We don't know if it was personal or political. We don't know that whoever hurt Tim wouldn't be willing to hurt one of us. Don't go doing anything that could put you at risk."

"If you think I'm going to lock myself away in my house while Tim's killer is running around loose, beating up or killing every gay teenager he can get his hands on, think again. That's not who I am. I think you know that," she said.

"You see?" Nathan asked.

"Yeah. She's pretty relentless," I agreed. "Listen. I need to be really frank with you two. Given what happened to my apartment, it's hard to imagine that this isn't some kind of radical anti-gay political agenda, especially when it happened so soon after we appeared on the radio. But after talking to Van, we can't rule out the possibility that this is something much smaller, much more personal. He seems to think it could well be someone here at the school."

Nathan's eyes looked as though they might pop out of his head. "He thinks a student killed Tim? Why?"

"Van thinks Tim might have been involved with a student in a, uhm, physical sense and that the student may have been more attracted to Tim than Tim was to the other student. I don't know myself. It doesn't sound all that plausible, but I'm only telling you two because you're out there in the student population."

"You think we might be able to hear something or find something out," Sara mused.

"I'm thinking it's possible you're at risk. If we have an unstable teenager who killed Tim, he may be willing to kill again, especially if he thinks we know who he is. And Tim did tell you on the phone on Friday night that he was going to meet with someone who had information about the graffiti on the side of the school. It does make some sense that it would be a student."

Sara was deep in thought.

I continued. "Or it could be a ruse from someone outside the school to get Tim where he wanted him to be. I really have a hard time thinking one of our students is capable of this much violence, but I want you to be careful."

Sara spoke as though completing ignoring my admonition. "I wonder if we let word get out that we were on to him, we could flush him out."

"Sara, listen to me. He's probably not an idiot."

"He doesn't sound like a master of intellect. He's an ignorant homophobe."

"Who so far has gotten away with at least a homicide and we don't know what else. If you were on to him, he'd know the police would already be here to arrest him. Letting it slip that you know 'who done it' isn't going to suddenly get a killer to confess."

"Still …" she said, her voice fading as a plan seemed to be formulating in her head.

"Nathan. Can you talk some sense into her?"

"Yeah, right," he replied. He had a point.

The bell rang to start the afternoon classes.

"Listen. It still seems pretty far-fetched to me. Just be careful out there and don't do anything stupid. If you think you hear anything at all, call me and I'll pass it along to the detectives."

"Yeah, cuz they've done such a great job so far," Sara harrumphed.

"We're working on it," came an all-too-familiar voice from the doorway. "Of course, if people would stop trying to play amateur detective, the big boys would clear this case a lot faster."

"The big *boys*?" Jasmine Smythe chided her partner.

"You know what I mean," he growled in response.

"Why, detectives, what a pleasant surprise. If I'd known you were coming I would have had lunch prepared, or at least coffee and cookies."

"The pleasure of your company is always sufficient, Mr. Patrick," Smythe cooed. Though she was being sarcastic, I might have blushed a little. If she ever gave up detecting, she surely had a career as a DJ for a jazz station — if only Vancouver had a jazz station.

"I take it you'd like to speak with me?"

"I'd like to kick your scrawny ass and then speak with you, but my partner thinks it would be a bad idea," said Furlo. "Though I'm pretty sure I promised you an ass kicking if you got in the way of our investigation again."

I turned to Nathan and Sara, who were watching the exchange, Nathan in shock and Sara with a look of righteous indignation. "Guys, can you step outside for just a couple of minutes before class begins? I need to talk to these two fine detectives for a moment."

Nathan looked like he couldn't get out of the room fast enough, but Sara stopped directly in front of Furlo. She had to look up into his face to deliver a threatening glare. "You know, I'm certain I don't have to remind you about the legal rights of citizens contained in the Charter, but it sounds like you do need reminding of the 'Code of Professional Conduct' regulation in the Police Act. You're a public servant in a public building speaking in front of students. Your threatening and unprofessional language could well bring the reputation of the police into disrepute. And I hope to hell that if you ever get around to catching Tim's killer, you don't use that kind of threatening language and get his conviction thrown out of court." Furlo said nothing, but I could almost smell his blood boiling.

"I will see to it that we do not," Smythe said gently. "You're right. There's no need for us to speak uncivilly to one another." Sara stepped around Furlo and walked out of the room. It seemed an appropriate moment for a door slam, but she took the high road and closed it gently behind her. Smythe tossed a warning glance in my direction to ward off any sarcastic comment. Code of conduct or no, anything I said could well put my health at risk. It was one of those rare occasions when I listened to common sense and said nothing. "I hope we weren't interrupting," Smythe said when a suitable amount of time had passed.

"Not at all," I replied in the civil tone Smythe had promised would be the mode of discourse. "We were just checking in on each other to see if we were all okay."

"And are we?"

"They're definitely hurting. Nathan is the most gregarious kid you would ever meet: always laughing, joking, talking too loudly, a real bull in the china shop. Today he can barely speak. I guess he should have stayed home, but at least here he's with his friends so they can support each other, especially Sara. She's masking her grief with some determined resolve to see justice. I know you don't want her or us anywhere near your case, but talking like a crusader I think is what's helping her hold it together. It's a grieving thing."

"And you? You didn't complete the 'we' in that equation."

"I'm fine."

"Are you? Don't try to pretend it doesn't affect you, that Tim was just a student. I know you better than that."

"Should we pull a couch in here so you can provide therapy, Doctor?" Furlo interjected.

"Dear god, no," I replied, trying to keep the conversation safely jovial for the time being. "My students already fall asleep in class. The last thing they need is comfortable seating to make it easier."

Smythe chuckled politely. Furlo did not. "Just what the hell did you think you were you doing on Saturday? Didn't we tell you to keep the hell away from our investigation? What do I have to do to keep you away, slap you with an obstruction of justice charge?"

I bit my tongue and tried to smile with polite understanding, but it was difficult when dealing with Furlo. I ignored his question and pressed on. "Would you like to hear what we learned?" Deep down, beneath all his bluster, Furlo was first and foremost a good cop. He sighed, ran his hand through his thick hair, reached into his coat pocket, and withdrew his notepad and pen. Smythe already had her BlackBerry out, ready to take notes. It was like watching two generations of police investigation side by side, though Smythe was the elder of the two detectives.

"Tell us what you know, in detail," Smythe said. The second bell rang to begin the period.

Sara poked her head back in the door. "Can we come in?" she asked.

I looked at the two investigators. "I do have a class. Let's switch places with them." I waved Sara into the room while Furlo, Smythe, and I walked across the room, out the rear door of the classroom into the hall to talk while the students filed in.

"I don't have a lot of time."

"Make time," Furlo demanded. The last of the students wound their way into their classrooms, leaving the three of us more or less alone in the corridor.

Smythe glanced around the hallway, assessing our limited privacy. "Tell us what you've learned." I did, in as much detail as I could recall. Furlo even smiled briefly as I described Sandi's ultimately futile efforts to integrate me into Celebrities culture. He was less amused when I suggested that he might want to consider speaking again to Mark Kansky and Van Pedersen to firmly pin down their whereabouts, especially given Van's reluctance to provide an alibi.

"We had thought of that," Furlo snapped. "We've done this before."

I figured he was being hypersensitive because he knew I was right, but that was likely my own ego getting the best of me. "Is there any way we can identify the text message that was sent to him?" I asked.

"I'm not certain," Smythe replied. "That's a little beyond my telecommunications knowledge. We haven't found his cell phone yet. It wasn't in his car. We searched the surrounding area, and we've got techs searching wider in the park, but so far we've had no luck."

"Did you try calling it?" I asked brilliantly.

Smythe smiled. "Gee, what a good idea."

"Oh," I conceded. "You *have* done this before. So where do you go from here?" I was careful to use the second person rather than the collective first. I didn't need yet another lecture or physical threat from Furlo.

"For now, for today, we'll be here talking to students, friends, teachers, seeing if there's anything they can tell us that might help point us clearly to a suspect."

"Do you think that will help?"

"Nope," Furlo chimed in. "We'll probably spin our wheels all day, with the added benefit of hanging out with twelve hundred smelly teenagers."

It didn't sound promising, and my dejection must have shown, because Smythe addressed it. "Winston, this is what we do. We talk to everyone. We look around, we theorize, we talk to everyone again, and we play with the pieces of the puzzle. We start with the corners, then the edges, and then we fill in the middle as we understand how the shapes fit together. We've got the frame, we're working on the middle now, and it's the hardest part, but I'm pretty sure we'll put it all together."

It was a valiant attempt at a pep talk, but I was glum. "We really don't need this, especially at this time of year. Graduation ceremonies are on Thursday night. Kids are supposed to be celebrating, and they're all wrapped up in another homicide. I don't know how much more they can take."

She nodded knowingly. Furlo just looked bored. "I understand. Kids are remarkably resilient. I know mine are. But we'll be as gentle as we can, especially if we find we're heading towards someone in the school, student or staff." I thought I detected a note of caution in her voice.

I wondered if they had already ruled out suspects from beyond the school, the political rather than the personal assailant, but I knew they weren't going to tell me anything more. I hoped Andrea would clear her current homicide quickly enough to stick her nose back into Furlo and Smythe's case. "Okay, Winston. We'll let you get back to your class. You'll call us if you find out anything new?"

I nodded.

"And we trust you won't be out trying to find out anything new," Furlo commanded.

I nodded again. Smythe gave me one gentle touch on the side of my face and turned to walk away. Her partner rolled his eyeballs before joining her. I took a deep breath: this next class was Tim's and was the one I'd been dreading most. But standing out in the hallway for the next seventy-five minutes seemed counterproductive, so steeling myself for the emotional onslaught to follow, I went inside.

Often, when a teacher leaves a class unattended, there is a reasonably good chance of chaos ensuing. My Law 12 Class was the exception to the rule as I entered, and barely a sound was detectable beyond a slight murmur. I would have been pleased to be hit by an errant paper airplane. Students looked at me expectantly as I moved to the front of the class. I paused, not really sure how to begin, then reached onto my desk to pick up the assignments I had marked and was ready to return to the class.

"Okay. Why don't we begin by handing these out, and I can answer any questions you have?" The silence became a stunned silence.

"Mr. Patrick?" came the soft voice of Sharanjeet. "Don't you think we should talk about other things first?"

"Okay, Sharanjeet." We'd been told in the staff meeting about how to talk about the "incident," but with Tim's class, everything we had prepared seemed trite. I eventually opted to toss the ball back into their court. "Is there anything anyone wants to talk about or ask?" There was no immediate response, not even so much as heads turning towards one another to see who would go first. Not even Sara and Nathan responded. "Of course if anyone feels a need to speak with one of the counsellors, they're still available. I recognize this is an extremely difficult time." Another moment or two passed before finally someone spoke.

"I heard Jordan was arrested," said Aaron Bradshaw, another muscle-bound student who looked like he lived at the gym. I didn't yet know if charges had been laid against Jordan, but I knew word would travel quickly, so there was no point in denying it, even if police had not yet made that information specifically public.

"I understand that's correct."

"Did he kill Tim?" another student asked.

I thought for a moment before answering. Not only had I believed his impassioned denials on Saturday morning, but also the fact that Furlo and Smythe were still so actively interviewing and prowling around the crime scene told me they didn't think so either. Still, I wanted the kids to at least be prepared for the possibility that one of their classmates had killed another.

"I honestly don't think so. But I don't know what the police are thinking," I admitted.

"Then why was he arrested?" Aaron wanted to know. It occurred to me only then that Aaron and Jordan spent a lot of time together and were probably friends. It then occurred to me that Aaron might already know about Jordan's assault on Tim, and I wondered if he had participated.

The class continued to look to me for answers. "Because he confessed to assaulting Tim and tying him to the goal posts on the field." A wave of murmurs travelled across the room, and I did nothing to stop it. Even Aaron appeared shocked by the revelation, which brought me some relief.

"Then why don't you think he killed Tim, if he already confessed to assaulting him?" Sharanjeet asked with a quick glance towards Sara and Nathan.

"He has an alibi for Friday night that the police have probably already confirmed. Besides, he seemed completely surprised when I told him about Tim's death." I realized too late what I had just revealed and hoped it might slip by unnoticed.

No such luck. "He confessed to you?" Aaron nearly shouted. "Why the hell would he have done that?"

I sighed. If there had been any hope that I might be a calming, comforting presence, I was soundly blowing it. "I guess the pressure of holding that in had become too much for him so when the opportunity presented itself, he just let it out." I was trying to be sufficiently vague.

"What opportunity?" Aaron demanded.

"We were at his house on Saturday morning."

"We?" another student asked.

"My friend, who is a Vancouver Police detective, and I paid Jordan a visit on Saturday morning."

"So you did suspect him of killing Tim," Tim and Sara's friend Lissa added from the back of the room. It was a statement rather than a question. So much for being sufficiently vague.

"We were trying to rule out all possibilities. I was simply trying to help the police in the initial phase of the investigation."

"Are we all suspects too?" Sharanjeet asked.

"No, of course not." A barrage of questions came out at once, and I felt like facing the media scrum outside the building might be a bit easier than the group currently interrogating me. I raised my hands and tried to restore some semblance of order. I had a feeling that my lesson on family law was likely not going to happen, but nonetheless, after more than half the class was spent on a question-and-not-very-satisfying-answer session, I finally managed to direct the students into a half-hearted attempt to complete the assignment I had planned. It wasn't scintillating, but I hoped it would be a welcome break from the trauma.

The class continued to talk more or less quietly as it began the assignment, and I booted up the relic of a computer that sat on a table alongside my desk. I had planned to update my students' marks while they were working, but given that I had neglected to turn on the beast when I arrived, I knew I had at least seven minutes to burn while it went through its ritual dance of attempting to connect with the school's network. It was why I normally did the computing portion of my job at home. I longed for my own computer, which had been destroyed alongside the rest of my belongings. The very thought of my shiny iMac singed beyond recognition made me cringe. As I sat staring blankly at the blank screen, Benjamin MacDonnell, a quiet but very dedicated student, ambled up beside me.

"Mr. Patrick?" he quietly asked. I figured he wanted to see his marks, a not unreasonable request but one I would be technologically incapable of responding to for probably at least five minutes, and I told him so. "No," he continued. "I wanted to ask you about something else."

"What's that?"

He glanced nervously around the class before responding. "I don't know. It may be nothing." Ben usually spoke quietly enough that I had difficulty hearing, but today was proving to be extra hard.

"Try me. Are you okay? Do you want to talk to a counsellor?"

"God no." He said that loudly enough that he drew the momentary attention of two students in the nearest desks. I rolled my desk chair — purchased by me to save my scrawny butt from the perilous discomfort of the wooden variety — backwards the remaining foot or so to the corner of the room to afford us at least some semblance of privacy.

"What is it, Ben?"

"I was just wondering if you had talked to Tim's counsellor." Both boys would have been assigned the same school guidance counsellor, Steve Plum.

"No, not specifically. Do you think he might know something that would help us?"

"It's just that …" I waited for him to continue but he didn't.

"It's just what, Ben?"

"It's just that he's a raging homophobe." I tried not to let my eyes bug out of my head, keeping my best lawyerly face on. I didn't know Steve well, but I also had had no reason to believe he was anything but a respected member of the counselling staff.

"That's a pretty severe statement."

"I'm sorry."

"Don't be. I'm just saying that's not the kind of thing you want to be saying lightly. What makes you say Mr. Plum is, uhm, homophobic?"

He looked at me carefully for a moment then seemed to decide I was trustworthy enough to continue. "Because when I went to him with some personal issues, it became clear."

"How so?"

He sighed, exasperated that I needed the picture drawn so clearly. "I was just coming out of the closet, and the experience was causing me some grief."

"You're gay?" I asked naively.

He smiled a little for the first time since our conversation began. "Man, where have you been?" I tried not to stare at him to search for the clues I had obviously missed. I wondered if he kind of looked gay but realized I still really didn't know what that was supposed to look like. Then I remembered I was not really supposed to think that being gay looked like anything in particular. Then I worried Ben would think I was a raging homophobe. Then I was just confused. "Mr. Patrick? Are you okay?"

"Yeah. You were saying?"

"When I talked to Mr. Plum to tell him what I was going through and, I don't know, tried to get some kind of support from him, he tried to talk me out of it."

"Of being gay?"

"He told me it was just a phase I was going through."

"We have a gay phase?"

He laughed. "Apparently, according to Mr. Plum. He told me all about how it was an unhealthy lifestyle, and if I really wanted help he could find people who could cure me."

Holy crap, I thought. "Holy crap," I said out loud.

"And I know that he told Tim the same thing more than a year ago. The guy obviously has some kind of a hate on for gay men."

"How do you know he told Tim the same thing?"

"Tim told me after I came out. He was very supportive, especially after I told him I had talked to Mr. Plum."

"Were you and Tim … uhm … involved?" I hated myself for asking, partially because I didn't want to think of another of my students as a potential suspect but also because I really didn't want to know.

"Tim? Oh no. We're just friends." I noted he spoke of their friendship in the present tense, which may have meant nothing more than his still being in grief and shock.

"Are you sure?" I pressed.

He sighed with more exasperation. I tended to bring this out in people. "Yes, Mr. Patrick, I'm sure. Just because two people are gay doesn't automatically mean they sleep together."

"Sorry," I said. "I'm perpetuating a stereotype, aren't I?"

"A little bit, yeah."

"Does that make me a raging homophobe?"

He softened a little again. "No, it doesn't. A little ignorant maybe, but we can work on that."

"I will. I promise."

He smiled. "I think the work we did in class on Tim's lawsuit was probably the best thing I've ever learned in school." It was my turn to smile.

"I'm glad. Listen, Ben, I'm glad you told me this. I don't know what it means, if anything, but I'll be sure the information gets to the right people. And I'll be discreet."

He looked relieved. "Thank you." He paused a moment. "Do you think you'll catch the guy that did this?" I liked the faith he had in me, though I know Furlo wouldn't.

"I like to think the police will," I corrected him. "They sounded pretty confident when I spoke to them." That seemed to satisfy Ben for the moment.

"Okay then. Maybe it's nothing. I just thought I would tell you."

"Thanks, Ben. I'm glad you did." He returned to his seat and I turned to my computer. It had finally reached the point when it could actually be used, so I distracted myself by updating students' marks in the computer and calling students up to my desk to show them their letter grade. Given all that had happened, it seemed a bit callous, particularly for a few of them, but it seemed it would give them something else to think about. As the bell rang, the class shuffled past, Sara and Nathan lurking at the end.

"Did you find out anything new from Starsky and Hutch?" Sara asked. I couldn't help but smile, primarily because I knew Sara's comparison of Furlo and Smythe surely referenced the Ben Stiller comedic satire rather than the original.

"Nope. They wanted to know what I know, and I told them what I'd already told you."

She looked disappointed. "And I don't suppose they would tell us anything, even if they did know something."

"I don't suppose."

"You'll call me if you hear anything, right?"

"I won't hear anything."

"Still, just in case. Or send me a message on Facebook. It forwards to my cell phone."

"Sara, I don't have a Facebook page, and I don't plan to get one."

She laughed. "Come on, Mr. Patrick. Get with the twenty-first century. Everyone's on Facebook. Just think of all the people who could catch up with you."

"I think enough people have caught up with me lately. I don't need anyone else tracking me down."

"Sara, let's go," Nathan prodded.

"Are you okay, Nathan?" I asked. "I know this is really hard on you. Do you think you want to go talk to one of the counsellors?"

"I'm fine," he muttered. "We've just gotta get to class."

"He's right," I told Sara. "What are you trying to be late for?"

"Calculus."

"Go. And guys? I mean what I said earlier: don't do anything that's going to put you at risk. Watch your backs. And if you hear or see anything that makes you feel at all unsafe, call me or call the police."

"Yes, Mr. Patrick," Sara moaned as she headed out the door, and I couldn't help but think she sounded a bit like me when I was talking to Andrea.

I ended the day with a preparation period and, having hidden out in my room since early morning, I opted to commit a contractual faux pas and sneak out of the building early, figuring I could check on the status of my insurance claim, figure out how long I was going to be without a home of my own, and while I was at it, how long I'd be driving the rolling gymnasium that had become my transportation. My mistake lay in forgetting that my car was parked several blocks away due to my pre-school avoidance of the media. As I walked toward the staff parking lot, I unwittingly met the still-swarming horde of media types awaiting opportunities for more shots at grieving students and their frightened parents. Before I could correct my mistake, they were on me.

"Mr. Patrick? Did you find it difficult coming to school today?"

"Mr. Patrick. How were the students in your classes?"

"Do you think someone at the school is responsible?"

"Do the police think the same person who burned down your home is responsible for Tim Morgan's murder?"

Among the barrage of questions, I managed to mutter a standard "I have no comment at this time," principally because the comments I wanted to make would not make it to air uncensored, and my employer would surely not be pleased to see me cussing out the media in front of the school. On the other hand, I was sure back-pedaling away from the press scrum wouldn't exactly play well either. Within a moment, reporters and camera operators had formed a circle around me, making exit a perilous option, and for surely the millionth time in my life, I allowed common sense to sit mutely in one corner of my brain while I answered a few questions as non-committally as I could.

"Obviously I am very saddened by the events of this past weekend. It's an unspeakably cowardly act that has been committed, and I am confident the police will bring the perpetrator to justice." *There you go, Furlo: a vote of confidence from my court. You're welcome.*

"What role are you playing in the investigation?"

"None whatsoever."

"Is it true the police have made an arrest related to the case?"

"You'd have to ask them."

"Do you believe someone at the school is involved?"

"I have no reason to believe that is or is not the case." Lawyer-speak.

"Why the hell are you making a gay issue out of this?"

I didn't have a quick comeback to what seemed an odd question. Even the rest of the media was momentarily quieted by the hostile outburst. "Excuse me?" was all I could muster.

"It's obvious this is a gay bashing. Tim Morgan was murdered because he was gay. Why are you investigating members of the gay community?" I felt the heads of the reporters turn back to me as the verbal ball landed on my side of the court.

"I'm not investigating anyone or anything," I reiterated. Like an audience at Wimbledon, the media's heads once again turned back to my inquisitor. I looked at the young man who had suddenly garnered all of our attention, trying to recognize him. He held a notebook and pen and one of those over-the-shoulder tape recorders with a microphone pointed in my direction.

"Then why have you been investigating Tim Morgan's boyfriend, the same boyfriend you went to court for to ensure he could accompany Tim to the school grad dance?"

So much for my Saturday evening soiree at Celebrities staying on the down-low. "Once again, I reiterate I am not an investigator."

"But you did talk to Tim Morgan's boyfriend?" This time it was another reporter who asked the question, picking up on the scent of a fresh angle introduced by the reporter I assumed came from the "gay press."

"I have spoken to Mr. Pedersen, yes." This would have seemed as good a moment as any to lie outright, but it was clear at least the one reporter had information to the contrary. Besides, Mr. and Mrs. Patrick raised a lawyer, not a liar, though I had had plenty of police officers assure me they considered the terms more or less synonymous.

"What was the nature of that conversation?"

"I won't comment on that."

"Do you consider Van Pedersen a suspect in Tim Morgan's death?"

"It's not for me to determine who is or who is not suspect in an open homicide investigation."

"So you don't think this is a hate crime?"

"I think any time someone is murdered, it's a hate crime."

"Why were you questioning Tim Morgan's friends and associates at a gay nightclub when this is so obviously the work of a homicidal homophobe?" The other reporters again dropped their questions and turned to the newcomer. I tried to look for a clear pathway through the throng to make my exit. None materialized. Great. My mother would see on tonight's news that I was spending my Saturday evenings in a gay bar. I would be sending her to an early grave. Or at least that's what she would be telling me as soon as she saw the news. I wondered how quickly I could change my cell number. "Hasn't Vancouver's gay community been through enough without you tarnishing its image, you of all people?" I knew he meant that I had been representing Tim in his legal challenge, but my mother wouldn't see it that way. Would it be inappropriate to have Ingrid phone my mother to tell her she'd kissed me?

"I have no further comment."

"Mr. Patrick? If you're not investigating the crime why were you at ...?"

"Celebrities," the inquisitor helpfully provided.

"Why were you at Celebrities talking to Tim Morgan's friends?"

"I have no comment."

"So you do think the murderer is a member of Vancouver's gay community?"

"No comment." Seeing no exit, I began pushing my way through the reporters back toward the school, not wanting the mob to follow me on my four-block journey back to my rental mini-van. Bad enough I was being "outed" in the local media; I didn't need people seeing my ride too. I might never date again. I was remembering now why I always advised people never to talk to the media, especially if it was spontaneous and not in a controlled interview setting.

"So do you think this was a lover's quarrel?"

"A jealous boyfriend?"

"Is there a suspect in the school? Do you think it was a student?"

"Or a teacher?"

I almost stopped to respond, but I knew anything I said would somehow be distorted. I hoped that particular query would not make it onto the evening news; my refusal to respond to the question would surely deliver the message that I did, in fact, think a teacher was involved. Damned if I answered, damned if I didn't. Why are all the jokes about lawyers instead of reporters? I continued to push my way gently through the group of soundbite-hungry bodies, ignoring their questions outright, and as my foot found purchase on school property, I could feel the pack come to a halt, though the questions were still shouted at my departing back. I wasn't too surprised, I suppose, to find Bill Owen in the school doorway observing my interaction with the fourth estate. Reading his expression, I gathered he was not pleased.

"What the hell are you doing?" he hissed at me as I got to the door. My mood-reading skills were in top shape.

"Going into the school. And how are you this afternoon?" I stepped past him and opened the door, anxious to leave behind the scolding sure to accompany his expletives but figuring I'd be able to limit its ferocity by putting myself within earshot of students. Don McFadden had been lurking just inside the door.

"You're holding press conferences in front of the school now? The school district has an official spokesperson, and it isn't you," Owen continued. My plan to avoid further confrontation by moving indoors had failed. The heads in the nearest classroom with an open door all turned towards the hallway and Owen's not-so-muted attack.

"I wasn't holding a press conference. I was going to my car, and they stopped me. I forgot I'd parked a few blocks away to avoid the media in the first place."

"You forgot?" Owen asked sarcastically.

"Yeah, I forgot. I've kind of had a lot of things on my mind today, you know, what with being more concerned about my students than the coverage we're receiving in the local media." You know when you're hoping to insult someone with a cutting remark but it just comes out as babble?

"And where were you even going? School's not over yet." He had me there.

"I had some business I had to take care of," I offered up lamely. Owen smiled like a spider that had just watched the fly drop right into his web. He was about to speak when he was beaten to the punch by the principal.

"It was school-related business, I'm sure," Don McFadden more stated than asked. I tried not to smile.

"Of course."

Owen looked again like he might just explode at any moment. "Give me a break."

"If there's nothing else, I'll be going. I think I'll head out the back of the school and escape across the field."

"Good idea," McFadden agreed.

And I did. I managed to manoeuvre my way once again through the school's adjoining side streets to my mini-van.

The full onslaught of rush hour had not yet commenced, though by two thirty in the afternoon, the volume was already reaching the state of mayhem that faced commuters as they fled the downtown core for the relative affordability of the suburbs. I found myself driving toward my old apartment building. Not having seen it in the week since the fire, I wondered if they'd begun restoring it. Even as I made my way into Kitsilano, I found myself longing for home. It had only been a week and already I missed the vibrancy of my neighbourhood, the people on the street, the proximity to the beach, and the variety of homes and styles that made it such a unique place. Sandi's place was luxurious but lacked the character of the bustling streets around my condo. Even when we were together, we'd lived in the same neighbourhood, though in a decidedly larger and fancier version of home.

I wasn't sure exactly what I was expecting, but it was more than what I encountered as I pulled up in front of the ruins of what had once been a reasonably upscale condominium. Though I was aware the fire had pretty much obliterated the third floor, it was clear the entire building was beyond repair. Through the windows of second floor apartments large chunks of debris from the ceiling could be seen protruding into the suites. Even from the street, the damage to the second floor caused not only by the fire but by the water was obvious. The whole western corner of the building was open to the elements. It hit me for the first time that the building would need to be torn down and rebuilt. My knowledge of structural integrity being limited to renovation shows on the Home and Garden channel, I'd figured they could simply rebuild the third floor on top of the second. The yellow tape that still enclosed the entire building told me otherwise.

"It's pretty unbelievable, isn't it?"

I turned in surprise, wakened from my contemplative melancholy. My neighbour from down the hall, Yoga Lady, as I'd dubbed her in the heat of the escape moment, had quietly sidled up to me with Aspen in tow.

"Yes. It's unbelievable. Hi, Aspen. How are you doing?"

In response Aspen flung herself at me in that way only small children really can. I squatted down to receive her hug. "Winston!" she squealed. Apparently I had made a friend. I picked her up in my arms to face her mother.

"You know, I never really got a chance to say thank you for what you did that night."

"It's nothing," I started, but Yoga Lady cut me off.

"No. Don't say that. It was something. It was everything. That night will haunt me forever. I was just so stunned I didn't know what to do. The thought that I might have made it out and she wouldn't have...." She turned and looked at the building again.

"Hey," I told her quietly. "She did make it out. You did as you were ordered, and that's the right thing. Besides, I don't think I could have held onto you on the edge of the balcony."

She paused while she composed herself then turned back to me with a slight smile. "I'm pretty heavy, huh?"

"No, it's not that. I just meant ..."

"I know what you meant." She laughed a little. "Winston, I'll never forget that. You saved Aspen's life, and by doing so you saved my life. So just let me say thank you."

"You're welcome." We savoured a moment of satisfied silence. "So did you find a good place to stay?"

"We're staying with my parents until we figure out what happens next. It's a bit awkward going back home again, but we make do. How about you?"

"I'm staying with my ex-wife, who's pregnant and ready to give birth in about a week to some new guy's kid, so I may have you beat in the awkward department."

She laughed. "You win."

She seemed really nice, and I kicked myself that this lovely woman had lived just a few feet away from my front door, and I'd never taken the chance to really meet her until our lives had been burned apart.

She sighed as she looked at the remnants of our home. "It really was a great location. Despite the leaks and the tarps and god knows how many thousands we've paid into renovations, I'm going to miss living here."

"Yeah. Me too." Whatever lift in mood her short visit had brought me was beginning to dissipate as I remembered her home was destroyed because of the events in my life. I might as well have lit the match myself, though she didn't say so.

"Winston, are you going to come visit us?" Aspen asked suddenly.

There was an awkward pause as I looked back and forth from Aspen to her mother, whose name I could not yet recall, making it seem all the less likely I would be remaining in touch.

"I'd like that, Aspen, especially since I don't get to see you in the hallways any more." Yoga Lady smiled at my response. Maybe the way to a woman's heart was through her child. Aspen let out a little "yay."

"Listen," I told her quietly. "I feel awful about what happened here. I've caused you and everyone else a lot of turmoil. If I had any idea this would have happened, I …"

"You what? Wouldn't have helped out your student? Wouldn't have stood up for his rights?" I must have appeared stunned. "Yes, Winston. I heard about your cause. I heard you on the radio and saw you in the papers. I was proud to be your neighbour. If I was going to lose my home, at least it was in support of a worthy cause." This woman had an amazing ability to put a positive spin on her world coming apart. Maybe I needed to take up yoga.

"We'd better get going," she said. "I hope we can keep in touch. Who knows how long it will be before we're right down the hall?" She reached into her purse, pulled out a business card and handed it to me. "Give me a call sometime."

"I will," I promised and felt the little lift in my mood. Positive attention from members of the opposite sex was not something to which I was generally accustomed, so when it came, I tried to relish the moment. The three of us turned back toward the sidewalk, where we'd left our respective vehicles. Yoga Lady loaded her daughter into a sleek little black Volvo I had seen in the parking garage.

"Wow," she said as she headed for the driver's door. "I guess you do see kids in your future."

"What do you mean?" I asked.

She pointed to the beige wonder on wheels. "You're all set up. A man who plans ahead." I laughed with her as she got into the car and drove away. I looked at the mini-van and told it, "Okay. You've got one mark in your favour." As I sat down in the faux velvet driver's seat, I looked at the business card in my hand and was disappointed by what I saw: Kitsilano Yoga Studio, with an address and telephone number.

I still didn't know Yoga Lady's name.

Chapter Nineteen

Super Cop was awaiting me when I walked through the door to Sandi's apartment. Sandi was sitting on the couch opposite, regaling Andrea with stories of the life of a pregnant woman. To her credit, Andrea was doing her polite best to appear interested, but from the apartment doorway I could tell she was less than enthralled with the conversation; she'd leapt to her feet at my arrival.

"Where have you been?" she demanded, and though the subtext was intended to be "bodyguard worry," the tone told me her question was more accusatory at my complicity in having her spend alone time with my ex-wife.

"It's three thirty," I told her. "School ends at three. Shouldn't you be praising me for heeding your wishes and coming straight home?"

"As if you got out of there and down here in half an hour."

"I had a last period prep."

"So you left early."

"Yep."

"So you didn't come straight home."

"You *are* a detective. I stopped by my old place to see how it was doing."

She didn't look terribly pleased. "You don't think that was dangerous?"

"I didn't go in. There's not much left to go into."

"Whoever burned it down knows where you lived, remember?"

"And they've probably seen the damage they did. You don't think the person is going to hang out in front of a building that's no longer inhabitable just in case I happen to show up?"

"It's possible. You did show up."

I shook my head. "Fine. Good point. Hi Sandi," I said, finally acknowledging my ex-wife. I was sure she would have something to say about how long it took me to notice her presence.

"I was starting to think I was invisible." See?

"Invisible?" *Look at the size of you* was the line wanting to come out of my mouth. I may be a wise-ass on occasion, but I'm no idiot. "Why, you're a glowing vision of loveliness."

"Ha, ha," she replied. You can't even pay a pregnant person a compliment.

I turned back to Andrea. "Why are you here anyway? Shouldn't you be out clearing the streets of unwanted gang-bangers?"

She smiled at me. "Super Cop strikes again."

"You caught someone?"

"Last night. I spent the night and today on paperwork. Slam dunk, baby."

Andrea was notoriously meticulous filing reports after an arrest. After working for days straight, one would think that a night's sleep was earned, but she always wanted to get the paperwork done right away while the adrenaline was still flowing. Of course, I realized she would now have time on her hands to baby-sit me, so I ought to stroke her ego a little to keep her in a good frame of mind.

"I thought these gang-on-gang shootings rarely get cleared?"

"They do." She spent the next fifteen minutes regaling us with her account of her foray into Vancouver's seedy underworld of drug dealers and traffickers, unravelling the business dealings of her victim until she had a clear trail to her suspect.

"Did you get a confession?"

"Didn't need one. I've built an airtight case. His lawyer'll tell him to cop a plea once he sees everything I've got on him."

"Yes, we're known for that."

"If you were, we could unclog the ridiculous court system and lock up more bad guys."

"And solve those pesky inflated real estate prices by simply filling up vacant land with more prisons."

"You'd rather have them out on the street?"

"We could start by addressing the problems that led them to crime in the first place."

"Oh please," Sandi interrupted, hauling herself up off the couch. "You're not going to get into one of those conversations again?" She waddled off into the kitchen. She was right. We'd hiked that argumentative trail many times with no clear victor. Now it was more or less habit; I think we'd even changed sides a couple of times just to keep it fresh.

"Hormones," Andrea mouthed.

"Dare you to tell her that."

"I took off my Kevlar at the station."

"Chicken."

"Damned straight. How were things back at school for the first day?"

I filled her in on the events of the day, including my visit from Furlo and Smythe, which raised a smile, and Ben's assertion the school counsellor was a "raging homophobe." She may have just cleared a major Vancouver homicide, but by the time I had finished describing what little more I knew — or thought I knew — she already had her game face on and was in detecto-contemplative mode.

"So are you liking anyone new for this?"

"I don't even know who I was liking before."

"Boyfriend's clean, at least as far as priors go."

"I thought you were working your own case?"

"I told you I finished up. I poked around a little. So what about his counsellor, the raging homophobe, as your student calls him?"

I shrugged. "Can't say as I know him very much other than to say hello. I've had very little contact with him beyond the odd memo."

"And his memos don't scream 'I hate homos' in the subtext?"

"Not that I've picked up on, but then I'm not a trained supersleuth."

"True."

"And it's a long way to go from 'I think I can counsel gay kids into being straight' to torching my apartment and killing a kid."

"Also true," she said. "You've given this some thought. Still, he might be worth looking at. I'll run him tomorrow and see what pops up."

"Nothing will. We all did criminal record checks. He's not going to have anything that hints at child abuse or violence or he wouldn't be there."

"Assuming your system works."

"You're doubting the system?"

"I'm doubting your system, not *the* system. *The* system works. I'm living proof of that. Did you mention it to Furlo and Smythe?"

I thought about it and realized my conversation with Ben had taken place after they had left. "No. I suppose I ought to call them. Unless ..."

"Unless?"

"Unless it's too trivial and would distract them from the real detecting. I could just talk to him first, feel him out."

"Sure, and if he's the guy that killed your student and torched your place, that shouldn't put you at any risk whatsoever."

"I'm pretty sure he isn't."

"Oh well, as long as you're pretty sure, it should be okay."

"I'm just saying I don't want to unnecessarily expose one of our teachers to a police interrogation. The kids need counselling right now. I don't want to see this guy's reputation ruined over an allegation. I'll talk to him. If I think there's anything to it, I'll call them right away."

"Fair enough. Just make sure you do it at school, where he's unlikely to do anything to you."

"I'm not completely incapable of taking care of myself, you know."

She muttered something that could have been meant as encouragement but was much too sarcastic to be seriously considered so.

"What about the dad? I really got a vibe that he was not okay with Tim's sexuality when I talked to him about the threats and the original assaults."

"I don't know," I admitted. "I've never met him. He didn't come to parent-teacher interviews, and I didn't see him at the hospital."

"What about a memorial service? Any word on that?"

It struck me just then that there had been no mention of a funeral or memorial for Tim. "You know what? I haven't heard anything from the school or parents."

"That strike you as odd?"

"A little, yes."

She nodded again. "Oh, well. We've got lots to work on."

"I think you mean 'they' have lots to work on. Remember those colleagues of yours who don't take kindly to having you meddle?"

"I'll be careful. After I drop you off at school tomorrow, I'll poke around some."

"You're dropping me off?"

"And picking you up. I'm back on guard detail."

"Great."

"I thought you'd be happy. Come on. Let's eat."

We walked up to Georgia Street and went to the White Spot near Denman. Despite its recent attempts to move moderately upscale, the venerable chain to me would always be about "legendary" burger platters and milk shakes served in those 1950s vintage stainless steel cups. I tried to limit my "Spot" experiences to preserve my cardiac well-being, but it always pleased Andrea to take me there, because it was kind of a cop-food place to go. We talked about her case some more and what she referred to as my case.

Having Andrea drop me off at work the next morning at least achieved the small victory of avoiding the press outside the building, what with reporters seeking the beige wonder. Having seen myself quoted in the *Vancouver Sun* and the *Globe and Mail,* I knew some follow-up from reporters would be sought. As a general rule, I didn't bother with local television newscasts, but I was fairly confident that if the print media had bothered to pick up my *faux pas* in the sidewalk scrum, I had likely made the local television news as well and would be less than popular with my colleagues. Avoiding the staff room even more than usual seemed prudent, at least for a couple of days. I hoped perhaps fellow teachers would recognize my comments as being taken out of context and would know I wasn't suspicious of them.

Good luck was either with me or laughing in my face. After avoiding the expected media hordes, I walked headlong into Steve Plum, our allegedly homophobic counsellor, as he made his way down the hallway. "You're here early," I said by way of greeting, trying to keep an accusatory tone from my voice.

"Ceremony's in two days," he said, his Australian twang not at all masked despite his decade in Canada. "Somehow I've become in charge of it for the past five years. I'm not quite sure how it happened, but once you get tasked with grad, you never really get to let it go, unless someone's just busting to have a go at it. You're not busting to have a go at it, are you?"

"I'm rarely busting to have a go at anything besides surviving my first year in the classroom, which I do by frequently busting open a bottle of red wine."

"Yeah, first year's a real bugger," he said wistfully, sounding more clichéd than even the most trite beer commercial. I wouldn't have been surprised to hear him offer to toss a shrimp on the barbie. "Sorry about Tim, mate. I've been meaning to check in with you, but with all the kids needing our support, I'm afraid I've let staff needs slip. How are you holding up?"

"I'm fine, really. Thanks for asking, though." He seemed perfectly genuine in his concern both for the kids and for me. It was hard to imagine he was the gay basher described by Ben, let alone one who could kill, but I didn't know what a homicidal homophobe ought to look like. This seemed like it might be the only opportunity to bring up the uncomfortable topic. "Say, Steve. Did you ever counsel Tim?"

"I did. He was in my caseload, so I certainly had dealings with him. We weren't close or anything." I thought I detected a shift in his tone, that he might have become a bit reserved. "Why do you ask?"

Why indeed. I thought it might go better if I was little less than completely forthright. "I just wondered if maybe he had given some indication that there were problems, maybe with someone here at the school."

He looked at me cautiously. "What kind of problems?"

"I don't know. Personality conflict, a falling out he might have had with another student or …" I hesitated briefly. "Or maybe a teacher."

"Jeez, mate, you're a piece of work, aren't you?"

"Excuse me?"

"You think one of your colleagues killed a student because he was gay?"

"I think no such thing, Steve," I tried to insist.

"Then why are you asking me about teachers if you don't think they're guilty?"

"I don't believe there's a cabal of educators attacking kids, no," I continued in the calm, lawyerly voice I generally reserved for hostile witnesses in pre-trial depositions.

"So you think it's just one?" He stared me down. A picture was forming in my head of the kind of anger this admittedly large Australian could generate. How cool would I be among my students if I got into a fight with one of the other staff members, I wondered. Looking at the imposing counsellor, I realized the answer was not very, considering the pounding I would be likely to take. "Shit, you think it's me, don't you?" he continued when I didn't immediately respond.

"Steve," I began, but he cut me off before I could get any further.

"Why the hell would I want to kill one of my students?"

"Steve …"

"My job is to help kids, not to hurt them. I don't even know you. How in the hell could you have formed such a low opinion of me already?"

"Steve …" I said, and wondered if that would be the only word I'd be able to say, however long our conversation lasted.

"I worked with that boy since the eighth grade, and I've been nothing but helpful to him. I'm offended you'd suspect I'd have done anything to harm him."

"I never suggested any such thing," I blurted out quickly, skipping his first name, as that had only served to have me cut off. "If you had worked with him, it was possible he might have told you about people with whom he was experiencing difficulties. That's all I was trying to find out. You don't think the police are going to ask you the exact same question?"

"They already did, mate. But at least they were just doing their jobs." He turned and walked away from me, seething. I debated letting it drop, but my conversation with Ben niggled away at the back of my head, information Furlo and Smythe would not have had when they questioned Tim's counsellor.

"Steve, wait." I had to hustle to catch up to him as he strode angrily up the hallway. He was fast. No wonder his fellow countrymen go on walkabouts all over the world: at the rate he was going, he'd surely run out of Australia before he ran out of steam. I came alongside and matched his pace. "Look, let me be honest with you."

"Oh, great. So you've been lying to me thus far?"

"Well, I am a lawyer." Try the self-deprecating humour route.

He stopped. Everyone likes a good lawyer bashing. "That's true."

I sighed. "A student, who shall remain nameless, referred to you as kind of homophobic."

"So you think that makes me a killer." It wasn't really a question.

"The student says you tried to counsel him out of being gay, that you could get him help realize he was making a mistake. He also told me you tried the same approach with Tim."

He stared hard at me again, and while my dig at my fellow members of the bar had brought momentary pause, it was clear he was still fuming. "Teenagers are often confused about their sexuality. I don't want them making a big mistake that could harm them the rest of their lives."

"You think being gay is a mistake, a phase they're going through?"

"I do, most of the time, yes."

"Steve, that's ridiculous," I said before I could stop myself.

"Oh, I see you're an expert in human sexuality now?"

"Are you?" I always hate it when someone answers a question with a question, but when debating with a lunatic, it can be an effective rhetorical device. Or at least it fills the air while one tries to grapple with the idiocy of the argument.

"There is plenty of research that shows many gay teenagers can be turned back with the right counselling."

I could imagine the type of lunatic fringe research he referred to in justifying his opinion. Maybe I was more progressive than I was giving myself credit for. "So when kids come to you with anxiety over their sexual preference, you try to talk them out of it? That's absurd."

"I present them with options. That's what a good counsellor does."

I tried to press forward. "So in those option-presenting sessions, Tim never gave any indication he was having difficulty with anyone in particular?"

"We haven't had those kinds of conversations in a long time. And no, he didn't tell me there was a homophobic teacher stalking him."

"And your conversations weren't at all heated." I knew I'd crossed the line before the sentence even finished leaving my lips. It was a sixth sense I had about the impact of words. Unfortunately it was a delayed sixth sense. I'd yet to manage to train it to engage before my mouth was put in gear.

"Heated?" he nearly shouted. "Heated as in 'did I yell at him for being gay and then kill him a year later?' Jesus, not only is that offensive, it's stupid. If I was going to kill Tim because he was gay, don't you think I would have done it when we were actually talking about it rather than a year later? I hope you're not planning a third career as a detective, because you might just be an idiot."

I figured this wouldn't be the time to float the idea of the Ingrid Svetlik and Winston Patrick Detective Agency that had seemed so promising just a few nights earlier. "A year ago Tim wasn't receiving the kind of attention he was now."

"So now I've gone homicidal not just because a student is gay but because he's gay and in the media? That's just fucking stupid. I'd be more likely to want to kick your arse than his."

"So now you're threatening me?"

"Christ, mate, it's a bloody expression. Fucking lawyers. You're unbelievable." He took a deep breath. "If you don't mind, I've got work to do, and if I keep talking to you, I might just end up popping you one." He gave me what was probably a little shove on the chest but the effect was enough to make me stumble backwards. As he turned and walked away from me, I opted not to follow. If his little shove was any indication of the amount of force Steve Plum was capable of producing, I didn't relish the thought of being 'popped' by him, which could only mean a punch. I gave him a moment to get well ahead of me then turned the hallway corner and nearly tripped over Nathan Donaldson, who was sitting with his back up against a locker. "Good morning," I said feebly.

He looked up at me. "Sounds like that went well."

I realized, apart from how much I'd pissed off a colleague, how brutally unprofessional we'd been in having a heated argument in a public hallway. It was early in the morning, but one never really knows what early morning activities might bring students into the school when one least expects them to be there. One more mental note to add to my checklist of things to do as an educator: don't accuse fellow teachers of committing hate crimes within earshot of students. There was just so much to remember in this job. "What brings you here so early? Got a practice or something?"

"Couldn't sleep. Figured I might as well get up and come to school. Thought it might be a quiet place to hang out this early. Guess I was wrong on that one." It sounded like just a touch of his usual humour might be returning.

"And yet you don't even have your law textbook in front of you. Just imagine how you could have been getting in some studying for your final exam." Might as well make this a teaching moment.

He looked down at the floor. "Yeah, imagine." I slumped down onto the floor next to him, noticing how dirty it was and wondering what the ass of my new pants would look like when I got up and how unseemly it would seem to be brushing my own butt as I walked down the hallway. "How are you doing this morning?"

He sighed. "Oh, I'm fine. I just didn't want to sit at home, cuz I knew Sara would probably call and pester me. Ironically, I figured I'd come here to get away from all this, and I got to hear your interrogation of Mr. Plum. And of course Sara has texted me about ten times since I got here anyway. I haven't bothered to read them."

"Is Sara okay?" I asked.

"She's organizing some kind of march for justice for Tim. Her and some members of some gay pride group are gonna descend on the art gallery demanding Tim's killer be brought to justice or something." He waved his arms in disdain. I wondered what Sara hoped to achieve. It isn't uncommon for vigils and marches to be held after someone is killed, as though if people gather together and yell, police will be better able to capture the perpetrator. For Sara it was no doubt part of her grieving process to get involved in something she thought might help.

"I take it you don't think it's a good idea."

Nathan sighed. "I just want it all to be over. I don't want to fight causes any more. I just want to get through these last few weeks and get the hell outta here."

"Yeah," I said, and lacking anything more profound to offer, I said nothing. We sat for several minutes staring silently at the lockers.

"Well, I'm sure you've got things to do," Nathan finally said, essentially giving me permission to leave.

"Are you okay?" I asked lamely.

"I'll be all right. Thanks for listening to me vent."

"Any time." I got up, dusted myself off as best as I could and walked quietly away. I didn't feel great about leaving him alone, but I'd run out of things to say, and Nathan looked as though he needed some alone time. For the next hour and a half, I spent my time squirrelled away in my classroom, absorbed in marking student work, but neither my heart nor my head were really into it. About every three minutes I got up and looked out the window at the diminishing members gathered on the sidewalk. Tim's murder was now three days old, an eternity in press time. About fifteen minutes before class began, I saw Sara on the sidewalk with a circle of reporters around her. I turned on the radio on the ancient portable stereo on my shelf, but no one was carrying her address live.

By the time classes began, the press had drifted away in pursuit of other stories. Though there were fewer outward displays of uncontrolled grieving by students, most were less than their normally unfocused selves as I tried hard to push through my lessons for the day. As I ventured down to the office at lunchtime to check for messages, I sensed both students and teachers clearing a broader path for me than needed. For much more than the first time since my arrival, I felt my presence in the building was less than welcome, the students no doubt viewing me as mobile bad karma, the few teachers I'd passed eyeing me suspiciously. There was only one other teacher in the letter tray room, a business education teacher named Jack, whose greeting was limited to turning his back on me and heading to the photocopier in the corner. I quickly tried to gather my paperwork from the letter tray and disappear before I made anyone more uncomfortable than they needed to be, but before I could make it to the door, Jack addressed me.

"I have an alibi for Friday night."

"Excuse me?"

"Just thought I'd clear that up in case you were looking at me for Tim's murder," he snorted. It was an invitation to an argument.

"Good to know," I offered in place of a retort. I had one hand on the door handle, but my colleague wanted to continue.

"Because I wouldn't want you thinking I'm some sort of gay-bashing killer."

"Definitely."

"I even have witnesses." I could sense his frustration at my lack of engagement.

"Okay then." I opened the door to step out in the hallway.

"You're an asshole," he said to my back, loud enough that students hanging around in the hallway on their lunch hour turned and looked our way. I let the door close and stepped back into the room.

"You'd have no difficulty finding others with the same opinion," I told him. "Particularly my ex-wife."

"How can you believe I'd be a killer?"

I hadn't given him any specific thought. In fact, I wasn't sure I even knew his last name. "I have no reason to believe you're a killer."

"But I'm a suspect," he insisted.

"Are you?" I asked, trying to turn it around.

"Well, you're investigating the staff of the school, particularly Tim's teachers, from what I hear."

"Then you hear incorrectly. I'm not investigating anyone. I'm teaching. Do I want to see Tim's killer caught? Absolutely. But do I think I'm the one who's going to catch him? No."

"So you don't think it's one of us then?"

I sighed. I really didn't want to lie to him and tell him I thought it impossible, but I had to work with these people. "I have no specific reason to believe it's a teacher, no."

"Typical lawyer talk," he hissed, and I knew further conversation was pointless. I should have stuck to my original plan of not engaging him and just walked away.

"Yeah," I told him. "I got an A in Weasel Words 101." I turned and exited. It was going to be a long week.

I managed to spend the rest of the day and all of Wednesday without communicating with any of the teaching staff beyond a courteous nod or "good morning" to those I passed in the hallways. Many of the greetings were ignored. I didn't keep an official tally, but I estimated more than half those I encountered either ignored me or sent hostile glares my way. I managed to pick up messages from my mailbox early enough that no one was present to berate me. It's hard to conceive of being completely isolated in a workplace with over a thousand people, but I felt empathy for the new kid who found himself completely alone in a sea of people. I was nearly ready to leave when Sara appeared at my doorway.

"Hi," I said.

"Are you coming?" she asked.

"Coming where?" I had been sufficiently absorbed in my self-pity that it had slipped my mind that Sara's rally for justice was going to take place at five o'clock, just in time for the height of the afternoon rush hour. She looked at me with the kind of exasperation I normally got from Sandi or Andrea or my mother. "Oh, right, the rally."

"Yeah, right. The rally."

I hadn't planned on attending. As a general rule, I don't like crowds. I find rallies annoying when I see them on television, and I seriously doubt their effectiveness in criminal justice matters. I had attended one student protest in my entire university and law school career; when they broke into "We Shall Overcome," it was more than I could take, and I had to leave. I had really only gone because of my desire to impress the attractive woman in my Law 270 Civil Procedures class. Neither the rally nor my attempt to attract my classmate had borne fruit. Looking at Sara standing in my doorway, one hand on her hip, I didn't see a way I could gracefully decline. "Of course I'm coming. I wouldn't miss it." Chickened out again.

The doubts I'd had on the cab ride downtown about how much promotion a high school student could produce to get recognition for her cause were quickly dispelled. For reasons difficult to ascertain, the Vancouver

Art Gallery was the site of nearly every significant protest that occurred in the city, and they were varied and frequent. On any given day, pedestrians walking by the steps of the turn-of-the-twentieth-century building could find at least one group handing out pamphlets, holding signs or singing songs of advocacy. When large protests needed a place to gather, the steps and lawn on the north side facing Georgia Street were most often utilized, though it displaced the street kids who made the steps their daytime home.

I arrived shortly before five o'clock to find a crowd I estimated to be a few hundred strong already gathered and ready to listen to the speakers assembling on the stone steps. I was expecting a group looking much like the party-goers Ingrid and I had encountered at Celebrities — and they were there to be sure — but the crowd was a much broader mix: students, grandmothers, young-to-middle-aged office workers, and the professional protesters that appeared at any and every rally, regardless of cause. A few tourists from the Alaska cruise ship runs lingered on the fringes of the crowd, expensive cameras wrapped around their necks, probably wondering if a concert was about to begin. I scanned the crowd looking for familiar faces and wasn't sure if I was disappointed or relieved that I didn't see any. I suddenly felt very much out of place. As I worked my way forward, a few people I could clearly identify as members of the gay community recognized me and offered either their thanks for my efforts at bringing Tim's original cause to light, or less than gracious epithets for what they perceived as my attempt to refocus the investigation as a gay community issue rather than a hate crime. To both I simply smiled and kept moving.

I was nearly at the front when I heard Sara's voice coming through the pole-mounted speakers. I couldn't yet make her out through the assembled masses. As I reached the front of the assembled protesters, I saw a man who Tim would have become, had he survived another twenty-five years. Tim's father was standing just off to the side of the steps, beside his wife, who I'd met briefly in the hospital. Nathan Donaldson stood more or less with them, staring away from Sara, whose speech was just concluding. As she introduced a prominent member of some activist group, I managed to approach Tim's parents. "I'm so sorry for your loss," I practically had to yell due to our proximity to the loudspeakers.

"Thank you," I think I heard Mrs. Morgan mutter, though I couldn't be sure.

I introduced myself to Tim's father, who stood stoically observing the crowd with what seemed a mixture of anger and disgust. "I know this must be difficult for you," I said.

"More than you know," he told me, scowling. "I'm only here because Sara managed to drag us. My wife thought it would look bad if we didn't come."

"How so?"

"Because we'd look like we don't care if Tim's killer is caught. At this point, I really don't."

"I understand you're grieving, but don't you think Tim would have wanted his killer brought to justice?"

"Why the hell would that matter? Now if they catch someone, we just get to parade Tim's life in front of the media even more. Do you have any idea what that's going to be like for our family?"

Andrea had told me Tim's father was gruff. I had been expecting his gruffness might have been muted, given the loss of his son. Apparently it ran deep. "Still, in the interest of protecting someone else who may be hurt, it's important that we continue to search for his killer." He grunted some sort of half-hearted agreement. I turned towards his wife, whose grief at least appeared to be more genuine than her spouse's. "Are you planning a memorial service?" Someone on the platform began singing a cappella, trying to get the crowd to sing along. It wasn't a song I'd heard, nor apparently had the crowd, as only a few voices managed to join in.

Tim's father interrupted his wife before she could respond. "What would be the point?" he demanded. "Inviting all of these people to make a spectacle of our family one more time?" He swept his arm derisively towards the crowd. My back was to the protesters, so I couldn't see if anyone was aware of his gesture.

I nodded, trying to show my understanding. "I take it you didn't approve of Tim's, uhm, lifestyle?" For the first time, Nathan seemed to notice my presence, though he'd been standing right next to Tim's mother the whole time. As I asked the question, his eyes kind of widened, as though sending me a signal not to proceed.

"No, Mr. Patrick. I did not approve of his lifestyle, as you call it. Obviously you did, with your little lawsuit project."

"It really wasn't my place to approve or disapprove of Tim's sexuality," I told him, and the word seemed to send a jolt through him. "We were engaged in the pursuit of a higher principle," I declared self-righteously. I wondered if I was trying to convince Tim's father or still working on assuaging my own guilt.

"Well, good for you," he growled. "Now look what you've done." He nodded again with disdain towards the throng of people, which I could now see from my peripheral vision was at least swaying in unison to the song being badly performed through the sound system.

"Once again, I cannot begin to adequately express how sorry I am that our efforts may have contributed to Tim's death."

"You've put my family through hell. Everyone knows all the sordid details of his life. It's humiliating." Tim's mother touched her husband's arm lightly, gently chiding him for his outburst, but to no avail.

"With all due respect, sir, Tim's constitutional rights were being violated. I believed I had an obligation to protect those rights, not just as a teacher but as a still-current officer of the court."

"Constitutional rights? What a load of shit," he declared. "Where in the constitution does it say he can bring his fag boyfriend to a dance?"

"Anthony!" Mrs. Morgan said in a voice meant to be forceful but which had an undeniable note of resignation.

"This isn't the place for this kind of debate," I said, trying to keep my own anger in check. Given that a funeral didn't seem imminent, this might be my only opportunity to ask questions of this angry man. "I was hoping you might have any ideas about who might have wanted to hurt Tim."

"I don't know. Maybe he charged extra for that," his father hissed. Sara had joined our little group and was watching the exchange with horror. The crowd had broken into "We Shall Overcome."

"You know, sir, whatever you or I or anyone else may think of what Tim was doing online, or anywhere else, he didn't deserve to die for it."

"Maybe he did. Maybe it's better he died this way than a prolonged death from some disease he'd pick up along the way. Maybe he was spared that."

"You can't mean that. You don't really believe Tim is better off dead."

He leaned in close to me, anger burning in his eyes. "Don't tell me what I can and cannot mean. I'd rather see my son die quickly than through a long, slow, agonizing death that would nearly kill us all." The possibility of saying something I would surely regret was incredibly high. I should have left before that could happen, but too late. Out it came.

"I'm sure you have an alibi for last Friday night?" Anthony Morgan's eyes widened, and if he'd taken a swing at me, he could hardly have been blamed.

"Mr. Patrick!" I heard Nathan's voice from beside me intervening for the first time. "Leave him alone." I turned, looked at Nathan and nodded.

"I apologize," I said to Tim's father. "That was totally out of line." I stepped away from him before our debate could resume. Nathan and Sara were immediately at my side. I shook my head in disgust.

"Are you okay?" Sara asked me.

"I'm fine."

"You don't really think Tim's dad could have killed his own son?" Sara asked as we moved out of earshot.

"I don't know what I think," I admitted.

"That's ridiculous," Nathan insisted. "I've known Mr. Morgan my whole life. He's been like a second father to me. He can be an asshole, but there's no way he could kill Tim."

"Are you even fucking kidding me?" I heard an angry voice say from behind, and before I could greet Detective Furlo, my arm was grabbed and I found myself being pulled away from the steps of the building. When we were well away from the front of the crowd, Furlo finally stopped moving and spun me so we were face to face. I wasn't entirely sure my feet had been on the ground as we'd moved. "You're questioning suspects now?" he demanded, and his face looked even angrier than Mr. Morgan's had.

"I'm not questioning anyone. I'm here supporting …"

"Supporting what, a cause? An overthrow of the government? A little singalong so the cops'll catch the bad guys?"

"I'm supporting my students, who have organized this rally in memory of their friend, whose parents can't be bothered to memorialize him." Jasmine Smythe materialized from behind her partner. "And let go of my arm," I demanded.

"What the hell were you thinking?" Smythe demanded. She looked as angry as Furlo. "You were questioning the Morgans. You're going to jeopardize our investigation."

"I wasn't questioning anyone," I insisted again. "I offered my condolences to the parents. The conversation kind of went sideways from there." I paused a moment. "You're looking at Tim's dad?"

"What?" Furlo snarled.

"You said 'suspect' before. He's a raging homophobe," I said, employing my student's definition of the high school counsellor, "but do you really think he could have committed his son's murder?"

Furlo continued to boil. "How much fucking clearer can we make it? *We* investigate. *You* stay the hell away."

"I'm just saying ..."

"For god's sake, Winston," Smythe interjected. "Everyone is a suspect. Unless we've entirely ruled someone out, any conversations you have with any parties could screw up a potential case. You know that."

She was right. I did know that and I quietly chastised myself for allowing my guilt or ego to cloud my legal judgment. But that same guilt or ego wouldn't permit me to apologize for that lapse in judgment in front of Furlo. I made a mental note to do so privately to Smythe when I got the chance. I offered an olive branch instead. "One of my students mentioned something to me I thought I should tell you about." I told them about Benjamin's description of Steve Plum's plans to cure him of his sexual preferences. Despite their initial anger, both detectives listened intently.

"When did he tell you this?" Smythe asked politely.

"On Monday, just after we spoke," I replied innocently.

"And you're just telling us this now?" Furlo growled. He was right again, of course, but I was neither sufficiently brave nor foolish to inform them that I had neglected to pass on this information because I'd wanted to check its veracity myself. I offered a lame excuse that I'd been busy instead. Furlo was not impressed. "Well, shit, Patrick. We wouldn't want to interrupt your busy life with our little homicide investigation," he said.

"All right," I told them. "Message received. Loud and clear this time. I will stay out of your investigation and immediately pass along any information I'm able to obtain." Furlo opened his mouth. "Strike that," I continued. "I will immediately pass along any information that comes my way through no action on my part whatsoever. Scout's honour."

"Your honour has been a little compromised," Smythe replied. From Furlo, it would have been a snide comment, but coming from her it was a stinging rebuke. "Come on," she ordered, and I obediently followed her and her partner towards Robson Street. At least during this walk both my arms were free. Smythe waved at a young constable standing next to his police cruiser, who just as obediently rushed over. "Please take Mr. Patrick home," she said, reciting Sandi's address from memory and sounding much like Andrea, added, "Please ensure he is safely inside the suite before you leave. If he tries to resist or evade you, shoot him."

"Ma'am?" he asked.

She glanced at me without humour before replying. "You heard me."

True to his instructions, the young recruit — they all seemed young to me when they were in uniform, but this one still had acne — more or less wordlessly escorted me right to Sandi's door. I knew I was going to catch hell from Andrea for not waiting for her to pick me up at school at the end of her tour. When I closed the door, I looked out the peephole to see the officer was taking his duty seriously and posting himself in the hallway to ensure I wouldn't make a break for it. I couldn't tell how long he was going to stand there. Andy might be able to shake him loose if he didn't leave of his own accord.

Sandi and Ingrid were bustling away at crib design and room borders as I went into my room and lay down on the bed. Much to my surprise, I fell asleep long enough that when I woke it was dark, which, given that it was May, actually meant I'd had at least a few hours of sleep. Glancing at the clock, I noticed it was just past midnight. I'd had nothing to eat, it was late, and I knew the likelihood of further sleep was slight. I also knew the chance of me making it out of the apartment to go find food while Andrea was heavily armed and sleeping lightly on the living room couch was even less. I had no marking to do, no newspapers to read for several hours, my encyclopedias had burned in the fire, and getting out of the house was not an option. I was beginning to gain an appreciation for prison life. And my cell came with a view of Coal Harbour. I managed to read a Salman Rushdie novel I'd found in the back of the guest room closet, and despite its tediously descriptive language and overwrought narrative, it failed to bring more sleep. It was beyond a relief when morning finally came, not only to end the torture of Rushdie's book but because I managed to convince Andrea to allow me to drive myself to work, given that the graduation ceremony was in the afternoon and I was expected to attend. I had barely gotten in the door when both Sara and Nathan appeared in the classroom.

"Oh my god," Sara declared. "You're okay?"

"I'm fine," I assured her. "Why wouldn't I be?"

"We thought you got arrested last night."

"*She* thought you got arrested last night," Nathan corrected. "I figured she was being melodramatic again."

Sara shot her friend a warning glance. "When those two detectives took you away, they were so mad I thought for sure they were going to give you a beatdown."

"I'm sure at least one of them would have liked to, but deep down they're both good cops. They're just trying to do their jobs."

"And you were just trying to do yours," Sara insisted.

"No, Sara. They're right. I'm related to their investigation. I was Tim's counsel of record in his legal battle. If Tim's dad was in any way involved, my questioning could potentially taint their investigation."

"I guess I'll have to change the topic of this morning's press conference, huh?" My eyes widened enough that Sara blurted out, "I'm kidding." She paused, cocked her head then asked, "So what do you think?"

"I honestly don't know. I hope they're closing in on someone, but Sara, we have to let the police do their jobs."

She nodded at me conspiratorially. "I see. Let them do their jobs. You'll just keep things on the down-low."

"Sara, let it go," Nathan demanded. "Come on, let's leave Mr. Patrick to his work." He was handling his grief much less stoically than his friend.

"What about your little friend?" Sara asked. Andrea would hardly have been amused to hear of herself being referred to as my "little friend."

"I'm sure she's as unwelcome in the investigation as I am, maybe more so. Listen. Tonight's the grad ceremony. I'm sure I can't tell you not to think about Tim's murder, but try to at least focus a bit on the good things that are going to happen today. You guys have been through enough. Try to divert your attention at least a little bit."

Sara looked suspiciously at me but nodded her assent. "Okay. We'll try to do that. You keep us informed." I wasn't sure, but I think she winked at me. Nathan rolled his eyes in the way I recognized from class.

"See ya later," he said, pulling Sara by the arm. He turned at the door and said quietly, "You're coming tonight, right?"

I nodded. "Of course." He seemed satisfied, and the grieving friends left.

I spent the rest of the day holed up in my classroom, and it felt not a whole lot different than being trapped in my bedroom all night, the obvious difference being that my current cell was packed with adolescents, most of whom wanted to be there even less than I. Travelling the hallways didn't seem like an option. I wondered if I'd ever find myself a welcome member of the teaching staff. I guessed I could request a transfer, but word travels fast; I could be a pariah no matter what school I went to. I felt sorry for myself all afternoon and was packing my newly acquired briefcase after the bell rang when my cell rang. Glancing at the call display, I saw Andrea's number, and I was tempted to ignore the call and forego a lecture about looking over my shoulder and taking care of myself. But then, the ceremony didn't start until five o'clock, and I had time to kill. "Hello, Ms. Croft," I said.

"First, a test: how much do you love me?"

"Is this multiple choice? What are the options?"

"A: you love me because of my radiant beauty. B: you love me because of my physical prowess. C: you love me because I'm a master detective. Or D: all of the above."

"Hmm … that's a tough one."

"Do you want to know what I know or not?"

I surrendered. "D. All of the above. What have you detected?"

"I was poking around a little this afternoon."

"Don't get yourself in shit," I said.

I could almost see her waving me off. "Yeah, yeah. Just a couple of hours or so ago, some evidence techs came in. They found your boy's cell phone."

"What? Tim's phone? I thought they've been scouring the park for days."

"They have. Apparently some dumpster diver found the phone in the neighbourhood near the crash and tried to pawn it. Local patrol picked it up and turned it over to the evidence guys."

"Now what happens?"

"Normally they turn it in to the tech lab guys, and when they can get around to it, they do their best to recover any information they can find. It can take days."

"Shit," I complained.

"Hang on," she told me. "It can take days unless you can persuade the techie boys to drop everything they're currently working on and recover information."

"How did you manage to do that?"

"Did you not just take that multiple choice test?"

"Computer geeks have a thing for Super Cop?"

"Doesn't everyone?"

"Excellent point. Do they know who sent the text message?"

"Not exactly."

"Shit," I complained again.

"Hang on. They don't know exactly who the sender is, but they know where the message came from. Even though it was a text message, it wasn't sent from another phone. It was sent from a website. They were able to trace the exact IP address of the computer that sent the text message using some sort of encrypto-static-demobilizer thingmy. The point is, the location might be able to tell us a lot."

"Where did it come from?"

"Your school's library."

The library had seen better days. At least I hoped it had. It was a point of pride in the school that our library collection was so large, given the state of funding available for those anachronisms known as books. Like most libraries, the number of computers seemed to be competing for space with the stacks. The room also smelled a bit like the musty attic in a grandmother's old house. Still, Candace, our librarian, soldiered on in her valiant attempt to make it a welcome refuge for students or staff who needed a quiet place to work, study, or read.

The library was completely devoid of students, though Candace always kept it open beyond the four o'clock closing time. With the graduation ceremonies due to begin in a couple of hours, the senior students were all engaged in primping and preening, the juniors having long since abandoned the building. I had kind of been hoping to find the library empty so I could snoop around, though I had no idea how I would find the computer that sent the email to Tim's phone. I found Candace working alone at her desk. She looked up and smiled as I entered.

"Hello, Winston." She was always eager to help any teacher who would give her the opportunity to do so.

"Hi Candace. Sorry to bother you so late in the day. You're not going to the commencement?"

"Oh yeah. But I live out in Richmond, so it's not worth going home beforehand. I'm just catching up on some paperwork and then I'll head down." She cocked her head. "How are you doing? You've had a really tough time again lately."

"I'm all right. Thank you for asking."

I stood awkwardly, looking around the room at the rows of computers. I had no idea how to proceed. Candace allowed me to wallow in my awkwardness for a moment before offering assistance. She would have made a good retail salesperson.

"Can I help you find something?"

"I just need one of the computers," I told her.

"Help yourself," she said, but she sounded skeptical. I did have just as crappy a computer available to me in my classroom. I took a tentative few steps forward and stopped. "You're welcome to use any one you'd like," she offered helpfully.

I peered at a couple of the machines. Their blank screens stared back at me, revealing nothing about who might have sent the message inviting Tim to his death. "I'm looking for a specific one."

"They're all available. Be as specific as you want."

I sat down at a machine, flicked it on, and waited an interminable amount of time in silence as Windows started. When it finally allowed me access, I opened a browser and clicked on the "history" menu. It was blank. I was officially out of ideas.

"The history is wiped clean every day at four o'clock. Otherwise the server gets filled with thousands of bookmarked urls from the kids." I turned and saw Candace looking at the screen over my shoulder.

"Oh," I replied.

"Why don't you tell me what you're really looking for, and maybe I can help."

My choices were limited. Probably the VPD's tech guys could, in fact, look at the computers and the school's server and ultimately find the text message they were looking for. But that would take time, a warrant, and probably a hearing with the school district's legal counsel, who would try, at least for appearance's sake, to resist the potential invasion of student privacy before ultimately giving in to the interest of justice. If Candace could help me, colleague-to-colleague, I might get the same information without being poisoned by a lack of probable cause.

"Someone sent a message to Tim Morgan's phone from one of these computers on the day that he died.

The email address was anonymous. I was hoping I could find out which computer so we could trace the user login and find out who sent the message."

She nodded. I was expecting a barrage of questions, but she appeared to take my explanation at face value. "I think I can make it even easier." She turned and walked into the small glassed-in office off the side of the room, returning a moment later with a red binder in hand. "I make all the students sign in before they're permitted to use one of the computers, and sign out when they're done. That way if some kind of damage is done to one of them, I know who to go after. When was the message sent?"

"Last Friday afternoon, around four o'clock."

She smiled. "That shouldn't be too difficult. We don't have a lot of customers late on a Friday afternoon." She thumbed back a few pages. "Here. There are only two names to choose from." I looked down at the page. One was a grade eight student whose name I couldn't pronounce. The other was a name I knew well.

Nathan Donaldson.

Chapter Twenty

The Orpheum Theatre is the jewel in Vancouver's theatrical crown and is the repository of the city's theatrical history. Currently it is the highbrow cultural centre, home to the Vancouver Symphony Orchestra and the Vancouver Opera, two institutions no one wants to see depart but which few are willing to pay to support. Thus the grand old site takes in some of its funds by renting itself out as a venue for guest lectures by retired politicians, touring comedians with renown too large for the comedy club but not famous enough for the stadium, and during May and June, high school graduation commencements; or, in the modern-day inclusive parlance, the "school leaving ceremony." The theatre's gilded moldings, antique chandeliers, and assorted trappings from a bygone era loaned the ceremony an air of dignity that would be lacking in a school gymnasium. It is located in the heart of the not-yet-respectably-gentrified entertainment district on the Granville Mall, but its interior more than makes up for the rather derelict surroundings.

When I arrived at the theatre, my lack of police cruiser parking privileges meant I had to scurry from block to block seeking a parking spot, increasingly difficult at the best of times, but with the influx of John A. Macdonald parents, nearly impossible. I finally settled on a metered street spot some seven blocks from the theatre. By the time I made my way through the traffic, the ceremony had started. The afternoon sun managed to deke out from behind the labyrinth of buildings, beating down sufficiently to drench me in sweat. I was surprised to see Ingrid standing at the entrance to the theatre lobby until I recalled she had asked to come to the ceremony. My mission to talk to Nathan about his message to Tim was momentarily forgotten as I vainly attempted to re-shevel my appearance.

"I was starting to worry I'd been stood up," Ingrid said sweetly. "It was starting to feel like high school all over again."

"I find it impossible to believe anyone would ever have stood you up."

"I was a bit of an ugly duckling," she said.

I filled her in on what I'd learned at the school library. "I'm hoping he's here," I concluded.

"I don't know. Nathan and the kids are all dressed in blue gowns. It's kind of difficult to tell them apart."

I nodded. "Let's go inside, and I'll see if I can spot him." I was headed for the door when Ingrid grabbed my arm.

"Should we wait for Detective Pearson?" In my excitement I had, of course, neglected to call my super cop amigo, an omission I would surely hear about later. The delay waiting for her arrival didn't seem warranted, given the low risk of approaching my student in a crowded theatre. Besides, I still couldn't bring myself to believe Nathan had actually killed his close friend. But I needed to know why he had coaxed Tim into meeting him that night. We might well have had

Tim's killer right away if he'd come clean. I wondered who he was protecting.

"No. Let's go inside. I want to make sure he's here and doesn't leave before I can talk to him."

I opened the door to the auditorium to see Don McFadden addressing the audience with what surely were congratulations and "life is just beginning" platitudes. A few heads in the back of the theatre turned as we entered, a few lingering longer on Ingrid before returning their attention to the event. If McFadden was aware of my late arrival, he made no show of it, and I was glad the lights on the stage shielded me from his view. We took seats near the back, and I scanned the room as best I could, trying to identify Nathan from the back of the grads' heads, their fabric-covered cardboard caps and tassels bobbing as they fidgeted through the dignitaries' speeches. There was no way I could go down front to speak to Nathan without drawing attention, so I settled in to experience my first high school graduation from the "other side."

It was about as exciting as I remembered my own seventeen years earlier.

I was actually starting to believe this event might make serious inroads into curing my sleeping disorders when Bill Owen, who was officially emceeing the event, announced the presentation of the graduating class. Each student would be called individually to cross the stage to receive a meaningless piece of paper that would be replaced after exams and students knew they had actually graduated.

Knowing we'd be in for a long haul, given the number of grade twelves who had to cross the stage, I settled into my seat, trying to get comfortable. I was about to attempt to nod off when I noticed one of the stage crossers, rather than returning to her seat, had snuck up the side aisle and headed out the back. I guessed that having crossed the stage, had her picture taken, and shaken hands with the principal, she couldn't be bothered to stick it out for the announcements of award winners and the valedictory address. I was silently chastising her shallow self-involvement and simultaneously applauding her chutzpah when I noticed a second student do the same. I suddenly worried that Nathan too might make an exit after he crossed the stage. Not wanting to miss my chance to talk to him, I excused myself and made my way down to the side of the theatre, joining a couple of colleagues already stationed along the wall offering private words of congratulations to their students. I smiled and nodded to my students, trying to remain inconspicuous. Nathan Donaldson being towards the start of the alphabet, I didn't have to wait long.

My plan didn't extend beyond following Nathan out into the lobby if he left prematurely, which, given the hundreds of people in the theatre, might actually have been more desirable than trying to track him at the end of the ceremony. Andrea has told me she enjoys playing cards with me because I have the worst poker face. Her assessment proved to be correct, as Nathan crossed the stage a few minutes after I had made my way to the side of the theatre. Our eyes locked as he hit the halfway mark of the decorative proscenium, and the big, dopey smile he was sporting dropped from his face, as though my very presence was enough to ruin the celebration of the event.

I smiled and nodded in what I hoped was a congratulatory manner, but it didn't put him at ease. He nearly crashed into Don McFadden, whose outstretched hand caught him and pulled him back to the mark, smiling for the camera positioned in front of the stage to capture the moments for a fee. Nathan produced a feeble smile for posterity and limply shook the principal's hand. McFadden, whose smile was pasted and practiced, faltered only a brief moment, then looked past Nathan to the next student, whose name was already being announced. Nathan rushed across the stage. I worried he might zoom past me, and I'd create a scene bolting out after him. But he didn't descend the stairs. Instead he left the stage at the side, disappearing into the wings.

I panicked momentarily. As I glanced around the theatre, Ingrid caught my eye from her seat at the rear, gesturing at the door behind me. Taking her cue, I slipped as surreptitiously as possible through the door, finding myself in an exit hallway. A set of stairs went up to the right, where an open doorway appeared to lead to the stage proper. I fairly hopped up the stairway and stepped gingerly through the doorway, but my arrival was undetected by all except a stagehand who turned and looked at me as I arrived.

"You looking for the kid that came off the stage?" I nodded. "I tried to stop him. He's not supposed to be back here, but he went down towards the dressing rooms." He pointed past a gigantic black curtain that looked as though I might find the Wizard behind it.

"Thanks," I said and trotted off in the direction he had indicated. There wasn't much to the back stage area of the theatre, a few doors into what I assumed were dressing rooms, and each one I checked was locked. I made my way down a long passage that paralleled the back wall of the stage before finding a stairwell. Figuring this was the only way Nathan could have gone, I took the stairs two at a time, hoping I could catch him before he left. I hated that I had spooked him, partially because it was confirming my suspicions and partially because if they were wrong, he was missing out on his graduation. Opening the door at the bottom of the stairwell, I stepped out onto Seymour Street at the rear of the theatre. Pedestrian and vehicle traffic was still heavy, but there was no sign of Nathan. He was an athletic kid to be sure, but I was no slouch in the running department either. He was either much faster than I had expected or had gone out a different exit.

Of course, the door I had exited automatically locked behind me, so I found myself locked out on the street. Frustrated, I made my way back to the theatre entrance and convinced the usher on duty that yes, I was a staff member and had already handed in my ticket to the event. It took a couple of minutes of persuasion and a flash of my school district photo identification before I could make my way back to the lobby, where a few parents and students, bored with the ceremony, were milling about taking photos to add to the family album. I found Ingrid standing in the foyer. She waved me over.

"Did you talk to him?" she asked.

"No," I replied. "I lost him. He must have gone out through another exit, and by the time I made it to the street, there was no sign of him."

"That's okay. The school has records of where he lives. Detective Pearson will know how to find him."

"What the hell is going on?" a voice demanded from beside me. I would have assumed by the tone that it was one of my immediate supervisors, but the voice was too familiar and female.

"Sara, what are you doing out here?" I asked. "You're supposed to be graduating from high school in there."

"I just crossed the stage and came out here. I saw Nate disappear off the side of the stage then you trotted off after him. What the hell is happening?"

I looked to Ingrid for some wisdom. How much should I tell her? Was it wise to alarm her about the text Nathan had sent when I didn't even know for sure he had anything to do with Tim's murder? How was she likely to react? With Andrea all of those questions would have been readily readable from my face, but Ingrid was not yet practiced enough in exchanging glances with me to read or respond to unspoken queries. I decided honesty was the best approach.

I sighed then gently explained what I had learned about the message, from where it had come, and from whom it now looked like it had come.

Sara's face registered little shock at the information. Instead she just nodded. Finally she said, "Son of a bitch." That seemed a more or less appropriate response, but I had been hoping for a little more insight.

"What?" I managed.

"I thought he had been acting strangely," she muttered more to herself than to Ingrid and me.

"Well, he did just lose a friend, just like you did. He would be understandably upset."

"No," she insisted. "It's not that. He just seemed … I don't know, not right, like he wasn't grieving the way I would have expected." She looked hard at me. "Christ, do you think he actually killed Tim?"

"No," I answered reflexively. "I mean, I don't know. There could be a hundred reasons why Nathan sent Tim a text message. It doesn't mean he killed him." Then I added. "But I do want to talk to him. And the police will want to as well when they find out he's the one who sent the message."

"They don't know yet?" she asked.

"No. At least I didn't tell them. I was hoping to talk to him first, get his side of the story."

I could almost hear the pieces falling into place in Sara's head. She looked ashen against the sky blue of her graduation gown. "This is unbelievable," she muttered, then without another word, she turned and marched away.

Ingrid and I watched her descend the lobby stairs. We stood around awkwardly, waiting to see if she would return. Ingrid asked, "Do you think she left?"

"I don't know." I knew this would have hit her particularly hard. She, Tim, and Nathan were the best of friends. To find out one may be at least in part responsible for the death of the other would certainly throw any normal person into shock. I wouldn't have been surprised if she was feeling sick. I wondered aloud if she'd gone to the washroom.

"Do you want me to check?" my companion offered helpfully. I nodded and followed Ingrid down the stairs to the women's washroom on the floor below. A moment or two later, she returned. "She's not here. I asked a woman at the counter if any students had come in, and she said she hasn't seen anyone."

"Shit. Where the hell did she go?"

"Do you think perhaps she went to try to find Nathan?"

"Yes."

"Do you think this Nathan might be dangerous?"

"Hell, I don't know what to think. It's hard to believe he would do anything to Sara. They're best friends."

"But if he already killed his other best friend…." She didn't need to complete the thought.

"Come on. Let's go." I started for the nearest exit.

"Where are we going?"

"To Nathan's house. With any luck he went home."

Of course the Donaldsons were not listed, and no amount of cajoling the directory assistance operator was going to get her to break her telecommunications vow and provide me with their unlisted number, let alone her address. This late in the day, there was no one answering the phone at the school, and Andrea was not answering her cell phone, so I could not get her to work her secret police address search magic. The best I could do was leave a voicemail message for her, telling her it was urgent she contact me, and carry on towards the school. I debated calling Furlo and Smythe, but knew I would be lectured on my failure to contact them sooner and to stay the hell away from Nathan, something I had no intention of doing. If Nathan was innocent, I didn't want him getting nailed for withholding evidence in the investigation, at least until I was able to advise him on how to proceed.

Stopping at the school, I banged on one of the doors loudly enough that one of the crew of evening custodians allowed me to enter. Ingrid and I stood awkwardly while we waited for my classroom computer to go through its multitude of booting tasks.

"I guess this must be why you come into school so early every morning," she offered.

"Pretty much," I agreed. At very long last, the computer was ready for the limited action I needed it to perform. I entered my student marks program and wrote down Nathan Donaldson's home address and phone number. "Okay, let's go."

We quickly made our way outside and raced the couple of kilometers to the Donaldson home on East 53rd at the corner of St. Georges. We arrived at the same time as Nathan's mother, a woman I had met a number of times. She was going in the front door. There was no car in sight, though in this neighbourhood most of the homes had garages or carports in back lanes behind all the houses. Like a growing number of people, she did not look at all pleased to see me.

"Mrs. Donaldson?" I asked.

"That would be the woman currently married to Nathan's father. It's Ms. *Antonsen*, you might recall." I should have recalled, given I had just written it down barely ten minutes before on the piece of paper with Nathan's address. "What the hell happened back there at the theatre?"

"I really don't know. Nathan saw me and ran."

"And you ran after him. I waited around the theatre like an idiot with his idiot father, and he never went back to his seat or came back to meet us after the ceremony. I finally just gave up and came home. Just what is going on?"

Talking to parents as a teacher is frequently unpleasant, especially when a lack of academic progress needs to be reported. I'd had plenty of conversations with parents as legal counsel, usually telling them about the inevitability of prosecution and the need to accept a plea bargain to diminish the length or likelihood of incarceration. But conversations in which I was reporting my investigation of parents' offspring as a suspect in a homicide I was completely unprepared for, so I chose the approach that seemed most appropriate: obfuscation. "I really don't know. For some reason he just panicked when he saw me. I thought maybe he came back here."

She looked at me with well-warranted suspicion. "So nothing's going on. You just thought you would pop by your student's house and say hello after that student bolted from you in front of a couple of thousand people?"

"That's right," I replied feebly.

She sighed in exasperation. "Well, I just got here, and Nathan's car isn't out back. You might as well come in, and we'll see if by some weird chance he came home without his car or left a note about where he might have gone." She opened the door and allowed us in, introducing herself to Ingrid as we passed. The Antonsen-Donaldson home was not terribly spacious but was well decorated, tidy without being fastidious, fashionable without relying on trendiness to make a statement. Ms. Antonsen left us in the living room and ventured off to search the house. As I expected from my first impressions, it didn't take long. "He's not here," she said. "Now, Mr. Patrick, why don't you tell me what you're really doing here?"

I glanced at Ingrid. She cocked an eyebrow and gave the slightest nod. She wasn't a cop but she hadn't led me astray yet. And she was present. "Ms. Antonsen. I know this has been a really difficult time for Nathan and his friends with Tim being killed last week. But I need to ask you: has Nathan been acting unusual? Has his behaviour changed?"

She looked at me with ever increasing wariness. "As you said, Mr. Patrick, Nathan lost one of his best friends in a brutal homicide. He hasn't exactly been a happy camper, if that's what you mean, but I would think that is totally understandable."

"Yes," I agreed. "I'm just wondering if his reaction to Tim's death has seemed in any way unusual to you, beyond or different from what you would normally expect from someone who is grieving the loss of a friend."

"What the hell are you getting at, Mr. Patrick?"

I honestly didn't know, so I finally surrendered and went with outright straightforwardness. "Ms. Antonsen, a short time before Tim was killed, he received a text message that prompted him to go meet someone at Queen Elizabeth Park. That message came from within John A. Macdonald Secondary."

"And?"

I sighed. I'd come this far. "And when I went to check who had been using the school library's computers at the time the message was sent, there were only two students who had been there. One of them was Nathan."

She chewed on that for a moment. "And you were going to ask him about that at the theatre this afternoon." It wasn't a question, so I didn't answer it. We stared at each other for at least a full minute before she continued. "And you think it's possible that my son killed one of his best friends."

"I'm afraid I don't know what to think. It's why I need to talk to him. It certainly appears that could be a possibility. It's also why I think it would be better if I talked to him before the police do."

"And the police know about this?"

"They will."

"You haven't told them."

"Not yet. I will."

"Why?"

"Because I have to. I think you know that."

"And if you didn't tell them?"

"They're on the verge of figuring it out anyway. If I could find out, you can believe their computer technicians can. Better yet, they'll just ask the librarian who was there, which is what I did. And I'll be charged with obstruction of justice, something I'd rather not have happen."

"But you're okay with my son being charged with murder." Her final word hung in the air like the echo from a slap.

"If he committed one, I'm afraid so, yes."

"This is bullshit," she sputtered feebly.

"What is, ma'am?"

"The notion that Nathan could have killed someone. Why would he do that? You don't really believe Nathan killed Tim."

I wanted to offer her some hope but not too much. "I don't know, Ms. Antonsen. I think I know Nathan pretty well, and I find it hard to believe he'd be capable of something like that. That's all the more reason I'd like to talk to him."

"Do you have a daughter?" Ingrid asked out of the blue. Antonsen's attention turned to Ingrid as though just remembering she was present.

"A daughter? No. I have two sons. Why do you ask?"

Ingrid got up and walked over to a side table near the door to the living room, just a few feet from where we had entered. "I noticed the purse you were carrying when you came in is still beside you on the floor. I was wondering who this purse belongs to."

I walked over. I felt a tug of recognition at the recesses of my consciousness as I looked at the small black bag. "This isn't yours, Ms. Antonsen?" I asked her.

She stood up and joined us. The three of us stood staring at the purse on the table like it was some sort of radioactive container. "No," she answered. "I don't know whose that it is." We stood staring a moment longer before Ingrid took the initiative.

"Let's find out," she said. She reached into the purse and pulled out a wallet. Opening it to the card section, she began to pull out the B.C. Driver's Licence. Before she could even raise it to read out the name, the hint of recognition I'd felt on seeing the bag came clearly into focus. I had seen it every other day for nearly a year now, including the day I'd met with its owner at CKNW radio's downtown studios.

"Sara Kolinsky," Ingrid said. I reached for the bag and quickly rummaged through its contents. In addition to the wallet there was Sara's tiny little cell phone, along with makeup, car keys, and assorted bits and pieces I assumed made up the average teenaged purse.

"Ms. Antonsen, did Sara come here before the graduation ceremony? Did she go to the Orpheum with you and Nathan?"

She looked stunned. "No. Nathan and I each went alone and met up with his father and stepmother. Why?"

I glanced again at Ingrid, and a flash of concern bordering on panic crossed her face. It confirmed that my own fears weren't at least entirely unreasonable. "Ms. Antonsen, does Nathan have access to any weapons?"

"What the hell are you saying? Just because Sara's purse is here doesn't mean he did something to her. She's been here dozens of times, probably hundreds of times. They probably just went out for something to eat."

"Without her purse?" Ingrid asked.

Nathan's mother was momentarily stunned. "We have a gun," she nearly whispered.

"What?" I demanded.

"It … it's his father's. I got it in the divorce settlement. It was more out of spite than anything else. I didn't want it. I just didn't want him to have it."

"Do you keep it in a particular place?" She nodded. "Please. Go see if the gun is here."

"He wouldn't take it. He and his brother know they're not allowed to touch it. I don't keep it loaded, though …" She faded off.

"Though what?" I demanded.

She looked at me fearfully. "We do have bullets for it. In a box. Next to the gun."

"Go check," I demanded. When she left the room, I retrieved Sara's cell phone from her bag. Scrolling through her contacts list, I hit "dial" when I landed on "Nate." The call went immediately to voicemail, where I heard Nathan's familiar, jovial, almost ridiculous voice urge callers to leave him a message or send him a text. As I hung up, my own cell rang in my pocket. I had barely flipped it open when I heard Andrea bark.

"Where the hell are you?" I brought her up to speed as quickly as I could. I had just finished telling her about Sara's purse when Nathan's mom returned to the room. She looked shocked. I didn't have to ask, and she didn't have to tell. She told us anyway.

"It's gone. The gun is gone. So are the bullets."

I took a gigantic breath. "Andrea. We have a problem."

Chapter Twenty-One

While she put out an all-points-bulletin on Nathan and his car, Andrea had expressly ordered me to stay put, sweetening the directive by assuring me I was waiting at his house in the event Nathan decided to return home. Of course, I knew that wasn't about to happen and that Andrea was attempting to keep me out of harm's way. I couldn't bring myself to sit and make idle chit-chat with Nathan's mother, so Ingrid and I sat in the mini-van discussing what to do next.

"I'm sure Sara will be all right," Ingrid tried to reassure me for at least the third time. I only nodded. Finally she said, "What are we going to do?"

I turned and saw her staring intently at me. For a brief second it occurred to me this was some kind of trap, like if I announced my intention to do anything other than what I had been instructed to do, it would be reported back to Andrea or Sandi. Then I realized I had been hanging out with Andrea way too much. Or Sandi. Or both. Still, caution was in order.

"Well, Andrea figured Nathan might come back here."

"You don't believe that, do you?"

I smiled a little. "No."

She smiled back, and the interior of the vehicle warmed a little more. "Then we need to come up with a plan. Do you think we should check Sara's house?"

I shook my head. "I'm sure Andrea would have sent someone there to check that out. It seems unlikely he would take her there. In fact, I'm sure Detectives Furlo and Smythe will be here any time now to search Nathan's room."

"We already looked there. We didn't find anything." She was right. We had searched it and found no missing clothes, no missing backpack, or anything else to indicate he had packed and hit the road.

"Still, barring any other information, this is likely where they'll start."

"So you have an advantage over them and we're sitting here not using it."

I looked at her questioningly. "An advantage?"

"You know him," she said. "You've worked with him all year. You've worked with teenagers all year. You probably have better insight into how they think than the police do."

I paused to consider her reasoning. In theory, she was correct. In practice though, I wondered if I'd been so wrapped up in my own need to survive my first year of teaching that I'd barely taken the time to really get to know Nathan, or any of my other students, for that matter. "I wish that were true," I finally confessed. "I don't know how teenagers think beyond some of their abysmal taste in music. Oh, and that they think Seth Rogen's movies are actually funny."

A little jolt of heat pulsed through me when she reached across the enormous chasm between the two front seats and placed her hand on my arm. "Give yourself some credit. You obviously mean a lot to these kids.

They didn't come to trust you because you're a warm body in the classroom."

I wasn't so sure, but it didn't help to argue, and I didn't really want her to take her hand away from my arm.

"I know this is difficult," she continued, "but let's operate on the assumption that Nathan did kill Tim. Why would he do that?"

"I don't know."

"Don't be so quick. Think, Winston. I know you're a thinker. You don't spend hours awake each night thinking about nothing." It was both alarming and comforting how much Ingrid seemed to know about me. I'm sure Sandi had told her all about my somnambulous wanderings with a none too flattering spin, but I preferred to think Ingrid had observed me on her own and formed better impressions.

"I don't know," I insisted. "They were good friends."

"Could he have been bothered or threatened by Tim's sexuality?"

"No. In fact, it's surprising how little it seemed to bother most of the kids. In my day, which wasn't that long ago," I interjected self-consciously, "being gay would have been a surefire path to isolation. But he seemed pretty popular. I never really noticed anyone giving him a hard time because he was gay." Of course, I hadn't really noticed he was gay at all until he had told me in class just a few short weeks ago, so the likelihood I would have noticed him being harassed was slim. "But Nathan certainly knew. He was involved in defending Tim's right to bring his boyfriend to the dance."

She thought about that for a moment. "Do you think he knew about Tim's online business?"

"I don't know. Everyone seemed surprised by that, even Sara. But if he knew Tim was gay, would finding out Tim was prostituting himself really make him that much more upset?"

"I don't know," she admitted. "What exactly did Tim tell you when he phoned the night he was killed?"

I thought about it. "He said he thought he knew who painted the pictures on the side of the building, and he was going to talk to him. So Nathan must be our graffiti artist."

"And they met in the park because this was a place they sometimes hung out on weekends to a party?" Her sweet, accented voice made it sound so innocent, like the kids were sipping tea and eating homemade cookies late at night in the woods of Queen Elizabeth Park.

"I suppose so."

"So the park might be a place they hold in special regard, a kind of secret meeting ground."

I realized where her line of thought was taking her. "And if so it might be a place Nathan would go when he needed someplace familiar or comfortable." I started up the mini-van and headed out onto the street. "It's as good a place as any to start looking."

It was early evening, but rush hour in Vancouver was long. We were already inside the park drive before I was able to approach a good speed. As we approached the top parking lot of the Conservatory, I was already sensing futility, but as we rounded the corner, I was surprised to see a familiar Crown Victoria parked alongside the curb.

I pulled in behind it and put my hazard lights on. Ingrid and I stepped out onto the sidewalk. Across the concourse, near one of the fountains, a small crowd of tourists had gathered in a clump, more than a circle, around a form on the ground. I broke into a run and pushed through the people, nearly all of whom were on cell phones, and made my way to where Andrea was lying.

"Andrea! What the hell happened?" I realized I was nearly screaming as I kneeled down beside her. She seemed to be barely conscious as she held her upper thigh.

"He shot me," she hissed angrily. She was holding a jacket around her left leg.

"Who shot you?"

"Your fucking student shot me. I didn't even see it coming." It was hard to tell if she was angrier with Nathan for shooting her or herself for not anticipating that he might. I was more worried the bullet might have hit her femoral artery, though not having passed a science class since tenth grade, I couldn't have identified just where the femoral artery was. I only knew from watching *ER* that it was bad.

"Just hang in there," I said soothingly. "It'll be all right."

"Of course it'll be all right," she said, but her voice was losing its power. "It's clean. Paramedics are on the way." She looked up at the small crowd. "Can you back these people away?" Ingrid started coaxing people away.

"Win," she said in a near whisper, "he's got Sara with him. And clearly he's armed."

"Shit," I sighed. "Did she look like she was with him voluntarily?"

"No. She screamed when he shot me, and he dragged her away." She nodded past the Conservatory building to the woods beyond.

"I've gotta go talk to him," I said.

"No." Her head started to tilt back and her eyeballs rolled skyward. She managed to shake it off. "He's wild, Win." Ingrid kneeled beside Andrea and began placing pressure on the now red-stained suit jacket around Andy's leg.

"Andy!" I barked at her. "Hold on. Help is on the way."

She managed to grab hold of my arm. "Make sure you point out which way he took Sara." She winced, and her nails momentarily dug into my flesh, even through my suit jacket. "Christ, Win. Don't let him kill her too." Her head lolled backwards, and she closed her eyes.

Ingrid looked at me with concern as she examined Andrea's wound. "She's in shock," she told me calmly. "But if they get here soon, I'm sure she'll be fine." I took comfort in her nurse training.

I looked in the direction Nathan and Sara had apparently run. He had shot a police officer. His situation had just gone from bad to worse. "I need to try to go after them, see if I can talk him into giving up."

"Winston," Ingrid began but I cut her off.

"I know. It's not safe. He's not thinking straight. But I think he'll listen to me. I have to try."

"I was going to say you should take this," Ingrid said, and she pulled Andrea's gun from where my friend, ever the cop, had secured the weapon underneath her good leg.

"I'm just going to talk to him, make sure he doesn't hurt Sara. He wouldn't hurt me. I don't think he'll hurt Sara either."

"You said yourself he's not thinking straight. Take it." Ingrid slid the gun surreptitiously into my hand. "Go," she ordered again. "Be careful."

I stood up and ran off, the gun feeling like a ship's anchor in my hand. At the far end of the Conservatory, the sidewalk ended abruptly and the hillside sloped steeply away. A small path, barely discernible, led into the forested park below. I glanced around, but there was no indication of where they could have gone. For a moment I paused and pondered the ridiculousness of my situation, standing on a hillside, shiny new shoes and suit, gun in hand, pursuing my own high school student. For the second time in as many weeks, I listened for the sirens I was sure were on the way but heard none. I knew that when an officer went down, the response would be quick, but it struck me too that after an officer was shot, the police would hit the park en masse and Nathan's chances of coming out alive would be greatly diminished. I trotted off down the hill.

The trail sloped sharply away from the public area above, and I could see how students would find this an ideal party location, given its isolation from late night sightseers and the roadways where passing eyes might report their activities. Every neighbourhood has its teenage hangouts where kids assume their privacy will be undisturbed. I ran as quickly as the terrain would permit, stepping over logs that had fallen across the trail. The forest was littered with deadfall, some massive in size that had no doubt come down in the now infamous windstorm that had destroyed so much of Vancouver's parkland wilderness a few winters back. I looked from side to side for any sign that Nathan and Sara were hiding off the path. I had only descended a short distance when I heard Sara's voice ahead and to the right off the trail. I couldn't make out what she said, but it was comforting at least to hear her. Because police work is not my forte, I called out her name out of instinct. There was no response, but I headed further down the path then veered off to the right toward where the voice had come from. "Sara?" I called again. A large tree trunk lay on the ground in front of me, its upturned root system creating a wall at least a foot higher than my head. I was about to step around it when I thought of Andrea being taken by surprise and for the first time I doubted my original assertion that he wouldn't fire on me.

"Sara?" I called one more time.

This time she responded. "Mr. Patrick?"

"Shut up!" I heard Nathan hiss.

I considered my options. I could wait for the police to come barreling down the path I had taken, flag them over, and let them deal with the situation. But I also knew that if they did, there was a real possibility of Sara getting hurt either by Nathan or in a crossfire. "Nathan," I called out, surprised by how calm my voice sounded, considering the pounding in my chest, "I'm coming around. Just stay calm." I took a deep breath, and before I could change my mind, I stepped around the fan of the tree base and stepped into a very small clearing. Across the clearing, on the edge of a small hill, Sara was lying on her stomach, Nathan kneeling beside her, pressing her shoulder down. She craned her neck to look up at me, and Nathan stared in alarm. They both were still clad in their graduation gowns, the formality of their attire clashing with the ragged fallen timbers around them. It had been sunny and bright for their ceremony, but now the forest was growing darker, despite the lengthening late spring daylight hours. Glancing up, I could see clouds had begun to close in. I felt a few drops of rain.

"What are you doing here?" he demanded.

"Looking for you," I said soothingly. "You ran away from me at the theatre. I just wanted to talk. Why don't we go home and talk?"

"How did you know? As soon as I saw you, I knew you knew."

"You sent Tim the message to meet him at the park. Here. Is this where you met?" I looked around. There were some discarded beer bottles and what appeared to be a small fire pit.

"But how did you know?"

"The police found his phone."

"But I didn't even text him from my phone."

"No," I said. "You sent it anonymously from the school. But they traced the IP address. All I had to do was see who was on the computer at that time. They would have found you."

"Nathan, why the hell did you do that? Why did you send a message from the school? You *planned* to kill him," Sara said, her voice a mix of fear and outrage.

"No. It wasn't like that," he pleaded, and his voice sounded again almost comically squeaky, like it did when he was creating fictitious excuses why his homework was incomplete or he was late for class. It was always good for a class laugh; now it just sounded sad. "I just didn't want him to know it was me until we could talk."

"Just before he came here, he told me he knew who he was coming to talk to," I said.

"I know. He was surprised to see me. He was sure he was coming to see Jordan Kansky. He couldn't believe it when I told him I was the one who did the graffiti on the side of the school. But I didn't come here to kill him, I swear I didn't."

"Then why did you bring a knife?" Sara demanded angrily.

"I didn't. It was Tim's knife. He brought it here with him. I guess he figured Jordan might be violent."

"Give me a break," Sara said, starting to rise. Nathan's anger suddenly returned, and he shoved her hard back onto the ground.

"Just shut up!" he yelled. He was beginning to sound hysterical.

"Nathan," I said again, trying to regain control of the conversation. "Calm down, okay? We're just talking here."

"Shoot him," Sara directed me forcefully. "Just shoot him." I had forgotten Andrea's gun was in my hand, and I had to look down to confirm it was even there. It looked embarrassingly limp and useless in my grip.

Nathan too seemed to notice for the first time I was armed and raised his gun towards me. "What are you doing with that?"

"Shoot him," Sara insisted.

"Calm down, both of you. I'm not going to shoot him. Nathan, I'm not going to shoot you." Sara started to move, and Nathan turned the gun back on her. It seemed to shake in his hand, and I realized how heavy it must be. It had a longer barrel than the one I carried. I wondered what that meant in terms of firepower. Or masculinity. "Nathan, what happened when you came to talk to Tim?"

He kept looking back and forth between Sara and me. Finally, he seemed to need to unburden himself. "I was so angry when I found out he was whoring himself out. I mean, you think you know a guy."

I couldn't think of what to say, so I just stood there in the intensifying storm shower and waited for him to continue.

"I was so angry when I found out that I just vented and took it out on the school walls. I don't know why. It was stupid."

"Then why did you ask him to come here?" I asked.

"I felt like an idiot for what I'd done. It was even less mature than usual." He smiled a little for just a second. "I just wanted him to stop. I wanted him to know how I felt about it, and I wanted him to stop." He looked again at Sara on the ground then back at me. "Shit. I gotta get out of here."

"Nathan, wait. What happened when you guys got here? Why did you attack him?"

"It wasn't like that," Nathan insisted.

"What was it like?"

Nathan looked back and forth between Sara and me, and I thought I heard a slight moan. "I told him … I told him … I loved him."

"What?" Sara and I asked simultaneously.

He looked between us pleadingly. "I know. I know. It sounds crazy. Maybe it is crazy. Maybe I just ... maybe I'm just confused." He sounded like he needed reassurance his feelings were okay, and given our situation, it seemed prudent that I offer it.

"It's not crazy, Nathan. It's okay." It sounded like a weak assurance, even to me. Teacher-training programs don't cover a lot of things. Dealing with a gun-wielding, emotionally distraught, hostage-taking student now seemed like a glaring omission.

I quietly digested this new information. The rain wasn't heavy, but it made sounds like static on the forest floor and on the leaves above us. A particularly cool drop snuck down the collar of my shirt.

Sara spoke quietly from her position on the ground. We barely heard her. "Then why did you kill him?"

There was a long pause, long enough that I wondered if he'd heard Sara's question. "He laughed," Nathan eventually said. "He laughed in my face." He looked like he was hearing Tim's laughter in the raindrops.

Sara and I both waited for Nathan to continue. "He was so mad that I'd drawn that shit on the school, he just laughed at me when I told him."

"Then what happened?" I asked, trying to keep him talking.

"He said he was going to tell everyone. He was going to tell everyone I was gay." Sara and I were quiet again.

"You don't understand," he insisted. "This would have killed me. The guys on the basketball team wouldn't have wanted me around. I've got a scholarship to U-Dub.

I would've lost all that. I would've lost everything. My parents. My brothers. Everything."

"No, Nate, you wouldn't have," Sara pleaded. "You would still have had me. You would still have had him," she pointed towards me. "You wouldn't have lost everything."

"No," Nathan persisted. "He was mocking me. He was going to tell everyone about what I'd done … and why I'd done it. I couldn't let him do that. He wouldn't listen to me. I just lost it. I started hitting him."

I waited for more information that didn't seem to be coming. "How did you end up stabbing him?"

Nathan looked pleadingly at me. "He pulled out the knife on me. I don't blame him. I was hitting him. And then I took the knife from him and I stabbed him. And I stabbed him again. And then I realized what I'd done. You have to believe me. I helped him to the car. I wanted to take him to the hospital. He wouldn't let me. He told me to fuck off. I tried following him, but he drove so fast. Then when he crashed …" His voice tapered off.

We waited in the rain, listening to nothing but our individual images of Tim's final moments. Then I finished his thoughts for him. "You stopped and took his phone. The police said there was another car on the scene briefly. That's why they initially thought it was a road race."

"I panicked," Nathan said softly. "I don't know why I took it. I threw it in a dumpster."

Sara spoke first. "Come on, Nate. Let's go." She started to rise.

"What?" he said. "No. Stay down."

"Nathan, come on," I urged. "It's time to go."

"No. I just … I just gotta think of a way to get out of here."

"Nathan, what are you going to do? You shot a cop. Are you gonna shoot me and Mr. Patrick too? Don't be an idiot. You won't even get out of the park. They'll shoot you before you even make the road. Just put down the gun, and we'll walk out of here."

"No," he said louder, pointing the gun close to her face. "I'm not going to jail. It was an accident."

I tried to urge her with my eyes just to lie still and not say anything that would make him more upset. She either wasn't reading my signals or heeding my advice. "Where are you gonna go? Mexico? Live on a beach wondering if the *federales* are about to spring on you?"

"Just shut up," he ordered, and I willed her to do the same. "I'll figure something out. I just need time to figure out what to do. I know some places I can go."

"Oh please, Nate. A high school teacher figured out you killed Tim. You think the cops are gonna have any difficulty tracking you down?" Fair comment, really, so I took no offense.

"I am not going to jail," Nathan said, his voice rising almost to a shout. "They'll kill me in there. I'd rather die than go to jail." The faulty logic in his statement threw up a red flag.

"Nathan," I said, trying to urge calm. "You don't need to die here or in prison. I can help you. If Tim's death was an accident, then you'll get the best legal help, and we'll make sure you get to tell your side in court." The legal counsel in me didn't want to promise him he'd get off, though if that's what it took to get him to walk out of the woods in one piece, I was willing to bend that little piece of truth.

He considered that long enough that I thought he might actually be ready to surrender when he shook his head. "No. Everything will come out. Everyone will hear about what happened. They'll hear about me. No. I can't go through that. I'm getting out of here. You two stay here."

"Nathan, listen to me, please. Sara's right. The park is no doubt being sealed off even as we speak. You won't get out of here. And if they see you with a gun, it's over. Just walk out with me, and we'll get you help. Everything will be fine."

"I'm sorry," he started to say when movement caught the corner of my eye. "No!" Nathan shouted. "Who are you?" I turned to see Ingrid had stumbled into the clearing and was staring terrified at Nathan and the gun he had raised in her direction.

"Nathan, no!" I shouted. He turned his gun back at me briefly then turned it again and pointed it at Ingrid, raising his left hand to the gun so both hands held the weapon in a firing stance.

In the confusion that followed, I was fairly certain I heard a familiar voice yell "Police," and I saw Ingrid's face contort in fear. I'm not sure I even heard the shot, but I saw Nathan fall backwards, the enormous gun flying from his hands as he crashed over Sara, who still lay on the ground. Detectives Furlo and Smythe came smashing through the clearing, guns pointed at Nathan, who lay across Sara, unmoving. With strength I wouldn't have thought possible, Smythe grabbed Sara under the arms and hauled her out from under Nathan with one arm while still pointing her gun at Nathan as her partner ensured he was down. I turned and saw Ingrid shakily getting up from the ground. I scanned the clearing. Everyone was okay, everyone except Nathan, who remained lying on the ground, his head pointing downhill away from me so I was spared seeing his final expression. Furlo stood up, shook his head slightly at his partner and holstered his weapon. I saw him recover Nathan's father's gun from the ground, flip open the cylinder and shake his head in apparent disgust.

"It's not loaded," I heard him tell Smythe.

"How the hell did he shoot Pearson then?" his partner demanded.

"Guess he only had time to load one bullet. Or maybe he didn't know there was only one in there. Guess we'll never know." He turned, looked at me, and walked wordlessly to where I stood. Reaching out, he took Andrea's gun from my arm, still pointed to where Nathan had fallen, and in a voice more soft than I'd ever heard from him, said, "It's okay, buddy. You did the right thing."

He caught me before I could fully fall and lowered me gently to the ground, holding my head between my legs as I tried to recover my breathing, then getting up as Ingrid sat down beside me, wrapping her arm around my shoulders and graciously pretending not to hear me as I wept in the woods.

Chapter Twenty-Two

In death, Nathan had become as famous as he feared, though we managed to keep the nature of his motive for killing Tim mostly under wraps. Tim's death was described as no more than a violent act visited upon a young person by another young person, and the editorialists reminded the public about the increasing senseless violence among youth and how parents, schools, the justice system, and the 7-Eleven on the corner were doing too little to prevent it. It wasn't hard to agree with them.

It was decided, more or less with my agreement, that it would be best if I did not complete the remaining weeks of classes. Officially, Nathan had been shot during an arrest attempt when he pointed his gun at the arresting officers, which was essentially true, given that Ingrid had been leading Furlo and Smythe down the path. When the two detectives had arrived with other officers, Ingrid had run off after me, ignoring Furlo and Smythe's orders to stop. But I sensed people knew the fatal shot had come from me, though there would have been no reason to believe I had been carrying a police officer's gun into the woods while pursuing my two Law 12 students. Sara, who had lost her two best friends in her senior year of high school, was the one who had suggested we keep that piece of information from public scrutiny in the interest of having me eventually be able to return to the classroom. Her concern for me in the face of all she had lost gave me faith in the education system; if we could turn out kids like her, the nation would be just fine. In the immediate aftermath of the shooting it was a moot point to me anyway. I wasn't at all certain I intended to return to the classroom.

Andrea, for her part, caught enormous flak for her relationship with me and the fact that I had taken her gun. Though police investigators and crown counsel ultimately decided the shooting was "clean," and that any police officer in my situation would have taken the exact same action, they had to discipline her for not securing her weapon and essentially arming an untrained, unlicensed civilian. It was one of those nudge, nudge, wink, wink, situations: we all understand what had happened, but it really ought not to have. She was suspended without pay for two weeks. It gave us both time to heal, to sit back and consider our futures in our respective public organizations and mostly to run, when Andy was able to do so, which was, of course, remarkably soon.

Ingrid and I withdrew from one another in an awkward, teenage-like discomfort for the first few days after the shooting. It was difficult for me to be around anyone who had witnessed what I had done that day in the park, and the scene replayed itself hundreds of times each day, and even more so at night as I lay awake hour after hour. Only a powerful sedative, prescribed after the third day of wordless nighttime wandering, provided me with any rest, and only in two or three hour doses. It was on the fifth night that Ingrid emerged from her room and joined me at the floor–to-ceiling living-room window when she told me how she blamed herself for Nathan's death. It broke the veneer of my narcissistic self-pity to realize someone else was hurting, and we spent hours, sometimes by day, more often at night, walking and talking and helping each other move toward a place where we could forgive ourselves for what had happened. I've heard it said that tremendous friendships are born of crisis; ours was the case proving the rule.

A settlement with my insurance company was finally reached, and I half-heartedly began the search for a new home. Sandi insisted that it wasn't weird that ex-spouses live together indefinitely and that her home was my home, a statement I hadn't really believed even before our divorce, and both our names were on the title. Still, I had become reasonably comfortable and wasn't in any particular hurry to vacate the premises, packing up my few meagre possessions to move into a new apartment. I decided time was on my side, especially with the summer months, when I would decide not only my professional future but would have ample time to pick a new home where the demons might not be able to find me. So much had changed in my life in such a short span, I wondered if I didn't need a change of neighbourhood too: Kitsilano just didn't look the same any more. Even my favourite restaurant was gone. I had to wonder what else was keeping me there.

Some time later, I was sitting on the couch, looking at the real estate listings on Sandi's laptop, when Andrea arrived. The weeks had given her plenty of time for reflection but had also made her antsy, and I knew she couldn't wait to return to work on the coming Monday.

"Hey," she said, and from the bounce in her step and the gleam in her eye, I could see she had police work on her mind.

"How's it going?"

"Interesting. Have you changed your mind about tonight?" The Sir John A. Macdonald Secondary grad was that evening. I had to imagine it was going to be a subdued affair given all the graduating class had gone through that year. Having me present could only serve to keep those events at the forefront of everyone's awareness, and I had told Andrea, Sandi, and Ingrid so. All had disagreed, though in Sandi's case I suspect it had more to do with a potential opportunity to take me shopping for expensive evening wear.

"Nope."

"I think you should pop by at least. You could even have the best looking prom date." Andrea had taken to near-constant, reasonably good-natured ribbing about my friendship with Ingrid and her insistence on its romantic potential, none of which had materialized. Her teasing had not yet gotten completely annoying, but it was on its way there.

"Oh? Were you planning on joining me?"

"Hah! In your dreams. We wouldn't want to steal all the focus. Those girls spent a lot of money on their dresses. They don't want their dates to be ogling me all night."

"You said your day was interesting?"

She plopped down on the chair across from me. Kicking off her shoes, she reached out and with her toes delicately closed the lid of the laptop I'd been staring at. "It was. I just got off the phone with Smythe."

"Doing a little work off the books?"

"Just a friendly conversation. Turns out the car science tech guys finally got around to doing an up-close and personal look at your ride. You know how busy it can get with the crime tech guys."

"Sure, I'm forever frustrated by my inability to get forensic work done."

"Ditto. Anyway, the case against your car had become low priority again once Nathan was …" she paused to gauge my reaction.

"Go on."

"But Nathan and Tim's, uhm, situation, came after the attack on your car and your house, which meant that we still had your garden variety hate criminals roaming the city. But guess what they've determined?" I waited quietly through her game. "The damage done to your car was, as I said, done by something rubberized. But they've figured out what it was: the tip of a cane."

"My car was beaten up by an angry disabled person?"

"Know anyone who allegedly fits that description?" She paused while the pieces fell into place. It took a moment, but eventually there was almost an audible click.

"Holy crap!"

"Wanna take a ride with me?"

"Oh, yeah. Wait a minute. You're not back at work yet."

"A super cop is never really off duty."

"What about Smythe?"

"She called me. It was her idea. She thought it might cheer you up a little."

Through her extraordinary powers Andrea managed to determine the whereabouts of Andrew Senchek. He and his family were in the Champlain Heights area of South Vancouver, a step down from the Kitsilano neighbourhood we had shared, barely within the city proper, just a couple of blocks in from Boundary Road. We pulled up in front of a swath of row housing. Some gardeners were working on the common area, and true to form, Polish Sausage was standing vigil over their work. He didn't seem all that surprised to see us.

"Keeping busy?" I asked as we approached.

"What do you want?" was his terse reply. I guess he hadn't particularly missed me.

"Why, for starters?"

He turned his attention away from the corner, around which a young man on the riding mower had just disappeared. His look was an odd combination of resignation and contempt. "I was angry."

"That much is apparent."

"Don't be smug, Winston. It doesn't become you."

If I had a nickel for every time someone told me that.

"You have no idea how much I had wrapped up in that place."

"What?"

"I worked so hard since coming to Canada. We started a family, we saved, and even after all our years of both working, all we could afford was a condo. A beautiful one, yes, but it's difficult to raise a family in such a space. Then when the building started to come apart, it was like our life was crumbling along with the stucco."

"Andrew, what are you talking about?"

He barely heard me. "The bills for the reconstruction were more than I could handle on the disability pension. I just thought if the building was sufficiently damaged, it would help us speed things up, and the insurance would pay for the reconstruction or buy us out."

The police and I had been so focused on the arsonist being a homophobic hate criminal, it hadn't really occurred at least to me that someone at the building might have been responsible. Nathan had been ruled out since his whereabouts that night were known, as were those of Paul Charters and Krista Ellory, my original door vandals. But we were continuing to operate on the assumption the fire had been set by someone ardently opposed to our campaign.

"Andrew, I was here to talk about my car. You beat the shit out of it with your cane."

He sighed. "Yes. You know, you can really be a bastard sometimes."

"So I've been told." I glanced at Andrea, who had yet to say a word. I wondered if she planned to read him his rights. She made no move, so I continued. "But you're telling me you burned down the building? You tried to kill me."

"Jesus, Winston, everything isn't always about you."

If I had nickel for every time someone told me that.

"You started the fire outside my apartment," I insisted.

"That's because you had been an asshole. You never wanted to let us into your apartment, always questioning everything we did. Then with all of your silly gay causes on the radio, you were just convenient to me. But it was never about you." He paused a moment. "Okay, it was a little about you."

"You nearly killed me and other residents."

"That was unfortunate. It was not part of the intent."

"Then why did you disable the fire alarms?"

He shook his head at me as though I was an idiot. It was a look I was growing tired of seeing people use. "So the building would be sufficiently damaged as to have to rebuild the whole thing. It's really not that complicated."

For a brief moment I actually felt sorry for him, thinking about the struggling immigrant image he had tried to portray, raising his family against difficult odds only to see his home destroyed by the shoddy craftsmanship and design that plagued so many of Vancouver's buildings. But as usual, Polish Sausage was making it difficult to feel empathetic. I finally turned to Andrea. "You wanna step in here?"

She began to read him his rights, which he listened to with his head held high, giving us a look somewhere between defiance and resignation. "It doesn't matter," he finally said. "My wife and daughters have already packed up and are leaving. What have I got to stay out here for?"

"Stop talking now," I said, one last offer of humanity I could extend, "at least until legal counsel can advise you."

Andrea slipped cuffs onto his wrists and lowered him into the back seat of her unmarked cruiser. "You just can't resist being a lawyer, can you?"

"It's hard to shake."

She put in a call to police dispatch to officially get permission to bring in a prisoner while off duty. When she finished she turned to me. “Still not going to change your mind about going to the prom tonight?”

I leaned against her cruiser and thought for a moment. “You know what? Maybe I will. I’ll just pop by and say hello.”

Andrea smiled. “Good for you.”

My cell phone rang. Not bothering to check the call display, I answered. To my surprise, it was Sandi, breathing heavily and telling me the two words I’d known would come but really didn’t want to hear.

“It’s time.”

ALSO BY DAVID RUSSELL

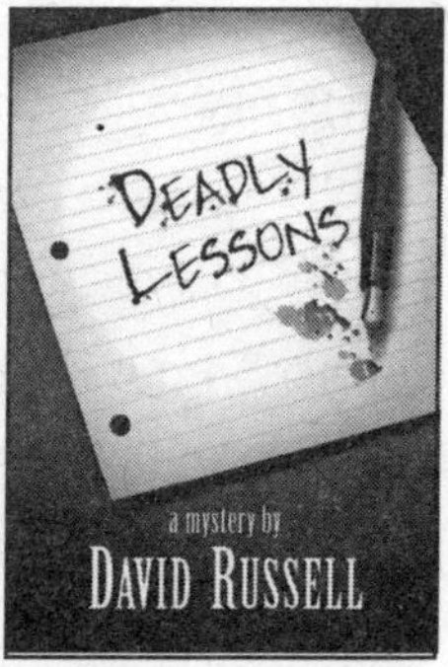

Deadly Lessons
978-1894917353
$13.95

Winston Patrick, a successful lawyer but dissatisfied with his career defending the downtrodden of Vancouver's criminal world, trades in the courtroom for the high school classroom. Soon Winston's past life meets his present when a student accuses a fellow colleague of a teacher-student love affair. Reluctantly, Winston agrees to provide legal defence, but the case takes an even uglier turn: the student is murdered, making her alleged lover the prime suspect.

And this is no ordinary student. With her family connections reaching as high as the Prime Minister's office, Winston and his friend Detective Andrea Pearson find themselves immersed in a murder investigation that could cause an international incident, if it doesn't cost Winston his own life first. Shortlisted for the Arthur Ellis Award for best first crime novel.

More Mysteries from Dundurn

Slow Recoil
by C.B. Forrest
978-1926607061
$16.95

Former Toronto Detective Charlie McKelvey is puttering through the first year of his forced retirement. His tedious life is torn wide open when a friend enlists his help in locating a recent Bosnian immigrant who has simply disappeared without a trace. Her teacher and recent lover, Tim Fielding, suspects foul play.

At first hesitant, McKelvey is quickly drawn into the case as the bodies and clues pile up. When the body of an unidentified woman turns up in Fielding's apartment — and Fielding is nowhere to be found — McKelvey finds himself a prime suspect in an increasingly obscure murder investigation.

Lake on the Mountain
by Jeffrey Round
978-1459700017
$11.99

Dan Sharp, a gay father and missing persons investigator, accepts an invitation to a wedding on a yacht in Ontario's Prince Edward County. It seems just the thing to bring Dan closer to his noncommittal partner, Bill, a respected medical professional with a penchant for sleazy after-hours clubs, cheap drugs, and rough sex. But the event doesn't go exactly as planned.

When a member of the wedding party is swept overboard, a case of mistaken identity leads to confusion as the wrong person is reported missing. The hunt for a possible killer leads Dan deeper into the troubled waters and private lives of a family of rich WASPs and their secret world of privilege.

No sooner is that case resolved when a second one ends up on Dan's desk. Dan is hired by an anonymous source to investigate the disappearance twenty years earlier of the groom's father.

The Tanglewood Murders
by David Weedmark
978-1926607092
$16.95

All Ben Taylor wants is to get away from the police force where he worked undercover for years. The RCMP has cleared his name in an Ottawa shooting, but that hasn't cleared his conscience. He arrives anonymously at Tanglewood Farms in Southwestern Ontario, where he worked in his youthful summers. Back then, it was a simple family-run vineyard, but it is a far different place today. The farm has become the hub of a powerful family empire.

When a body is discovered in a shack on the farm, Ben is drawn into the investigation. Meanwhile, the woman who was once the love of his life now lives as a recluse behind the darkened windows of the farmhouse. As she begins to reveal to Ben her own dark secrets, they become suspects in the eyes of the police, the migrant workers, and even each other.